EXIT STRATEGY

KELLEY ARMSTRONG

sphere

SPHERE

First published in the United States in 2007 by Bantam Dell,
A Division of Random House, Inc.
First published in Great Britain in 2007 by Sphere

A CIP catalogue record for this book
is available from the British Library

ISBN 978-0-7515-3812-0

Papers used by Sphere are natural, recyclable products made from
wood grown in sustainable forests and certified in accordance with
the rules of the Forest Stewardship Council.

Typeset in Minion by Palimpsest Book Production Limited,
Grangemouth, Stirlingshire
Printed and bound in Great Britain by
Clays Ltd, St Ives plc
Paper supplied by Hellefoss AS, Norway

Sphere
An imprint of
Little, Brown Book Group
Brettenham House
Lancaster Place
London WC2E 7EN

A Member of the Hachette Livre Group of Companies

www.littlebrown.co.uk

To Jeff

Mary

Mary Lee pushed open the shop door. A wave of humid heat rolled in. Another hot Atlanta night, refusing to give way to cooler fall weather.

Her gaze swept the darkened street, lingering enough to be cautious but not enough to look nervous. Beyond a dozen feet, she could see little more than blurred shapes. At Christmas, her children had presented her with a check for a cataract operation, but she'd handed it back. Keep it for something important, she'd said. For the grandchildren, for college or a wedding. So long as she could still read her morning paper and recognize her customers across the store counter, such an operation was a waste of good money.

As for the rest of the world, she'd seen it often enough. It didn't change. Like the view outside her shop door tonight. Though she couldn't make out the faces of the teenagers standing at the corner, she knew their shapes, knew their names, knew the names of their parents should they make trouble. They wouldn't, though; like dogs, they didn't soil their own territory.

As she laid her small trash bag at the curb, one of the blurry shapes lifted a hand. Mary waved back.

Before she could duck back into her store, Mr. Emery stepped from his coffee shop. His wide face split in a Santa Claus grin, a smile that kept many a customer from complaining about stale bread or cream a few days past its "best before" date.

"Going home early tonight, Miz Lee?" Emery asked.

"No, no."

His big stomach shuddered in a deep sigh. "You gotta start taking it easy, Miz Lee. We're not kids anymore. When's the last time you locked up and went home at closing time?"

She smiled and shrugged . . . and reminded herself to take out the garbage earlier tomorrow, so she could be spared this timeworn speech. She murmured a "good night" to Mr. Emery and escaped back into her shop.

Now it was her time. The customers gone, the shop door locked, and she could relax and get some real work done. She flipped on her radio and turned up the volume.

Mary took the broom from behind the counter as "Johnny B Goode" gave way to "Love Me Tender." Crooning along with Elvis, she swept a path through the faint pattern of dusty footprints.

Something flickered to her left, zipping around the side of her head like a diving mosquito. As her hand went up to swat it, she felt the prick at her throat, but it was cool, almost cold. A sharp pain, followed by a rush of heat. At first, she felt only a twinge of annoyance, her brain telling her it was yet another hiccup of age to add to her body's growing repertoire. Then she couldn't breathe.

Gasping, her hands flew to her throat. Sticky wet heat streamed over them. Blood? Why would her neck be—? As she bent forward, she noticed a reflection in the glass lid of the ice cream freezer. A man's face above hers. His expression blank. No, not blank. Patient.

Mary opened her mouth to scream.

Darkness.

He lowered the old woman's body to the floor. To an onlooker, the gesture would seem gentle, but it was just habit, putting her down carefully so she didn't fall with a thud.

Not that anyone was around to hear it. Habit, again. Like unplugging the security camera even though, when he'd been surveying the shop, he'd noticed there was no tape in the recorder.

He left the wire embedded in the old woman's throat. Standard wire, available at every hardware store in the country, cut with equally standard wire cutters. He double- and triple-checked the paper overshoes on his boots, making sure he hadn't stepped in the puddle of blood and left a footprint. The boots would be gone by morning, but he looked anyway. Habit.

It took all of thirty seconds to run through the dozens of checks in his head, and reassure himself that he'd left nothing behind. Then he reached his gloved hand into his pocket and withdrew a square of plastic. He tore open the plastic wrapper and pulled out a folded sheet of paper within. Then he bent down, lifted the old woman's shirttail and tucked the paper inside her waistband.

After one final look around the scene, he walked past the cash register, past the bulging night-deposit bag, past the cartons of cigarettes and liquor, and headed out the back door.

ONE

I twisted my fork through the blueberry pie and wished it was apple. I've never been fond of blueberry, not even when the berries were wild and fresh from the forest. These were fresh from a can.

Barry's Diner advertised itself as "home of the best blueberry pie in New York City." That should have been the tip-off, but the sign outside said only Award-Winning Homemade Pie. So I'd come in hoping for a slice of fresh apple and found myself amid a sea of diners eating blueberry. Sure, the restaurant carried apple, but if everyone else was eating blueberry, I couldn't stand out by ordering something different. It didn't help that I had to accompany the pie with decaf coffee—in a place that seemed to brew only one pot and leave it simmering all day.

The regular coffee smelled great, but caffeine was off my menu today, so I settled for inhaling it as I nibbled the crust on my pie. At least that was homemade. I shifted on my seat, the vinyl-covered stool squeaking under me, the noise lost in the sounds of the diner—the clatter of china and silverware, the steady murmur of conversation regularly erupting in laughs or shouts. The door behind me opened with a tinkle of the bell, a gust of October air and a belch of exhaust fumes that stole that rich scent of fresh coffee.

A man in a dirt-encrusted ball cap clanked his metal lunch box onto the counter beside my plate. "He got another one last night. Number four. Police just confirmed it."

I slanted my gaze his way, in case he was talking to me. He wasn't, of course. I was invisible ... or as close to it as a nonsuperhero could get, having donned the ultimate female disguise: no apparent makeup and thirty-five pounds of extra padding.

"Who'd he get this time?" the server asked as she poured coffee for the newcomer.

"Little old Chinese lady closing up her shop. Choked her with a wire."

"Garroted," said a man sitting farther down the counter.

"Gary who?"

The other man folded his newspaper, rustling it with a flourish. "Garroted. If you use something to strangle someone, it's called garroting. The Spanish used it as a method of execution."

I glanced at the speaker. A silver-haired man in a suit, manicured fingernails resting on his *Wall Street Journal*. Not the sort you'd expect to know the origin of the term "garroted." Next thing you know, his neighbors would be on TV, telling the world he'd seemed like such a nice man.

They continued talking. I struggled to ignore them. *Had* to ignore them. I had a job to do, and couldn't allow myself to be sidetracked.

It wasn't easy. Words and phrases kept tumbling my way. Killer. Victim. Police. Investigation. No leads. I could, with effort, block the words, remind myself that they had nothing to do with me, but the voices weren't so easy to push aside. Sharp with excitement, as if this was something they'd seen in a movie and the victims were nothing more than actors who, when the credits rolled, would stand up, wash off the fake blood and grab a cigarette before heading home to their families.

The Helter Skelter killer. Even the name was catchy, almost jocular. I bet he was proud of it. He'd risen from the ranks of the unnamed and now he was someone—the

Helter Skelter killer. I pictured him sitting in a coffee shop like this, eavesdropping on a conversation like this one, his heart tripping every time he heard his new name. My hand tightened on my fork. A burr on the handle dug in. I squeezed until pain forced my thoughts back on track.

It wasn't my concern. There were dozens of killers all across the continent, plotting crimes just as ruthless. Nothing to be done about it, and I was no longer in a position to try.

I took a swig of coffee. Bitter and burned, foul on my tongue, acid in my stomach. I took another gulp, deeper, almost draining the mug. Then I pushed it aside with my half-eaten pie, got to my feet and walked out.

I stood in the subway station and waited for Dean Moretti.

Moretti was a Mafia wannabe, a small-time thug with tenuous connections to the Tomassini crime family. Three months earlier, he had decided it was time to strike out on his own, so he'd made a deal with the nephew of a local drug lord. Together they'd set up business in a residential neighborhood previously untapped—probably because it was under the protection of the Riccio family.

When the Riccios found out, they went to the Tomassinis, who went to the drug lord, who decided, among the three of them, that this was not an acceptable entrepreneurial scheme. The drug lord's nephew had caught the first plane to South America and was probably hiding in the jungle, living on fish and berries. Moretti wasn't so easily spooked, which probably speaks more to a lack of intelligence than an excess of nerve.

While I waited for him, I wandered about the platform, taking note of every post, every garbage can, every doorway. Busywork, really. I'd already scouted this station so well I could navigate it blindfolded, but I kept checking and double-checking.

My stomach fluttered. Not fear. Anticipation. I kept moving, trying to work past it. There was no more room here for anticipation than there was for fear. It was a job. It had to be approached with cool, emotionless efficiency. You cannot enjoy this work. If you do, you step onto the fast slide to a place you'll never escape, become something you swore you'd never be.

I kept my brain busy with last-minute checks. There was one security camera down here, but an antiquated one, easy to avoid. I'd heard rumors of post-9/11 upgrades, but so far, this station had avoided them. Though I hadn't seen a uniformed transit cop, I knew there could be a plain-clothes one, so I spotted the most likely suspects and stayed out of their way. Not that it mattered—in addition to the extra padding I was wearing a wig, colored contacts, eye-glasses and makeup to darken my skin tone.

I'd spent three days watching Moretti, long enough to know he was a man who liked routines. Right on schedule, he bounced down the subway steps, ready for his train home after a long day spent breaking kneecaps for a local bookie.

Partway down the stairs he stopped and surveyed the crowd below. His gaze paused on anyone of Italian ances-try, anyone wearing a trench coat, anyone carrying a bulky satchel, anyone who looked...dangerous. Too dumb to run, but not so dumb that he didn't know he was in deep shit with the Tomassinis. At work, he always had a partner with him. From here, he'd take the subway to a house where he was bunking down with friends, taking refuge in numbers. This short trip was the only time he could be found alone, obviously having decided that public transit was safe enough.

As he scouted the crowd from the steps, people jostled him from behind, but he met their complaints with a snarl that sent them skittering around him. After a moment, he continued his descent into the subway pit. At the bottom, he cut through a group of young businessmen, then stopped beside a gaggle of careworn older women chattering in Spanish. He kept watching the crowd, but his gaze swept past me. The invisible woman.

I made my way across the platform, eyes straining to see down the tunnel, pretending to look for my train, flexing my hands as I allowed myself one last moment of anticipation. I closed my eyes and listened to the distant thumping of the oncoming train, felt the currents of air from the tunnel.

It was like standing in an airplane hatch, waiting to leap. Everything planned, checked, rechecked, every step of the next few minutes choreographed, the contingencies mapped out, should obstacles arise. Like skydiving, I controlled what I could, down to the most minute detail, creating the ordered perfection that set my mind at ease. Yet I knew that in a few seconds, when I made my move, I left some small bit to fate.

I inhaled deeply and concentrated on the moment, slowing my breathing, my pulse. Focusing.

No time to second-guess. No chance to turn back.

At the squeal of the approaching train, I opened my eyes, unclenched my hands and turned toward Moretti.

I quickened my pace until I was beside him. Tension blew off him in waves. His right hand was jammed into his pocket, undoubtedly fondling a nice piece of hardware.

The train headlights broke through the darkness.

Moretti stepped forward. I stepped on the heel of the woman in front of me. She stumbled. The crowd, pressed so tightly together, wobbled as one body. As I jostled against Moretti, my hand slid inside his open jacket. A deft jab followed by a clumsy shove as I "recovered" my balance. Moretti only grunted and pushed back, then clambered onto the train with the crowd.

I stepped onto the subway car, took a seat at the back, then disembarked at the next stop, merging with the crowd once again.

Job done. Payment collected. Equipment discarded. Time to go home ... almost.

Outside the city, I sat in my rented car, drinking in my first unguarded moment in three days. Although the scent of the city was overpowering, I swore I could detect the faint smell of dying leaves and fresh air on the breeze. Wishful thinking, but I closed my eyes and basked in the fantasy, feeling the cold night air on my face.

This was my first hit without a gun. Distance shooting was my specialty, but my mentor, Jack, had been pushing me to try something else. Carrying a gun these days wasn't as easy as it had been five years ago, and there were times when using one just wasn't feasible. So he'd trained me in poisons—which to choose, how to deliver it, how to carry the syringe and poison disguised as insulin. Then he'd encouraged me to find an excuse to try it. With Moretti, it hadn't been so much an excuse as a necessity.

The Tomassinis had confirmed that Moretti had suffered a fatal heart attack on the train. There had been some commotion and the police had been summoned, probably because Moretti had realized in his final moments that he'd been poisoned. That, Jack said, was a chance you took using concentrated potassium chloride in a public place, on a victim who knew he was a target. It didn't matter. With Moretti, the Tomassinis wanted to send a message, and it was clearer if his death wasn't mistaken for natural causes.

As for what else I felt after killing Moretti, I suppose there are many things one should feel in the aftermath of taking a life. Dean Moretti may have earned his death, but it would affect someone who didn't deserve the pain of loss—a brother, girlfriend, someone who cared.

I knew that. I'd been there, knocking on the door of a parent, a spouse, a lover, seeing them crumple as I gave them the news. Your father was knifed by a strung-out junkie client. Your daughter was shot by a rival gang member. Your husband was killed by a man he tried to rob. I'd seen their grief, the pangs made all the worse by knowing they'd seen that violent end coming... and been unable to stop it.

Yet in this case, it was the other victims I saw—the teens Moretti sold drugs to, the lives *he'd* touched. Killing him didn't solve any problems. It was like scooping water from the ocean. Yet, the next time the Tomassinis called, if the job was right, I'd be back. I had to.

It was the only thing that kept me sane.

On my way out of the city, as the lights of New York faded behind me, the radio DJ paused his endless prattle with a "special bulletin," announcing that the Helter Skelter killer may have struck again, this time in New York City. "Speculation is mounting that the Helter Skelter killer is responsible for the rush-hour subway death of Dean Moretti..."

My calm shattered and I nearly ran my car off the road.

TWO

Cool under pressure. If they posted employment ads for hitmen, that'd be the number-two requirement, right after detail-oriented. A good hitman must possess the perfect blend of personality type A and B traits, a control freak who obsesses over every clothing fiber yet projects the demeanor of the most laid-back slacker. After pulling a hit, I can walk past police officers without so much as a twitch in my heart rate. I'd love to chalk it up to nerves of steel, but the truth is I just don't rattle that easily.

But driving up to the U.S./Canada border that morning, I was so rattled I could hear my fillings clanking. How could Moretti's hit be mistaken for the work of some psycho? Any cop knows the difference between a professional hit and a serial killing.

Had I unintentionally copied part of the killer's MO? The case had been plastered across the airwaves and newspapers for a week now, but I'd behaved myself. If an update came on the radio, I'd changed the station. If the paper printed an article, I'd flipped past it. It hadn't been easy. Few aspects of American culture are as popular with the Canadian media as crime. We lap it up with equal parts fascination and condescension: "What an incredible case. Thank God things like that hardly ever happen up here." But I no longer allowed myself to be fascinated. In hindsight, it was a choice that warranted a special place on the overcrowded roster of "Nadia Stafford's Regrettable Life Decisions."

I'd driven all night, as I always did, eager to get home as soon as my work was done. It was just past seven now, with only a few short lines of early morning travelers at the border. As the queue inched forward, I rolled down my window, hoping the chill air would freeze-dry my sweat before I reached the booth. Somewhere to my left, a motorcycle revved its engine and my head jerked up.

Normally, crossing the border was no cause for alarm. Even post-9/11, it's easy enough, so long as you have photo ID. Mine was the best money could buy. Half the time, the guards never gave it more than the most cursory glance. I'm a thirty-two-year-old, white, middle-class woman. Run me through a racial profile and you get "cross-border shopper."

In light of the Helter Skelter killings, they'd probably look closer at everyone, but I had nothing to hide. I'd switched my New York–plated rental for my Ontario-plated one. I'd disposed of my disguise in New York. The Tomassinis paid me in uncut gemstones, which are small enough that I could hide them in places no border agent would normally look.

I pulled forward. Second in line now.

It would be fine. Let's face it, how many terrorists enter Canada from the U.S.? Even illegal immigrants stream the other way. Yet even as I told myself this, the agent manning my booth waved the vehicle in front of me over to the search area. It was a minivan driven by a white-haired woman who could barely see over the steering wheel.

I assessed my chances of jumping into another line, where the agent might be in a better mood, but nothing says smuggler like lane-jumping.

I removed my sunglasses and pulled up to the booth.

The agent peered down from his chair. "Destination?"

"Heading home," I said. "Hamilton."

I lifted my ID, but didn't hand it to him. Prepared, but not overeager.

"Where are you coming from?"

"Buffalo."

"Purpose?"

"Shopping trip."

"Length of stay?"

"Since Wednesday. Three days."

Now, I could have easily combined all this information in one simple sentence, but I never liked to display too much familiarity with the routine.

"Bring anything back with you?"

I lifted a handful of receipts, all legitimate. "A couple of shirts, two CDs and a book. Oh, and a bottle of rum."

The agent waved away the receipts, but did accept the proffered driver's license. He looked at it, looked at me, looked back at it. It *was* my photo. A few years old but, hell, the last time I'd changed my hairstyle was in high school. I didn't exactly ride the cutting edge of fashion.

"Passport?" he asked.

"Never had any use for one, I'm afraid. This is about as far from home as I get." I dug into my purse and pulled out three other pieces of fake ID. "I have a library card, my health card, Social Insurance number . . ."

I held them up. The agent lifted his hand to wave the cards away, then stopped. The wordless mumbling of a distant radio announcer turned into clear English.

"—fifth victim of the Helter Skelter killer," the DJ said.

"Sorry," I murmured, and reached for my radio volume, only to find it already off.

The agent didn't hear me. He'd turned his full attention to the radio, which seemed to be coming from the truck on the other side of the booth. As the announcer continued, in every booth, every car, the occupants seemed locked in a collective pause, listening.

"Police are searching for a suspect seen in the vicinity. The suspect is believed to be a white male..."

I exhaled so hard I missed the rest of the description.

"Although police are treating Dean Moretti's death as a homicide, they are dismissing rumors that he was the Helter Skelter killer's fifth victim. Yet speculation continues to mount after a witness at the scene claimed to have seen the killer's signature..."

The announcer's voice faded as the truck pulled away. I strained to hear the rest, but my agent had already turned back to me again.

I held up my fake IDs, gripping them tightly to keep my hand steady. "Did you want to see...?"

The agent shook his head. "That's fine. You should think about getting a passport, though. One of these days we're going to need to ask for it."

"Okay. Thanks."

The agent leaned out from his booth to check the backseat, his gaze traveling over the crunched-up drive-through bag. Necessary cover. A spotless car can seem as suspicious as one piled hip high in trash.

I held my breath and waited for him to tell me to pull over.

"Have a nice day," he said, and handed me my fake license.

In Fort Erie, I swapped the rental car for my own. Then I headed to the QEW, drove through Hamilton and kept going. My real destination was four hours away—past Toronto, past the suburbs, past the outlying cities.

I found CBC on my radio dial and kept it there, waiting for news of the Moretti case or the Helter Skelter killer in general. As I listened, my heartbeat revved as every news item concluded, certain the next one would be what I wanted.

For almost two weeks, this killer had been splashed across the news, even in Canada, and I'd been so damned good. I'd slammed the door shut, as I did on news of any particularly vicious or noteworthy crime—anything that might set a fresh match to that tamped-down fire in my gut.

But now I had an excuse to delve into the details of these crimes—and it was like a recovering alcoholic handed a champagne flute at a wedding and expected to offer a toast.

So I listened. And heard bitching about the softwood lumber dispute, bitching about the Kyoto Accord, bitching about the education funding formula, bitching about the provincial government, bitching about the federal government...No wonder immigrants landed here and hightailed it to the U.S. Our national broadcasts scared them away.

I stopped in Oshawa and grabbed a jumbo bag of Skittles, something sweet to keep my hands and mouth busy. Finally, as I got back into the car, the ten o'clock morning news brought word of the Moretti case.

"It is expected that police will provide a description of the man wanted in connection with yesterday's subway killing. Authorities stress that the man is wanted only for questioning. He is not considered a suspect, but police believe he may have witnessed..."

Amazing how that "wanted for questioning" line actually works. I've known perps who've shown up at the station, thinking they're being smart, then been genuinely shocked when the interview turns out to be an interrogation.

Unless they really *were* looking for a witness... What if someone had seen me? No. It had been a good hit, a clean hit.

The newscaster continued, "Yesterday's subway killing is believed by some to be the fifth in a series of murders that began over a week ago."

Okay, here it comes. The recap. I turned up the volume another notch.

"The last confirmed victim was sixty-eight-year-old Mary Lee, who was found strangled in her Atlanta convenience store yesterday morning. Up next, a panel discussion on the problems with health care in this country..."

I whacked the volume button so hard it flew off and rolled under my feet.

Four killings in less than two weeks, in different states, seemed more like a cross-country spree killer than a serial killer. How were the police connecting the murders? Why would they think the hit on Moretti was part of the series? An elderly woman strangled in her shop and a Mafioso punk injected with potassium chloride in a subway? How did you connect those?

I spun the radio dial, searching for more information, but, for once, the media was silent.

In Peterborough, I stopped at my storage shed and dropped off my subcompact workmobile. A few blocks away, I picked up my regular wheels: an ancient Ford pickup. Then I left the city and drove north until the beautiful fall foliage ceased seeming jaw-droppingly spectacular and became merely monotonous. Ontario cottage country. My year-round home.

I slowed near a rough-hewn sign proclaiming Red Oak Lodge: No Vacancy. Well, that was a surprise. This time of year, the lodge was rarely at more than half-occupancy, even on weekends. Not that the lodge would make me rich anytime soon. It had yet to break even. In fact, my contract work with the Tomassinis was the only thing that kept it open.

Three years ago, I'd almost declared bankruptcy, hanging on for months fueled by a nearly irrational desperation. I'd destroyed my life once. To rebuild it only to lose it again?

When that first job offer from the Tomassinis came, under circumstances I can only chalk up to fate, I took it, and the lodge and I survived.

Distant staccato cracks of gunfire sent a pair of pheasants jetting into the sky. Red Oak used to be a hunting lodge. But hunting for sport went against my admittedly warped code of morality, so under my ownership, the lodge had been reborn as a wilderness retreat and state-of-the-art shooting club. I still played host to hunters—that was unavoidable if I wanted to stay afloat—but they had to bag their prey elsewhere.

I signaled my turn, but before I could steer into the lane, the roar of tires accelerating on dirt sounded behind me. I glanced in my rearview mirror to see a car pulling out to pass me. A small car, which around here meant tourists. I grimaced. Why come up for the autumn colors if you're not going to slow down enough to see them?

As the car zoomed up beside mine, gravel clinked against my fender. I raised my hand—my whole hand, not just my middle finger. Being semidependent on tourists for your livelihood means you can't afford to make obscene gestures, no matter how justifiable.

In midwave, I caught a glimpse of the driver. Dark-haired. Male. Features shaded into near-obscurity by the tinted glass, but the shape of his face was familiar enough to warrant a double take. The man leaned toward the window, so I could see him better.

"Jack?" I mouthed.

He nodded. I stopped the truck, but he'd already pulled away, message conveyed. He wanted to talk to me, but no such conversation would take place until the sun set.

Jack. Most professional killers prefer a nom de guerre with a bit more pizzazz. I swear, every predator that survived the flood has a hitman namesake. A few years back there was one who called himself the Hornet. Didn't last long. In this profession, it's never a good omen to name yourself after something with a short life span. Most people assume Jack is short for something, maybe Jackal, but I figure Jack is exactly what it sounds like—the most boring code name the guy could think up.

In the world of professional killers, there are a million shades of mysterious. In my own zeal for secrecy, I'd be considered borderline paranoid. Compared to Jack, though, I might as well be advertising in the Yellow Pages with a photo. In the past two years, Jack had visited me over a dozen times and I'd never seen him in daylight. If he wanted to come by, he'd phone pretending to be my brother, Brad, which worked out well, since Brad himself last called me in 2002. For Jack to just show up meant something was wrong, and I was sure that "something" had to do with the Moretti hit.

THREE

I parked around back, beside the minivan owned by my live-in caretakers, the Waldens. Before I got out, I rolled down my window and inhaled the crisp air, resplendent with pine and wood smoke.

To my right, Crescent Lake glistened through the trees. As I watched, a canoe glided past. A dog barked, the sound carrying from a cottage on the far side. I could make out the faint figure of someone on my dock, tying up a rowboat. Owen Walden, my caretaker, judging by the stooped shoulders. Out fishing, maybe escorting a guest or two.

As I turned, a rabbit loped across one of the many paths Owen and I had carved through the forest and meadows, hiking and biking trails for guests. A sharp wind whipped up the dying leaves, and the rabbit shot for cover.

I took one last look around, acclimatizing myself. Forget the Helter Skelter killer. Forget what happened in New York. Forget who I'd been in New York. This was home—and with home came the other Nadia. The Nadia I should have been.

When I reached for the door handle, I heard the crunch of gravel underfoot. Silence. Then softer footfalls, careful now, but the grinding of stones still unmistakable. I opened my door and stepped out.

Something jabbed the middle of my back.

"Police," a man barked. "Against the car and spread 'em."

I kicked backward, hooking his leg and yanking it. He toppled to the ground. Before he could move, I planted one foot on his chest.

"Haven't lost your touch," he said.

"Maybe you're losing yours." I smiled and helped him to his feet. A good-looking guy: wavy blond hair, just starting to recede, a solid build and a knee-weakening grin. Mitch Dylan had been coming to the lodge since the summer I opened it—the same summer he'd been in the midst of an ugly divorce and needed a retreat as much as I did.

"I saw the No Vacancy sign," I said. "You must have brought a full squad with you."

"Pretty much."

He leaned into the cab, grabbed my duffel bag from the passenger seat and started listing names. All cops. Mitch was a Toronto homicide detective. A good cop, and I say that with all sincerity. I like cops—I used to be one.

He led me the long way to the lodge, giving us time to chat. After five years, I won't say there wasn't an attraction, but it never proceeded beyond flirting with the idea of flirting. Nor would it. These days, there was no place in my life for anything more serious than a summer fling—and lately even those seemed more trouble than they were worth.

The lodge was a guy place—a rectangular block of a log cabin, completely lacking in architectural beauty. I don't mind that, though I had added a wraparound deck and porch swings, so I could sit out on summer afternoons, drink iced tea, let the breeze ruffle my hair and get a good dose of girliness...right before I needed to split logs for the evening beer-and-hot-dog bonfire.

The front doors opened into the main room—a huge area dominated by a stone fireplace. The room was jammed with places to sit and places to set down a beer or coffee, none of it matching, little of it bought new. No one seemed to care, so long as they were comfortable. That's what people come to a lodge for—comfort.

When Mitch and I walked in, the room was full of guys. They sprawled over the couches and chairs, feet propped on anything that didn't move and some things that might. There were two women with them. I was pleased to see Lucy Schmidt—one of the few policewomen who didn't act as if my professional disgrace was a gender-specific contagion. She walked over and hugged me, her sturdy, six-foot frame enveloping my five-six.

"Hey, you made it," one of the men called from the sofa. He'd been here in the spring and I struggled to put a name to the face. "Mitch said you'd take us rappelling after lunch."

"He did, did he?"

As I walked toward the stairs, I noticed three men who looked more like corporate management than cops. They probably were. Other lodge guests often joined in with Mitch's group. I'd have to check with Emma, make sure our insurance was up-to-date. Last time Mitch's bunch was here, their visit had coincided with a firm's annual getaway. Four accountants had ended up with non-life-threatening injuries. Fortunately, none sued. Two even had me take photos of their wounds, oozing blood and dirt, to show their friends back home.

A young man with a crew cut came bouncing down the stairs and stopped in my path.

"You must be Nadia," he said, face splitting in a grin that made him look twelve. He extended a hand. "Pete Moore. Etobicoke. My first year."

I shook his hand.

"You know, you're quite a celebrity over at the police college. We did a case study on you."

From the corner of my eye, I saw Mitch bearing down, not-so-subtly gesturing for Moore to zip it. Moore didn't notice.

"Couple months ago, we had this kiddy rapist, a real nasty piece of shit, and I said to my sergeant, 'Man, this is one of those times when you really wish you had someone like Nadia Stafford on the team.'"

Mitch grabbed the duffel from me, put a hand against my back and propelled me up the stairs, body-checking Moore so hard the young man yelped.

"Kid's got a bad habit of opening his mouth before engaging his brain," Mitch said when we got to the upstairs hall.

"It's okay."

"I'll talk to him."

"Don't." I pushed open the unlocked door to my room. "Really, it's okay. He thought he was paying me a compliment."

I took the duffel bag and turned, cutting Mitch off before he followed me into the room. "Give me an hour to shower and unpack and I'll be down."

I'd lied about having a shower. My bathroom only had a tub. If I installed a shower, I'd use it—and my life needed less harsh efficiency and more hot baths with orange-blossom bubbles. Except for the bathroom, my quarters are the very model of efficiency. Because the lodge is a live-in business, there's a self-contained apartment on the first floor, but this I gave to the Waldens. I used one of the twelve guest rooms, and ate my meals in the dining lounge with everyone else. Most of my day was spent outdoors and, with 120 acres, I had all the living space I could ask for.

The first thing I needed was not a bath, but information. I knew Jack could tell me more about the Helter Skelter killings, and how much danger I was in because of the Moretti connection, but I couldn't wait for nightfall.

I took my laptop from the safe under my bed. I'm not a big believer in locking up valuables simply because they're valuable. To be honest, I'm not much of a believer in valuables at all. The only reason I have a safe is for securing the two items I wouldn't want a wandering guest to find: my handgun and my customized laptop.

Computer booted, I started typing a list of search terms: Helter Skelter New York Dean Moretti. Halfway through "Moretti" I stopped. My Internet connection was supposed to be secure. Jack had recommended someone to me, and I'd paid dearly to ensure no one could trace my signal or follow my virtual footsteps. Twice-yearly updates kept me ahead of the latest security-busting technology, or so I'd been told. But was it enough?

The Helter Skelter affair was an FBI case. The Feds knew a lot more about technology than any local police department. If anyone ever tracked the Moretti killing to me, I didn't want my computer records showing that I'd taken an undue interest in the Helter Skelter case. Yes, I'm sure that at that very moment, thousands of people were researching the same thing, but I had to be more careful.

I'd need to wait and get my information from Jack.

I spent the rest of the day in agony. I love being the host/guide at a wilderness lodge, but that day nothing would have pleased me more than if my guests had all packed up and left, so I could hop in my truck, barrel down to Peterborough and find every newspaper, magazine and online source that so much as mentioned the Helter Skelter case.

I could ask. Hell, I was surrounded by cops. Half of them probably knew every detail of the case, even if it was unfolding across the border. Yet I couldn't take the chance.

It'd been a clean hit. I hadn't left a single clue behind. Or had I? If the cops thought the Moretti hit was the work of the Helter Skelter killer, they'd have their best and brightest working the scene with every tool at their disposal. I was good, but was I good enough to stymie the best crime investigators in America?

Rappelling helped clear my mind. Ten years ago, if someone told me I'd be ricocheting down cliffs or jumping from airplanes or rocketing along rapids, I'd have told them they'd mistaken me for someone else. Nadia Stafford did not take chances. Ever. She was the girl who did as she was told and always looked both ways—twice—before crossing the road.

My cousin Amy had been the risk taker of the family. I don't think Amy ever looked before crossing a road in her life. She didn't need to; she had me to do it for her. That's why we were best friends—we complemented each other perfectly.

Though she was a year older, I was the responsible one, the one who kept her safe. Her job was keeping me from retreating too far into my comfort zone, to prod me out into the world. The last thing she ever said to me was: "Come on, stop worrying; it'll be fun."

It was at the pit of my downfall, after my dismissal from the force and before I bought the lodge, that I discovered extreme sports. I opened the paper, saw an article on sky-diving, got into my car and drove down to sign up. I can still remember standing in the hatch for the first time, knowing that I'd prepared with all the care I could, both mentally and physically. And yet, standing there, looking down, I knew there was still a chance that all my preparation could be undone by the whim of fate. So I jumped.

It wasn't about wanting to die or having nothing left to live for; it was about letting go. You live your life doing what you're supposed to do, following the rules, following your conscience no matter what your gut tells you—and most times, that's okay. Control is good. It allows you to believe in certainty and absolutes, like lining up the perfect shot. But when you hold on for so long, and hold on so tight, every once in a while you have to close your eyes and jump.

After dinner, I helped the guys set up their poker game, but begged off participating, claiming fatigue from the long drive. I'd rest in my room, then join the evening bonfire.

Once in my room, I locked the door, opened the window and slipped out. My feet automatically found the grooves in the logs and I was on the ground in seconds.

I spent the next hour just inside the forest, waiting for Jack. I'd come out too early. Yet I needed this time alone to sit in the forest, listen to the leaves rustle and the distant call of the loons and owls.

Almost an hour had passed when the faint scent of smoke cut through the smells of the forest. Not wood smoke, but that of a cigarette, some foreign brand with a scent so distinctive I'd recognize it in the smokiest blues bar.

I looked over. The lights from the lodge silhouetted a

dark figure stood poised between the trees, a few feet from my shoulder.

"Can't just say hi, can you?" I said.

He arched his brows and said nothing. Muffled laughter rippled from the lodge. Jack frowned, then hooked a thumb south and started walking. I followed.

FOUR

We walked toward the lake. No words exchanged, just walking.

Objectively, I knew I was walking into the forest with a professional killer—a dangerous man made even more dangerous by knowing my secret. The problem was that the concept was hard to reconcile with Jack.

He didn't *seem* threatening, and I'd spent the first year fighting the urge to trust him. That was...confusing for me. At one time, I'd instinctively trusted people, but experience is the best teacher, and even the most trusting child can grow into an adult who's always wary—even as she hides behind open smiles and friendly conversation.

So why this sudden urge to trust Jack, of all people? Maybe it was more a need than an urge. For six years, I'd been so careful, holding myself close and tight. Of all the people in my life I should trust, Jack probably ranked at the bottom. Maybe that's why I did. Like jumping from a plane. I know it's dangerous. I know it can kill me. And I don't care. I close my eyes, take the leap and fall.

We stopped at a fallen oak by the lake. Once we'd made ourselves comfortable, Jack glanced in the direction of the lodge.

"Full house," he said. "Cops?"

"It's not a problem."

"Not for me."

He had a faint Irish brogue. Did that mean he was Irish? Probably not. There was nothing about Jack I took at face value, except maybe his size, which would be hard to fake. He was a couple of inches under six feet and well built. Beyond that—the brogue, the black hair, the dark eyes, even the angular face, too irregular to be called handsome—all could be faked. For all I knew, he wasn't even a smoker.

He opened his mouth again and I knew what was coming, some more pointed comment on my choice of guests.

"Speaking of problems," I said quickly. "It seems I have a big one."

"Yeah. Wondered if you'd heard. You okay?"

"A bit freaked." I paused. "No, a lot freaked."

He nodded, took out a cigarette and lit it. The match flared, illuminating the angles and shadows of his face. He passed the cigarette to me. I'd quit six years ago, but that doesn't stop me from sharing the occasional one with Jack. I'd never told him I used to smoke. Maybe the drooling gave it away.

I took a few deep drags, then handed it back. He inhaled once and held it out again. I guess he realized I needed the nicotine more than he did.

"I've been away," he said. "Out of the country. Got back. Heard the news. Wanted to warn you. Then this."

"Warn me about what?"

"Cops think he's a pro."

"The Helter Skelter killer? The Feds think he's a hitman? Shit."

I tapped the ash off the cigarette, then looked down at the burning ember and stubbed it out against the log.

"Is that why people think Moretti might have been part of the pattern? There has to be more to it than that."

He shrugged. "Not important. You did fine. Cops will make the mob connection. They'll back off. But if the Tomassinis come calling again…"

"It'll be the new year before I hear from them again anyway."

"Good. Cops are coming down hard on pros. Dragging in every guy they ever suspected. Couple have already gone. Old charges. Circumstantial evidence. Lot easier to make that stick right now."

I glanced up at him. "Are you in trouble?"

"Nah. But what's bad for the business? Bad for everyone *in* the business. Word's already leaking. Jobs are drying up. It goes public? They think he's a pro?" He shook his head. "Gotta be stopped. Some of us are gonna try."

"Finding the killer?"

Jack nodded. "You want in?"

"Me?"

"I know you've got a legit job. We'd work around it. There's a payoff, too. Expenses plus, covered by an interested party."

My hands slid out to either side of me, as if adjusting my seating—steadying myself as the world seemed to sway. But I kept my face impassive, gaze down as if considering his words.

Beside me, Jack took out a cigarette. Calm and patient, unaware of what he'd just offered. The chance to hunt this killer. The excuse to tell myself it was just a job.

I inhaled deeply. "Well, I'm flattered, but compared to you, I'm a rookie. There's nothing I could add."

"You were a cop. You're good. Careful." He took out another fresh cigarette. "Could use you."

He glanced at me. When I said nothing, he lit the cigarette, one elbow resting on his thigh, and smoked while staring out into the forest. Several minutes passed. Then he cocked his head my way, waiting for an answer.

"I don't think so," I said.

"Fuck." He breathed the word. "What's the problem?"

"You know this is just a part-time thing, something to cover the bills until the lodge starts making money. I just ... I don't think it's a good idea."

He shook his head, lips parting in another curse, this one a silent puff of smoke. He finished his cigarette, then glanced my way again. When I didn't speak, he stood, stubbed out the butt and stuck it into his jacket pocket. From the same pocket he pulled a white envelope and handed it to me. I opened it. Inside was an airline ticket and a fake passport.

"For tomorrow night," Jack said. "Give you time to think."

I nodded.

He zipped up his coat. "I'll be at the airport. If you're there, you're there. If not ..." He shrugged. "If not, I'll see you later."

I knew I couldn't take this job, and it had nothing to do with the possibility it offered. I simply couldn't afford to get involved with other hitmen.

It was bad enough that Jack knew so much. Only two people in the Tomassini organization even knew I was a woman: the head of the family and his nephew—my original contact. So how did Jack find out who I was? All he'd say was that my security precautions were fine, that my cover hadn't been blown, and I shouldn't worry about it. Damned reassuring, that.

Two years ago, I'd gone out back to gather logs for the furnace and found Jack there. Why did he track me down? Sussing out the competition maybe, but I suspected it was the "nature" of this new colleague that set off his radar more than any competitive instinct. My name and some cursory research would have revealed my background. Maybe he thought I was a cop trying to infiltrate the ranks. Maybe he'd come out here to kill me. He probably had. As for why he'd changed his mind, I can only speculate that perhaps he'd decided I wasn't a threat. I might even prove a valuable contact. Or maybe not so much valuable as entertaining. With Jack, one could never tell.

As reluctant as I'd been to engage in any kind of professional relationship with Jack, I hadn't been fool enough to reject his overtures. That could be taken as an insult, and he knew too much about me to risk that. So, despite severe misgivings, I had to accept that if he'd wanted to kill me, I'd be dead already.

And whatever had brought him to my door in the first place, the relationship had its benefits. He'd suggested I start taking my fee in gemstones—harder to trace and easier to transport. He then exchanged those stones, taking his cut and putting an extra layer of protection between my cash flow and the Tomassinis. In addition, he offered invaluable training and advice. The cost of that? A few bottles of beer, maybe a slice or two of Emma's pie, and keep him amused with stories of life at the lodge. An odd arrangement—but as satisfying a business relationship as I could want.

As for strengthening that relationship by working alongside him, though . . . that wasn't a step I was ready to take. Trusting Jack as my mentor was one thing; trusting him as a partner was another. And I definitely didn't want to get involved with more hitmen.

Yet the promise of Jack's offer started gnawing at my gut the moment he walked away. Maybe this was what I needed. What I did for the Tomassinis served its purpose—stamping out the fire for a little while. Between hits, I had my skydiving and rappelling and white-water rafting. But that was like taking medication for a cold—temporarily covering the symptoms while doing nothing to cure the root problem. And if there was a cure, maybe this was it. To do what I'd failed to do twenty years ago, for Amy.

Or was that just an excuse? Telling myself I wanted to pursue a cure when all I really wanted was to scratch the itch?

As I started hauling logs out for the evening fire, I considered putting an end to the matter right there—starting the blaze with the ticket and fake passport. But I didn't. I set up the logs, letting Mitch help when he came out, then left him in charge of fire burning while I excused myself.

I headed to my room and locked the ticket and passport inside my safe. Then I announced the bonfire and gathered volunteers to help me carry out supplies from the kitchen.

Conversation around the fire soon turned to cop talk, at the instigation of the corporate trio. That was to be expected. Put a law-enforcement group in a social setting with civilians, and it's never long before the civilians start asking, "What's the biggest case you've ever worked?" The trio had avoided such questions all day, curiosity warring with consideration—knowing these guys were on vacation—but when the beer started flowing, the queries came, and so did the anecdotes.

Usually, I love these war-story bonfires even more than my guests do. It's like curling up with a cup of hot chocolate and a warm blanket. I'm transported back to my childhood, wedged between my father and one of my uncles or cousins at some get-together, listening to their stories of life on the force—more heroic and exhilarating to me than any tales of knights and dragons.

Today, it was like settling in with my cocoa and blanket... and finding the milk curdled and the wool rough and scratchy. Now the stories only served to remind me that I wasn't part of that life and never would be again.

I'd learned to deal with my grief, and most of the time, I truly did love my new life. But tonight the old impulse was gnawing at me, along with that plane ticket in my bedroom.

Jack was right. Between the two of us, we had the skills to find a hitman turned serial murderer. He knew that underground world better than any federal agent. And me? I didn't just know how to be a cop; I knew how to be a killer.

"You were on the force when that happened, weren't you, Nadia?"

I looked up from picking the black crust off my burned marshmallow. It took a moment to remember which story someone had been recounting.

"The Don Valley rapist? Yep. I wasn't in that division, though."

The corporate trio turned to look at me.

"You were a cop?" one—Bruce—said.

I nodded.

"Retired," Mitch amended.

Bruce laughed. "Retired? Already? You can't be much more than thirty—let me guess. Struck it big in the dot-com explosion, and got out before the implosion, right?"

I laughed with him.

"The rest of us just come out here to look, drool and dream," Mitch said. "Seven more years, Stafford, and I'm buying that woodlot down the road, building a lodge of my own and putting you out of business. You watch."

A few others joined in, joking about retirement plans, partly in earnest, partly to steer conversation away from me. I appreciated the gesture, but one of the first lessons I'd learned when I'd opened the lodge was that anyone who cared to find out my past would.

If my name and face didn't tweak their memory, it would tweak another guest's. Or, failing that, they only had to stop at Mullins General Store down the road and mention where they were staying. Ever since her husband had tried to get me to pay my renovation bill in currency of another kind, Lisa Mullins had decided it was her sworn duty to ensure all my guests knew of my past. "You're staying with Nadia Stafford? Oh, she's such a sweet girl, isn't she? Hard to believe she's a . . ."

As I leaned toward the flames, I could almost feel Lisa's breath on my neck as she whispered, "Killer."

I couldn't sleep. Too many thoughts banged around in my head, so I went outside and wandered the paths close to the lodge. The night was cold, crisp, the same fresh air I'd fantasized about the night before, sitting outside New York. Yet here was the real thing, and it did nothing to clear my head or lift my thoughts.

If I could help find this killer, I wanted to. But did I dare?

This job could be a dream come true, a chance to set my dark side at rest, douse the embers for good. Or would it? What had happened to me has happened to countless others, and how many of them had turned into professional killers? We are the sum total of a lifetime of experiences, and while there may be those events that change our lives forever, they are still tempered and molded by all the rest.

If I indulged my fantasy, helped catch the killer and

found justice—if not for Amy, for others like her—would I emerge renewed? Would I be just like everyone else, reading about horrible crimes and thinking "what is the world coming to?" but feeling no compulsion to act on that horror, that outrage? Did I *want* to be like that?

Twigs crackled and I froze. My first thought was "Jack" and hope zinged through me. I could talk to Jack. Get more details, work this out—

"Nadia?" a voice whispered. "It's Mitch."

I hesitated, then said. "Over here."

"I didn't want to spook you," he said as he approached. The moon lit his wry smile. "Never a smart move with someone who knows aikido."

I tried to smile back. Probably succeeded.

"You okay?" he asked. "I heard you leave the house."

"Just getting some air. Couldn't sleep. Lagged from the drive, I think."

He moved closer. "You seemed a little off today. Is it what that kid said?"

"Kid?" It took a moment to realize he meant the rookie's comments. "No, no. Just the trip." I managed a smile. "I'll be fine tomorrow, just in time for the shooting range. Gonna kick your ass again."

"Nothing new there." Now he was the one struggling to return the smile. "I know it must be hard for you, still hearing stuff like that, after all these years, but—" He tilted his head, looking away, as if trying to decide whether to continue. "I just— For five years, I've kept my mouth shut, Nadia, not wanting to upset you, but I saw how you were today after that kid's dumb crack, so I'm going to say it. What happened to you could have happened to me or a dozen guys I know. Circumstances pile up and..." He waved his hand. "Things happen. Maybe you snap. Maybe you slip. Point is, it could happen, and we all see how it could happen."

I nodded. Struggled to look grateful. I knew what he was trying to do, but he saw only that single event. It hadn't been a slip, but an escalation, culminating in one explosive, career-ending move.

I said a few words. Can't remember what. Just token sentiments, meant to reassure him that he'd succeeded in reassuring *me*. He moved closer, on pretext of blocking the cold night air—so close I could feel his breath, warm on my cheek. I knew he was struggling to put words to something else, something more personal, but I pretended not to notice. It was easier that way. Easier for me. Easier on him.

Maybe five years ago, he would have been the answer to my prayers. Today, I knew myself better, and knew there was nothing I could ever really share with a guy like Mitch Dylan.

So I waited until he decided this wasn't the time or the place, then I made some joke—I don't know what, it didn't matter—and led him back inside.

I passed the plate of cold cuts to Mitch. Lunch. My first meal of the day. At breakfast I hadn't been able to do more than push food around my plate. After that, I'd kept busy with my guests, hoping the knot in my stomach would wither from lack of attention.

"Would December be too early?" Mitch said as he forked roast beef slices onto his plate.

"Might be," I said. "With this mild of a fall, I wouldn't count on snow until January. Plus we get a busy spurt over the holidays. I don't think you guys want to mingle with the 'romantic country Christmas' crowd."

Pete Moore walked into the dining room.

"Finally," Mitch said. "Get lost on your way to town?"

Moore slapped the day's *Toronto Star* onto the table. "It wasn't him."

Mitch shook his head. "Put that away and sit down before all the food's gone."

"Wasn't who?" someone down the table asked.

"The New York subway killing. They've confirmed it wasn't the Helter Skelter killer. Rumor has it some witness was running around claiming he saw a page by the body, but it was just a piece of paper."

"Page?" I said.

"From the book."

I longed to ask "what book?" but didn't dare. A natural enough question under the circumstances, but I told myself it was still better not to take an interest. I could look it up later.

"So it's only four," one of the businessmen said.

"For now," Moore said, pulling out his chair.

"Well, four murders, the best cops on the case, they must be getting close," I said.

Silence answered. I looked down the table, at the faces of the most seasoned officers there. They concentrated on their plates, eyes downcast as if in reverence for the victims to come. My stomach twisted.

"Nadia's right," Bruce, the corporate guy, said. "They've got to catch this bastard soon, huh?"

Mitch finished chewing and swallowed. "It doesn't look that easy. He's not leaving them a damned thing to go on."

I speared a pickle. "I heard a rumor he might be a professional killer. That true?"

"A hitman turned serial killer?" Lucy said. "God, I hope not."

"Or this sure as hell won't stop at four," someone muttered.

When the last of my guests trickled out later that afternoon, I spoke to Emma. Something had come up, and I had to leave for a few days. During the week, the lodge would see only a few guests, so it was easily handled.

As for where I was going, she didn't ask. According to Emma, I spent far too much time at the lodge anyway. I should take advantage of slow times to travel and get together with friends—preferably male ones. So when I did slip away mysteriously now and then, she only smiled and told me to have a good time.

I stayed to help with the post-weekend cleaning, then left for Toronto that evening.

I had a plane to catch.

FIVE

I turned the page on my in-flight magazine and wished I'd picked up a newspaper so I could acquaint myself with the basics of the case. I'd been worried about displaying too much interest in the matter but I seemed to stand out more by *not* taking an interest.

The woman in the aisle seat leaned toward her husband, voice low to avoid waking those lucky few who'd managed to fall asleep.

"I'm only saying—" she began.

"That you're afraid," her husband boomed. "Christ almighty, Anne. No one's going to break into the hotel room and kill you while I'm at my conference."

"The newspaper says we shouldn't be alone. That's the one thing all four murders had in common. The victim was alone."

Her husband managed to raise his voice another notch, in case the pilots and first-class passengers couldn't hear him. "So he's going to pick you? Out of the three hundred million other people in this country?"

"I was just thinking—"

"Well, don't."

I turned from the window. The wife ducked my smile and sank into her seat. I put on my headphones, leaving one fewer witness to her humiliation. But before I could turn up the volume, the husband continued.

"Do you really think these are random killings?"

"The paper says—" she began.

"Bullshit. There's no such thing as random murder.

These people, they did something wrong and it got them killed. The police will find the link. Drugs, I bet."

"I can't see that, George. Not that poor old woman in Atlanta."

"Ran a shop, didn't she? Who knows what she was selling? That third one? The Russian? Police admitted he had a record. Then there's the college girl, and we all know what kids do in college."

"What about the second one? The accountant."

"Stockbroker. And black. That says it all—" The man had the sense to stop short and cast an anxious glance around. "Stockbrokers, I mean. How do you think they make so much money?"

"I don't know, George . . ."

"You don't need to know. I've met my share of criminals and I can tell you, one look at those photos in the paper, and it's obvious those 'victims' were on the wrong side of the law."

A serving cart jangled down the aisle and stopped beside us.

"Two coffees," the husband said. "One cream. Two sugars."

He looked over at me. I tugged the headphones from my ears and smiled at the hostess.

"Coffee, please. Just cream."

As she poured, the husband leaned toward his wife, voice dropping a notch. "You don't need to worry, Anne. If you ever got within fifty feet of a killer, you'd see it in his face."

The hostess held out my coffee. The husband took it and passed it to me. Our eyes met.

"Thanks," I said.

He nodded, returned my smile and took his own cup from the hostess.

I exited the plane, swept along in the tide of passengers. Inside the terminal, I looked around and groaned. A crowded major American airport, and Jack hadn't specified a meeting spot. Plus he'd be wearing a disguise. Wonderful.

Did Jack expect me to be incognito? I stored all my things in New York, having no need or inclination to play dress-up at home. I took out the passport and checked the photo again. Shoulder-length auburn curls. Hazel eyes. Not smiling, but dimples threatening to break through. Yep, definitely me, so he obviously hadn't intended for me to wear a disguise. Hey, where'd he get a picture—? I shook my head. Better not to know.

I looped back toward the exit gate. Halfway there I spotted Jack. Something—maybe his posture or the tilt of his head—tripped a wire in my head. Normally I'd peg Jack at late thirties. Now he'd aged himself another decade, deepening the lines around his eyes and mouth, roughening his skin. His hair was dark blond, pulled back into a ponytail. A Vandyke beard covered his chin. He wore jeans and a long-sleeved pullover pushed up to his elbows to reveal a garish forearm tattoo. He looked like an aging biker who'd retired from the life, settled down, bought himself and the missus a honky-tonk bar. I really hoped I didn't have to play the missus.

He stood back from the crowd, sipping coffee from a Styrofoam cup. For at least a minute, I stood there, just watching. This was one huge step up from sitting with him in the forest, taking lessons. Could I trust Jack enough to work alongside him? Did I *dare*?

I closed my eyes and took a deep breath, then started toward him.

As his gaze scanned the last trickle of exiting passengers, his mouth set in a firm line. The flow of passengers petered out. Jack strode to a garbage can and crushed the cup. It wasn't empty, and coffee spurted on his hand. He glared at the mess, pitched the cup into the trash and swiped his wet hand across his jeans. Then he stalked toward the exit. I slipped through a small crowd and put myself in his path. He nearly mowed me down before stopping short.

"Nad—" He rubbed his hand across his mouth, as if erasing the mistake.

"Surprise."

"Right." Pause. "Luggage?"

I lifted my carry-on. "Just this."

He glanced around, as if uncertain what to do next.

"You really didn't expect me to get off that plane, did you?" I said.

"That look you gave me Saturday? Figured it was a no go."

"I could get on the next flight."

A slow quarter-smile. "Gotta earn your way home."

"I plan to. Where to first?"

"Breakfast."

Jack offered to grab food while I used the washroom.

When I emerged, Jack was still in line at a bagel place. I caught his attention and waved to a spot out of the through-fares. He nodded and I hefted my bag to my shoulder and walked to stand between a group of young men and a sun-glasses kiosk.

"—like I told the cop, it was an accident," one of the young men was saying.

"Yeah," another answered. "Bitch's arm got in your way and next thing you know, it's broken. Whoops."

A chorus of snickers. I turned the other way, getting a look at them through the mirrors on the kiosk. Three guys, maybe early twenties, all white, dressed in baggy clothes, do-rags and shades. Gangsta wannabes, trash-talking at full volume, thinking it's cool to brag about breaking a girlfriend's arm.

Then I saw the kid half hidden off to the side. No more than eleven, probably younger, dressed like the big boys—probably a cousin or nephew. He stared up in rapture, absorbing every word.

"...restraining order. Can you believe it? Won't fucking let me see my own kid, all because she's pissed off about a broken arm, and if she thinks that's going to stop me, bitch better think again, because a restraining order ain't no magic security system. Ain't gonna stop me from bustin' into her place whenever I want to, and if she don't like it, a broken arm's gonna be the least of her worries."

"You tell her."

They continued, ignoring the glares from people passing. No, not ignoring the glares—reveling in them, because that's what it was all about, getting attention, making people scared of you.

I glanced again in the mirror, focused on the young man doing all the bragging and felt a familiar swirling in my gut.

What if he was a target, a hit?

First, I'd have to get him away from the pack. There was always an opportunity. Nature would call. Or he'd decide he needed a Coke. Maybe a cigarette. Or he'd whip out his cell and step outside for better reception.

Once away from his pack, I'd need to be able to identify him from a distance or find him in a crowd, even if he was with twenty guys who could pass for his brothers. Distinguishing features? A puckered scar on his left earlobe, as if he'd pierced it himself, then changed his mind. I noticed the wear pattern on his navy high-tops, the soles worn along the outside of the heels, as if he walked slightly bow-legged. His clothing could always be changed. Yet someone suspecting a tail rarely changes his footwear. Shoes and jewelry. Always make a note.

As he talked, a jangling underscored his words, and I traced it to a chain hanging off his belt. I closed my eyes and memorized the sound. Then I noted the sound of his voice, the inflection, the accent.

My target said something to his buddies, stepped away and headed for the doors.

"You ready?" Jack's voice startled me. He lifted a tray of coffees and bagels.

One last glance after my target, then I nodded and followed Jack out of the terminal.

We dined on stale bagels and lukewarm coffee, consumed in the ambience of engine thunder and jet fuel fumes.

"So what's the plan?" I said as I perched on the hood of Jack's rental car. "Have you met with the other guys? Come up with some theories?"

"Nah. Figured you'd want to do that."

I stopped licking cream cheese off my fingers. "Meet the others? If I can avoid it, I'd really rather—"

"Not meet them. I agree. Stay under the radar. Work with me. That's it."

"So you and I . . . we'll be working together?"

He looked over at me. "Thought that was understood. Watch each other's backs. That a problem?"

"No, I just . . . I wasn't sure. I know you work alone, so I thought maybe you'd just set me on a trail or a lead. But working with a partner is how I'm used to doing things— or was, as a cop, so that's fine by me. How are we going to coordinate this with the others, then? A conference call to toss around theories, come up with a plan of action, divide the work . . ."

I stopped, glancing over at Jack, who was staring out at the runway, face impassive.

"There's no meeting, is there? Long distance or other- wise."

He shook his head. "These guys? Not much for team- work. Me neither."

"And I totally get that. But in this case, we need to coor- dinate our efforts, if only to ensure we cover everything and . . ." I met his gaze. "And it's not happening, is it?"

He shook his head. "One guy I tried pulling in? Already in custody. Better keep to ourselves."

"Well, what's *our* game plan, then?"

"Start by filling me in. Who's he killing? Where? Patterns? Methods?"

"I don't know a damned thing about these killings, Jack. I've told you I've been trying to forget that part of my life, stop following the cases."

"Oh."

"Ah, you thought I'd just *said* I'd stopped. I know he's killed four people in the past week or so, and that the last one was strangled."

"Four states. Four methods. That's all I know."

"Shit, we really are starting from ground zero, aren't we?"

Once we were on the highway, Jack handed me a bag. I reached in, pulled out a wig and sighed.

"Figures. Get a guy to buy a wig, and he's going to go blond every time."

"Small store. Two choices. Blond or red."

"I like red."

"Fire-engine red."

"Cool."

"Be thankful I didn't pick clothing. Almost did."

"What were you going to get? Miniskirt and fishnets?"

I put on the wig, then looked at the rest of my outfit. I wore jeans, a plain white T-shirt and a denim jacket—an all-purpose ensemble that, with the right accessories, could run the gamut from preppy-casual to biker-chick-trashy. Normally, I'd fall somewhere in the middle: the nature-girl look, with wash-and-wear hair, fading summer tan and tinted lip gloss. Given Jack's choice of disguise, more makeup was a must. I opened my makeup case, applied enough to scare myself, then took a tissue and pared it back a layer or two.

"Good?" I asked.

Jack glanced over and grunted. Not the most enthusiastic endorsement, but at least he didn't say I looked so much better in a platinum wig and half-pound of makeup.

"One thing missing," he said.

"Stilettos? Or a whip?"

His mouth twitched as he passed me a heavy wrapped bundle.

I unwrapped it to find a Glock 33. "Oooh. Serious bondage gear!"

"Got a waistband holster. Should fit under your jacket. Keep it on, all times."

I found the holster and slipped into it, then double-checked my makeup application in the visor mirror, making sure the faint, thin scar on my neck was hidden. "Not bad. I have to work on my aging techniques, though. I can never get it right. You'll have to teach me sometime."

He made a noise in his throat that I took for agreement, then turned into a strip mall so we could get some research material.

Joyce

"I can try, but..."

The dry-cleaning clerk shrugged, bit back a yawn. Given that it was barely 6:30 in the morning, the yawn and the heavy-lidded eyes could be excused, but Joyce knew it wasn't lack of sleep that was causing the younger woman's attention to wander. She just didn't give a damn.

"Look," Joyce said. "You opened five minutes ago, so you can't possibly be overbooked yet. Your sign says you offer same-day cleaning. I need same-day cleaning."

"We *are* overbooked. With regular customers." A slow quarter-smile. "If you were a regular customer..."

"I *am* a regular customer. I've dropped off clothes every Friday for the past three months."

The clerk's eyes narrowed behind her microframed glasses. "I work Fridays and I've never seen you."

"Of course you have. I talk to you every week!"

The young woman's expression didn't change. "I've never seen you."

Joyce pulled back and shoved her hands in her pockets, torn between crying and screaming. Maybe she should do both. Throw a hissy fit, see if that made her more memorable next time. She sized up the clerk, considered throwing herself at the young woman's mercy, telling her the truth. Look, I've just been through the world's shittiest divorce. I have my first date tonight and this old black dress may not look like much to you, but it's the only thing I have to wear.

Joyce imagined saying the words. Imagined the clerk's reaction. Imagined the smirk, the glitter of condescension.

Imagined her response, "Oh, I'm soooo sorry, but no. Can't do it." Another smirk. Now piss off, you old cow. No twenty-year-old ever imagined herself sinking so low, her self-confidence puddled around her ankles, her ratty apartment and divorce petition exposing her failures as a wife, a woman.

"Piss off to you, too," Joyce muttered under her breath, gathering her dress from the counter and swooping from the store with as much dignity as she could muster.

The door swung closed behind her. Joyce paused, and looked up and down the street, hoping another "same-day cleaning" sign would miraculously appear. There must be other places in town, but she had no idea where they were. She'd only moved there three months ago to take a job from a sympathetic friend.

She inhaled sharply. Okay, maybe she didn't know where there was another cleaner, but she could find out. Joyce strode to the nearest phone booth, pushed open the doors, reached for the phone book... and found an empty chain.

"God-fucking-damn it!"

She hiccuped a laugh. Now that felt better, didn't it? She glanced down at the dress slung over her arm. Ten years old. Ten years out of style. Made for a woman ten years younger. Screw this. If she was going on a date, she was doing it right. Break the bank and buy a new dress. Maybe something from the sales rack at Barneys. She checked her watch. Not yet seven. If she started work early, she could take an extended lunch hour, use the time to buy a dress. She smiled. Problem solved.

Joyce drove into her office building's underground garage. The lot was almost completely empty. She shivered as she walked toward the elevator. Picked up her pace. Slid her car key between her index and middle fingers, the way her daughter had taught her after taking a self-defense course at college. Any guy jumps you, Mom, go for his eyes.

Joyce reached for the elevator button, then paused. Was this such a good idea, getting onto an elevator so early in the morning? What if it stopped between floors and she was stuck there alone? Or what if she wasn't alone? Yes, it was silly, but still... She glanced toward the stairs. A five-floor climb. It wasn't like she didn't need the exercise.

As she rounded the second flight of stairs, she caught sight of something on the step. Folded green paper. She paused, leaned over. Twenty dollars. She laughed, the sound echoing through the empty stairwell. Twenty dollars toward a new dress. How perfect was that?

As her fingers brushed the bill, a current of air swished behind her. She looked up to see a blur flying toward her head. Over her head. The world went white. She opened her mouth, but something jammed against it. She bit down, tasted plastic. A plastic bag over her head. A hand or arm pressing it into her mouth, cutting off her screams.

Her hands flew up. Too late she felt the keys slide from her fist, heard them tinkle against the concrete. She panicked, clawing, kicking, but hitting only air. She tumbled forward. Felt a hand between her shoulder blades. A shove. Her head struck the sharp edge of the step. Light and pain flashed. Her daughter's face. Go for his eyes, Mom. Darkness.

* * *

The man looked down at her body, sprawled awkwardly over the steps, skirt shoved up to reveal one cellulite-pitted thigh above her knee-highs, her arm stretched over her head, fingers grazing the twenty as if, in death, still reaching for it. He almost laughed.

A twenty placed at eye level. A human trap, guaranteed to catch the first person who climbed these stairs. There was an element of risk here, something he'd never allowed himself before. If she hadn't been alone, he'd have had to scrap the whole plan. But the thrill of it, the purest surge of power, came from knowing that if this attempt failed, it made no difference in the overall plan. Kill this person, kill another. Kill here, kill there. Kill now, kill then. For once, it didn't matter. There was no contract, no obligation. He could take risks, enjoy them even, and, to his surprise, he found that he did.

He looked down at the woman. His penultimate strike, perhaps even his last. That was the plan anyway. He'd make this last hit and then, if all went well and the police stayed stumped, he'd stop here. If it didn't go smoothly—and one always had to plan for contingencies—he had one more victim in mind, someone who could take the blame.

But now he wasn't so sure he should stop. He told himself it wasn't the unexpected thrill of this newfound power—that would be unprofessional. Instead, he wondered whether he hadn't been shortsighted. Perhaps five wasn't enough. He'd gotten this far and the Feds were still chasing their tails. Why not add another couple of bodies? He always had the backup hit—his scapegoat—if things went bad. And, more likely, another body or two would only add to the confusion. Then he could stop, free and safe.

He smiled and walked away, leaving her lying there, the

bag still over her head. As he passed, he glanced down at the twenty lying by her outstretched hand. Let them tie up their labs pulling scores of fingerprints from it, running them through the database. They wouldn't find his . . . on the bill or in the database. He took the folded book page from his pocket, unwrapped it and tucked it under her hand, beside the twenty.

One last visual sweep. All clear. He adjusted his driving gloves, picked up his briefcase, then walked down to the main floor door, cracked it open and peered through. Closed doors, darkened windows, an office building still slumbering. He straightened his tie and walked out.

SIX

I ran into the convenience store and bought *Time, Newsweek* and *Cosmopolitan*. No, Cosmo wasn't running an in-depth analysis of the Helter Skelter killings. I'm sure they would have, but, apparently, the breaking news of "10 Ways to Drive Your Man Wild in Bed" took precedence.

As I climbed into the car, Jack plucked the magazines from under my arm. "*Time. Newsweek.* And...?"

He looked at the half-naked supermodel on the cover of *Cosmopolitan.* Most guys would have looked closer. Or at least looked interested. Jack frowned.

"Chock-full of articles on catching a man," I said. "I thought it might help us."

Jack shook his head.

"Hey, in this outfit, do I strike you as a *Time* and *Newsweek* kinda girl? But if you see anything in there that interests you, it's all yours."

Another head shake. He turned the key in the ignition and the subcompact's engine puttered to life. "I'll drive. You read."

The articles contained only a single line on each victim, descriptions so brief even Jack would be hard-pressed to condense them further. That's not to say the articles were short. Each magazine contained not less than three separate pieces on the case, each running several pages. So what did they write about? The killer. Theories, motivations, expert opinions, editorial comments.

The list of victims was almost identical in both publications.

Alicia Sanchez, 21, Hispanic, college student, suffocated in her dorm room, October 5, Beaumont, Texas.

Carson Morrow, 36, African American, stockbroker, stabbed in a parking lot, October 8, St. Louis, Missouri.

Leon Kozlov, 53, Caucasian, retired, shot in his apartment, October 12, Norfolk, Ohio.

Mary Lee, 68, Asian American, business owner, strangled in her shop, October 14, Atlanta, Georgia.

Four lives and four tragedies reduced to factoids.

I studied the four minuscule photos and wondered what they'd been doing the days they'd been killed, what they'd been thinking, planning, dreaming.

In just over a week, four lives had been taken and countless more thrown into turmoil—husbands, wives, lovers, children, parents, siblings, friends, wondering why this had happened, and what they could have done to prevent it, and whether their loved one had suffered, and why hadn't they said something more meaningful the last time they met. And, most of all, *why*. Just why.

Four lives taken, countless more awaiting justice. But when I read that article, I saw no end—no justice—in sight. Just more deaths. More victims. More mourners. More questions.

Neither magazine mentioned the possibility of a hit-man killer, but that likely wasn't a theory investigators would release to the media. The murders, though, had all the earmarks of professional hits—the deaths clean and cold.

"Four murders in four parts of the country, four very different victims, four separate methods," I said. "Linked by a calling card. A page from *Helter Skelter*."

"Yeah. Heard about that."

"It's a book, isn't it?"

"About Manson."

"Charles Manson? The freak with the cult? He killed some actress, didn't he?"

"Before your time, I'm guessing."

"The sixties. Peace, love and drug-induced murderous rages. Hippie stuff."

"Now I feel old."

"Right, like you were more than a baby yourself. From what I remember, the Manson case was textbook disorganized crime. Definitely not the work of a pro. So what's the connection?"

"None, other than that it scared the shit out of a lot of people. Like this guy's doing."

I glanced over at him. "According to *Newsweek*—or their contacts, at least—the Feds have evidence suggesting there's something to the Manson connection."

"Then we don't ignore it. But don't focus on it."

"Okay. So where do you want to start?"

A small frown my way. "No idea. That's your area. Yeah, you weren't a detective. But you think like a cop. Good enough. We'll work something out."

So we did, laying out theories. We had a hired killer making random hits. Option one: system overload. When a pro chess player goes nuts, he becomes obsessed with the game. A pro killer goes nuts? No mystery what might obsess him. Option two was more likely. Why does a hired killer kill? Because he's been hired to.

"The guy beside me on the plane mentioned that Leon Kozlov had a record," I said. "That's a good place to start—checking criminal records and arrests. I have contacts in U.S. police departments—lodge regulars—but I'd *really* rather not use—"

"Agreed. Last resort."

"Good. There are legit ways we can check for criminal backgrounds, though it'll take some time and legwork."

He stared out the windshield, fingers drumming on the steering wheel.

"Got another way," he said finally. "Contact. Couple hours' drive. Find out about Manson, too."

We pulled off at a diner for coffee. We had to be getting close to Jack's contact, and I certainly wasn't hungry, but Jack insisted.

As I sat there, coffee untouched, I swore I could hear my watch ticking. For one person, somewhere out there, time *was* ticking. How much longer before the killer took another life? Judging by his schedule so far, maybe a day.

Time was passing and somewhere my target was planning his next kill while I sat in a diner, across from my "partner," who looked as anxious to get to work as any time-card puncher on Monday morning.

I vented my frustration with chatter.

"—two hours, not a single nibble and my butt is frozen to the ice. So I check the guys' hooks, and no one has any bait. 'Bait?' one says. 'What for? We don't want to catch anything. We just wanted an excuse to toss back a few before lunch.'"

Jack opened his mouth, but a burst of static cut him off. Across the room, a server moved a portable radio onto the counter. The three customers there all leaned forward, like fans listening to the last inning of the World Series. I caught the words "number five" and "Boston." A game this early in the day?

"Turn it up," someone yelled.

The server obliged. I made a face, then caught the first rush of the announcer's words and stopped with my coffee cup halfway to my lips.

"—received confirmation that this is definitely murder number five. It appears the Helter Skelter killer has taken another victim—"

"Fuck," Jack muttered.

"—Boston. Police have released few details at this time. They will say only that an unidentified woman has been found suffocated in the stairwell of her office complex."

Customers crowded around the counter to hear better. Not so much as a fork clinked against china.

"—approximately 7 a.m. Police have confirmed that a page from the book *Helter Skelter* was found with the body. A news conference is scheduled for later this morning. More details are expected at that time. We return now..."

Jack pulled his chair forward, legs scraping the linoleum. He jerked his head toward the door.

Jack got into the car and drove. Not a word about what had happened inside. Yet the news had been enough to get him up and moving.

After less than a thirty-minute drive, Jack pulled into Fort Wayne, Indiana. He drove to a strip mall and parked far enough from the storefronts that no one would notice or care that we were taking up a spot and not shopping.

He got out. I followed. He looked at me over the roof.

"Uh, let me guess," I said. "When you said 'stop by' the pronoun you left off was 'I' not 'we,' right?"

"You want to come?"

"I'm not going to spend this investigation hanging out in the car, getting secondhand information. But I'm not in a hurry to be introduced to all your underworld contacts, either. You know this guy—it's your call."

"You should come." He locked the car. "Get it over with."

Before I could say anything, he was already striding across the parking lot, leaving me jogging to catch up.

We stood before a small two-story house on a street that was mostly brick bungalows, with the occasional two-story thrown in for variety. An old neighborhood in every way, from the massive oaks that looked as if they'd seen the first colonists to the front porches adorned with wicker rockers, mobile scooters and wheelchair ramps.

Down the street, an army of young men worked their way from lawn to lawn, mowers and hedge-clippers in tow. A patrolling security car slowed to give us a once-over, then drove on. It looked like an upper-middle-class retirement community, where the owners kept their houses small, saving their money for Alaskan cruises and European vacations. A strange place for an underworld contact meeting.

"Something I should tell you." Jack peered up at the house. "Things I didn't mention before. Probably should have. But..." He paused, then shook his head. "Too late now. You'll understand or you won't."

With that, he headed for the front steps.

SEVEN

White curtains in the windows. Fresh dark green trim to complement the yellow brick. A black metal mailbox. The space for an engraved surname under the brass door knocker was blank. Jack motioned for me to knock.

"This contact," I said. "Is he a civilian or…"

"Pro."

I adjusted my jacket, making sure my Glock was in place, then banged the knocker. Inside, a dog barked, then another joined in. They sounded big.

A distant door opened, then shut. The barking resumed, now coming from the rear yard.

"What should I call myself?" I said. "I need a name, right?"

Before he could answer, a dead bolt clanked. The door opened. There stood a petite white-haired woman wearing a silk blouse, wool slacks and leather pumps. She looked from me to Jack, back to me, then pointed a finger at Jack.

"You are in deep shit, Jacko."

The woman stepped back and Jack propelled me through the doorway.

She smiled at me. "Let me hang your jacket. Gun on or off, it doesn't matter. A guest's comfort comes first." Her blue eyes sparked. "Though I'll be flattered if you think you might need it."

I handed her my coat and kept my gun holstered.

"I'll join you in the living room," she said. "Jack can hang his own damned jacket, though he might be wise to keep it, in case I decide to boot his ass into the yard with the dogs."

I glanced at Jack. He waved me in. I walked along the

hall and turned into the living room. Thick navy blue carpet, smoke-gray walls, yellow leather sofa set, high-end stereo, Apple computer and built-in bookcases.

If I had my own living room, this is what I'd want it to look like. Scary thing was, this *was* what it would look like: immaculate and organized to the point of compulsion. The computer was turned off, keyboard shelf closed, all cords tucked out of sight. On the bookshelf, every spine was aligned with its neighbor, the books grouped by subject, alphabetical within each subject. Though I couldn't read the rows of CDs behind the glass stereo doors, I knew they'd be organized the same way.

I'd assumed this woman lived with our contact. Seeing this room, I knew I'd been wrong—she *was* the contact.

Jack pointed to the love seat, then sat beside me. I turned to whisper a question but, before I could, the woman joined us. She took a seat across from us, sat and waited. And waited.

"How long do we have to sit here before you do the courtesy of performing introductions?" she finally said.

"Dee, Evelyn. Evelyn, Dee."

"Oh yeah," she said. "That helps. Fucking rude mick. And what the hell kind of name is Dee?" She turned to me. "He picked it, didn't he? I just hope it doesn't stand for Diane."

I frowned.

" 'Jack and Diane'?" she prompted.

"Ah, the song. John Cougar. Or whatever he calls himself now."

"Melonhead or something like that. A perfect example of the importance of names. Cougar, you remember, but the minute you decide to call yourself Melon-shit..." She shook her head. "Names create an impression. Dee makes me think Sandra Dee, and that's all wrong for you. Now Diane wouldn't be so bad if you made it Diana. Goddess of the hunt. That would work."

Jack snorted.

"Shut up or get out," Evelyn said. "You screwed me over. It'll take a lot of ass-kissing to make up for this one." She shifted to face me. "I'm the one who tracked you down."

"What—?"

I looked from her to Jack. Jack met my gaze and dipped his chin, eyes dark with something like apology.

Heart hammering, I turned back to Evelyn. "How—?"

"When it comes to finding people, I'm the best there is. I could tell you where Jimmy Hoffa is . . . but it'd cost you."

"She didn't *find* you," Jack said. "Frank Tomassini mentioned you."

"But I found her from there, didn't I? Frank didn't exactly hand me her name and address."

"He told you about me?"

"Special case. He wouldn't mention it to anyone else."

"But how do you know Frank—?"

"As I was saying, I found you. Women in this business always interest me, and your background was . . . intriguing. Unfortunately, travel to Canada is a bit problematic for me. Some bad business in Quebec back in the seventies, which I'm sure your authorities have forgotten all about, but I prefer not to test that theory. So I decided to send my favorite protégé—"

"Favorite?" Jack muttered. "Only one still talking to you."

"I sent Jack to check you out, to assess your suitability as a protégée. He comes back and says, 'Nah. Forget her.' Which"—another lethal glare at Jack—"apparently meant that *I* was supposed to forget you, not that he planned to.

How long have you been traipsing across the border, cultivating my contact?"

Jack shrugged.

"Often enough, clearly. When were you going to tell me?"

"Brought her here, didn't I? We need information."

She laughed. "Don't you love this guy? He lies to me, steals from me, then has the gall not only to bring you here, but to ask me for help."

Evelyn didn't sound betrayed or even surprised. The look she gave Jack reminded me of a parent complaining about a rebellious teen, exasperated pride masquerading as pique.

"There's a fresh pot of coffee in the kitchen," Evelyn said. "Pour us some, and I'll think about talking."

Jack heaved himself from the love seat and headed into the hall. Evelyn watched him over her shoulder, then turned to me.

"Don't tell her anything," Jack's voice floated back. "She knows what she needs to know. Rest is idle curiosity."

Evelyn mouthed an obscenity. She listened for Jack's movements in the kitchen, as if gauging whether he could still overhear.

"Let's just talk about a decent nom de guerre, then. How about Diana? That's better than Dee, isn't it?"

"Honestly? It makes me think 'dead princess,' not 'Greek goddess.' I'm not sure 'princess' gives off the right vibe, and that 'dead' part is definitely not a good omen."

"You have a point. Hitmen aren't known for their classical educations. We'll stick with Dee until I think of something better."

"Charles Manson," Jack called from the kitchen. "We need details."

"Ah, so this is about the Helter Skelter killer." She turned to me. "Now there's a name. Say the words 'Helter Skelter' and everyone of a certain age immediately thinks Manson, and everything that goes with that. For a killer—"

"Yeah," Jack said, rounding the corner with the coffees. "It's about him."

"You're going after him?"

Jack passed me my mug. "Someone's gotta. Feds are clueless. They'll round up every pro . . . except the killer."

"From what I hear they already are, which is why I've been trying to get in touch with you for a week now. You've been ignoring me."

"Wasn't ignoring you. Busy. Setting this up."

She leaned forward. "So who's in? No, let me guess. Felix, Angel, Quinn—but only because you need him for his contacts. You didn't ask Sid and Shadow, did you?"

When Jack didn't answer, she rolled her eyes. "You did. I don't know how you can put up with those two. Not a full deck between them."

"But they're good. All that counts. Angel's out. Got picked up."

"By the police? On what charges?"

"Jaywalking."

"Don't be smart. You know what I mean. Angel's as careful as they come and if he's been charged with one of his old hits—"

"Then we're all in shit. That's the point. Now, about Manson . . ."

"Well, I can certainly tell you everything you need to know about Charles Manson. But if you're chasing down this alley because your killer uses a silly quote—"

"*Newsweek* says there's more," I said. "According to their sources, the Feds have uncovered a possible connection between the killer and Charles Manson."

Evelyn looked at Jack. "What does Quinn say?"

When Jack didn't answer, she swore under her breath. "You're investigating a case where federal investigators have an important lead, and you haven't even asked Quinn about it yet?"

"Who's—?" I began, then remembered Evelyn's list of names. "He's one of the other pros working this, right? How would he—?"

"Manson, Evelyn," Jack said. "What do you know?"

EIGHT

◆

Charles Manson was a career criminal of the lowest order. During those rare times in his teens and twenties when the state wasn't paying his room and board, he pimped and drug-dealt his way through life. It seemed Manson never committed a crime for which he didn't do the time. You'd think these early signs of ineptitude would make a guy sit back and go, "Hmmm, maybe I'm not cut out to be a criminal mastermind after all." Apparently not.

Manson was a classic predator. He knew how to sniff out the weak and tell them what they wanted to hear. By 1969 he had over two dozen followers, most of them teenage girls. The second greatest question of loyalty after "Would you die for me?" is "Would you kill for me?" In August 1969, Manson put his followers to that test. First, four of them killed Abigail Folger, Wojciech Frykowski, Steven Parent, Sharon Tate and Jay Sebring. The next day, three killed Leno LaBianca and his wife, Rosemary. On April 17, 1971, Manson returned to jail, where he remains.

When she was done explaining, Evelyn sipped her now-cold coffee. "If I had to guess at the connection, I'd look at hero worship."

"I hope by 'hero' you don't mean Manson," I said.

"Even after all these years, Charles Manson receives more mail than any inmate in the system. At the time of the crimes, it was even worse. Some underground papers hailed him as a revolutionary, a martyr of the people and for the people. A cult of Manson still exists today, if you know where to look for it."

"You think one of them—?"

Evelyn cut me short with a wave. "No, no. Losers and lunatics."

She stood, walked to her bookcase, pulled out a volume and tossed it between Jack and me. I picked it up. *Helter Skelter,* by Vincent Bugliosi.

"Manson's minions didn't try to hide anything," she said. "Even the cops couldn't fuck up this case and, believe me, they seemed to be trying their damnedest. Those murders have nothing to do with this Helter Skelter killer. Opposite ends of the spectrum."

"Fine," Jack said. "Just background anyway. More important? Criminal connections. Third victim has a record. Who else?"

"And you want me to look that up for you out of the kindness of my heart? You aren't bringing me the best damn job in a decade, picking my brain and walking away. I want in."

"Already got a team—"

"And not one of them wouldn't welcome me if you asked. Now go make lunch. I have work to do."

Jack asked whether I was hungry, and when I said I wasn't, he ignored Evelyn's complaints that *she* was, and ushered me outside for "some air."

I could hear dogs around the back, but couldn't see them through the fence. The wind was icy and I buttoned my jacket, but didn't complain, knowing he'd brought me out here to talk privately.

He led me to the front of a midsize car I presumed belonged to Evelyn, and we sat on the hood. He patted his jacket pocket, as if looking for his cigarettes, then made a face.

"Played that wrong," he said. "Should apologize."

"I won't say otherwise." I glanced at him. "I wish you'd told me about her. Getting down here, presuming you're the only one who knows about me..."

"Wish you hadn't come?"

I stared at the fence for a minute. "No. Had I known, I definitely would have wanted to meet her, to put a face to a threat. But...it makes me uncomfortable."

"Figured that. Hard to tell. You're good at hiding it."

"So after you met me, you told her I wasn't a suitable—"

"Never said that."

"You told her to forget about me, which you knew she'd take to mean I wasn't suitable. And this thing about 'stealing' me...I'm not exactly a theft-worthy contact. That means you didn't want me connecting with Evelyn. Why?"

"Evelyn bores easily. Always looking for projects. You were new. Didn't need her shit. Now?" He shrugged. "Up to you."

Jack made sandwiches for lunch while I helped. He didn't ask what Evelyn wanted, just walked in and started fixing them. The kitchen was as immaculate and well ordered as the living room. It was stocked with staples, but low on perishables, giving the sense that Evelyn ate out more than she cooked. What perishables I saw were all of the "grab-and-eat" variety, like fruit, breads and cold cuts—things for snacks and quick lunches.

As we ate, Evelyn told us what she'd dug up. Kozlov's early record showed a few sporadic arrests, but no convictions. That changed when a twenty-one-year-old liquor-store clerk had refused to sell to Kozlov. Already staggering drunk, Kozlov broke a bottle and slashed the young man. Kozlov ran. The kid bled to death. The DA had argued for murder, but Kozlov's lawyer plea-bargained down to a ten-year manslaughter term. After his parole, he hadn't been heard from again until he wound up dead on his living room floor.

With the others, we didn't get so lucky. When the first victim, college student Alicia Sanchez, had been killed, one paper speculated a drug connection, claiming Sanchez had been racking up frequent-flier miles at local drug hang-outs. It was later revealed that she had attended exactly one campus party where several students, excluding Sanchez, were arrested for marijuana possession. Victim number two, Carson Morrow, had been arrested on loitering charges following a sit-in protest during his own college days. The charges were later dropped. Attending a pot party and a protest rally—neither classifies as a hanging offense.

"So the easiest link is out then," I said. "But if it was that obvious, the Feds would already be on it. We need to look wider—unreported criminal activity or . . ." I looked down the list. "Given that most of these don't seem like criminal types, a direct link might not be the answer."

"Warning hits," Jack said.

I nodded. "Whether they were the target or messages to the target, it still seems too random for a single job."

"Might not be."

"Then why connect them with a calling card?"

"Advertising."

Evelyn cut in. "There are a few ways a hitman can make a name for himself, fast. One is to leave a calling card, pref-erably something only the mark's associates will find and recognize. When Jack started, I wanted him to use the jack of spades—"

"Not my style."

"You have no style, which is why you refused. The way I would have done it would have been subtle. That's the key. Not like this Helter Skelter thing." A twist of her lip. "This is crass. And reckless. He's obviously doing more than working through a job list."

"Maybe the point," Jack said. "Advertise big. Advertise wide."

I scanned the printouts on Joyce Scranton. Though the press conference had been held only an hour ago, people had already dug up and posted everything they could find on the latest victim.

I looked up from the pages. "How far is Pittsburgh from here?"

" 'Bout . . ." Jack squinted, then looked at Evelyn. "Five, six hours?"

"And we pass through Ohio. Perfect. We can check out Kozlov's town, then move on to Pittsburgh, see what we can dig up on Joyce Scranton." I lifted the page. "She was living in Boston, but she's a recent transplant. All her family is in Pittsburgh. We can ask around, get a feel for the woman and her life."

Evelyn eased back into the sofa. "Waste of time."

Jack glanced my way. I looked back, my face impassive. He studied me for a moment, then pushed to his feet.

"Gotta start somewhere," he said. "Dee? Grab your jacket."

NINE

Norfolk was a city of about thirty thousand within commuting distance of Cleveland, small enough that every cop would know all the case details of Leon Kozlov's murder, and small enough that a stranger could call the police station front desk, ask what time the day shift ended and get an answer without so much as a "who's asking?"

There are two kinds of women who could show up in a cop bar and get the guys talking. First, the handcuffs-and-pistols groupies, women who start bar conversations with, "Have you ever shot anyone?" I don't understand the groupies, so it's hard to impersonate one. Besides, the guys don't take such women seriously—not outside the bedroom anyway—and those who *are* interested will tell them anything to get them there, so the reliability factor is shot. I'd go with type number two. The female cop.

Evelyn had a cache of contact lenses, but I stuck with the ones Jack bought for me. All the cleaning in the world won't make me use someone else's contacts, though I did accept her offer of a new wig. I'm not keen on wearing another person's headgear, but that platinum blond job had to go, so I'd taken a long-haired, dark brown wig and plaited it back.

When it comes to disguises, I know all the tricks. What shade of hair color or eye contact color works best on me. How to wear a wig so it doesn't slide around. Where to add padding so it looks natural. All the cosmetic variations of skin tone, freckles, moles, scars. I'd mastered the nuances, too. Regional accents, altering stance and mannerisms, everything it took to become another person.

I owe a large part of that to my older brother. As a child, Brad had set his sights on an acting career. Every time our family entertained guests, he'd practiced his craft with a live performance. Being his only sibling meant being recruited into these plays and given multiple roles, so he could concentrate on the lead. He'd even bullied me into taking acting classes and joining the school drama club so my ineptitude wouldn't ruin his performances. All this ended in ninth grade, when I got a role in the annual school play, and Brad got a place in the chorus. After that, Brad declared himself too mature for home dramas, and Mom declared my acting lessons a waste of money.

I found the bar easily enough. It was what I expected: a dark, decrepit pub with little to recommend it except that its unrelenting dinginess ensured the BMW and Prada crowd was unlikely to wander in and start ordering martinis. And, really, when it comes to a good cop bar, that's the only qualification that counts.

When I stepped inside, I paused to let my eyes adjust to the semidark. A blond, beefy rookie at the bar was telling a story loud enough to drown out the television, earning him a few glowers from other patrons, but nothing more, as if they still remembered the day when they'd been up there relaying the tale of their first big takedown. The bar smelled of sweat, aftershave and fried food, with the faint scent of cigarette smoke wafting from the side hall, probably the bathroom—though in a place like this, it was just as likely to be coming from the kitchen.

I walked to the bar and ordered a beer from a grizzled, mustached bartender. A few sets of eyes followed me, more curious than anything. Lacking the requisite blue eye shadow and gelled-to-the-rafters hairdo, I was unlikely to be mistaken for a groupie but, to avoid any lingering misconceptions, I met each look with a polite, professional nod and took my beer to a booth alongside the bar. Then I pulled a law enforcement magazine from my purse, laid it on the table and began to read.

I flipped through the magazine, glancing up now and then. Approachable, but not screaming for attention. A trio of fortyish men stood at the bar. Detectives, judging by the department-store suit jackets draped over the back of their stools. When I caught them looking, I favored them with a polite smile. It took only a few minutes before they appeared at my booth.

The first one, a beefy redhead, gestured at the magazine. "What force?"

He injected a healthy dose of friendly curiosity in the question, but I knew it was more test than interest.

"OPP," I said, closing the magazine. "Ontario Provincial Police."

He nodded. I had details at the ready, but he didn't ask. Canada was only a few hours' drive north, but it might as well be Iceland, for all he cared.

"Mark Waters," he said, extending a hand.

I smiled and shook his hand. "Jenna Andrews."

The other two men introduced themselves as Chris Doyle and Brad Cox. Good small-town cop names, WASP-bland. They reflected their names—solid, average-looking guys, both with short brown hair and blue eyes, both bloodshot, either from overwork or overdrinking. For Cox, I was betting the latter. He was fast developing the watery eyes and sloppy gut of a cop who had a bottle stuffed in his locker and another in the glove box of his car.

Doyle's bloodshot eyes didn't look like anything a good

night's sleep wouldn't cure, but from the strain lines around his mouth, I doubted he'd be getting that rest anytime soon. It was him I looked at when I waved at the opposite bench and invited the men to join me. Waters, the ringleader, claimed the seat beside me. Doyle slid into the opposite side, Cox beside him.

"Just passing through?" Waters asked.

"Visiting some cousins in Cleveland," I said. "When the family togetherness started getting to me, this seemed like a good place to escape to."

Waters laughed. "They won't follow you here, that's for sure. Pretty quiet tonight... though it sure wasn't like that last week."

He waited, a smug half-smile on his lips, as if his city's recent claim to infamy was a personal accomplishment.

"The Helter Skelter killing." I shook my head. "Helluva thing."

Waters's lips parted, needing only a word of encouragement to start expounding on the case.

"Bet the TV crews descended like vultures on roadkill, eh?" I said. "We had a serial killer up north, passed through our town, grabbed a girl. You couldn't walk down the street without having a microphone shoved in your face."

Cox leaned across the table. "I thought you Canucks didn't have serial killers."

"Everyone has serial killers these days," Doyle said, his voice soft. He lifted his gaze to mine. "You've got one big case up there now, don't you? Out west?"

"The pig farmer," I said with a nod. "Gave some of the biggest parties around. Lots of hookers came. Not all of them went home."

"What's this?" Waters said.

Fortunately, this was one case I *did* know about. Although there was a publication ban, Lucy and I had discussed it on the weekend. She had a friend in Port Coquitlam who'd filled her in on the details, which she'd passed on to me, and which I now passed along to these guys, solidifying my credibility.

Doyle asked a few questions, and I focused my attention on him, leaning his way, making plenty of eye contact. This was the guy I wanted to talk to. Part of that had to do with the wedding ring on his finger—an easy excuse if he expected more than a friendly chat. And part of it was that if I had no other agenda in mind, this would be my choice, not a blowhard like Waters who probably wore his gun to bed, or a cop like Cox who'd surrendered to the bottle. I wanted the one who still cared enough to lose sleep over his cases.

After a few minutes, Waters seemed to notice the way the tide was turning. He play-punched Doyle's arm.

"We'll be at the bar," he said, and jerked his head at Cox.

Doyle watched them go, then looked back at me. Uncertain, but not uninterested, as if it had been a long time since he'd been left alone with a woman in a bar, and he didn't quite remember what to do next. Before I could say something, he grabbed my empty glass.

"Can I get you a refill?"

I nodded. "Miller, thanks."

"Lite?"

"Never."

He smiled, the worry lines around his eyes fading. When he returned, he'd recovered his nerve. We chatted for a while and, without any prodding, talk turned to the biggest news in town.

"When the uniforms called it in, the last thing I was thinking was that it was this Helter Skelter killer. I knew

Kozlov. He killed that boy just after I transferred to this force." Doyle looked at me. "You hear about that?"

"No. What happened?"

"Up in Cleveland. Kozlov held up a liquor store. Kid behind the counter grabbed a baseball bat. Kozlov slashed him up with a broken bottle and left him to bleed to death." Doyle shook his head. "Kid was in his last year of college, working to pay for his tuition. Over a thousand people at his funeral. Dozens of classmates, all crying their eyes out. Only people showed up at Kozlov's funeral had cameras."

"And who's the one people are going to remember?"

Doyle met my eyes, nodded. "Exactly. No fucking justice."

"At least he didn't die in his bed. There's some justice in that."

"Yeah." Doyle sipped his beer. "When the call came in, saying he'd been shot, I thought 'Sure, what do you expect?' Guy like that bought himself a .22 to the temple years ago."

"A .22? I read it was a .38 . . . or did you just mean, hypothetically . . ."

"Nah, it was a .22. Reporters fucked up a few things on this one. First guy on the scene was from the local paper—just a kid. He scooped it, and a bunch of stringers followed his facts. I think some later reports got it right . . . but yeah, it was a .22. Hitman's special."

"Hitman?" I gave a half-laugh, as if testing whether Doyle was joking.

"Yeah. Feds are trying to keep it quiet, but that won't last. What I heard, they were already suspicious, but this one sealed it."

"But a hired killer? For a guy like Kozlov? Was there anything in his history to . . . ?"

"Explain why someone would pay even a nickel to off him? Maybe back when he was with the Russian mob."

"The mob?"

Doyle took a long draft of his beer. "I've heard rumors. Probably racist bullshit, you know? Guy's a petty criminal, looks like a thug, Russian background. If it's racism, he played it up. Used to talk big when he was in his cups, yammer on about his glory days with the mob."

"Are the Feds checking this out?"

"Maybe. But even if it's true, it's ancient history, and it doesn't explain how he wound up dead a couple of decades later. I thought about taking a peek but . . ." He shrugged. "No time to satisfy idle curiosity. This case I'm working on now takes up all my time. As it should." He wrapped his hands around his mug. "Kiddie porn. Fucking sick shit."

"There's nothing worse," I said.

"Big-city cops, maybe they get used to it. But me? I've seen some stuff before, but not like this. Nothing like this. My wife—" He stopped. Shrugged.

"You can't talk to her about it."

"Gotta play by the rules. I'm supposed to leave it at the station, not let it affect me, but, Christ, of course it affects me. Then I go home and I'm moody, snapping, she gets mad, and I . . . I can't explain, right? So I left."

"Ouch."

"There's more than that, but . . ." Another shrug. A gulp of beer.

Doyle nodded and we talked some more, about the case, about his wife. Any hope of circling back to Kozlov was gone, but I didn't rush to leave. By the end of his third beer, he pushed the mug aside and smiled ruefully.

"Guess this isn't going anywhere, is it?" he said. "My first shot, and I spend it talking about my marriage."

I pointed at his ring. "If you're still wearing that, you're not ready." I checked my watch. "I should be getting back soon. My cousins will wonder what happened to me."

"I should go, too."

I cast a sidelong glance at his two friends, still at the bar. "You want me to walk out with you?"

A small smile. "If you don't mind."

TEN

Doyle walked me to my car in the parking lot, where we talked for another ten minutes before he left.

I unlocked the rental-car door.

" 'Bout time," said a voice to my left. "You shaking down a witness? Or making a new friend?"

"With cops, I'm better at making friends," I said, turning as Jack slid from a pickup truck's shadow. "What happened to picking you up at the coffee shop when I was done?"

"Drank enough coffee."

He started heading toward the passenger door, but I pulled him to a stop and handed him the keys.

"And I drank enough beer."

I told him what I'd learned.

"I'm betting the rumors aren't just rumors," I said. "Maybe not the Russian mob, but Kozlov's record does scream organized crime. Sporadic arrests, never convicted, then after one conviction, a downhill slide."

"Washed their hands of him," Jack said.

"But he may have earned enough clout for them to hire a lawyer for that murder charge. Either way, I shouldn't be seen poking around Norfolk asking more questions, so maybe you—"

"Put Evelyn on it. We have an appointment."

"Who—?"

"Called Quinn, too. He's not talking."

Jack's voice and expression were passive, but his hands tightened on the steering wheel as he turned the corner.

"Not talking...? Oh, you mean about the Manson connection."

"Yeah. Confirmed it. Won't explain it. Protecting his sources."

I stared out at the passing streetlights. "This Quinn. He was a cop, too, wasn't he? Had to be, if he's your go-to guy for police intel."

"Not was. Is."

Cold blasted down my spine as I swiveled to face Jack. "Jack, don't tell me I'm working with——"

"You aren't. That's why." He paused. "One reason."

"For not meeting the others, you mean."

"Yeah. Quinn's legit. Not working undercover. But you two meeting?" He shrugged. "That cop at the bar? Fine. More police contact? Not if we can help it."

"In case he recognizes me?"

Jack nodded. It took me a moment to unclog my throat and answer.

"It made national news at home." My voice sounded odd. Like a newscaster reciting a story that had long since lost emotional impact. "And, yes, it was picked up in the States. But what makes headlines in Canada isn't a big deal down here. No American cop would have recognized me a month later, and it's been over six years."

"That's what I figured."

I turned back to staring out the window, into the night. The distant wail of a police siren rose above the rumble of the car. I tracked the sound, wondering if it was coming or going. Unlike everyone else on the highway, I wasn't glancing in the side mirror or checking the speedometer. For me, the wail of a siren evoked memories of home and childhood, the best and most comforting of both.

I sounded my first siren when I was three. Riding in our

town's Santa Claus parade, tucked into the front seat between my grandfather and my father. Granddad was chief of police. Dad had just made detective. An uncle and an older cousin walked behind the cruiser, stiff in their dress uniforms, struggling not to smile.

I don't remember ever deciding I wanted to become a cop, no more than my friends consciously decided they would grow up to marry and have children. We simply assumed that was what we would do, what we needed to complete our lives.

I enrolled in police college right out of high school. My brother had already headed off to New York to pursue acting, having never shown any interest in the "family business." When I graduated, Dad was so proud, he didn't stop grinning for a month. My mother says it's a good thing he died three years later, or "what happened next" would have killed him. Maybe she's right, but I'll never forgive her for saying it.

"What happened next" began when my partner and I were first to a crime scene. Dawn Collins, fifteen years old, brutally raped and murdered. I'd seen murder victims before. I'd seen far worse cases than this. And yet, when I walked into that room and saw Dawn, naked and curled up in the corner, her dark hair falling over her face, the cord around her neck the only sign she hadn't just fallen asleep, something in me snapped. Not a loud snap. Not even a hard one. Just a tiny little snip, like someone had flipped off my power switch and I just...shut down. Couldn't think. Couldn't process. Couldn't react.

My partner, a seasoned constable nearing retirement, had taken it in stride, presuming I was in shock and just letting me follow him as he processed the scene, calmly explaining each step, and letting me play student bystander.

By the time the others arrived, I'd snapped out of it enough to do my job.

That night, the nightmares came. I'd lived with them for over a decade by then and, usually, they were the same images played and replayed—running through the forest, running for help, help for Amy, help that would never come in time. But that night after seeing Dawn Collins, I wasn't running. I was back in the cabin, a man's face over mine, features contorted in laughter as I screamed. Screamed in terror, in pain—screamed for Amy, screamed for my father, for anyone.

I woke up screaming. Bathed in sweat. Shaking so badly I had to gasp for breath. Twenty minutes later, two officers from my own precinct showed up at my door, responding to a call from my neighbor. By then, I was calm enough to convince them it hadn't been me—maybe someone down the hall or a too-loud television. They bought it—even joked about it later, at the station, teasing me about who I'd been having sex with to make me scream so loud. And I laughed with them, because that's what they expected, and because I knew no one would ever guess the truth. Nadia Stafford was not the kind of girl to wake up screaming from anything.

That night, I gagged myself before I went to bed. I knew the nightmares would come again, and they did. That crime scene had reminded me too much of Amy's death. Once I fell asleep, I felt her panic, her terror, her agony. Knew what it was like to be a victim.

And when they caught the guy a few days later, I knew what I needed to do to make the nightmares end. I had to see Dawn get the justice that had been denied Amy. So I asked for and received permission to be in on the arrest. I wanted to see his face at that moment when he knew it was over, that justice had prevailed and he was going down.

Only it didn't happen that way. When we picked up Wayne Franco, he was downright gleeful in anticipation of the glory and recognition to come. There was no justice forthcoming. I'd been a fool to think so. Being arrested didn't mean you would pay the price for your crimes. Amy had taught me that.

As I stood there, watching Franco grinning, I knew I hadn't come here to see Wayne Franco arrested. I'd come here to see Dawn Collins get justice. So I waited. And when he made the mistake of reaching into his pocket, I put a bullet between his eyes.

By waiting for my mark to make that fatal move, I'd given the department the excuse they needed, and they fell on it like shipwreck survivors spotting a lifeboat. They claimed I was acting in self-defense; who knew what the killer was pulling from his pocket? No one ever asked whether I thought my life was in danger. I'm sure they suspected the answer. In the end, they were able to take my history, couple it with a psychiatric evaluation and claim post-traumatic stress disorder, allowing me to "retire" from the force.

The media hadn't been nearly so magnanimous.

After six months of hell, I'd cashed in my meager retirement savings, taken ten grand in "get out of our lives" money from my mother's new husband and put a down payment on the Red Oak Lodge.

By the time we reached a motel, my reflective mood had blown over, leaving only wisps of cloud. I'm no good at brooding. After "the Incident" I think I disappointed some people by not falling into a fit of depression like some Victorian heroine, retiring to my bed and wasting away until nothing remained but a melancholy epigraph for my grave. Then there were those who wanted to see me rage into battle, fight the establishment, middle finger extended to the world. When I'd simply shrugged and started over, I robbed both groups of the chance for some classic "wronged woman" drama. But I hadn't been wronged. I'd made a choice. I'd paid the price.

Given the chance to do it over, would I—could I—do any differently today?

Probably not.

Jack and I shared a motel room. I'll admit when he broached the "one room or two" question, my instinctive response had been to say "two . . . of course." And that wasn't because I suspected Jack wanted more out of this partnership. In two years he'd never looked at me in a way that suggested he'd even *noticed* I was of the opposite sex.

Yet sharing a room required a whole new level of trust. If we were partners, though, this wasn't the time to say, "Sorry, I don't trust you enough to sleep in the same room."

So I'd taken a deep breath, told myself "In for a penny, in for a pound" and asked him what he thought we should do. One room was safer, he said. In the future, he'd try to find suites with separate bedrooms and pullout sofas, to give me privacy, but it was too late for that tonight. So one room—two beds—it was.

The next morning after breakfast I called Emma at the lodge to check in. Then we headed out to our first stop of the day—a meeting with a contact of Jack's in a business district that looked as if it hadn't done much business in a while. The For Lease signs just barely outnumbered the pawnshops. After a half-block of silence, I cleared my throat.

"This guy we're meeting, am I allowed details? Like who he is and why we're talking to him?"

Jack skirted a trio of slow-walking seniors and didn't speak until we'd outpaced the three by at least twenty feet.

"Saul's retired," Jack said. "Like Evelyn. Old pro. But more . . ." He paused. "Involved. Keeps his ear to the ground. Listens to gossip, rumors. These days? Nothing else to do."

"So you trust him."

"Don't distrust him."

Jack stopped in front of a dilapidated coffee shop, checked the address—or the portion of it that hadn't peeled off the window—then opened the door.

To my surprise, the coffee shop was running at over half capacity. For a moment, I thought, *Must be good coffee*. Then I looked around at the customers, most of whom looked as if their current seat was the closest thing they had to a permanent residence. Not so much good coffee, then, as free refills, an unusually cold day and a management policy that didn't discourage loitering.

The shop looked better inside than out. Still shabby, but clean. A pregnant server made the rounds with a coffeepot in one hand and a dishrag in the other, relentlessly hunting for half-filled cups and dirty tables. Someone was baking in the back, the sweet smell of banana muffins overpowering the faint stink of unwashed bodies.

Jack nudged me toward a late-middle-aged man sitting alone near the rear of the shop. Presumably Saul. He had the newspaper spread across his table, doing the daily cross-word as he nursed a black coffee.

Balding with a fringe of white hair, Saul wore a frayed button-down shirt that had been through the laundry cycle a few too many times. Maybe he was dressing down to fit in with the other clientele, but something about his ensemble—right down to the cheap watch and worn loafers—looked more lived-in than put-on. His sallow complexion didn't speak to many sun-drenched retirement getaways, nor did the frown lines etched into the corners of his mouth.

When Jack said Saul had retired, I don't know what I expected, but it sure wasn't this. The man had spent his life working a job that paid more than a surgeon's salary.

As we approached the table, Saul looked up from his paper. His gaze went to Jack first and his frown lines rearranged themselves into a smile. He rose, hand extended. Then he saw me. He looked between Jack and me, as if measuring the distance between us. Then he leaned slightly to the side, to look past me. Jack walked over and clasped Saul's hand, which he still held out in forgotten welcome.

"Saul. This is Dee."

Saul snuck another peek behind me, as if double-checking to make sure I was really the person Jack was introducing. The frown lines reappeared. Deepened to fissures.

"Have you lost your mind?" Saul hissed. "What the hell are you doing, bringing a . . . ? Goddamn it, Jack. I don't believe this."

"I told you I was bringing someone," Jack said.

"A partner," Saul said. "A work partner, not a play partner."

"Play?" Jack looked at me, then back at Saul. "Fuck. I wouldn't bring— Dee's— We're working together."

Saul looked from me to Jack, then shook his head.

"You're getting old, Jack," he said. "Of all people. Jesus."

He slapped a five on the table and walked out.

"Wait here," Jack said to me. "I'll bring him back."

I shook my head. "That's not going to help. Give me the keys, and I'll wait for you at the car."

Jack craned his neck to watch Saul through the windows. He dropped the keys into my hand. As he stepped away, I surveyed the table, made sure Saul, in his anger, hadn't left anything behind. Then I wiped the coffee ring off the table, straightened the sugar and napkin containers and picked up the mug to take it to the counter.

Out of the corner of my eye, I saw Jack stop by the door. He walked back to me.

"Careful," he said, keeping his voice low. "Rough neighborhood."

Anyone else, I would have assumed he was joking and laughed. Jack's expression was dead serious.

"I'll be fine," I said. "Thanks."

Thirty minutes later, Jack joined me. I turned the radio down.

"Did he come around?" I asked.

Jack fastened his seat belt. "He doesn't know anything."

ELEVEN

When we drew near enough to Pittsburgh to get the local stations, we learned that Joyce Scranton's visitation was scheduled for that afternoon. It seemed early—they certainly wouldn't have released the body—but a call to the funeral parlor confirmed it. Getting into that visitation would be the best way to learn about Joyce. As both the radio and the funeral parlor stressed, though, it was a private affair, for family and friends only. I thought that would make Jack veto the idea, but he only insisted on a good story and a good disguise, then left me to it.

Joyce Scranton's visitation was a rush job. Mismatched flowers, refreshments still in the bakery boxes, a guest book provided by the funeral home and only a single photo of Joyce, standing in for her body, which was still in Boston. One look around, and you knew someone had said, "Let's just get this damned thing over with." Two looks around, and you could figure out who that "someone" was.

When I'd first come in, I sought out Joyce's estranged husband, Ron, to offer my condolences. Easier to get information if you're forthright. I'd had a story at the ready, explaining a vague connection to Joyce, but Scranton's gaze had moved past me before I said more than my name.

I walked to the picture to pay my respects, straightened it and picked up a discarded napkin someone had left beside it. Then I'd headed for the refreshment table, eying the unappetizing array of day-old cupcakes and brownies and wishing I'd grabbed one of those fresh muffins at the coffee shop. As I pretended to graze, I watched Scranton work the room, moving from person to person, offering fake-sad smiles, one-armed hugs and backslaps before quickly moving on, gaze lifting, now and then, to the clock on the far wall. A pretty brunette in her early twenties dogged his steps anxiously, as if she might misplace him. The college-age daughter, I assumed, until he veered over to a young red-eyed woman huddled in the corner with an elderly couple, and made a show of embracing her, before she slipped his grasp and hurried to the washroom. The elderly couple hurried after her, but not before unleashing lethal glares on Scranton.

At a mutter beside me, I turned to see a woman, silver haired but no older than late forties, skewering Scranton with the same deadly look.

"That was Bethany, I suppose," I murmured, gaze sliding after the disappeared girl. "Joyce's daughter. I'd seen pictures, but they were old school ones..."

"That's Beth. Poor thing. And Joyce's parents with her."

I nodded at the brunette following Scranton. "Is that...? I thought there was only one daughter..."

The silver-haired woman snorted.

"Ah," I said. "Not a daughter, then."

As a group approached the table, she waved me to a quiet corner. "Can you believe he brought her here? The divorce not even final?"

Joyce Scranton—victim in life as in death. Stripped of her dignity even at her memorial. I swung a glare on Scranton, my nails digging into my palms, then shook it off and reminded myself why I was here: information.

"The divorce settlement was pretty much done, though, wasn't it? I haven't—" I forced a blush. "I hadn't talked to Joyce in a while. I kept meaning to but..."

"We always think there will be more time, don't we? Well, there wasn't any time left with the settlement, either, though Joyce was finally showing some spunk, digging in her heels and asking for her fair share. She didn't expect to *get* it, but she was making the effort."

I spent a few more minutes with the woman, a school friend of Joyce's, then moved on, hoping to get a better insight into the victim. The results were mixed. I certainly got the impression she'd been well liked. Yet even this memorial was like the media reports of her murder—the circumstances of her death overrode the importance of her life. After an hour of "What kind of madman is doing this?" and "Oh, God, if this can happen to Joyce, is anyone safe?" I headed outside to meet Jack.

"I like Scranton for it."

I propped up my jacket collar against the wind and leaned down to my takeout coffee, masking my face with the steam so Jack wouldn't see how *much* I liked Scranton for it. There were a million Joyce Scrantons out there, betrayed by someone they'd trusted. While I knew I shouldn't let that cloud my judgment, it didn't keep my jaw from tensing as I watched the family walk from the funeral home down the road.

I continued. "Not only do we have a change in the wind where the divorce settlement was concerned, but there's life insurance to consider, too—whether she still has him listed as the beneficiary. And, if it's not Scranton, I'd consider the girlfriend. I doubt she liked that wind change."

He dumped his coffee, watching it pool on the cold

ground, then pitched the empty cup. "*Could* be insurance work. Saul used to do that."

"There's some kind of specialty in insurance work?"

His gaze shifted to mine, and I could feel the weight of mild rebuke. No, rebuke—even mild—was too harsh. His look reminded me that I was dealing with hired killers, men who didn't just take out the occasional Mafioso, but who made their living killing whomever they were paid to kill. And although I'm sure he didn't intend it, the "rebuke" reminded me that I had no right placing myself above guys like Saul. I, too, killed for money.

After a moment of silence, Jack let me off with "Shitty work. But it's out there."

"So that's one possible motivation. Take a bunch of separate insurance jobs and string them together to look like the work of a serial killer. That'd be one surefire way to avoid insurance investigations. Could this guy *be* Saul?"

He shook his head. "Nah. Got arthritis. In his hands. Had to retire early. Even before that?" Another head shake. "Going downhill. Couldn't do the work."

"But someone else? Could one hitman get enough insurance jobs to tie this together?"

"One guy? On his own? Doubtful. Through a broker? Yeah. They specialize, too."

I drank the remainder of my coffee and threw out the cup. "Okay, we'll get Evelyn to do some searching, see who benefited from the other deaths. Did we get anything more from Evelyn when you called?"

"Yeah. The stockbroker. One of his clients. Didn't just invest in stocks. Drug connections. Set her on Kozlov, too. Check out a mob connection."

With that, we should have been ready to leave. But Jack just stood there, staring off into space.

He'd been quieter than usual since our visit to Saul, and I'd thought he was just off balance, that an old comrade would think he'd lowered himself to the "female student" ploy. But that didn't seem like Jack, to be so bothered by what someone else thought.

"Saul *did* give you a lead, didn't he?"

"Yeah." He pulled out one hand to pat his breast pocket, then made a face, remembering he didn't have cigarettes. "Rumor. Wanted to run it by Evelyn first."

"And...?"

He jerked his chin toward the road. "Tell you on the way."

As Jack drove, he told me the story of Baron, a former hitman. Not a friend, but an acquaintance, someone he seemed to respect. Ten years ago, Baron had gotten out of the business. Voluntarily.

That's rare, Jack said. Like being an actor or a politician, you tell yourself you're going to get out when you've accomplished some goal or tired of the job, but the truth is, hardly anyone leaves until he's forced out. The money's too good and the adrenaline rush is too addictive. Your ego wants you to get out while you're at the top, but you keep holding on just a little longer. Then the fall starts—you screw up, you slow down, you're off your game—and you tell yourself you'll retire just as soon as you climb that hill again so you can do it from the top. Only you never get back up, and you hang in until you're at the bottom, like Saul.

But Baron got out. He met a woman—a single mother working in a strip club while she took college classes. Maybe he looked at her, saw someone working to get out of the life and thought "if she can, so can I." They fell in love.

They married. He retired from the life. He bought a business restoring old cars. They started a family.

"Helluva story, huh?" he said. His gaze was on the windshield, face expressionless, but he gave the words a twist of something like bitterness.

"No happily-ever-after in this one, is there?"

"Should be. You think..." He shrugged. "Cynical side says bullshit. Won't work. The hitman and the stripper? Like a bad movie. But that optimistic side?" Another shrug. "Says good on them. He got out? He's happy? Good."

"Everyone likes a fairy-tale ending. To think someone beat the odds and came out on top. It makes a good story."

"Yeah. And that's all the fuck it is. A good story."

"It didn't last?"

"Thought it did. Until Saul said otherwise. Few months ago? Baron came back to the life. Sniffing around for work. Wife took off. Kids with her. Which came first? Who knows."

"Whether they left because he was talking about turning pro again, or whether he decided to turn pro again because they left?"

"Yeah. Doesn't matter. Point is, he didn't get back in. Gone too long. Can't find work. New middlemen? Don't know who the fuck he is. Older guys? Don't give a shit. You been gone that long, you start over. From the bottom. Prove yourself."

I remembered what Evelyn and Jack had said about "advertising." "And that's why Saul mentioned it to you. Because it's possible that this killer is Baron—his way of proving himself."

"Yeah. And there's more."

He turned from a secondary highway onto the interstate. I waited impatiently for him to continue, but he didn't until he'd merged into traffic and resumed his speed.

"Couple months ago, Baron went to see a guy. Middle-man Saul and I know. Guy named Cooper. Wouldn't give Baron anything good. Just shit work. Gotta prove yourself, he says. So Baron says fine. Takes him on the street. Says pick a target. Give me thirty minutes and I'll prove myself."

My gut went cold. "Kill a random person on the street. And he did?"

"Nah. Cooper said fuck off. Prove yourself another way."

I sat there for a minute, heart racing so fast I could barely breathe. "Where do we find Baron?"

"No idea. But I can find Cooper."

"Then let's do that. Where does he live?"

"Heading there now."

TWELVE

Music from the nearby tavern boomed into the streets. Old-time country, the sort that reminds me of howling coyotes. Ask me where I'd expect to find a middleman/drug dealer and I'd have picked some funky new-age bar, with go-go dancers and bathroom sinks sprinkled with powder that didn't come from a Javex can.

Talking to Cooper wasn't going to be as easy as I'd hoped. Yes, he knew Jack. Yes, he'd talk to Jack. But unlike Saul, Cooper couldn't be trusted to keep his mouth shut, which is why Jack used him for information only.

Cooper was a businessman to the core. He'd buy and sell anything, meaning he'd happily give Jack what he wanted, only to run out and resell the information that Jack was on the trail of the Helter Skelter killer.

Cooper had no stomach for violence—so Jack *could* threaten him into keeping his mouth shut but, as he said, that kind of behavior didn't foster good contact relationships.

When I came up with an idea for keeping Jack out of it, I expected him to balk but he'd only said, "Yeah. That'd work. Just keep in shadows. Don't wanna have to kill him after. Bad for business."

So now I was waiting outside this Kentucky bar as Jack scoped it out from the inside. After ten minutes, he exited.

"Cooper's there," Jack said. "Usual place. Now, we need—"

"A suitable place for friendly conversation. I've scouted out two potential meeting rooms already." I walked to the end of the alley and spokesmodel-waved my hand south. "In that direction, we have the ever popular abandoned warehouse. Spacious, yes, but you run the risk of unwanted roommates, particularly at this time of the evening." I gestured north. "In this direction you have my personal favorite, an empty shop. Cozy, but secure."

"Let's see the shop."

I led him down the alley to a steel door. "The shop fronts onto the street, but I've looked through the window and there are a few rooms back here. From the looks of the For Lease sign, it's been vacant for a while. The only security system is a barred front window."

Jack examined the lock on the steel door and shook his head. "Can't do it." He lifted the tool pouch he'd brought from the car. "Wrong tools."

"That's okay. I'm sure it opens fine from the inside. Here. Trade."

I handed him my purse, took his tool pouch and glanced inside.

"Perfect."

I wriggled out of the tight cowboy boots, flexed my toes and looked up. Ten feet over our heads was an unbarred, unbroken window. I walked to a Dumpster a yard away and climbed onto it. With the flashlight from the pouch, I took a closer look at the wall, locating a couple of toe- and fingerholds, where the brick had broken. Flashlight off and in the pouch, pouch strap looped over my arm, and I crawled onto the wall.

Once at the window, I grabbed the wide cement sill and hoisted myself onto it. With one hand, I unzipped the pouch. Out came the glass cutter. Out came the suction cup. Then, very carefully, out came the window.

I slid the pane through the sill and lowered it to the floor beneath. Then I climbed through and sprinted into the hall.

A minute later, I was at the rear door. A simple dead bolt lock. I allowed myself the faintest smile before I opened it.

Jack shook his head. "You make me feel old."

"It's the makeup. Spend too long looking that age and you'll start to feel it."

I was damned tired of talking. We'd been nursing our drinks for almost an hour, and I'd done nothing but talk.

What else was there to do in a bar? Dance? Jack would sooner shoot out the bar lights for target practice. We couldn't drink; we had to keep our reflexes and wits sharp. So that left conversation—which wouldn't have been so bad, if Jack had actually participated.

After a while, I'm sure everyone around us pitied the poor guy stuck with the ditz who wouldn't shut up. When I tried to stop, though, he'd always prompt me with a question.

Under normal circumstances, this wouldn't have been a problem. Talking is good. It fills the silence, keeps the brain from sliding into places you'd rather it didn't go. But I didn't want to talk. I was on a trail and my prey was sitting only twenty feet away.

Cooper was a contact, not a job. Yes, he was a drug dealer, but from what I saw, his customers were willing enough. And he was a middleman, but he'd turned down that "offer" from Baron, so he wasn't a complete scumbag. Yet none of that mattered because what swirled about me, as heady and intoxicating as peyote smoke, was the scent of prey.

"So you've been taking these courses in Peterborough..." Jack prompted.

His voice was sharp and I surfaced abruptly, my brain snarling at being disturbed. I tried to retreat, to pull the mask back on, but it was too late. Yet his eyes never left mine, just fixed me with a level stare.

"Your courses, Dee. What have you taken?"

"Umm . . . sociology, English, a classics course that I will never have any use for—" I stopped. "We have a likely customer."

Jack looked at the mirror beside our table. The mirror allowed Jack to stay hidden in the corner of the booth, and me to keep the back of my head to the bar crowd while I watched them, focusing on a forty-something dark-haired bearded man in a black suede cowboy hat and matching shirt. Cooper.

I'd been here long enough now to establish Cooper's sales pattern. Customer walks up. Customer engages in requisite two minutes of small talk. Customer leaves out the front door. Two minutes later, Cooper heads for the bathroom, located next to the rear exit. Five minutes later, Cooper would be back in his seat, his stash lighter and his wallet heavier.

We'd been waiting for the right kind of customer, and this one looked like it: a middle-aged man in pressed blue jeans and a cowboy hat that probably saw the outside of his closet only when he needed his fix.

While Cooper's customer went through the small-talk portion of the ritual, Jack headed out the front door. I could swear I heard a round of cheers as he escaped the living Chatty Cathy doll.

A minute later, the middle-aged customer left, and so did I, but I veered toward the bathrooms as he hurried to the front.

Moving slower, I crept to the back door, then stepped out into the night. The middle-aged customer hovered at the edge of the parking lot, near the alley, casting anxious glances into its dark depths, unwilling to enter until Cooper was there to protect him.

Keeping in the shadows to hide my face, I strolled toward him, humming a Cowboy Junkies tune, which I don't think qualified as country, but it seemed suitable, under the circumstances.

Hearing me, the man started. I looked over at him, smiled and slid my jean jacket open, giving him a peek at my holstered Glock.

He bolted.

I took his place.

I held myself still and silent in the shadows. Every dry leaf skimming over the pavement sounded as loud as crumpling newspaper. Water plinked into a puddle nearby. No, not water, antifreeze, dripping from a parked car, the sweet smell wafting past. Somewhere to my left, a streetlamp flickered and buzzed. Yet none of this distracted me, only brought the world into sharper focus.

The rear exit cracked open, then stopped. A voice. Cooper's. I listened, unable to make out words, but memorizing the sound. A woman laughed. I strained forward, gaze glued to the dark rectangle of the opening door. Then he stepped out.

Cooper walked into the parking lot and looked around. As he glanced toward the alley, I gave a small wave, staying in the shadows. He stopped, head tilting, as if thinking I didn't *look* like the guy he'd sent out. I discreetly flashed a few folded bills, and he decided he wasn't going to be picky.

As he approached, I slowly backed into the alley. He followed. When he reached the alley mouth, I gestured to the alcove with the unlocked door. Then I stepped into it, out of his sight, and opened the door. He rounded the alcove and saw the open door, but didn't backpedal, just frowned at me.

"What—?"

I grabbed his arm and twisted it, bringing him to his knees.

"Jay-sus!" Cooper's twang turned the oath into a southern revival shout.

I switched holds, getting his arm behind his back, and twisting again. Then I shoved him into the room and knocked the door shut behind me. When he tried to pull free, I gave a warning twist, then kicked the back of his kneecap. As he buckled, I used the momentum to drop him face-first to the floor, still holding his arm.

"Scream, and I'll snap your wrist," I said.

The door opened, and Jack slipped in. A click as he locked it behind him.

He glanced at Cooper, then moved alongside the wall, gun drawn. He took up position out of Cooper's sight, but where he could cover both us and the door.

"The money's in my back pocket," Cooper said through his teeth. "Some product there, too."

"I wouldn't touch your 'product' or the money from it." I leaned over him, letting more of my weight fall on his back. "A guy came to you, looking for—"

"Lost of people come to me. Looking for lots of things."

A small twist on his arm. Just enough for him to let out a hiss.

"That wasn't a question," I said. "Pay attention, and we'll get through this a whole lot faster. This guy goes by the name Baron. Wanted to 'prove' himself to you. Offered to do a random hit..."

Cooper audibly swallowed. "I want a lawyer."

I leaned down to his ear, still staying behind where he

couldn't get a look at me. "Is this how cops usually roust you, Cooper? You have a pocket full of something that would get you in very big trouble...if I was a cop. But that's complicated. So this is how it works. I'm not a cop. You're not a drug-dealing death broker. I'm a concerned citizen. You're a concerned citizen. We're going to share our concerns about Mr. Baron. He isn't a client of yours, is he?"

"Shee-it, no. He's lost it. Right over the fucking edge. I'm staying clear."

"Good plan. And as a concerned citizen, you want to make sure he isn't a danger to anyone else, so—without admitting to any association with the man—you'll tell me how I can get in touch with him."

A moment of silence passed. I knew Cooper was weighing his options. He could claim he hadn't taken any contact information from Baron. Or he could provide false information. But after about twenty seconds, he said, "He gave me his number. It's on my cell phone."

He directed me to the phone in his pocket. I took it out, then slid it back to Jack. As Jack checked it, I waited, gun to Cooper's head. He'd know then that I had a partner, but showed no sign of surprise. Cops always had partners, and he thought that's what I was, no matter what I said to the contrary. It was a fair game—cops pretending to be civilians so they don't have to follow the rules, which meant he didn't need to worry about getting busted.

Jack nodded, telling me the number was in there. He punched it into the address book on his prepaid throwaway phone, then erased it from Cooper's, and slid it back across the floor.

I put it into Cooper's pocket. Then I took out the bills Jack had given me to pay for the information. I didn't see the point, but Jack insisted, and it was his money, so paid Cooper would be.

Yet even as I stood, bills held out, I found myself hesitating. I expected Jack to grunt or give me some sign to pay the guy and get on with it. When he didn't, I looked over and saw him there, expressionless and patient. Waiting.

His gaze met mine. I looked away and let the bills flutter down beside Cooper.

THIRTEEN

—

On the drive back to Evelyn's, Jack stopped at a desolate rest area pay phone to try the number Cooper gave us. I sat in the rental car, sipping bitter coffee and watching him at the booth, hunched against the cold night air, his back to me, breath streaming like smoke signals. I rolled down my window, but was too far to overhear him. A night bird squawked. I turned to gaze at the woods surrounding the rest area and thought of home.

When he came back, he was frowning, gaze distant in that way that I'd learned meant I had to be patient.

We were on the highway before he spoke. "Someone answered. Wasn't him."

"Cooper gave us the wrong number?" I shook my head before Jack could answer. "No, I guess that's not very likely. He'd have no reason to keep a false number and if it was in some kind of code, he'd have said so. He didn't seem to be holding out. So either Baron gave him the wrong number—which doesn't make sense—or Baron's changed it." I glanced over at Jack, reading his expression. "Or none of the above."

"Was Baron's number. Just not him."

I considered venting my frustration in a comment about Jack's own code, and the mental gymnastics required to crack it, but he didn't seem in the mood for jibes. He'd gone quiet again, probably thinking about Baron.

"The person who answered, did he seem to *know* Baron?"

He blinked, then shook it off, glancing over to give me his full attention. "Hard to say. Guy started spitting questions. Who's calling? What's this about? Where'd you get that name?"

"And it definitely wasn't Baron?"

Jack shook his head.

"Is there any way to trace the number?"

"I'll put Evelyn on it."

"What? Jack being cheap? Can't put you up in a motel for the night?" Evelyn said as she stepped back to let us in.

She had her hand on the collar of a muscular German shepherd. When I hesitated, she waved me in. "They're trained. If I don't give the signal, they won't attack."

I glanced over at the other one, an even bigger shepherd peering back at me from the other side of the hall. "Any chance I might 'accidentally' give the signal?"

"Get inside." Once I was in, she released the first dog's collar. "This is Ginger. That's Scotch. Girls? Say hello."

I stretched out my hand, fingers extended. They snuffled it.

"Now off to bed," she said.

They turned and headed up the stairs, one behind the other.

I walked into the living room, then stumbled as a sudden cramp from the long drive took my calf muscles hostage. Jack caught my arm, but I waved him off, hopped over to the sofa and collapsed onto it.

"You want your coffee extra strong?" Evelyn asked. "Or through an intravenous?"

"I got it," Jack said. "Dee? You talk."

"Ah, so you've finally realized the advantages of having a partner," Evelyn said. "If nothing else, it saves you from the supreme effort of speech."

Jack kept walking. I pulled my leg up and started massaging the muscle.

"If you want something for that, just ask. I've got a damned cupboard full of crap. The days when muscle rubs and ointments replace massage oil and lubricants... Never thought I'd see it." She leaned back in her chair. "So, what happened with Baron?"

I glanced over at Jack, but he kept walking. So I told Evelyn.

"Well, that's priority one, then. Finding him." She seemed ready to go on, then glanced toward the kitchen. A pause, then she turned back to me. "I made some progress myself. Leon Kozlov, former associate of the Nikolaev family. A small family, but an old one. One of the first in America."

"You know them?"

"I know folks associated with them, which is how we're going to get the story on Mr. Kozlov."

"He got insurance?" Jack called as he retreated into the kitchen.

I told Evelyn about our theory.

"Well, not really a *theory*," I said as Jack returned with our coffees and sat beside me. "At this point, it's just one more avenue to explore."

"A good one. People die, someone always benefits, and usually it's money. Let me see what I can dig up. First, though, I'll find Baron. Pathetic fuck."

One could say those two words with sadness, even empathy. Evelyn did not. Jack's shoulders tightened and he pushed to his feet as if to hide the reaction.

"I told you this would happen," she said. "Didn't I?"

"Yeah." Jack headed for the computer and turned on the monitor. "Let's get looking. Find him."

Evelyn turned to me. "When Baron retired, I told Jack it wouldn't work. It never does."

"Didn't argue," Jack said.

"You gave Baron the benefit of the doubt."

"Nothing wrong with that. Want me to log on?"

"You don't know my password."

"Yeah?"

They locked gazes, but Evelyn only shook her head, refusing to be distracted.

"You have a sentimental streak, Jack."

"An optimistic streak. And it's not fatal. Dee doesn't need to hear this shit. You want me to say it? You were right. Now log on or—"

She stood. "Get away from my keyboard before you break something."

Baron's number didn't lead anywhere. Not immediately at least. Evelyn put in a few cybercalls for more information, both to trace the phone number and to track Baron through the criminal network.

"But that won't bear fruit today, so you can go and check that cartel lead while Dee and I check out Kozlov and research the insurance theory."

"You don't need her."

"Neither do you. There's no need to take her along, especially on something like that."

"Evelyn's right," I said. "I can't help you shake down a drug cartel source, and probably shouldn't—especially after how Saul reacted. I'd rather stay, search for insurance links and help Evelyn with the Kozlov lead."

His back to Evelyn, Jack looked at me and gave a small shake of his head. I knew what he meant. Evelyn didn't need my help. It was only an excuse to get me alone, away from him.

* * *

Jack left before dawn. So I was alone with Evelyn, doing research. In school, I'd always been a struggling B student. As a cop, I'd never aspired to detective-hood, if only because of the sheer amount of desk work involved. Now, in my thirties, I had returned to academia, taking college courses, but only because my days were spent outdoors and active, and I could spare some time to develop my brain.

Yet when it came to solving this case, I had minimal interest in poring over Internet printouts and visiting a retired hitwoman's old pals. Another victim's life was expiring, and I wanted to be with Jack, interviewing—or interrogating—a source.

As for whether I trusted Evelyn enough to stay with her, the answer was no. I didn't see Evelyn as a threat—not at her age—but neither did I know her. Still, I was okay with that. In my years as a cop, I'd had a couple of partners I hadn't trusted even after that initial discomfort of working with someone new had passed. I'd spent almost a year partnered with a dirty cop—someone I suspected was more likely to shoot my back than protect it. I'd learned to deal with that, and never gave him any cause to think I didn't trust him. More than once I'd heard him snicker with his buddies about how naive I was. But when he'd tried to pin something on me, I'd seen it coming and turned the tables so deftly he'd never figured out what had gone wrong. If I'd worked with him and emerged unscathed, I could do the same with Evelyn.

So, first, we researched the insurance claim theory. There were legitimate ways to get that information, but legitimate means slow, and always leaves a trail. Evelyn knew shortcuts through the dark alleys of the information highway.

By breakfast time we had our list of victims, insurance claims and beneficiaries. None screamed "murder for money." Carson Morrow's wife would collect his, but it was only fifty thousand, not nearly enough when you had two kids and he was the family breadwinner. Mary Lee's family would collect a quarter of a million. A tidy sum . . . if it wasn't to be divided among five children and eleven grandchildren. Leon Kozlov's ten-thousand-dollar policy would cover burial costs, with little left over.

So far, the cases didn't seem to support an insurance-based theory. Maybe Morrow's wife had other reasons to kill him, and the insurance money would just be a bonus. Maybe multiple members of Lee's family had conspired to have her murdered. Maybe Kozlov had a richer policy elsewhere.

Then there was Alicia Sanchez, whose coverage did raise red flags. I wasn't certain, but I suspected that insurance on an unmarried college student was relatively rare. And a quarter of a million dollars went way beyond burial costs. I couldn't imagine any parent killing his child for insurance money. But Sanchez did have two brothers, one with a criminal record. One way to get a "loan" from Mom and Dad would be to make sure they had the money to lend. And after grieving for one child, they'd be reluctant to refuse to help another. Not a perfect theory, but something worth further investigation.

Midmorning, we left to visit Evelyn's Nikolaev family contact. She pulled into the driveway of a town house complex, less than an hour from her place.

"That was quick."

"At your age, you want to keep lots of distance between you and your colleagues, so no one makes the connection. By our age, no one cares anymore, and it's a hell of a lot easier to get together for coffee when you don't live five states apart."

She turned from one short, narrow road onto another, heading for the rear of the complex.

"Maggie and Frances are a couple girls I know from way back. Not girls anymore, mind you. They're more retired than I am, but they still dip their hands in when the rocking-chair life gets dull. Not hitwomen, of course— there were never more than a few of us around. Maggie and Frances used to—" A smile played at her lips. "I'll let them tell you. They'll like that."

I scanned the town houses. The sign out front said they were condos, but the units had that run-down "don't-give-a-shit" look that I always associate with temporary residents. The one Evelyn pulled up in front of, though, shone with pride of ownership. The shoe-box-size front lawn had been replaced with a perennial garden, English-cottage style. There were cobblestones instead of crumbling walkways. A well-maintained, ten-year-old Honda sat under the carport, atop a cracked, but recently resealed, driveway.

"So they both live here?"

"They're partners."

"After all these years? Most marriages don't last that long, let alone business partnerships. Or I guess, by now, it'd be more friendship than business."

"More than friendship or business."

"Oh?" I paused. "Ah, 'partners.' Right."

Evelyn opened her door. "It's a shitty word, isn't it? People think things have come so far, and we're still stuck using euphemisms like 'partners.'"

"Probably better than what they called it fifty years ago."

Evelyn snorted. "Pretty much the same thing they *did* call it fifty years ago."

I climbed from the car. "So Maggie and Frances worked for the Nikolaevs?"

"No, they hung out with a couple of wiseguys who did. Gay wiseguys. The mob takes a dim view of gays, back then and now. Frances and Maggie gave them convenient girlfriends to parade around. In return, they got protection and contacts in the Russian Mafia."

Russ

Toilet paper.

Before Russ Belding had left the house, his wife had asked whether there was anything else they needed from the grocery store. Now, watching his mutt-terrier, Champ, squat in the bushes, Russ remembered that he'd put the last roll of toilet paper on the holder the day before and forgot to add that to Brenda's list. He pulled his cell phone from his pocket and caught sight of the time on it: 7:57. Too late. Brenda liked to go shopping as soon as the store opened at eight, before it got busy, and she didn't have a cell phone.

Should he pick some up on the drive home? He hated leaving Champ in the car. It was a cool fall day, but here in Florida, "cool" didn't mean the same thing it had back in Detroit. Even with the window open, that blazing sun would turn the car into a furnace.

Would they have enough paper to last until tomorrow? A full roll, put on yesterday, would last approximately—

Russ stopped himself and chuckled. Thirty years in the navy and his engineering skills were reduced to calculating the rate of toilet paper consumption. The joys of retirement.

At the sound of his master's laugh, Champ bounded across the grass and twined his lead around Russ's legs. As Russ untangled himself, he thought of a better use for his abundance of free time: dog training. A squirrel darted through the bushes and Champ shot after it, nearly yanking Russ to his knees. Amazing the amount of velocity one small dog can produce. Now there was a scientific question worth considering.

Russ walked off the path to check the spot where Champ

had squatted. Even before he could see anything, the smell of dog shit wafted past him. He reached into his pocket for a baggie and found... nothing.

Getting old, captain, Brenda would say. Memory is the first thing to go.

A furtive glance around. This stretch of path was empty, as it almost always was since the town opened the new park. Joggers flocked there for the trails, and parents and children for the playground equipment, leaving this dark, overwooded bit of green space for those who preferred privacy to scenery.

Russ looked down at the brown pile, steaming in the crisp morning air, then sighed and picked up a big oak leaf. Leave a mess on the deck and someone's bound to slip in it. As he bent over to pick up the dog shit with the leaf, Champ barked.

"You want to do it, sailor? Be my guest."

Something hit the base of his skull. One split second of blinding pain, not even enough time to form a thought. Then darkness.

The man slid the gun back into its holster and pulled his shirt down over it. As he did, he glanced around, reassuring himself that the path was still empty. The small dog yipped hysterically, darting between him and the body on the ground.

The body lay where it had fallen, a few scant feet from the path. He tugged the folded page from its plastic covering. One more look around before he leaned over and tucked the paper into the dead man's rear pants pocket. Then he proceeded north, walking alongside the path on the grassy edge where his running shoes left no mark.

FOURTEEN

———◆———

Evelyn and I walked up the cobblestone path. A cartoon Halloween black cat hung from the wreath hook on the door, with a Pull Me sign dangling from its tail. I obliged. The cat screeched and quaked, eyes rolling in terror. I smiled. Evelyn shook her head and rang the bell.

A moment later, a handsome woman in a wheelchair pulled open the door. As Evelyn leaned down to kiss her cheek, another woman scurried from a back room. She was smaller, rounder and plainer, with a mop of white curls and faded blue eyes.

"Frances!" she said. "I told you I'd get the door. The locks are too high."

The first woman shook my hand. "You must be Dee. I'm Frances. This hovering mother hen is Maggie."

"I'm not hovering. The doctor said you aren't supposed to lift yourself. You'd have to lift yourself to reach that lock."

"I'm almost six feet tall. I can reach the lock on my frigging knees." Frances looked back at me. "Forgive us. The wheelchair is, I'm afraid, a recent development and Maggie isn't adjusting well."

"Me?" Maggie sputtered. She swept past Frances, beamed a wide smile at us, embraced Evelyn and clasped my hand between hers. "So you're the new hitwoman. Lovely. We're so pleased to meet you."

Frances rolled her eyes and looked at me. "Bet you've never had that greeting before."

Maggie shooed us into the living room. As with the exterior of the house, one could see that great effort had been made to transform substandard housing into a warm and inviting home. An Oriental carpet, perhaps once worth thousands, now faded and threadbare in places. Jewel-toned pillows adorned an antique sofa and chair set, their upholstery patterns rubbed clean at the edges, their wood trim smooth with wear and shiny with polish.

Unlike at Evelyn's house, these walls bore no artwork. Instead, they were decorated with photographs. Picture frames were everywhere, covering the walls, the end tables, the fireplace mantel, frames of every description, from dime-store plastic to contemporary wood to silver antiques. A lifetime of memories.

"Coffee for Evie," Maggie said. "And you, dear? Coffee? Tea? Cold drink?"

"Coffee's fine, thank you," I said. "Cream or milk, please, whichever you have on hand."

"How polite. Evie, are you taking notes?"

Evelyn opened her mouth, but Maggie vanished before she could respond. I continued to look at the pictures, then zeroed in on an old one propped next to the telephone. In it, two young women grinned before Mount Rushmore. Maggie and Frances. I could tell by the smiles, which hadn't changed in the forty-plus years since the photo had been snapped. Age had favored Frances best. In the old picture, she was severe looking, her features too strong for her youthful face. And Maggie? She'd been jaw-droppingly gorgeous, with blond curls, dimples, flawless skin and a figure that could have body-doubled for Marilyn Monroe.

"A knockout, wasn't she?" Frances said. "Of course, she still is."

"Nice save, darling," Maggie said as she pushed through the kitchen door. "Time has not been kind to this old broad, but it got me what I wanted."

"An early and comfortable retirement," Frances said. "We didn't make a fortune, but we did well enough."

Maggie grinned wickedly and slid her fingers down Frances's arm. "That's not what I meant."

Frances blushed and dropped her eyes like a sixteen-year-old, then quickly grabbed two coffee cups from the tray Maggie had laid on the side table. She leaned forward to hand me one.

"Has Evie told you what we did in the old days?" Frances asked.

I shook my head.

Maggie held up a hand, motioning for Frances to let her explain. "A variation on the oldest and best female confidence scheme in the books. First, you find a lonely rich man . . . and believe me, all rich men are lonely. Then you send in someone who looks like that." She pointed to her image in the old photo. "She wrangles a private invitation back to his house, and makes sure the doors are left unlocked behind her. While she's busy cooing over cocktails, in comes her partner and cleans the place out. Frances could pick a mansion clean in thirty minutes."

Frances grinned. "And Maggie could tease for thirty-five, so it worked out fine."

"Thirty-five? Darling, I could tease for sixty and do no more than peck his cheek."

Frances rolled her eyes. "Sixty? Remember that Swede? In Atlanta? If I hadn't—"

"I'm sure Dee and Evie didn't come to hear us reminisce," Maggie said. "How may we help you ladies?"

"We need to talk to someone who would have been with the Nikolaev family in the seventies. You still keep up with Peter, don't you?"

"We're going down to Florida next month to see him

and Chance." She frowned at Frances. "Is it Chance? Or Enrico?"

"Doesn't matter," Frances said. "Since Ivan died, it's a new Chance or Enrico every time we meet him. Eighteen-year-old pool boys. Some men hit a certain age—straight or gay, it doesn't matter—they'll empty their wallets on the first flat stomach that comes along."

"But we don't need to call Peter to find you a Nikolaev contact," Maggie said. "Little Joe is in an old-age home outside Detroit."

"A retirement home?" Evelyn said. "Little Joe is Boris Nikolaev's brother, isn't he?"

"Hell of a thing to do to your own brother," Frances said. "But Boris never had much use for Joe. Not that I blame him. There was some scandal a couple of years back, Joe flapping his gums when he shouldn't have. Boris shipped him off to a fancy rest home. Joe was never the sharpest tool in the family shed, but if you're looking for someone to talk, he'll talk all right. Problem always was getting him to shut up."

"Will there be a problem getting in to see him?" I asked. "They'll have him under security still, won't they?"

Frances shook her head. "When the family puts some-one out to pasture, he's persona non grata. They'll visit him, keep up appearances but, as far as they're concerned, he's out of the business. They won't tell him anything, so there's nothing he can tell anyone else. On current events, that is. The past? Well, no one cares much about the past these days."

Frances searched the Internet for private rest homes in the Detroit suburbs until she found the one that tweaked her memory. Then we took our leave and prepared for a trip to Michigan.

"He's an old man," Evelyn said as she pulled into a mall parking lot. "Flash him some T and A, and he'll tell us everything we want to know."

"Great," I said. "We'll find you a push-up bra and miniskirt."

She pinned me with a look. "After a certain age, all the push-up bras in the world don't help, as you'll discover. With a man like Little Joe, the horseflesh has to be young and it has to be firm."

"Did I mention I don't do Mata Hari?"

"Dee..."

"I'm not pulling some feminist bullshit. I can't play the seduction card—I don't have the look for it. When I was on the force, Vice nabbed me once for undercover, stuck me in a microskirt and halter top, put me on the street corner. I looked like the world's only crack ho with a personal trainer."

"We can skip the microskirt."

"And the halter top?"

A sigh. "And the halter top. Let's see what we can find."

I folded my sandwich wrapper into quarters, tucked it into the take-out bag and folded that into a neat square. Then I leaned forward to shake the crumbs from my cleavage. Amazing what they can do with bras these days. Slap together some elastic and some underwire, toss in a couple of gel-filled "contouring pads" and I felt like I should be ticketed for false advertising.

Evelyn had picked out my sweater—a low-cut job that was 50 percent Lycra, 20 percent angora and 100 percent skanky. She'd completed the ensemble with skintight jeans, ankle boots, red press-on nails and jewelry that clanked when I walked.

Back at her place I'd finished up with hair and makeup. I'd considered Jack's platinum wig choice, but it tweaked the outfit over the line to street whore. So I'd kept on Evelyn's long brown one, borrowed a curling iron and hairspray, and teased the wig until it looked like what I'd worn for my eighth-grade yearbook photo—a shellacked ode to the era of big hair and heavy metal. Mafia bait. All I needed was a wad of bubble gum and a Jersey accent.

We'd taken turns driving, picked up lunch and arrived at Glory Acres just past three-thirty. The place had once been a home—a real one—occupied, undoubtedly, by a real family. It appeared to have begun life as a two-story Victorian but, like most of us, had spread with age. There was an addition here, a wing there, none of it the same style as the original building. Two skeletons of porch swings were propped against the house, seats and cushions gone. Burlap covered the shrubs and rosebushes. Birdbaths had been emptied and turned upside-down. A house in hibernation.

"I'll talk to him alone first," Evelyn said as we walked up the front steps. "I need to refresh his memory on some... past deeds of mine. So he knows I'm not conning him."

"Maybe you can get him to talk to you, skip my role altogether."

She said nothing, and I had the feeling it wouldn't matter if she could get Little Joe to talk—she'd still bring me in. Testing me. Or showing me who was boss. Probably both. Typical "new partner" bullshit. One reason I liked working with Jack—he never pulled this crap.

"It might take ten, fifteen minutes, so use the washroom, freshen up." She gave me a once-over. "Put on more lipstick. And pull the sweater down."

"If I pull it down anymore, I'll fall out."

"All the better."

"So what's my story?" I said as I pulled open the front door. "Your niece? Nurse? Tax accountant?"

"For occupation, we'll stick with the truth."

I stopped, the door half open. "Seriously? Dressed like this?"

"He'll love it."

FIFTEEN

I waited in the atrium. The nurse had said there was a sitting room, but I preferred to stick close to the door, where escape was within sight. The smell is what did it to me, that unforgettable mix of disinfectant, overcooked vegetables and mortality that hits you in the gut and screams "run, while you still can!"

The last time I'd set foot in one of death's holding pens—sorry, "retirement homes"—I'd been thirteen, visiting my great-aunt Anna. The same Aunt Anna who'd sworn she'd die if her kids ever put her in a home. She didn't belong in a retirement home. First, she'd never retired, having run a cake-decorating business right up to the minute her kids stuck the For Sale sign on her front lawn. Second, though she was ninety-one, her brain was as sharp as ever, which was part of the problem. With her body wasting, she needed live-in help and she could be difficult. When the third nurse quit, Aunt Anna's children gave up and put her in a home. Two weeks later, the old woman's prediction came true. She died. There's a moral in there somewhere. I think it's "don't have kids."

Evelyn came to collect me about ten minutes later.

"Now, he knows what you are," she whispered as she steered me down the main hall. "But I didn't give a name. Don't use Dee. That'll be your official name and we don't want him knowing that." She stopped outside a room and grasped the handle. "We could go with—"

"I've got one," I said and pushed open the door.

The door opened into the living room area of a hotel-size suite. A couch, a chair, a coffee table and art prints on the wall, all very Holiday Inn, reasonably new, but definitely bargain-basement quality. A decent enough place to spend the night...but the rest of your life? I fought back a shiver.

A man sat in the chair, his back to the door, affording only a view of a liver-spotted bald head. He stood as we came in. I blinked, and hoped my surprise didn't show. He was three inches shorter than me, and I was only wearing one-inch heels. With a name like Little Joe, maybe this doesn't seem surprising, but blatant irony is the favored form of criminal nickname humor. Any guy with the words "tiny" or "little" in his moniker was certain to be six feet plus. Obviously the Nikolaevs didn't share the usual sense of mob humor.

Like many undersized criminals, Little Joe had over-compensated in the weight room. He'd pumped iron for so many years that even now, stuck in a rest home, his biceps would be the envy of a man a quarter his age. He had, however, neglected the lower half of his body, which left him looking like a balloon character squeezed from the bottom, a massive chest topping spindly legs. His eyes were sunken brown dots that glittered when he saw me. He smiled, revealing a perfect set of fake pearly whites.

"Is this her?" he asked, his gaze dropping to my chest and staying there.

"Jess," I said, stepping forward and extending my hand. "But my friends call me Jezebel."

He wheezed a laugh. "I bet they do." He vice-gripped my hand. I squeezed back and he fairly licked his lips, eyes never rising above my neckline. "I bet you are very good at your job, no?"

"The best. No one ever complains."

I extricated my hand from his and sashayed to the sofa.

Evelyn tried to take the seat beside me, but Little Joe slid into it with the speed of a twenty-year-old.

"Now this, Evelyn, this is how a hitwoman should be," Joe said, waggling a finger at her. "Not dressing up like a man, running around, shooting people. She must be subtle. Use her assets." A sidelong look at my "assets." "Yes, this is how it should be."

I wriggled like a praised puppy. Joe sidled closer.

"Evelyn tells me you're a very important man," I said.

My use of the present tense didn't go unnoticed. Joe preened and regaled me with a few glimpses into his former life. As he talked, I was aware of time ticking past, but also knew this wasn't someone who could—or should—be rushed into answering questions. I took my cue from Evelyn, who settled into her chair as if not expecting to rise for a while.

Little Joe was the older brother of Boris Nikolaev, long-time head of the Nikolaev family. To hear Joe tell it, he'd voluntarily abdicated his role as heir because he didn't want the responsibility. My guess was that he'd been passed over, like a Fortune 500 CEO's screw-up son—given a big corner office and invited to all the meetings, but never asked to actually do anything.

After about a half-dozen surprisingly boring mob stories, Joe made the segue himself.

"So you girls need help, you come to Little Joe. This is good. I may be old, but I can still help. You said it was about a former associate of my family?"

"A man who worked for you. Leon Kozlov."

"Kozlov?" Joe's face screwed up and I expected him to make the connection with the Helter Skelter victims, but instead he said only, "From the seventies?"

"Late seventies, maybe early eighties. He seems to have

parted ways with the family. Kicked out, probably. His for-
tunes didn't exactly improve after he left you."

"Kozlov. Leon Kozlov."

Joe's eyes rolled back, as if searching his mental files.
Then he turned his head and spat. Didn't just make the
motion. Actually spat. Fortunately, in the opposite direction. He muttered something in Russian. I didn't need to
know the language to know it wasn't a compliment.

"The Fomin hit," he muttered. "Sasha Fomin."

Evelyn frowned. "Kozlov was a hitman? I don't think—"

"No, no. Kozlov, he was not a hitman. He was security. A
bodyguard. Not for the family, but for our associates, people we wanted to protect. Only he didn't do so good a job."

"So this Fomin got whacked on Kozlov's shift?" I said.

Joe squeezed my thigh. My upper thigh. Upper inner
thigh, to be precise. I resisted the urge to squirm back into
the sofa cushions . . . or break his fingers.

"Smart girl," he said, kneading my thigh. "I said she was
a smart girl, no?"

"How did the hit go down?" Evelyn asked.

"Hit-and-run. Looked like an accident, and this Kozlov
tried to tell us that is what it was, but we were not fooled.
The Nikolaevs know accidents. Remember that senator?
From Texas? Now that, that was genius. First, we—"

"About Kozlov," Evelyn said. "Do you remember anything else about him?"

Joe puckered his lips, obviously displeased with being
cut short. I turned toward him, pulling my elbows in to
spring my breasts up closer to the old man's face. His eyes
zeroed in on target, lips smoothing in a smile. I inched
back before my cleavage caught drool.

"Did you know Kozlov well?" I prompted.

A snort. "As you say, he was not an important man. Not

important enough for me to know." He hesitated. "But, if you wish to know more, there was a man who worked for us, was friends with this Kozlov. Volkv. Nicky Volkv."

"Any idea where I'd find him?"

"More than an idea. You will find Mr. Volkv is a guest of the state, serving a life sentence for murder. Like Mr. Kozlov, he did not do so well after he left our organization."

Evelyn found out where Volkv was being held, then she thanked him and rose. "You've been a great help. If there's ever anything I can do for you..."

Little Joe turned his gaze on me. All over me. He grinned and opened his mouth, but I pressed my finger against his lips.

"I don't think you're ready for that," I said. "You look like you still have a lot of good years left ahead of you."

He barked a laugh. "Maybe, someday, if that changes, I will call you. Send me off in style."

I grinned, pressed against him and kissed his cheek. "It would be a pleasure."

As we stepped outside, Evelyn murmured, "Seems someone is quite the accomplished actor. Jack give you lessons?"

"Jack?"

"He doesn't seem the type, does he? Like you." A sly look my way, as if expecting a response. When I didn't comment, she continued. "Now, me? I bet you think I'd make a good actress."

"Probably."

She took out her keys and opened the car door. "Well, I'm not. I can't stand it, and no amount of practice makes it any easier." She slid into the driver's seat and waited for me to get in before continuing. "I just never could get the hang of being someone else. Nearly blew a job over it once."

She started the car and pulled from the lot. I expected the "story" to end there but, when she reached the main road, she continued.

"I had to hit a mark at a big party. I was about your age. Now I was never what you'd call pretty, but there are ways to make men forget that. Under the circumstances, what's the easiest way to make the hit?"

"Honeypot."

"Exactly. A little vroom-vroom—like you did in there—lure your mark away, then take him out while his brain's hiding in his trousers. So I bought the dress, put on my disguise, showed up at the party, got my first really good look at the old geezer and knew there wasn't a hope in hell I could pull it off."

"Ugly?"

"Made Little Joe look like a fireman's calendar centerfold."

"So what'd you do?"

"Waited until he found a little morsel he liked, let her do the dirty work, then shot him while she was in the bathroom cleaning up afterward. Improvisation, Dee. That's what I'm good at—not acting. The point is, everyone has strengths. Jack can teach you some. I can teach you others. There's no need to limit yourself." She slid a look my way. "But remember I'm the one with the teaching experience. Jack's only ever played the pupil."

I nodded and said nothing.

By the time we made it to the jail where Volkv was being held, visiting hours would likely be over. Besides, this wasn't a "fly by the seat of your pants" type of mission. It would require planning.

As we switched places and I drove back to Evelyn's, she kept me amused with stories about Little Joe, none of which were complimentary and all of which wouldn't have been nearly so funny if I'd hadn't met the man.

"—nearly blew a year's worth of planning," Evelyn said. "And why? So he wouldn't have to pay for the goddamned blow job."

"Isn't that the same story he told us? The payroll heist?"

"Now you know why the man's stories are so boring. He takes out all the parts that make him look like a moron, which means there's no goddamned story left. Between making things up and letting things slip . . . Volkv! Yes!"

Her sudden outburst nearly had me wearing my Coke.

Evelyn waved an apology my way. "I've spent the last hour trying to figure out where I know the name Nicky Volkv from. Thinking about Joe's loose lips just reminded me. Volkv tried to turn pro after he left the Nikolaevs. His first hit, he screwed up big-time. Put a car bomb in the wrong car, killed a young couple."

"Sounds like Volkv and Kozlov would have hit it off well. Two Mafia incompetents."

"It's the mob. Competence is a recessive gene. That's what keeps us in business."

I changed lanes, carefully passing a school bus. "You did mob work?"

Evelyn waggled her hand. "Fifty-fifty. For contract killers, mob hits are like office work—steady employment, decent pay . . . and boring as hell. There's far more lucrative and interesting work out there." She glanced my way. "Even for someone with her own rules. Drug cartels, political assassinations . . ."

I said nothing. To Evelyn, I suppose this made sense. If I didn't mind killing thugs, why not just kill bigger ones? But that would take me places I didn't want to go.

Didn't want to go? Or wasn't ready to go?

I shook off the thought and concentrated on the road.

Evelyn sipped her coffee. "Do you like working for the Tomassinis, Dee?"

"They treat me well. When they give me a mark, I check it out, and it's always exactly what they say it is. No tricks."

Evelyn gave a slow nod. "The Tomassinis are good. A small, old-fashioned family. Not many of them left. They haven't changed much from back when I worked for them."

"Ah, so *that's* how you know Frank Tomassini."

Her eyes glinted. "It didn't seem strange to you that a Mafia don had no problem hiring a woman? You have me to thank for his enlightened employment policy and, believe me, it took work to bring him around. I spent a year pretending I was a man before I told him. When I did, he fired me . . . until he had a job no one else could do."

"And hired you back."

"Frank always said I was the best damned hitman he had, which I was—and which is why he probably jumped at the chance to hire another woman."

"I guess I should say thanks."

She snorted. "You'll do better than that. You owe me, and I'm collecting."

"I'd *owe* you if you got me the job. You made it possible, but you didn't get it for me. That I did myself."

"True, which begs the question. How the hell does a New York Mafia don find a Canadian girl living in the middle of the goddamned forest, and recruit her as a contract killer?"

I let out a small smile. "Fate."

"That better not be all I'm getting. We have an hour left, and I expect to be entertained with a damn good story, especially considering what I'm offering in return."

"Which is?"

Her gaze still on the windshield, she lifted her coffee cup to her lips, but not before letting an enigmatic smile slip out. "Questions answered, as I said. Specifically, one question for one question. A fair exchange of information, that mightiest of commodities."

"And what information will I get?"

The smile tweaked the corners of her lips. "That depends on you. On what you want to know. For now, give me your story."

I hesitated, but could see nothing in the tale that could satisfy more than idle curiosity. She could always find out through the Tomassinis. Better for me to give it, and take something in return, some knowledge or skill I could use.

So I began. "The offer came through Frank's nephew, Paul..."

SIXTEEN

As for how Paul wound up at my lodge, that I *do* chalk up to fate. He'd come up with two of his cousins—also Tomassini wiseguys—for deer hunting season. They'd checked into a lodge 50 kilometers from the Red Oak. But the place hadn't been up to Paul's standards, and someone had recommended mine. He came, he liked, he stayed...even if he had to do his actual hunting off the property.

I figured out that they were Mafiosi pretty fast, but Paul and his cousins were quiet, well-mannered guests—better than those with the corporate team-building getaway I was hosting at the time—so I didn't care. Deer season ended, and Paul booked a week for duck season. Then he reserved the deer season for next year. Paul's cousins kept their distance from their ex-cop host, but Paul and I hit it off well—not friends, but friendly.

By his fourth visit, I could see foreclosure on the horizon and was scrambling to push it off a little further, but had finally come to realize I was only postponing the inevitable. My second life was about to crash—not as spectacularly as the first—but all the more devastatingly. I'd kept my problems to myself...until Paul tried booking his next visit, and I had to admit the lodge might not still be around.

The next day, when I was out back chopping wood, he'd appeared, looking dapper and well groomed even in a lumber jacket and jeans.

"Got another axe?" he asked.

I wiped sweat from my cheek and shook my head. "Just the one. Wouldn't be good for liability."

"Let me take a turn." He flashed a grin. "Never know when axe-wielding might come in handy."

I handed him the axe and showed him how to use it.

"I'll grab the pieces as they fall," I said. "Just watch my fingers."

For a few minutes, he just cut wood, alternating between cursing and laughing. Guys like Paul swing moods like they swing axes, swiftly and decisively, the smiles no less sincere than the scowls.

"You want me to take over?" I asked.

A mock glower. "When I'm just getting the hang of it?" He swung and embedded the axe in the stump I used as a chopping block.

"Hate to see you lose the lodge, Nadia," he said. "You work your ass off, and you've got a great setup here. It's the damn economy. You just need a little cash, to get you past this."

I nodded and grabbed the split pieces.

He wiped his brow, then pulled the axe out of the stump. "We might be able to help each other out. I have a problem that needs a solution, and I'm thinking maybe you could help with that."

I felt his gaze on my back as I added the pieces to the woodpile. He waited until I turned, giving him my full attention.

"A couple of years back, we had this young man start work for us. My sister's brother-in-law's stepson. A tenuous connection but..." A shrug. "Still family."

He put another log on the stump.

"The kid's not with us six months and there's trouble. An associate tells us he's been roughing up whores, paying them with bruises. My uncle's not happy but he thinks

'Who knows how the kid was raised? He just needs to be set straight.' So we set him straight. And it seemed to stop."

Paul swung the axe, shaving a sliver off the next log.

"*Seemed* to stop... until the kid's arrested for beating on a whore, and he's not just using his fists anymore. Almost killed the girl. So my uncle's furious, but still, the kid's family, just needs help to make better choices."

He swung again, taking off yet another slice.

"Kindling," I said when he swore.

I picked up the pieces.

"You know what's coming with this story, don't you?" he said.

"I've got a pretty good idea."

"We're kicking ourselves for not seeing it. To a cop or shrink it's probably obvious as hell. But us? We're optimists. Always trying to see the good in people, their ability to change."

I didn't dare comment on that.

Paul continued. "So what happened, as you cops or shrinks might say, was your standard escalation of violence, and now we've got ourselves one dead whore and a kid who doesn't seem to understand what he did wrong. After all, he says, she was only a whore."

My hands tightened around the log I was holding.

"You and I both know it isn't going to stop at one. My uncle, he knows that, too. He wants the matter resolved." Paul put the axe down, headfirst, and leaned on the handle. "I'm thinking maybe you could help us with that."

It's a testament to my desperation that I even considered the offer. For all I knew, I was being set up. But at that point in my life, on the brink of losing everything, it was a chance I had to take.

* * *

When I finished, I drove for another five minutes before Evelyn reminded me that she now owed me an answer.

"I think I'll save mine," I said. "I don't know what you can do, what you can teach me. When I find something, I'll ask."

"Professional knowledge?" She put her empty coffee cup in the holder. "Stop being so damned polite. When I offered information, I meant an exchange in kind. Personal for personal."

"Something about you?"

"I suspect I don't interest you that much. I'm an old woman whose sole importance is how I can help solve this case and what I can do for you professionally, and I don't take any offense at that. But I'll bet there's someone you *do* want to know more about." A small, unreadable smile. "Jack."

I turned onto the off-ramp. "You're offering me personal information on Jack?"

"Nothing *too* personal, of course. Ask me who he is or where he lives or how to find him when he doesn't want to be found, and I'll tell you to go to hell. But I can't imagine you'd ask that, so the point is moot. What I can offer is some...smaller answers."

"No, thank you."

She laughed. "How very polite you are. Let me guess. You don't want to pry; when he wants to tell you, he will. If that's what you're waiting for, you're a fool. He won't tell you anything."

"Then I guess he doesn't want me to know."

"Oh, I wouldn't say that. With Jack, it's not so much a

matter of not wanting to give things away as assuming you wouldn't be interested in hearing them. But if you are..."

I said nothing, but I could feel her gaze boring into me.

"You are interested, aren't you?" she said, voice deceptively light.

I turned and met her gaze. "If I want to know anything, I'll know who to ask."

"This isn't an open-ended offer, Dee."

"You said Jack doesn't talk about anything personal because he assumes I'm not interested. So if I *am* interested, all I have to do is ask him. First thing Jack taught me? Avoid the middleman. The price might look reasonable, but you'll end up paying more for it than you expect."

Evelyn went around front to collect the mail as I headed for the rear door. I'd barely cracked open the gate when a black-and-tan torpedo hit the other side, nearly slamming my fingers in the gap. A dark nose squeezed between the slats, snuffling like a pig finding truffles.

"Hello, girls," I said, heaving the gate against their dead weight. "Come on now. Get back so I can get in."

Scotch stuck her head through the opening and tried to wriggle through as Ginger danced and whined behind her. I turned to Evelyn as she came up behind me.

"I thought you left the dogs inside," I said.

"I did. Seems someone made it to his contact and back in record time."

We stepped through the back door into the kitchen. Jack looked up from the newspaper.

"See, she's still in one piece," Evelyn said. "I haven't devoured her yet."

Jack's gaze flicked over my outfit. "And I got shit for the *wig*."

"It was a necessary evil," I said. "Very necessary. Very evil. If you'll excuse me, I'm going upstairs to burn this sweater before anyone can suggest I wear it again." I glanced at Jack. "Unless you have news."

"It can wait."

I climbed from the shower and changed into jeans and a pullover. As I tried to finger-comb my curls, a brown blob looked back from the mirror, swirling in the steam. I groped at the wall, fingers searching for the fan. Flicked a switch. The room went dark.

I pulled open the door to get some air just as Jack crested the stairs.

"I seem to have a sauna going here," I said. "Is there a fan?"

"Nah."

I retreated into the bathroom, expecting him to take his duffel wherever he'd been heading. He laid it on the hall floor.

"Need a blow dryer?" he asked.

"Not unless I want an Afro." I raked my fingers through my shoulder-length curls. "This is definitely wash-and-wear."

I sifted through my meager selection of nondisguise makeup and decided against it. If Evelyn was offended by the sight of my naked face, so be it. As for Jack, well, he was still standing there, getting a eyeful of what I looked like without it, so it was too late for vanity.

"Did Evelyn tell you what we found out?" I asked as I pulled on socks.

"Not yet."

Something in his voice made me look up. His face was impassive . . . and yet.

"There's been another one, hasn't there?" I said. "Another murder."

"Yeah."

"When did it happen?" I said. "Where?"

He nodded toward the stairs. "CNN's on. When you're ready."

I was crouched over, my sock half on. I yanked it up and he reached out, as if to help me keep my balance. I shook my head, slipped past him and down the stairs.

SEVENTEEN

That morning, retired naval captain Russ Belding and his dog had gone for their usual morning walk through a wooded park near his home. He was last seen at approximately 7:45 by a jogger. An hour later, two teens taking a shortcut through the woods had found Belding's dog, dragging its leash, and within minutes, found Belding himself, shot through the base of his skull. A bullet through the central nervous system—dead before he hit the ground.

At noon a courier delivered a registered letter to five major media outlets. Inside the envelope were two sheets of paper. One was another page from *Helter Skelter*. The other was a letter in which the killer claimed to be the son of Charles Manson.

During the next few hours, every so-called expert the news station could drag out of his lead-lined nuclear-bomb/alien-invasion/Ebola-outbreak underground shelter got his fifteen seconds of fame. We listened to a few of them spout paranoia, then Evelyn started turning down the volume.

Jack lifted a hand to stop her.

Evelyn arched her brows. "What? Don't tell me you're buying this son-of-Manson shit."

"There's more." Jack crouched beside the TV set and hit the channel button. Static fuzz filled the screen.

"It's satellite," Evelyn said, waving the remote. "In the twenty-first century, we use these. What channel do you want?"

"Just flip through. Look for breaking news." He checked

his watch and frowned. "Surprised it's not on yet. Leaked two hours ago."

"What leaked?" I asked.

"No idea. Heard about the letter, called Felix. Quinn said something—"

"Wait!" I'd caught a glimpse of the scrolling text that always accompanied breaking news. "Go back. No...one more. There!"

Evelyn stopped on two dour news anchors. Middle-aged news anchors. Never a good sign. When a network wants a report taken seriously, they always pick bleak and Brylcreemed over bouncy and blond.

"The FBI are refusing to comment, but a source within the department claims that completed DNA analysis on the hair found at the second murder..."

"Hair?" Evelyn cut in. "What hair?"

Jack shook his head and waved her to silence. The announcer droned on, regurgitating the details of the second Helter Skelter murder for all those hermits making their annual pilgrimage into town to get the latest news.

"As for that test, the results apparently confirm that the Helter Skelter killer is, as claimed in his letter, a close blood relative of notorious murderer Charles Manson, who is currently being held..."

Jack shook his head. "Fuck. Thought it was a hoax."

"What about this hair?" Evelyn said, cranking the volume. "Where did they find a hair?"

The announcer ignored Evelyn and proceeded to ensure that all those hermits knew who Manson was before continuing.

"We take you now to our regional bureau, where reporter Angela Fry is interviewing Dr. Frederick P. Myers, a leading Manson expert—"

"Screw this," Evelyn said, tossing down the remote. She crossed the room and turned on her computer. "Let's find out more about this hair."

The hair had come from a piece of duct tape used on the second victim. An arm hair. The tape had presumably brushed against the killer's arm.

As for what evidence the FBI could gain from a single arm hair, well, I bet they'd sweated over that themselves for a while. Limb hairs aren't the most studied source of evidence, and with only one, the results are often inconclusive. They could tell whether it was human or animal, where on the body it came from and whether it had fallen out or been pulled. The big question, though, would be whether they could get DNA evidence from it, but they obviously had.

Once we'd cleared up the hair mystery, I suggested we find that letter. It was probably pure bullshit, but it wouldn't hurt to see what the killer had to say. We located it on a media Web site.

The letter began without an opening salutation.

> *You call me the Helter Skelter killer. That name comes from the pages I've been leaving, but let me assure you there is nothing "helter skelter" about my methods, as you may have determined. I chose that book not for the title, but for a deeper, more personal reason. My father, Charles Manson, had a vision. My goal was to take that vision to a new level, which I believe I have accomplished. I am now willing to end the killings, in return for a small favor.*

It ended there. Evelyn checked copies posted on a few other sites, but they were all the same—stopping before he made his demand.

"He's playing with us," I said. "With everyone. Claiming to be related to Manson. Nattering on about taking his vision to a new level. Making unspecified demands. He said just enough to stir up speculation and panic."

"What'd you find?" Jack asked.

"Huh?"

"Today. Earlier." He flicked off the television. "Forget this. He wants people to panic? Fine. Doesn't work on us."

Right. I took a deep breath, and told him what Evelyn and I had uncovered. Then I asked about his trip. It turned out that Carson Morrow's "cartel client" was a nephew who'd gone straight, and been out of the business for years. So that lead was dead. When Jack asked whether Evelyn had heard anything on Baron, she checked her messages and found a few tips to check out.

"You do that. I'm gonna take Dee out." He looked at me. "Dinner?"

"Um, sure," I said.

"It's too early for Martini's," Evelyn said. "You know I hate eating there before eight—"

"Didn't invite you. Giving Dee a break."

He waved me to the back door as she sputtered an obscenity-laden answer.

Jaxson

"Jackson," he told the hostess. "With an x."

Even now, ten years after his agent gave him the moniker, he felt silly saying it. Invariably, the other person frowned, not understanding. It wasn't like saying "Brandy with an i." Who the hell put an x in Jackson?

"J-A-X-S-O-N," he said when the hostess's brow knitted.

"And your first name, Mr. Jaxson?" she said as she wrote it down beside the reservation list. Before he could answer, her baby blues went double-wide. "Oh, my God. *That* Jaxson. I'm so sorry. I should have recognized—"

"That's okay. Some days, I'm happy being anonymous. After *No Holds Barred*, I didn't want to be recognized for months."

Ba-dum-dum. A line he'd used a thousand times, and not worth a snicker, much less the guffaw the hostess gave it. That's the hell of being famous. Everything that leaves your mouth is profoundly witty, profoundly charming, profoundly profound.

"Will your guest be joining you later?" the hostess asked as she led him through the darkened restaurant.

"She just got a casting call about an hour ago," Jaxson said. "She might be late."

The hostess smiled, nodded, promised to keep an eye out, all the time doubtless wondering which starlet Jaxson (Jackson...with an x) was bedding now. He almost felt guilty, as if he were robbing her of some bit of gossip she could sell or barter on the social market. No one would be joining him. There was no starlet. There was Melanie, a med student, but she was neck-deep in her internship and had no time—or patience—for media.

Instead, he ate lunch with the *Washington Post*. He plowed through his garlic fettuccine—screw the carbs—and finished up with a slice of chocolate cake—double-screw them. He wasn't in L.A. today, so he didn't need to play by L.A. rules.

After lunch he signed an autograph for the server and left her a twenty as a tip—more than his meal cost, but not so long ago he'd been waiting tables himself. Since he'd graduated from rehab, he had precious little to spend his money on. He might as well give a bit to someone who could use it.

Onto the street. Not much danger of being hounded for autographs here. This town might be small but, having attained a certain cachet in Hollywood circles, it saw stars quadruple his caliber every day.

Earlier, circling for a parking spot, he'd seen a conservation area. He could use the solitude, and the exercise after that meal.

He turned around, orienting himself, then spotted treetops to the east and set out.

He'd been trolling all day. Time for a West Coast hit, and this town seemed as likely as any. For hours he'd browsed the shops, tossed bills to the street performers, amused himself running through his options. Tourist, townie, celebrity... tourist, townie, celebrity. There was much to be said for each choice. And there was much to be said for not choosing at all, for simply targeting the first person who came into view.

The woman in Boston had been his first taste of the

truly random. Set a trap and whoever falls for it, dies. The thrill of that still hadn't left his bones. The power of it. Power over even his own conscience. It didn't matter who'd walked through that stairwell door—an adolescent paper-boy, a pregnant woman, an old man—they would have died because that's what he'd decided and he wouldn't re-nege on the deal.

He'd been strolling the main street, savoring his op-tions, when he'd seen the young man. He wasn't the first actor to walk past. He wasn't the biggest. But the young man tweaked a memory of sitting in a dentist's office, flip-ping through an entertainment magazine. He'd been in there, this pretty-boy actor with the ridiculously spelled name. A chill of delicious déjà vu ran through him. Jaxson, model turned forgettable actor. Sharon Tate, model turned forgettable actress. Perfect.

He'd watched the young man, dressed in jeans and a sweatshirt, clean-shaven and polite, stepping aside for oth-ers, apologizing when he bumped a passerby, never disap-pointed when the object of his courtesy didn't leap up and ask for an autograph.

Better and better. The portrait of Sharon Tate painted in *Helter Skelter* was of a good, sweet-natured girl, the an-tithesis of the spoiled starlet. Maybe it was true, maybe it wasn't, but it mattered little how someone really behaved, only how she was remembered.

He thought about the page in his pocket. A court scene. No mention of Tate. Too bad . . . or maybe not. Think of all the overeducated experts he'd rob of a paycheck if he was too obvious. He could see them now, pale-faced professors scrabbling over their stacks of books. A jolt of excitement in flatlined lives. Who was he to take that from them?

Tagging along behind a group of chattering retirees, he

followed Jaxson to the edge of a conservation area. As the seniors stopped to snap photos, Jaxson's light gray sweatshirt disappeared down a wooded path and he had to bite his cheek to keep from laughing out loud. If he believed in ESP, he'd almost think that somehow he'd sent out signals, directing Jaxson to the best possible spot for a kill. The strong mind dominating the weak.

He allowed himself a brief smile, broke away from the tour group and headed into the woods.

In the beginning, there was a plan. And it was a good plan. But it wasn't very interesting. It wasn't supposed to be interesting. But, to his surprise, after all these years, the act of killing came with a rush of power, a charge of adrenaline, an excitement that bordered on the sexual. It was as astonishing as waking one morning and getting a hard-on from brushing your teeth.

Jaxson's pale shirt flashed between trees, appearing and disappearing like a lighthouse beacon in a storm. He kept his eyes trained on his target, ears mapping its path when that shirt slipped from view. Undergrowth crunched steadily under the young man's footfalls, and the birds quieted as he approached.

Time to get closer.

He was near enough to smell the actor's cologne, harsh against the subtle smells of nature. Near enough to hear him breathing. Inhale, exhale, the rhythm of life. Moving faster, closer, he felt the first twinge in his crotch, a spark of excitement that would remain but a spark. The power of control. He slid his finger along the ice pick and pulled it from his jacket.

Then, with only a curtain of forest between them, he stopped. It suddenly occurred to him that he had more choices than how to kill and whom to kill and where to kill. He could choose whether to kill. Push to the brink and stop.

When he stopped short, he expected the spark to dwindle, to recede into disappointment. Instead, it surged into a full-blown, fly-splitting erection. He stood there, the ice pick in one hand, and let the other fall to his crotch. One caress, so firm it made his eyelids flutter. Then he put the pick back in his pocket, turned and walked away.

The power of control.

The power of choice.

EIGHTEEN

It was only after we left Evelyn's house that I realized I was hardly dressed for dinner. The jeans and pullover were bad enough, but the wash-and-wear hair and zero makeup had me cringing. Jack was still in a variation on his "aging biker" getup, complete with garish forearm tattoo, so obviously we weren't dining at any place with a dress code, but I still vowed to make a dash for the washroom when we arrived.

As it turned out, I was glad I had some grooming supplies in my purse, because his choice of restaurant was a steak house. Not a "slap the meat in a frying pan" type, but one where the server brings out a steak for your inspection before cooking it. We had to wait as the hostess scrambled to clear tables for the extended family in front of us, so I had time to slip into the bathroom to touch up and to scrub for dinner. When I came back, Jack was still waiting.

"Is Evelyn going to be upset?" I whispered as the server showed us to our table. "Us taking off on her?"

"Nah. Not here. Hates this place. She likes fussy food. Fancy." He glanced over at me, frowning slightly. "This okay? With you? Should have asked."

"This is great. I like food that covers the plate, not decorates it."

A small smile. "Good."

The hostess tried to seat us near the kitchen doors, but Jack redirected her to a small room they hadn't started filling yet. Our table was tiny, but private, the noise of other diners only a distant murmur. The lights were low. Too low really. Nice for atmosphere—not so good for reading menus. When I noticed Jack squinting at his, I borrowed his matches and lit our oil lamp. It sputtered a moment, acrid smoke filling the air, then lit, casting a wavering yellow glow over the table.

Jack considered the wine list, but seemed relieved when I said I'd be having a mixed drink instead. I ordered a Caesar, then—seeing the server's blank look—changed it to a Bloody Mary. Jack got draft beer.

For our meals, we both chose steaks, with vegetables on the side and loaded baked potatoes. Add on an appetizer, plus the bread they brought with our drinks, and it was probably enough calories to last a week. But after grazing on fast food for days, I considered this healthy eating. At least there would be something green on my plate.

"Today go okay?" Jack asked when the server left.

"You mean with Evelyn?"

He nodded.

"It seemed fine."

He hesitated, his gaze sliding to mine, searching. After a moment, he broke away and nodded, satisfied.

"If you were worried she was going to pester me about the protégée thing, it didn't happen. She hinted about better jobs, but didn't pursue it. I think she's changed her mind about my suitability."

Another pause, butter knife raised. Then another nod. He speared one of the bread slices with the knife, offering it to me. I took it. Then the server arrived with the appetizer, and I asked how his trip to Illinois had gone.

As I sipped my Bloody Mary, I thought about how long it had been since I'd had something like a "date dinner." Not that I'd mistaken this for a date, but the general scenario—sitting in a semidark restaurant, enjoying drinks and conversation with a man over a long, leisurely meal—was one I hadn't experienced in a while.

Three years since my last relationship. Even that had been casual. My last serious one was six years ago, when I'd been "preengaged."

That had been Eric's word for it. He'd even bought me a preengagement ring. It'd been a joke, something to placate his mother, who kept looking at me with visions of grandchildren in her eyes, but after a while, I think it became reality for Eric, and maybe even for me, the idea that we really were headed toward engagement. I didn't need to get married. But I *could*, with the right guy. And if there was a right guy, Eric was it.

He was a firefighter. My first firefighter, I always teased. When it came to dating, I had a definite "type." Men in uniform, and it had nothing to do with symbols of authority setting my libido aflutter. I'd grown up in that culture. Lived it, breathed it, loved it. Born to a family of cops. Practically grew up at the station. Raised by the force, as they'd joke. So I'd dated cops, with the odd military officer thrown in for variety. I understood guys like that. I was comfortable with them. Dating a firefighter hadn't been much of a stretch.

It had been a good time of my life. The right time for someone like Eric. I had my problems, but I'd learned to control them. Then along came Wayne Franco.

When I shot Franco, Eric tried to hide his shock, tried to convince me—and, through me, himself—that it had been an uncharacteristic act brought on by overwork, stress and anxiety over Dawn Collins's murder.

In the aftermath, Eric stood by me, even when his superiors started "suggesting" he might want to take a vacation, get out of town while all this was going on. Seeing that pressure on him, I did the right thing. I told him I could handle this myself and suggested he step back. To my surprise and, yes, my disappointment, he'd done just that. And I'd realized that he'd supported me not because he believed in me, but because he believed it was the right thing to do, the noble thing to do.

After almost a week passed and he hadn't called, I phoned and told him where he could stick his nobility.

We never spoke again.

The food arrived as Jack and I were scraping up the last of the crab dip. My steak was a decent size—I'd turned down the "smaller" portion offered by the server—but Jack's took up most of his plate, so big they had to serve the potato separately.

We both started to eat, quiet for a few minutes, relishing the food. After a moment, Jack paused to watch me, as if making sure I was enjoying it.

"This is great," I said, tapping the steak. "I haven't had one like this in a long time."

"Yeah?" He waved his fork over his plate. "To Evelyn? This is workman's food. Me? Growing up? Rich people's food. We'd dream about eating like this. See it in movies, magazines." He cut off a generous slice. "I was a kid? Used to brag. Saying I'd be rich. Live in America. Eat steak every day."

I smiled. "Did you ever do that?"

"Tried. After my first big job? Ate at places like this almost two weeks straight. Made myself sick."

I laughed. "I'll bet."

I could have prodded more personal information from him, maybe asked if he'd known Evelyn at the time and what she'd thought of that. Innocent questions that I suspected he'd answer. But that seemed manipulative, tricking him into revealing more.

Was I interested in *knowing* more? Sure. Jack played a significant role in my life, yet I knew next to nothing about the man. Curiosity was a given.

When Evelyn had tempted me with details on Jack, goading me about being interested, I'm sure this casual curiosity wasn't what she'd meant. Was I interested in Jack? Physically attracted to him? Maybe to Evelyn the question should have an easy answer. He was a man, not unattractive, and available, at least in the sense that he was right there, with no immediate competition in sight. Maybe, to her, it was as simple as "yes, I'm interested" or "sorry, not my type."

Jack *wasn't* my type. Far from it. But when I looked at him, across the table, even asking myself "am I interested?" threw up a mess of incomplete and conflicting emotions... and an overriding sense that any time I spent untangling my feelings for him would be wasted, because he was clearly *not* interested in me.

I'd worked with enough men to sense, almost immediately, whether I was in danger of being cornered in a dark alley on patrol or followed to my car postshift with a shy "You doing anything tonight?" With Jack, that radar didn't even turn on.

When the server asked whether we wanted to see the dessert menu, Jack didn't consult me, just said yes, two please.

"What're you getting?" he asked after I'd surveyed mine for a minute.

"I don't think I could finish anything…"

"So don't finish. That's the point of dessert. You don't need it."

I smiled. "Are you getting something?"

"'Course. Eat like this? Gotta have dessert. Rich people do."

My smile grew, and I ordered an apple-caramel something-or-other and a coffee.

When it arrived, he asked, "So, the money. What're your plans? Something for the lodge?"

It took a moment to realize he meant the payment for this "job." "We need to catch him first."

"We will. Got plans?"

"I haven't thought about it," I said as I cut into my dessert. "The Moretti job will pay for the roof and prewinter repairs. I think I'll use this for extras."

"That deck by the lake? You mentioned that this summer."

"I did." I leaned back with my coffee. "I really want to work on snagging more of the romantic getaway market for summer. Winter is easy—couples just want to hole up in a warm room and have someone else cook comfort food for them. Summer needs more. Owen and I have plans for a picnic spot in the meadow. I'd been hoping by next fall I could afford a gazebo, for the following summer."

"There you go. Buy yourself one this spring. Get one for the deck, too."

"That'd be nice. A big deck at the waterfront, plus a gazebo over the edge. Maybe even upgrade to ones with screens for black-fly season and cooler weather. It'd make a great place for couples to have a drink or—" I tapped my pastry. "Coffee and slice of Emma's pie. It'd photograph well for the brochure. I'd take the picture of the meadow picnic spot when the spring flowers are out. And the other one by the lake at sunset."

My mind racing ahead, planning. All the tension and frustration from earlier, from hearing the killer's letter, had evaporated. Maybe it was the drink. Maybe it was the good food. Maybe it was just being away, comfortable and relaxed. Whatever the reason, the fire in my gut had stopped burning, and I could see beyond this case, to a time when it would be over and I'd be reaping the rewards—the monetary ones and the deeper, more meaningful ones.

I glanced at Jack. "First, we need to catch this guy."

"Still gonna get paid. Only difference? Afford two gazebos or four. I'd count on four."

I smiled. "You *do* have an optimistic streak." I sipped my coffee. "As much as I'm enjoying this break, should we talk about tomorrow?"

"Yeah. I'm going after Baron."

"Do you think Evelyn will have a lead for you?"

He shrugged. "Doesn't? I'll find one. Legwork."

"Evelyn wants us to talk to Volkv tomorrow, but I think Baron is the better lead. Where do you want me?"

He considered this as he scraped chocolate icing from his plate. "Shouldn't focus on one thing. Do I want you along? Sure. Need you? Hard to say. More than Evelyn will? No."

"So I'll stay with her. If you find Baron...I know you don't need backup..."

"I find him? I'll call."

NINETEEN

Again, Evelyn met us at the door. "About time. I'm getting a little tired of this, you two. I find all your leads, then I'm stuck in this damned house waiting for you to get your asses back and start investigating them."

"You find *all* our leads?" Jack said as we hung up our coats.

"Most."

"Is this one about Baron?" I asked.

She waved the question aside. "Later. I have something better—a fresh avenue."

I groaned. "The only thing worse than not having any theories? Having too many."

She herded us to the living room, impatiently waiting while we settled in, then said, "Earlier, you asked me to look into criminal records for the other victims. What you failed to ask for was arrest records—"

"I *did* ask. You said you'd look into—"

"I found one." She eased back in her seat and smiled. "Murder."

"Who?"

"Mary Lee."

"You don't mean the—"

"Old lady?" Her brows arched. "A murderous old lady? Heavens, what a thought."

Before she could have the satisfaction of drawing out the explanation, Jack walked to the computer desk, flipped through the papers, brought one to the sofa and sat down beside me where we could both read it firsthand.

Mary Lee had indeed been charged with murder, almost

twenty years ago. From the article, it wasn't clear whether the charges had been dropped or whittled down to something that hadn't shown up in our earlier search. We could tell only that the case had never gone to trial.

The victim? Lee's husband. Smothered with a pillow. She'd confessed to the crime even. But after every member of her family told a story of years of escalating abuse, backed up by medical records, the DA's office had decided that Lee had been in justifiable fear for her life and acted in self-defense. She'd been lucky. It didn't always work out that way, especially twenty years ago, but she'd been set free and gone on to live exactly as she had before, as a law-abiding member of society.

Evelyn said, "So we have six victims so far, and two confirmed killers—"

"I wouldn't put Mary Lee in the same category as Leon Kozlov."

She waved me off. "Details. They're both killers. Two out of six. Seems a little high for random sampling, don't you think?"

Jack shrugged. "Maybe. Maybe not. Depends on circumstance. Like Dee said—"

"There's more. What do those two crimes have in common besides being homicides?" She didn't wait for an answer. "In Lee's case, the charges were dropped. In Kozlov's they were reduced. Did the crime, but not the time."

Jack grunted. "I don't see—"

"No, but I'll bet Dee does."

As she said that, I realized what she was getting at and spit out the word she wanted. "Vigilantism."

Jack shook his head. "After, what, ten years? Longer for Lee."

I hated pursuing this, but it was an angle that needed to

be considered. "If that's what this is, vigilantism would likely be an excuse. Someone who's justifying his actions by choosing people one could argue escaped justice."

"Is that common?" Evelyn said. "Vigilantes as common killers looking for justification?"

I met her gaze straight on. "It's one explanation. Sometimes you'll find people ganging together to protect a neighborhood, calling themselves vigilantes, when all they really want is an excuse to bust some heads. It's a more likely explanation than 'pure' vigilantism—someone with . . . an overdeveloped sense of justice."

"Doesn't make sense," Jack said. "Hitmen kill. Don't need an excuse."

"Isn't money an excuse?" Evelyn said. "What if we're talking about a hitman who got to liking it, then needed to find another reason to keep doing it when no one was paying?"

"There may have also been a precipitating event," I found myself saying. "If someone close to him was recently the victim of a crime, and went unpunished, that may have set him off."

"Would it?" Evelyn's eyes turned my way.

I locked gazes with her. "Yes, it's one factor."

"Still not buying this," Jack said. "Two out of six. What're you telling me? The other four killed someone? If this guy found them—"

"Then it must be a matter of public record, which rules out more arrests because I haven't uncovered any. But there are a lot of ways for someone to be responsible for a death." She paused. "Something someone did. Something he failed to do."

I could hear my heart thumping, each breath getting harder to take. Was she mocking me?

I focused so hard pain exploded behind my eyes, but I

lifted my head to fix her with my calmest, most guileless stare . . . only she wasn't looking at me. Her gaze was fixed on Jack.

A look passed between them, but I caught only a glimpse of it before Jack shrugged, face blank once more.

"Maybe," he said. "Only way to find out? Check it out."

Jack followed through on his skepticism by heading off to bed. He had another long day coming and little sleep from the night before. If we wanted to research this angle, we could do it without him.

That meant I was left alone with Evelyn. I could have followed Jack, made the same excuse. But if Evelyn had anything to say to me, better to hear it now, and clarify where I stood with this new "partner."

She sat down at her computer and started flipping through sites, waiting just long enough to ensure Jack wasn't changing his mind. Then she turned to me.

"I offended you," she said. "With that vigilante angle."

I settled back in my seat, notepad on my knee. "I don't offend easily." I smiled to underscore my point. "But, yes, I can get a little prickly about the word. Chalk it up to my cop side. 'Vigilante' means some yahoo trying to do our job—implying that we can't handle it—and usually getting in our way."

"But the underlying concept is a person who takes justice into his own hands. Which I think you're familiar with?"

I considered my next words carefully, aware of the weight of her gaze on me. I could sing the "I'm only in it for the money" song. But take my past, put it together with my current line of work, and even Jack had known, from the start, why I was in this. That's why he'd never suggested I branch out, try anything more lucrative. Knocking off a couple of wiseguys a year? Sure. Killing someone's wife to convey a message? Never. Not even if that one job would equal years of work for the Tomassinis.

So I only looked at Evelyn and said, "Does that bother you?"

"Not a bit, as long as I'm not in danger of being murdered in my bed. I can't say I understand it, but it does have its advantages."

"Advantages?"

"Drive. Passion. Sometimes, in this job, it can be more important than keeping your cool. And certainly more interesting." She turned back to her computer. "Now, let's see what we can find."

I spent the next two hours with Evelyn as she cruised the information highway, letting me tag along at the far end of the towing rope. Evelyn bobbed between the two levels of the Internet, searching the mainstream Web and its underground tendrils. When she pulled a particularly clever maneuver, she'd pull in my towline and let me see what she was doing, but when it came to the nuts-and-bolts of surfing the underbelly, she'd block her keystrokes or shift in front of the monitor, all the while promising to show me this part "another time." In other words, she wowed me with fancy footwork, but held back on the basic steps, like a dance teacher offering a free lesson to encourage a prospective student to shell out for the full course.

Finally, we found something—a short article more than fifteen years old. In it, Carson Morrow, victim number two, was mentioned as one of four teens who'd been in a car when one of the quartet died in a single-vehicle accident. That was all we got. For once, the reporter had focused on the life of the victim, not the circumstances of his death.

Had Morrow been the driver? Had he somehow been responsible—maybe egging the driver on or supplying alcohol? The article didn't speculate, only listed him as one of the survivors and ending with a vague "no charges have been filed at this time."

Evelyn searched for more, but that was it. Not surprising—a motor vehicle accident involving teenage boys was tragic, but not newsworthy. We printed the article, and she sent out "feelers" to a source, someone in the St. Louis area who might be able to tell her more. Then she dove back into the Web, trolling for the others. The best we could find was a mention of Russ Belding as the commanding officer on a ship where a sailor had died in a port town. There was some possibility of "responsibility" there, but it would require more in-depth searching. Being an incident that involved the military, that might not be so easy, but Evelyn swore she had connections.

More insurance digging didn't help prove that theory. Sanchez's brothers didn't seem in need of money. Both were married, with decent jobs. The one who'd done time had apparently gone straight. We'd found no sign of another policy for Kozlov.

As for Russ Belding, he had a hundred-thousand-dollar policy, the same one he'd had for decades. I can't imagine anyone who's been married for thirty-five years killing off her husband for a hundred grand, just after he's retired from the navy and ready to spend his twilight years with her. According to Evelyn, though, that was a good reason *to* kill him.

"Pulled a job for that myself," she said. "Couple married thirty years. Some"—a dismissive wave—"banking family. Wasn't about money, though. Having money only meant the broad could afford my fee. He was set to retire and she couldn't bear the thought of the old coot hanging around all the time, pestering her and messing up her social calendar."

"So she hired you to kill him?"

"Wanted him popped as he left his retirement dinner. I thought it was symbolic or some shit, but she just wanted to be sure he wasn't going to change his mind in the middle of his farewell speech. So I told her I'd be in a perch watching through my scope. If she came out with her hat off, I'd withdraw. But she had it on, so..." Evelyn pulled an imaginary trigger. "Permanent retirement."

I tried to keep my mouth shut. But after a moment I said, "I bet he was really looking forward to enjoying his retirement, after working all his life."

"If so, then he shouldn't have stayed married to a woman who'd rather bury him than spend more time together. He was getting something out of that marriage, so he chose to stay in it and it cost him his life. Cold facts for a cold world, Dee. Spouses, children, friends, lovers—they'd all kill you under the right circumstances. Just a matter of finding their price."

I looked into her eyes, trying to tell whether she meant that or was just spouting more rhetoric, but she turned back to her computer.

"Speaking of murderous families, time to move on to sons of Charles Manson..."

While we'd been at dinner, Evelyn had discovered there were more than a few. She showed me the list, and said she'd already contacted a source she described as a Manson freak. Then we had to declare the evening at an end and, like Jack, rest up for the day to come.

* * *

I lay in bed, staring at the ceiling. Or, I should say, where I assumed the ceiling would be if I could see it. Evelyn had top-quality blackout blinds, and I'd closed them completely, hoping the darkness might convince my brain it was time for sleep, but so far, all it had done was give my brain time to wander. Naturally it went to the place I'd been trying to keep it from since our discussion.

Justice.

I grew up with a very clear understanding of what that word meant. The concept had been formed at that early age where everything is clearly black and white. Right must triumph. Wrong must be punished.

From the time I was old enough to open a bag of potato chips, I'd played hostess to my father's monthly poker games. As for whether it was appropriate for me to hear the conversations that went on over those games, I don't think anyone considered that. They saved the darker talk, the angrier debates, for later, after I'd refilled my last bowl of peanuts and curled up on the recliner. There I'd pretend to be asleep, knowing this was what was expected of me. Eyes closed, I'd listen as the best stories came out, the tales of battles between good and evil, and the knights who fought them.

The beer, rye and Scotch would flow, the hour growing ever later, the importance of the game dwindling as the stories took over. Most times, that's all it was: stories. But when the anecdotes didn't have happy endings, the course of the conversation would change. They'd talk about miscarriages of justice, usually in another town, a bigger city.

Sometimes it would just be a head-shaking "can you believe it?" and a spirited discourse on how the case could have been handled better. Now and then, though, head-shaking wasn't enough. If the miscarriage lay in some particularly

heinous crime—a serial rapist, a thrill killer, kiddie porn—
the talk took another turn, into the realm of biblical eye-
for-an-eye justice.

My father usually kept quiet during such debates. Then,
one time, the conversation turned more heated than I'd
ever heard it, over the case of a ten-year-old girl who'd
been tortured and murdered. That time Mr. Weekes—a
former law professor turned librarian—was the only de-
fender of mercy. When my father had tried to squelch the
argument, my uncle had turned to him.

"For God's sake, Bill. Are you telling me if some sick
bastard did this to Nadia, you wouldn't want to shoot him
yourself?"

Without hesitation my father said, in his usual quiet
voice, "Of course I would."

After Amy died, I wanted to sit in on her killer's trial.
My aunt—Amy's mother—had tried to talk my dad out of
letting me, but he'd only said, in that same soft way, "I want
her to see justice done."

I wasn't allowed to stay for the whole trial—my father
took me out during any parts he deemed unsuitable. But
even from what I saw, I knew things weren't going well.
Everyone thought it would be so simple. The police had
been on the scene moments after Amy's death, giving her
killer time to run but not to cover his traces or hide evidence. And they had me, an eyewitness.

Yet it hadn't been that easy. Those police on the scene
had included the father and uncle of the victim, not acting
as investigators and sealing off the scene, but rushing in
hoping to save her, hoping to catch her killer. Mistakes had
been made. Accusations of tampering were lobbed.

And I wasn't allowed to testify. As for why, I remember
only whispered meetings behind closed doors—the crown

attorney with my father, my father with my mother, my parents with Amy's. Then came the shrinks. Two of them. First one, gently taking me through that day. More whispered conferences with my father and the lawyer followed. Then came the second psychologist. More questions. More prodding. After that, the whispering stopped and the decision was made. I would not testify.

I can only presume they were afraid to put me on the stand. I'd been thirteen, kidnapped, seen my cousin raped, then escaped... only to fail to bring help in time. At best, I was a traumatized witness. At worst, I was a liar, coached by my father and uncle to accuse an innocent man.

Drew Aldrich was acquitted.

At first, I blamed myself. I'd failed Amy once, by running away, then failed her again, by not convincing the prosecutor and the psychologists that I was strong enough to testify. But they had my statements. That should have been enough.

It might have been different if I'd been able to add charges to the case. But Amy had been the victim, not me.

It didn't matter. Whatever I had done, or failed to do, justice would still be served. That was why I was here. To see justice. My father had promised.

Outside the courtroom, I watched Aldrich bounce down those steps, and I waited for the shot that would wipe the smug smile off his face.

It didn't come.

Not then. Not ever.

Aldrich left town that day. A free man.

They let him leave.

Amy was dead, and her killer lived, and no one—not even those men I loved and trusted, who'd spoken so passionately about justice—ever did a damned thing about it.

TWENTY

I rolled from bed and padded downstairs, moving quietly so I wouldn't wake Jack or Evelyn. I knew what I wanted, and I was sure Evelyn wouldn't mind me helping myself.

In the kitchen, I opened the pantry and scanned the contents. Nothing. Now what? I didn't feel right pawing through all her kitchen cupboards. There was tea and decaf coffee, but what I craved was cocoa.

That's what my dad always made me when I slipped downstairs at night. Though I'd claimed insomnia, the truth was, I often came down just for the hot chocolate...and the time with my father.

Dad never went to bed before one. After the eleven o'clock news, my mother retired, and Dad would head into the kitchen, retrieve his briefcase from the back hall and spread his case files across the table. Then he'd work.

As a child, I always harbored the suspicion that he wasn't really working, but was just taking advantage of some quiet time after my mother went to bed. I know now that his cases had kept him awake. He'd spend the next hour or two running through leads, twisting and turning them in his brain, struggling to fit the pieces together.

When I'd interrupt, he'd just smile, get up, fix the hot chocolate and we'd count how many mini-marshmallows I could cram in. Seventeen was my personal best.

If the case he was working on was child-friendly, he'd tell me about it and not only ask my advice, but act as if he took it seriously, jot down notes, promise to follow up and let me know what happened. He always did; solved or shelved, he'd tell me how it worked out.

I stood in the draft of the open fridge, staring at the milk container.

"Letting out all the cold air."

I jumped, the door slipping from my hand. Jack stood behind it.

"Have you ever had warm milk?" I asked.

"What?"

"I was looking for hot chocolate mix, but Evelyn doesn't seem to have any, so I thought maybe I'd try warm milk. They say it helps you sleep. Doesn't sound too appetizing, though."

"It's not." He skirted around me, opened a cupboard and took out two containers, one labeled cocoa, the other sugar. "Hot chocolate."

I looked from one container to the other. "Requires cooking skills, doesn't it? Maybe I'll just stick with—"

"Sit down." He grabbed the milk from the fridge.

"No, really, I wasn't asking—"

"I know. Hand me that saucepan."

I reached for a big copper pot hanging over the counter.

"No, the sauce— The little one."

Jack moved to the stove and leaned down to turn it on. As I handed him the pot he turned sharp, nearly colliding with me.

"Here's the—" I said. "Oh."

He wasn't wearing his biker-guy getup from earlier. Not surprising, given the hour, but it was only now, standing a few inches away under the harsh kitchen lights that I realized he wasn't wearing a disguise at all. The dark brown eyes, the short, wavy black hair, it was what I'd seen all those nights at the lodge. Even his face was pretty much as I remembered...except for one thing.

When I'd first gotten off the plane and seen Jack's biker

disguise, I'd been impressed by the first-rate job he'd done with aging—the crow's feet around the eyes, the lines around the mouth, the sun-weathered skin that changed him from a man in his thirties to one closing in on the half-century mark. Well . . . it hadn't been makeup.

"You're not wearing a disguise," I blurted before I could stop myself.

"Neither are you." He gave a half-shrug. "Seemed only fair."

There was something expected here, some response— any response—to an action that couldn't have been made lightly. I opened my mouth, hoping something intelligent would come out. When nothing did, I snapped it shut.

As I handed him the pot, I cursed myself. Was it too late to crawl back to bed?

Jack turned to stir the cocoa in and I found myself look-ing at the back of his head, noticing the silver mingled with the black. Why was I so shocked? If I'd been thinking logi-cally, I'd have realized long ago that Jack couldn't be any-where near my age, not with his reputation.

"I need pants," I said.

Jack turned and gave me the same "what?" look as when I'd asked about hot milk. Then he glanced down at my bare legs sticking out from under the oversized T-shirt I wore to bed.

"Sit," he said. "I won't look."

I slithered to the table and busied myself refolding the newspaper. When Jack shoved the cocoa and sugar back into the pantry, I got up and returned them to the cup-board, in the same places they'd been, labels forward.

As I sat down again, the dogs padded into the kitchen. They glanced at Jack, then slipped around the table, Scotch stretching out at my feet, Ginger pushing her nose under my hand for a petting.

"Snuck out of Evelyn's room." Jack laid a mug at my elbow, then pulled out the chair beside mine. "You should get one. A dog. For the lodge."

I shook my head. "I'd love to, but I have to consider my guests. I could get someone who's allergic and they wouldn't appreciate a house filled with dog dander."

"You have dogs? Growing up?"

Another shake. "My mom loved cats. Personally, I can't see the attraction. You feed them, pamper them, clean up their crap, and they still act like they'd be gone in a second if they got a better offer. Call me needy, but I want a pet that wants me back. I brought a puppy home once but... It didn't go over too well, so we had to get rid of it."

According to Brad, my mother had shipped the dog off to the pound while I was at school, though she'd told me it ran away.

"How about—?" I began, then stopped.

"How about me?" Jack said. "Pets, you mean?"

"Sorry, I didn't mean to pry."

"Wouldn't ask anything I minded answering myself." He stretched out his legs, earning a grunt from Scotch as he invaded her space. "Had barn cats. Don't really count as pets. Found a dog once. Should say, my older brothers found it. Gave it to me."

"That was nice of them."

"I thought so. Till I realized they just wanted someone to do the work. Feed it. Brush it. Take the blame if it caused trouble. Dog played with all of us. Didn't care who 'owned' it."

I laughed. "Smart brothers."

"Yeah." He smiled, then went quiet, traced a finger around

the circle his mug had left on the table. "Yeah, they were." Jack swiped away the condensation mark with his hand, then waved at Ginger, who was still sucking up my attention. "No reason you can't get a dog. Build a good outside kennel. You're outside most of the time anyway."

"I suppose."

"Should have one. At least for protection. That caretaker you've got? He's, what, seventy? Not much help. No security system. Fuck, I tried the front door once. Two a.m. Wasn't even locked. Then there's your jogging. You take a gun along?"

"Where I live—"

"Doesn't matter. You need to be careful. Those deserted roads? I remember—" Jack shook his head. "Wouldn't believe what guys can pull off."

"Such as?"

He lifted his brows.

"Come on. You set up a story, now carry it through. You've still got"—I glanced in his mug—"half a cup left. Tell me half a cup's worth of story and we'll call it a night."

And, to my surprise, he did.

HSK

He pecked at the keyboard with his index fingers. Slow but steady. His philosophy for all things, or so it had been ...

What was the cliché? You can't teach an old dog new tricks? Of course you could, so long as you provided the twin keys to change—motivation and desire. He'd never be a sixty-word-a-minute typist, but his two-fingered method suited his purposes just fine.

Five years ago he didn't even know how to turn on a computer. But then someone showed him how useful a tool it could be and so, with motivation and desire, he'd taught himself how to use it. Now he couldn't imagine how he'd survived all those years in the business without it.

There were places down there, deep in the Web, that most Internet-savvy criminals scorned and mocked. Places inhabited by interlopers in the criminal world. Wannabes—that's the word they used these days. Computer geeks who set up shop in the underworld and tried desperately to be part of it.

He could picture them, caffeine-hyper beanpoles with bad skin and thick glasses, surrounded by pizza boxes and Coke cans, fingers flying across the keyboard, ferreting out every bit of underworld gossip and lore, endlessly searching for some tidbit that maybe, just maybe, would impress someone in the business, someone who'd seen dead bodies that weren't just video game carnage. They lived in that hope, so they worked ceaselessly, improving their network of contacts, their data banks of information.

Ego being what it is, no success is a success unless it can be admired and envied by others. Lacking the audience they desired, these moles of the underground found another forum for their braggadocio. They talked to one another.

Tonight, as he sat in the Internet cafe, nursing a coffee, he'd prowled through three such chat rooms, ostensibly to get a heads-up on the investigation, hear the leaks, the rumors, the speculation. Perhaps, if he was being honest with himself, he'd admit to the thrill that came each time he saw his alter ego appear on the screen, each time someone typed the words "Helter Skelter killer."

In one of the chat rooms they'd been debating some esoteric angle of the crimes, something about the randomness of good and evil. A doctoral dissertation in the making. He'd snorted, and glided from the chat room unnoticed. In the fourth one, though, he'd entered in the middle of a conversation that made his fingers freeze on the keys.

He read slowly, deciphering their cyber-shorthand as he went.

DRAGNSLAYR: . . . getting together and going after this guy.

RIPPER: Going after HSK?

The three initials were what made him stop. His acronym. The Helter Skelter killer.

DRAGNSLAYR: Who the fuck else are we talking about?

REDRUM: You mean other assassins are going after this guy?

DRAGNSLAYR: Isn't that what I said? Fuck, maybe I should go find people who can read.

RIPPER: Who's your source?

REDRUM: Hey, guys, wouldn't that make a cool movie? Assassin versus assassin.

RIPPER: Been done.

REDRUM: When?

DRAGNSLAYR: Heard it from 22TANGO. Said those twins—Shadow and Sid—were going around to the brokers, asking questions, seeing if anyone hired this guy.

REDRUM: Shit. So why are they going after him?

DRAGNSLAYR: Who cares? It's a great fucking story.

REDRUM: Bet it's a job. HSK whacked the wrong guy. Now they're going to whack him. Man, that would make a great movie. You sure it's been done?

RIPPER: How about you go start writing it now?

REDRUM: Piss off.

He turned away from the monitor. His colleagues coming after him? There was something vaguely cannibalistic in that, something unfair, even treacherous. Yes, he had to admit, something hurtful. Why come after him? He hadn't trodden on any toes, hadn't stolen a job or offed a colleague. His attitude and behavior toward his fellow pros had always been respectful.

And yet...

True or not true, he'd have to take it into account. Maybe it was time to change gears. Consider the possibilities. Savor the power of choice.

One choice niggled at the back of his brain. The most intriguing of the lot.

In this game he'd created, he'd allotted himself a number of special moves. His trump cards. Perhaps it was time to play one of them, an ace he'd been saving in case things went wrong. The game had changed now, though, and it made no sense to play the card. And yet...

His father had been a gambler. Lost everything they owned. Yet his father always swore that Fortune had deserted him when he'd stopped trusting her, when he'd become nervous and started holding his cards too long. A smart gambler, he'd said, knows how to make a surprise play pay off.

A surprise play. He chuckled, then surreptitiously wiped down the keyboard with his sleeve, put on his coat, picked up his disposable coffee cup and left.

TWENTY-ONE

———

Jack left early that morning. Evelyn and I ate breakfast, then headed out. I'd threatened to burn my Mafia-bait outfit. Now I wished I'd followed through. I was indeed dressed again as a big-haired tight-jeaned boob-plumped Jersey girl. Evelyn swore that what had worked with Little Joe would work with Nicky Volkv, but I suspected she just liked forcing me to do things I didn't want to do.

After dropping Evelyn off on the way to talk to a nearby source, I stopped to call Emma at the lodge. It was Thursday now, the weekend coming and no sign that I'd be home in time.

Emma assured me that wasn't a problem—we were only half booked, and they were all fall foliage tourists, most of them seniors, none of whom had booked my extreme sports "extras" or access to the shooting range. She'd just tell any drop-ins that these services were unavailable this weekend, and offer a discounted rate if anyone complained. Everything else—supervising hikes, doling out bikes and canoes, hosting the bonfires—she and Owen could handle. I should just relax and enjoy my time away... and whomever I was sharing it with.

I arrived at the penitentiary just after morning visiting hours began. I parked the car, grabbed my new pleather purse and set out. Between the lot and the building was a postage-stamp bit of green space filled with staff on their smoking breaks and visitors psyching themselves up to enter the prison.

As I walked through the parking lot, my gaze swept across those faces, counting and memorizing. As both a hitman and a cop, you learn to take note of your surroundings. So, although I was still a hundred feet from that green space, I noticed when nine people became ten, and I knew that the tenth had not come out of the prison or stepped from the parking lot, but had simply appeared. That blip made me pay attention.

I sized him up. Burly with a trim light-brown beard and a forgettable face. Midforties. He lifted a half-smoked cigarette to his lips, but the way he held it marked him as someone unfamiliar with the vice. Something told me very few people took up smoking in their forties, and no casual smoker would brave today's bitter wind for a cigarette.

I saw his gaze slant toward me. His face was still in profile, his eyes cast to the ground, but shifting in my direction. Measuring the distance.

I forced myself to take three more steps. His left leg turned, toe pivoting to point my way, knee following, hips starting to swivel. I stopped sharp and winced, delivering the best "oh, shit, I forgot something" face I could manage without slapping my forehead. Then I wheeled and quick-marched back to the car.

I glanced into the side mirror of each vehicle I passed on the way. The first three times, the angle was wrong and I saw nothing. On the fourth try, I caught a glimpse of the man, following as casually as he could manage.

I reached into my purse and pulled out my prepaid cell phone.

"Hey, Larry, it's me," I said, voice raised, as if to compensate for a poor connection. "You won't believe what I forgot."

Pause.

"Okay, you guessed. I am such a ditz."

Pause.

"Well, you don't have to fucking agree with me!"

As I talked, I kept glancing in the mirrors. The man started dropping back, then disappeared, unwilling to attack while I was talking to someone. I scanned the parking lot, making sure he wasn't doing an end-run around me.

I recognized his intentions as clearly as if they'd been screen-printed across his jacket. If I hadn't turned around, he would have headed into the lot, his path intersecting mine as I walked between the cars. A tight passage, a quiet shot to the heart and I'd fall, too far from the building to attract attention.

Once inside the car, I locked the doors and took a deep breath, calming that part of me that was screaming "what the hell are you doing?" Escaping, taking refuge, turning down a fight—not things I was accustomed to. I had to clasp my hands around the steering wheel to keep from throwing open the door and going after him.

But in this case, the instinctive choice wasn't the wise one. So I glued my butt to the car seat, eyes on the mirrors, making sure no one snuck up on me, and concentrated on planning my next move.

Would he try again? I wouldn't. Even if the mark appeared unaware of the situation, an aborted hit meant a failed attempt. I'd try another way in another place. But, having seen him head back toward the building, I guessed he wasn't leaving yet.

If he was staying, then so was I.

I backed out and found the exit, then sandwiched the car between a minivan and an SUV, and waited.

Now came the big question. Who was trying to kill me? Start with "who knew I was here?" First, Jack. While I didn't like the idea of suspecting him, that didn't stop me from working it through objectively. But he'd only known Evelyn and I were visiting a former Nikolaev thug at a jail. We hadn't given him a name or location, and he hadn't asked. He'd also thought I was coming here with Evelyn, so if he set a hitman on my trail, it would be to kill both of us, which made no sense.

Then there was Evelyn. She knew exactly where I was and that I was alone. Why kill me? With Evelyn, I didn't dare speculate on motivation. I didn't know her well enough. But she was a viable suspect and I couldn't discount her.

There was a third possibility—another person who knew we were coming to visit Nicky Volkv: the guy who sent us here. Maybe we'd stumbled onto the solution to the Helter Skelter killer mystery without knowing it—he was a hitman hired by the Nikolaevs to clean up some unfinished business.

If that was the case, then this man following me had to be the Helter Skelter killer himself. Hitmen are predators, in the purest sense of the word. Most don't get a charge out of killing a mark, no more than a lion enjoys taking down a deer. It is a means to an end, a method of survival. As a human predator, we are at the top of the food chain. We hunt. We are not hunted.

When I realized there was a hitman after me, my instinctive response had been to turn the tables. To become the hunter. I may be misremembering, but I seem to recall some theorem about matter always wanting to return to its original state. That goes for people as well. We were chasing a predator. If Little Joe told him we were on his trail, he'd come after us.

And now, if I was lucky, he had.

My plan was to wait for him to drive out, then follow. I managed to stick to it for fifteen minutes before persuading myself I needed to make sure he was still around. So I got out of the car and scoped out the area first. I stood behind a van and waited for a car to leave the lot, listened to the *bump-bump* of its tires on the speed bumps and committed that sound to memory. If I heard it again, I'd know to look and make sure my target wasn't leaving.

It took some effort to find the right path—the one that would allow me to travel without being seen. After scouting the lot, I gave thanks for the North American preoccupation with vehicles big enough to carry a whole hockey team. I darted from minivan to SUV to oversized pickup, working my way closer to the doors while checking over my shoulder to ensure I could still see the exit.

At last, as I peered through the windows of a minivan, I could see the visitor doors. But there was no sign of my target. The *bump-bump* of an exiting car sent me scrambling back to the lane, straining to see the exiting vehicle. A carload of people, driven by a heavyset woman.

As my heart rate returned to normal, I caught the eye of a passing couple. The woman's gaze flitted past me, but the man's lingered, checking me out, the response seeming more reflex than interest. I flashed my usual friendly grin— the sort that encourages strangers to ask me for directions but is only mistaken for a come-on by the most deluded. The man nodded and continued.

I breathed deeply, cursing. Not seeing my pursuer, then hearing a car leaving, I'd panicked. I should be above that. Better I should lose my target than risk exposing myself.

I returned to my spot, only to resume a fresh round of mental cursing. There was my target, back in place, smoking, having probably only been moving around when I'd first looked.

As I thought of the passing couple again, I was reminded that I wasn't hidden, even here between the vehicles, so I pulled out my cell phone and put it to my ear. To anyone walking by, I'd look as if I was just making a call before I headed out.

Even as I set up my "excuse," my gaze never left my target. I scanned him from head to foot, noticing and memorizing. He looked older than I'd first thought. Maybe early fifties. Casually dressed in jeans, a pullover and a jacket. A generic navy blue jacket. No insignia or markings. Likewise there was nothing about his appearance to draw the eye—brown hair, short beard, nondescript looks.

When he walked out to the smoking area, no one would notice. When he left, no one would notice. If he lingered, someone might think only "Is that the same guy who was there an hour ago?" but it would be a fleeting thought, chased away by his very mediocrity and the conviction that he probably just looked like someone who'd been there an hour ago. That was the goal in our business—to blend in, to pass unnoticed.

While I had to admire his skill, it didn't make my task any easier. How would I pick him out from a crowd later, if I needed to? Even his sneakers were generic, and he'd probably be savvy enough to change them if he suspected a tail. I was too far to see distinguishing features—a scar, a tattoo, a crooked nose, a chipped tooth—and even if I could,

I couldn't accept them at face value. I'd been known to slap on a fake mole or birthmark just to give people something to focus on. Jack had taught me that. Witnesses love distinguishing features. If you can't avoid being seen, it may be smart to give them one.

All I could do with this guy was focus on what would be hard to disguise. General height was one thing—lifts can only give you a couple of inches. Bone structure, too. He was broad-shouldered and burly. While it's harder to fake being thin, his size gave me an attribute to remember. Facial shape was another thing. It takes a lot of work to change that—and it's not something you can do as quickly as pulling on fresh clothes. So I measured, taking mental notes until I was reasonably sure I could find him in a crowd.

So I could follow him. But could I kill him? Here? Now?

My free hand slid under my jacket, finding the gun I'd taken from the car. I pulled it out, getting a feel for the unfamiliar weapon. Tested the weight and slid my hand around the grip, my gaze still on my target, cell phone still at my ear, my mind only half focused on the gun, but automatically running through the details—how close I'd need to get, the quirks of this particular model. My fingers were as keen as a wine connoisseur's nose, recognizing the gun by feel, regurgitating everything I knew about this model.

There was a perfectly placed pickup in the front row, but with no vehicle on either side, it was too exposed. Next best location? The SUV one row away, with a minivan on the other side. Dark tinted windows meant I could creep up the side of the vehicle and take the shot over the hood, hidden behind the cab.

I slid the cell phone into my pocket and the gun into the holster. Then I set out, darting from oversized vehicle to oversized vehicle, leapfrogging across three rows. I slipped up along the SUV and checked my trajectory. Perfect. Target in sight and in line.

As I watched him, the world around seemed to constrict, like looking through a spyglass, everything focused on that one patch of the universe. The rumble of conversation from the smoking pit fell to a whisper. The bright sun faded, my eyes opening wider behind my sunglasses. The smell of cigarettes and exhaust disappeared. All I saw, all I cared about, was him.

I let myself hang there, in that pocket. One moment to revel in the exhilaration of total focus. Then, slowly, I closed my eyes, inhaled and shifted out of the bubble. As blissful as it was, I couldn't stay there. Too cut off from the world, too unaware of my surroundings.

I traced my finger over the gun grip, but didn't unholster it. Finding the perfect shot was step one. Deciding whether to take it was another.

This man still posed a threat. A hitman doesn't drop a job when the first attempt fails, not unless he's been made. So he'd try again, which was reason enough to kill him.

But killing him here was risky. Although I saw no cameras, this was a prison. There would be armed guards nearby. Yet should I decide he needed to die, all that would be merely obstacles, not barriers.

If I did this, though, I might never know who he was. A hitman hired by Evelyn? Someone sent by the Nikolaevs? Or the Helter Skelter killer himself?

I needed answers, and I wouldn't get them by killing him. So I closed my jacket and withdrew to my first hiding place. I watched him for another twenty minutes. Then after one lingering look at his watch, he took keys from his pocket and started walking. I hurried back to my car.

* * *

He pulled out of the lot in a gray rental. I noted his license number and details of the vehicle itself, then waited until he was nearly out of sight before pursuing.

I followed the car along the highway, up the off-ramp and through the city streets. I stayed far enough back that he never saw me, but close enough that I never lost sight of him.

Finally, the car turned into a city-run parking lot. I pulled down a side alley, only to discover that I couldn't see the sidewalk or the parking lot. No time to find a better place. I hurried from the car and crept alongside the building.

Near the end of the alley I dug into my purse and found what I wanted. Then I eased as close as I dared to the end of the alley, lifted the open makeup compact and angled the mirror.

The only people I saw were two elderly men heading toward me and a trio of teenage boys skateboarding in the opposite direction.

I was thinking of circling back when I caught a movement at the parking lot exit. A middle-aged executive, silver-haired, clean-shaven and bespectacled, briefcase swinging purposefully at his side. I sized him up against the man from the jail...then stepped back into the alley. Now I knew why he'd lingered in his car.

As I watched through my mirror, he crossed the road and marched away from me. A scant twenty feet later, he turned right, opened a door and went in. I eased out for a better look at his destination. A coffee shop.

It shouldn't take him more than two minutes to grab

takeout. Five minutes passed. Obviously, he wasn't getting his coffee to go. Time for my own quick-change routine.

I zipped down the alley and came out on the main thoroughfare. The first promising shop I saw was a drugstore with a window display of tourist wear. Good enough. Three oversized sweatshirts, one ball cap, cold cream, a scrunchie and a bag of penny candy, and I was flying back to my car.

All three sweatshirts went on over my skintight sweater, bulking me up, schlepping me down and giving me ample room to hide my gun. Wig off. Hair pulled back in a tiny ponytail that disappeared under the ball cap. Cold cream on; makeup off.

I knew enough to take off my watch and hoop earrings. But when it came to my ankle boots, I was stuck. All I could do was pull my jean cuffs over them.

Then I returned to my spot at the end of the alley, crossed the road, fell in behind two women close to my age and proceeded past the coffee shop window. One sideways look was all I permitted myself. My would-be killer sat just beyond the window, drinking coffee and reading a newspaper.

I ducked down the first side road and checked behind the restaurant for alternate exits. There was an emergency door, but it was unlikely he'd risk setting off an alarm. So I circled back to my alley, took out my bag of candy and settled in to wait.

Thirty minutes later, I was still waiting.

I'd slipped past the coffee-shop window a couple of

times to reassure myself the man hadn't left. But there he was, either determined to read that paper from cover to cover, or waiting for someone.

Evelyn had expected me to pick her up twenty minutes ago. Had I been in active pursuit of a potential killer, I could be forgiven for not swinging by to grab her. But now, hiding in the shadows, I had no excuse...beyond the fact that I hadn't ruled her out as a suspect.

If I called and said, "Hey, I'm across the road from a guy who tried to kill me," she could tell him to sneak out and finish the job. Or come and do it herself. And that's why I needed to phone her—to test my suspicions.

Evelyn picked up on the first ring.

"There better be a good excuse for this," she said before I could get a word out. "I'm freezing my ass off out here."

"You'd better get inside," I whispered. "Find someplace warm. I—"

"What? Talk into the mouthpiece, Dee. That's what it's there for."

"I'm whispering—"

"What?"

A notch higher. "I need to be quiet."

"Oh." A pause. "Wait, let me see if I can adjust the volume on this thing." Pause. "There. Now, what's going on? Is there a problem? Did you get to see Volkv?"

"No."

"No to what? No, there's not a problem? Or no, you didn't see Volkv?"

I considered hanging up but, after another check of the street, I said, "Someone tried to stop me. Permanently."

"Christ, Dee, you've been hanging around Jack too long. Speak in full sentences. Someone tried to—" She stopped. "Shit. Where are you?"

"Following him. He's having coffee."

"Good, good. How long has he been there?"

"Almost an hour."

"He'll be waiting to make his call, then. To report his failure. Where exactly are you?"

I gave her the name of the town and coffee shop.

TWENTY-TWO

It took Evelyn twenty minutes to arrive.

"Still there?" she whispered as she crept up the alley toward me.

"I think so. I've done three walk-bys, but I'm afraid of being too obvious."

"I'll take a turn, then. What am I looking for?"

I described him. She nodded and headed for the street.

Two minutes later, as she headed back toward me, the coffee shop door opened and the man walked out. I slipped back into the shadows. As soon as Evelyn appeared at the corner, I waved her over.

"He's—" I whispered.

"Yes, I know. Stay—"

I swung past her, slid to the end of the alley and pulled the compact from my pocket. Through it, I watched the man stride into a phone booth. He dropped his briefcase, picked up the receiver and dialed.

Evelyn appeared at my side.

"Making a phone call?" she said, without even glancing in the compact mirror.

I nodded.

"Does star-69 work at pay phones?" she whispered.

"No idea."

"Damn. Probably no time anyway. Where's he parked?"

I hitched a thumb in the direction. "Half a block down, on this side. The main exit is off this road."

"Here's the plan, then. We're ending this here. I'm going straight down this road, and you're going to circle around the back way—over the curb, through an alley, whatever will get you out on the other side. Then you'll wait for my signal. If you don't see me, let him go. That means it isn't safe. There's only one way out of town, so if he leaves, we can catch up with him. Now where's my car?"

I paused. Considered her "plan" . . . and how much sense it made.

"One lot to the west," I lied.

"Keys?"

I made a show of searching for them, knowing she'd given me the backup set and still had hers.

"I have mine," she said after a moment. "Just go."

I drove to the lot where Evelyn was hurrying along the rows, her keys in hand, her lips moving in silent curses as she searched for her car.

I didn't have time for this. Every moment I delayed was another moment for my target to escape. I should have left her here. I'd wanted to. The moment she'd given me the instructions, I knew she was planning to give me the slip and go after my pursuer herself, and I'd wanted so badly to say, "Fine, then," take her car and peel out after him myself, leaving her where she'd planned to leave me—stranded in some no-name town.

I'd have been justified in doing so. Jack would have agreed. But letting Evelyn out of my sight wouldn't be the smart move. After this, I trusted her less than ever. All the more reason to keep her at my side, where I could watch her.

So, I forced myself to turn into that lot, unclenched my hands from the wheel, forced my frustration—my rage—down, pulled up alongside her and put down the passenger window. She shook her head and reached for the door handle. I hit the lock button.

"Lean in first and toss your gun on the floor."

She glared over at me. "We don't have time—"

"I'm not the one playing games. Now get your gun out and on the floor or I go after him by myself."

She looked around, then dropped it onto the seat. I leaned over and laid it on the floor.

"Backup weapon, too," I said.

A colorful oath, but she took out the second gun and put it into the car. I unlocked the doors, and was moving again before she had hers closed.

"Leave your guns on the floor," I said. "You can reach them if you need to, but not without me seeing you."

She fastened her seat belt. "Nicely played. I'm impressed."

"Well, I'm not. I don't like games, Evelyn. Maybe you were testing me. Maybe you didn't think I was competent enough to come after this guy with you. Maybe you wanted to make sure I *didn't* go after him. If that's it, and you're protecting him or you're in on this—"

"Then I would have killed you in that alley."

"Maybe. All I'm saying is that just because I picked you up doesn't mean I trust you."

She smiled. "Good girl."

His car turned off at an exit ramp. I noted which way he turned at the top, then put on my signal.

"So who do you think this is?" she asked.

I told her. She pursed her lips, saying nothing.

"Doesn't that make sense?"

"It would certainly make our lives easier, wouldn't it?" Before I could reply, she pointed at the signs atop the exit ramp. "Well, either he's hungry or he's holing up for a while. There's nothing else up here."

We found his car in an Econo Lodge parking lot.

"Pull over behind that transport."

"Shouldn't I park in another lot?"

Evelyn shook her head. "You're not parking, just stopping and getting out. I saw a mall at the last exit. I'm going back for supplies while you watch which room he takes and keep an eye on it. I doubt he'll go any farther than one of these restaurants before I get back."

"So we're going to interrogate him, I assume."

"I prefer 'talk,' but yes, that's the general plan."

"What are you picking up?"

"Basic supplies," she said. "Gloves, duct tape, rope..." She met my gaze. "Is that a problem?"

"Better grab garbage bags, too."

Evelyn knocked on the motel room door. She hadn't altered her disguise from earlier—blue-rinse hair, pince-nez, polyester slacks, a flower-dotted cardigan and a purse big enough to defy airplane carry-on regulations.

When no one answered, she rapped again and called out in a querulous voice.

"Harold? Harold? I can't find my key."

The door cracked open, the chain jangling, then snapping taut with a click. Standing by the hinges, I could see nothing of the person inside, meaning he couldn't see me, either.

"No Harold here, lady."

"What?" Evelyn leaned forward, blinking nearsightedly. "Who are you? Where's my Harold?"

"You've got the wrong room."

The man started to close the door, but Evelyn's foot darted into the gap, leaving him no choice but to keep it open or crush her. Even cold-blooded killers have their limits.

"Look, lady—"

"Stop whispering, young man. I can't hear you. Where's my Harold? Open this door right now."

"You've got the wrong—"

Her voice rose to a screech. "Open this door!"

I tensed, listening for a certain sound . . .

"Lady—"

"If you don't open—"

Click. He'd disengaged the chain. I kicked the door open.

TWENTY-THREE

As the door crashed open, the man flew back. I swung in, gun raised, Evelyn covering me.

"On your knees," I said.

The man froze, but didn't drop. His gaze flicked down, presumably to the gun holstered under his jacket.

"Hands up and get on your knees," I said as Evelyn closed the door behind us.

Still he hesitated, and I knew what he was thinking. He wasn't about to drop for a couple of women—and one a senior citizen. Better to take the risk, pull the gun and trust that he could get the drop on us.

I pretended to glance toward Evelyn, as if getting her opinion. The moment I moved, he went for his gun. I kicked his kneecap and he dropped down with a grunt. When he looked up and saw my gun pointed in his face—and Evelyn's at the side of his head—he decided to raise his hands.

I ordered him onto his stomach, hands to his sides, palms up. Evelyn motioned that she'd stand cover while I bound him, but I shook my head. I wasn't lowering my gun and my guard while she had a gun. Not after that stunt in the parking lot.

As she bound him with the duct tape, I took a closer look at the man. Did he bear any resemblance to Manson? It was hard to tell, since I presumed he was wearing makeup. He was certainly bigger than Manson, but that could come from his mother. The age seemed reasonable.

Evelyn patted him down, removing a 9mm, a hidden switchblade and a wallet. When she finished, I repeated the pat down. If she was offended at my double-checking her search—and her binding job—she gave no sign of it.

I took the wallet. Inside were a half-dozen twenties, some smaller bills and a Virginia driver's license. The name and the license were fakes, but I had no idea how good a forgery it was. That's the beauty of using out-of-state licenses. If you get pulled over, chances are the officer who writes up your ticket wouldn't know a real license from a fake.

"Robert," I said. "Would you prefer Rob or Bob?"

The man only glared up at me.

"Bert, then," I continued. "You look like a Bert to me. So, Bert, not exactly a story you can barter for beer at the legion hall, is it?"

"You made me, didn't you?" he said, eyes on mine, voice as calm as if we were indeed discussing this at the legion.

"A takedown in a prison parking lot? In front of witnesses?" Evelyn shook her head. "Amateur hour."

"I could have done it," he said.

"But you didn't. You fucked up. Having a mark make you before you even get within firing distance? Unbelievable." Evelyn stepped forward, eyes trained on his. "But you didn't have all the facts, did you? You didn't know she was a pro."

"Pro?" Bert squinted at me. "She's a hitwoman?"

"No," Evelyn said. "You just got your ass kicked by the Avon lady."

His squint narrowed to a slit. "He told me she was a con artist." A sharp twist of the lips. "Paying me five grand to off a pro? Fuck, I deserve twenty for this."

"For what?" Evelyn said. "You didn't kill her."

Bert shrugged his brows as if he hadn't abandoned the hope of collecting.

"And for me?" Evelyn said.

"Two."

"Two grand? *Two*—"

I stepped forward, cutting her off. "Who hired you?"

Evelyn waved me back. We stared each other down for a few seconds, then I rolled my shoulders and moved beside Bert, gun at the ready. I'd already taken the muscle role. Too late to change my mind now.

"Who hired you?" she asked.

"I want to make a deal," he said.

"Do I look like Monty Hall? Here's your deal: either you tell me or you never leave this motel room."

His gaze shifted from Evelyn to me. "Look, if you're a pro, you know the score. If I go blabbing on my employer, my life ain't worth shit."

"And if you don't, it ain't worth shit, either," I said.

He turned his attention to Evelyn.

"You've got to understand," he said. "This isn't some nobody I'm dealing with—"

"Isn't it?" she said, taking a seat on the bed. "Perhaps he was a somebody once, but now he's a toothless old lion desperate not to cut his last years short. That's why he called you, isn't it?"

I glanced sharply at Evelyn, but her gaze was riveted on the hitman.

"You know then," he said. "So why are you asking me?"

"For confirmation."

"Yeah, it was Little Joe Nikolaev. He said you two went to see him yesterday and he let something slip. Something big. I don't know what it was, but he said if Boris heard, that was it. He'd shut him up for good."

So *that* was what this was about? That old hit Little Joe had let slip, the details of which I'd already forgotten?

For twenty minutes Evelyn prodded and probed, trying to find out whether there could be a Helter Skelter connection. She even asked point-blank if he knew anything about the killer, but it was obvious he didn't.

"All right then," she said. "You can't tell us what you don't know."

"I held up my end," he said, gaze lifting to hers. "Now it's your turn."

She nodded. "Fair is fair. Dee?"

I walked behind him, aimed the gun at the base of his skull and pulled the trigger.

TWENTY-FOUR

Thirty minutes of driving and Evelyn had yet to say a word. Finally, I glanced her way. "You think I made the wrong decision. Killing him."

"If you didn't, I would have. Let him live, and he'd only keep trying to finish the job. We humiliated him. In such a situation, there's no room for mercy."

"So the problem is ... ?"

After a moment, she murmured, "No problem. Just ... interesting."

As soon as I got back, I took a shower. While I was dressing afterward, the hall floor creaked. One creak could be blamed on the older house, but a second told me someone was out there. I tensed.

I knew I was alone with Evelyn, but that was all the more reason for being nervous. I still wasn't sure how to interpret her trick earlier.

I pulled on my shirt, unlocked the door as quietly as I could and cracked it open. There, at the top of the stairs was Jack, his back to me, hands in his pockets.

I released the door handle. At the soft click, he turned.

"Back already?" I said. "Do you need—?" I waved into the bathroom.

"Nah."

I backed up to the sink again, leaving the door open. As I took out my comb, he stepped into the doorway.

"Did you find Baron?" I asked.

"Yeah."

"Okay. So we'll need a plan—"

He shook his head. "Can't question him."

A glance over his shoulder, head tilting as if listening for Evelyn. When I sidestepped, giving him room to come in, he did.

"Baron's dead. Shot himself. A month ago."

"Oh, geez, I'm sorry."

As the words left my mouth, I realized how silly they sounded. Offering my consolations on the death of a colleague he hadn't seen in years, and had suspected of being a serial killer. Yet he nodded, gaze sliding to the side.

I rubbed SPF moisturizer on my face, then scrubbed my hands and repacked my toiletry bag. "Are we sure about Baron? I know faking your death sounds like something out of a movie, but is there any chance . . . ?"

"Slim. Talked to someone. Got the story. Looked it up. Found the obituary, picture. It was him. Other ways to check?" He shrugged. "No idea."

"Short of digging up a grave, that's probably the best we can do. Have you told Evelyn?"

He shook his head.

"We'll get that over with, then."

If Jack expected Evelyn to go off on her "see, I told you he was a loser" tangent about Baron, he was mistaken. She took the information in, said "Well, there's one fewer theory for you, Dee" and moved on.

Evelyn's source for Manson information had gotten back to her with a list of three possible Manson sons: a former Manson family member turned Nevada brothel owner, a drug dealer who boasted of an ongoing prison corre-spondence with Manson and a B&E artist who claimed to be Manson's illegitimate son.

"Door number three sounds promising," I said.

"He's probably bandying the story around to gain street cred," Evelyn said. "But we should look him up." She turned back to her computer. "What's the name on that sheet again?"

"Benjamin Moreland."

"State?"

"Right here in Indiana."

"Hold on."

Jack shook his head and sunk back into the couch. Five minutes of keyboard-clicking later, Evelyn stopped.

"Well, that's promising," she said.

She swung around from the computer and waved at a grainy, enlarged photo on the monitor. Jack and I peered at the screen. A thin, wide-eyed face peered back.

"That good?" Jack asked.

"You don't see the resemblance?" Evelyn said.

When neither of us answered, she sighed, retrieved the *Helter Skelter* book from the shelf, opened it to a page of photos and passed it to us. The guy did look like Manson, especially in the upper half of the face, through the eyes and hairline.

"Now, he could be trading on a coincidental resem-blance to back up his story," Evelyn said. "But I'd check it out. DNA is DNA."

Twenty minutes later, she turned from her computer again. "I found Moreland. Seems he's currently enjoying the hos-pitality of a mental institution outside Indianapolis."

"So he's Manson's son after all," I said. "Or, I suppose,

one could argue that claiming to be related to the man is grounds for committal in itself. Either way, it can't be him."

"Not so fast," Evelyn said. "We have no idea what kind of security this hospital has. If this was our killer, it would make one hell of an alibi."

She pointed to the screen. "He had a series of arrests in the late eighties, then nothing. Maybe he's moved up in the world. For all his fuckups, Manson was a bright guy. Let's assume his kid inherited those brains."

I glanced at Jack. "Do we have anything better to follow up on right now?"

He shook his head.

"How far to Indianapolis?"

"'Bout two hours." He checked his watch. "Leave now? Should make visiting hours."

We'd barely made it out of the driveway before Jack said, "Evelyn told me. What happened. At the motel."

"Ah."

He drove for another few minutes in silence, then said, "Something else, isn't there? With Evelyn."

"I don't think she expected me to shoot—"

"Not what I meant. About Evelyn. What'd she do?"

"Nothing I couldn't handle."

"Don't doubt that. What was it?"

When I didn't answer, he pointed at the glove box. "Can you grab—?"

I had it open before he finished. A box of American cigarettes nearly fell in my lap. When he nodded, I opened the pack and handed him one. Even lit the match for him. He nodded his thanks, took the first drag and made a face, lips curving in a silent oath.

I arched my brows. "Not your normal brand, I take it."

"Does it smell like it?"

"No, but I wasn't about to assume that what you normally smoke at the lodge *is* your normal brand." When he gave me a look, I shrugged. "Hey, if you smoked something different, trying to throw me off track, I wouldn't blame you."

"I don't pull that shit, Nadia. Not with you." He lifted the cigarette. "This? Just while I'm on a job. Other's too . . ."

"Distinctive?"

He nodded. "'Course, if I had any brains? Quit altogether. Worst habit a pro can have. Started quitting ten years ago. Got down to maybe one a day. Then . . . stuck."

Another drag. He shook his head and reached for the ashtray then stopped and held the cigarette out to me. I shook my head and he stubbed it out.

"About Evelyn," he said. "Whatever happened? Like to know."

He wasn't going to let that slide, so I told him about Evelyn's stunt in the parking lot, then said, "So what was that about? Testing me or trying to go after the guy herself?"

"Probably both. You spot her trick? You pass. You both go. You fail?" He shrugged. "Better to leave you behind."

He passed a transport, then turned back to the slow lane before speaking again.

"Either way? Fucking waste of time. You're pissed? Got a right to be."

"She likes games, doesn't she?"

"All there is. This investigation? A big game. That hitman? Smaller game. Testing you? Tiny game in that one. Like fucking nesting dolls. She pulls that shit again? Walk away."

TWENTY-FIVE

The nurse behind the desk worried her identification badge, the surface dulled from handling. She looked no more than twenty-one. From the way she flinched every time a patient walked by, this was the only job she'd been able to find, and she was counting the days until she could transfer.

"Mr. Moreland doesn't get many visitors."

"But he is allowed to have them, correct?" I said.

She shot a nervous glance around. I couldn't see the cause of her discomfort. There were no drooling, ranting, half-naked lunatics wandering the halls. The ID badges were the only way I could see to tell the patients from the staff.

"Mr. Moreland is permitted visitors, is he not?"

"Umm, right."

"And your evening visiting hours are 7 to 9 p.m., correct?"

A nod.

"Then forget this"—I gestured to my business card on the counter—"and consider me a visitor."

"Do you need a special room?" she asked.

"For privacy, yes, that would be best."

She fingered her badge and bit her lip.

"Is that a problem?" I asked.

"No, I guess not." She looked around, as if searching for someone. "Everyone's on break, but I guess—" She swallowed. "I guess I could take you."

So that was the problem. She didn't want to leave her protective cage. I hoped she got a new job soon...for the patients' sake.

After another worried look up and down the hall, she stepped out.

Nurse Nervous left me in a small windowless room that could have passed for a corporate meeting room. I studied the posters on the wall. Good taste on a budget. The furnishings were likewise a compromise between quality, comfort and cost: decent upholstered chairs and a sturdy conference table. A long way from padded rooms and leather restraints.

Outside the room, the silence was broken only by the occasional swoosh of a door and staccato clicks of staff passing by, their steps quick and purposeful. When I caught a whiff of cleaning solution, I thought of Jack and hoped he wouldn't have a problem finding Moreland's room.

While I waited, I ran through the list of questions I was going to ask Moreland. Basic queries, easily answered, none of which would reveal any hint of our suspicions because my main role was to get Moreland out of his private room long enough for Jack to get what he needed.

As footsteps squeaked down the hall, I listened. Voices drifted in, both female. The first I recognized as the young nurse.

"—ever tells me anything."

An older woman answered, her voice clipped with authority. The squeal of a cart covered her first few words. "—show up, demanding access to Ben, saying it's part of this horrible Helter Skelter killer mess. We've had to notify the director, round up every doctor Ben's ever spoken to, alert security—believe me, Angela, informing a junior nurse was the last thing on our mind." The women's footsteps receded around a corner. "Who did you say wants to talk to Ben now...?"

I nearly shot out of the room, but managed to stop myself at the door and crack it open for a quick peek before hightailing it out. I started marching in the other direction and got five steps before Jack swerved around a corner and grabbed my arm.

"Lawyer?" the older nurse's voice trumpeted down the hall. "Lord, that is just what we need. Where did you put—?"

"Fuck," Jack whispered, drowning her out.

Still clutching my elbow, Jack strode to the first door, checked it, then moved to the next. Another peek. Then he yanked it open and propelled me inside.

I caught a glimpse of brooms and buckets. Jack wheeled in, closed the door and the closet went dark.

"FBI," he whispered, breath tickling my ear.

"How many?" I whispered.

"Don't know. Just heard the nurses talking." A pause and he shifted, moving against my hip as he leaned toward the door.

I put my ear to the wall, but heard only pipes gurgling. The small closet made for very tight quarters. Warm, too. Much longer in here and we'd be putting our deodorant to the test.

The room already stank—of bleach, as if there was an open container or a small spill—and between the smell and the heat, my head started to spin.

"Hold on," Jack whispered. Like I was going anywhere.

The soft grate of a doorknob turning. A splinter of light lit Jack's face. He pressed his cheek against the gap, then pulled back. The light vanished and the door clicked shut.

"Nothing."

"You get some of Moreland's hair?" I whispered.

A shake of his head. "Don't need to. It's a match."

"Wha—?" I bit off my near-yelp of surprise.

"That's why Feds are here. Got a tip. Hair matches Moreland's DNA."

"Shit. So it was a plant."

"Yeah."

The word tickled my ear. He shifted, and his hand went to my hip for balance. As he breathed, that faint scent of the earlier cigarette wafted over me, and my pulse quickened. I told myself it was the smell of nicotine, but I suspected it had more to do with having a man pressed up against me, hand on my hip, breath against my hair . . . Like I've said, it'd been awhile.

Jack pressed closer as he shifted again, trying to get his balance or get comfortable. I could feel the heat of his fingers through my skirt. He leaned forward, listening, cheek a hairsbreadth from mine. I could smell him—the cigarette plus something faintly spicy: soap or shaving cream. He smelled very . . . male. When he moved again, his hand slipping on my hip, my imagination followed through where his fingers didn't: down my skirt, catching the edge—

I jerked upright. "Sounds quiet. We should go."

"Yeah." A moment's pause, then. "Nearest exit—"

"—is a staircase two doors on the other side of the meeting room, leading down to the first floor. There's an emergency exit right there, but it supposedly triggers an alarm. If possible, it'd be better to cut back across the first floor to the main doors. The only alternate route I see is to head into the basement and cut across to another stairwell."

A soft chuckle that reverberated along my back. "Good work. Basement's it, then. Hold on."

Putting his free hand on my other hip for balance, he opened the door and leaned into it. The sliver of light grew to a handsbreadth. Then he twisted back toward me, mouth lowering to my ear.

"Clear. Wait."

He took a broom from behind us, and eased from the closet, leaving the door open a crack so I could see out. As I picked up my briefcase, I looked down at my new pumps. Take the risk of someone hearing me clicking along the floors? Or the risk of being spotted in stockinged feet? I went for option two and slipped them off.

Broom to the floor, Jack swept briskly, moving fast. He kept his head down, concentrating on his work and hiding his face. The hall remained empty. A few feet from the end, he stopped and turned so his back was to the nearby nurses' station. Then he bent, as if to pick up something. As he leaned over, he peered under his arm, looking toward the station. Then he gestured for me to hightail it down there.

I crept out of the closet, closing the door behind me, and walked as fast as I could without breaking into a jog. I kept my face turned slightly toward the far wall. When I drew opposite the hall leading to the nurses' station, I caught a glimpse of two men in suits, talking to the nurse, their backs to me. I kept walking.

Ahead, Jack waited by the stairwell. As I took that last step past the hall junction, one of the FBI men moved. I caught only the flash of motion, not enough to know whether he was turning to watch me or scratching his ass. I picked up the pace. Footsteps sounded behind me.

I flicked my fingers at Jack, telling him to get out of the hall. He stepped into the stairwell, but held the door open. Six steps, seven, and I was there.

Behind me, shoes squeaked against the linoleum, making a sharp turn. As I ducked through the door, Jack grabbed my elbow and pushed me toward the stairs.

He paused behind me, presumably to double-check. I didn't wait for the verdict. I galloped down the steps as fast as I could without stumbling. As I rounded the first flight, Jack fell into step beside me, caught my eye and nodded. The Feds were following.

I lifted my forefinger, then swiveled my thumb down. "First floor or basement?" I mouthed. Jack pointed down. Basement. Above us, the door finally clicked shut, only to whoosh open seconds later. Footsteps thumped across the landing. I shifted to the outside, where I'd be harder to spot, and Jack fell in behind me.

At the first floor, I motioned for Jack to continue heading down, then turned toward the door. He caught my arm, but I motioned that I'd follow in a moment. I jogged to the first floor door, opened it as far as it would go, released it and turned to race after Jack. As we rounded the midflight turn, Jack glanced up. The door I'd opened was slowly swinging shut, where the agents would see it and assume we'd gone that way. Jack nodded his approval.

Above us, several sets of shoes clomped down the steps at double-time. When we reached the basement door, Jack waved me against the wall. He opened the door slowly and silently. We slipped through and he eased it shut behind us.

We turned to survey our surroundings. A typical industrial basement: big, semidark, full of wheezing, clanking machinery. Helpful signs on the wall indicated points of interest: furnace, laundry, storage, deliveries. Jack jabbed a finger at the last.

As we turned the first corner, a grating squeal cut through the mechanical roar, growing louder by the second. We looked around. To our left was a hall lined with old office equipment. We took refuge beside a filing cabinet.

The squeal turned to a steady squeaking. Wheels in need of oiling. Seconds later, the sound began to recede. I leaned out to see an employee wheel a metal cart of laundry onto an elevator. We waited until the doors clanked shut before we took off.

After years of being the hunter, it was strange being pursued—and by cops, no less. I felt an uncomfortable inkling of shame, not unlike when I was nine and Amy talked me into swiping a candy bar from the store. I hadn't been caught. I'd even snuck back later and returned it, without her knowing. Running from these agents, I felt the same twinge, mitigated only by the reminder that I wasn't committing a crime, but trying to solve one.

My ruse with the first-floor door wouldn't stymie the FBI for long, but it had bought us a few critical minutes. We made it to the delivery loading dock without incident. From there, escape was a simple matter of unlocking the exit door and walking out.

We stepped into the fading light and found ourselves at the foot of a small flight of stairs.

"I'll look. Wait here."

I nodded. Though I was quite capable of scouting, I was the lawyer who'd snuck out. No one was looking for a janitor.

Jack climbed the steps and disappeared. By the time I'd slipped my shoes back on, he'd reappeared at the top. He waved me up. I was just high enough to peek over ground level when two men in maintenance jumpsuits walked around the corner. I ducked so fast I nearly fell backward down the steps. Jack started to follow, then let out an obscenity.

He turned to me, said, "Wait," then strode off.

TWENTY-SIX

Had the maintenance men seen Jack, noticed his janitor's uniform shirt and called him over to help with something?

A moment's silence. Then a man's voice, raised just loud enough to carry.

"Drive where?"

"Just drive," Jack called back.

I walked up a few steps and stood on tiptoes to peek over the top. Jack and the two men were about twenty feet away, on the other side of a storage shed. I darted over to it.

"Not good enough," one man said. "Tell me where the hell I'm driving, Jack, or . . ."

I didn't hear the rest of it. My brain snagged on Jack's name.

Jack walked past the storage shed. Hearing the other man still talking, I swung back, trying to get out of sight. I stepped on a branch, the crack of breaking wood loud enough to make Jack turn. His gaze met mine. He looked away quickly, but it was too late. The two men in maintenance suits were behind him, now both staring right at me.

One of them was around Jack's age, average height and lean to the point of bony, with thinning ginger hair, a sparse beard and glasses.

The other man was closer to my age, a little over six feet with a solid build, light brown hair, and a face that was pleasantly handsome but no cause for second glances. Nothing about him screamed "cop"—no mustache, no brawny forearms, no steel-eyed glare of perpetual suspicion. But I knew that's what he was, the same way I'd know a Beretta from a Glock with a split-second glance.

The cop looked from me to Jack. "Your new partner, Jack? Either that's one hell of a disguise or there's something you forgot to tell us."

"Drive," Jack said. "North. First rest stop."

The cop opened his mouth to argue, but the red-haired man said, "We'll be there." He smiled at me, then shooed his partner toward the parking lot.

"That was Quinn, wasn't it?" I said as we got into the car.

"Yeah."

I fought the first bubble of panic rising in my gut. "Okay. Presumably, Quinn got the same message those Feds did, and came by hoping to find out what was going on. Bad timing, but now we have to deal with it. This meeting at the rest stop. Should I stay in the car?"

He pulled out of the parking lot. "Up to you."

"My first instinct is to stay out of their way. But he already got a good look at me, and he obviously figured out I'm your mystery partner. So if I stay in the car, that's going to arouse suspicion. They'll wonder if it's more than rookie nerves."

"Yeah."

I looked over at him. "Can I get some advice? Please?"

He drove for at least five minutes without answering, then did so slowly, as if with great reluctance. "Safer to meet them. Get it over with. You're in disguise. Quinn's a blowhard but..." A long pause, as if he'd rather not finish. "He's good. Trustworthy. You'll be fine."

Quinn and his partner were waiting when we pulled into the rest stop. Jack drove past them, circled to the rear of the building and parked on the far side. He looked around, then got out and headed for the picnic area that, given the cool season and the late hour, was understandably empty.

He gestured at the table in front of us. "Here good?"

"Seems okay. We're far enough from the buildings that no one should overhear if we keep our voices down. Watch the body language, though."

When I looked up, Quinn was bearing down on us, jaw set, fists balled at his sides.

"So much for body language," I murmured.

Jack stood, shoulders squaring. Quinn's partner headed our way, as if to intercept, but he was too far to reach us in time.

"What's this?" Quinn said, gesturing at me. "When you said you had a partner, we all figured you meant Evelyn or someone we knew. That"—his finger jabbed my way—"is neither."

"I'm vouching for her," Jack said.

"That's very nice. But we're taking a big risk, working with a stranger—"

"I said, I'm vouching for her."

They stared at each other. Last time I'd seen that look it'd been on a pair of feral dogs, in a battle for control of the lodge's garbage bins—right before I turned the hose on them. Some guys . . . you can teach them to walk upright, put them in nice clothes, but it still comes down to a good ol'-fashioned pissing contest. And me without my hose.

"Hey," I said, inching between the two. I fixed my smile on Quinn and upped the wattage. "What's a club without initiation rites? How about a test? Make sure I pass muster."

"You don't have to—" Jack began.

I put up a hand to stop him, never breaking eye contact with Quinn.

"Test me," I said. "Can't say I was ever any good at pop quizzes in school, but what the hell. Give it a try."

Quinn's gaze locked on mine. "You any good at distance shooting?"

"Got a rifle on you?"

The barest hint of a smile lit his eyes, but didn't reach his lips. "Not right now. So, what's the best silencer for Remington 700?"

"None."

His brows rose a quarter-inch.

"First, it's a suppressor. You can't silence a gun. Ignoring that, a real distance shooter wouldn't use one unless absolutely necessary. Most times, you're taking the shot from far enough away that a suppressor isn't necessary, and using one means you run the risk of throwing off your MOA."

"Minutes of angle," the red-haired man said with a smile. "She's right. I've told you that before, but you never listen."

I continued. "If you have to use a suppressed rifle, you'd be better off with a McMillan M89 or Steyr SSG. Their suppressors work okay, but personally I prefer—"

"All right, all right." He extended his hand. "Quinn."

"Dee."

The red-haired man took my hand with a smile. "Felix."

Quinn turned back to Jack. "So what the hell was that fuckup at the hospital?"

"Following a lead. Same as you."

"Well, that shit wouldn't have happened if you'd listened to me and we actually tried a little teamwork on this job."

Jack glanced my way, as if expecting a "told you so." I

looked away before I gave him one. As I scanned the rest stop, I slid between Jack and Quinn again.

"We have an audience," I said.

Quinn followed my gaze. Next to the building a middle-aged couple stood beside their car, watching us.

"May I make a suggestion?" I asked.

Quinn nodded.

"How about we sit down, I'll grab some cans of pop and we'll have a picnic."

"Good idea," Felix said. "You stay here, Dee, and I'll get the sodas." A wry smile my way. "You make a better referee."

Quinn waited until Jack was halfway seated, then picked up the argument where he'd left off. "I'm getting sick of this, Jack. I might not have the career you and Felix have, but on something like this, *I'm* the expert. You don't handle a criminal investigation by having all the teams chasing whatever lead catches their fancy. It's a cooperative effort, not a competition."

Jack's gaze slid my way. "Yeah. You're right. Time to team up. On strategy. Investigate separately. But plan together."

I expected Quinn to find a way to argue, but instead he smiled and relaxed.

"Thank God," he said. "And thank you. Now maybe we can make some progress, because Felix and I are just spinning our wheels. What about Sid and Shadow? I tried calling them yesterday, but they aren't answering the page."

"Same here."

Felix was approaching the table and overheard. "So either they've been arrested or they've changed their mind about doing this. Either is equally likely, I'm afraid, and little we can do about it, whichever it is. We'll continue trying to contact them, but for now we'll have to presume our investigation is down to four."

"Five," Jack said. "Evelyn's in."

Felix handed out our cans. "So you *did* manage to secure her participation. Excellent. Can we contact her with research questions?"

Jack nodded. They talked for a moment. As they did, I realized Jack sounded...odd. Had since we'd first met Quinn and Felix at the hospital, though it was only really obvious now, as he spoke more. It took a second to figure out what was different. Then it hit. The accent—or lack of it. Since meeting the others, he'd swallowed that trace of a brogue, as he did whenever we were out. With Evelyn, he let himself fall back into it. Everyone else got a standard undefinable American accent.

Quinn popped open his can. "Back to the case. The DNA is a match. That's confirmed, so the question is, how did Moreland do it?"

"He didn't," Jack said.

I could see Quinn's hackles rise, and jumped in. "It's unlikely Moreland did it. He's a diagnosed disorganized schizophrenic. If he did commit the murders, they'd be more like Manson's. Of course, that doesn't mean he's an ironclad 'no way,' but combined with the problem of getting out of the hospital for each murder..."

"Damned near impossible," Quinn said, nodding. "Feds are bound to figure that out soon."

"So the hair was a plant," Felix said. "Quite clever. Exceedingly clever, in fact, requiring only a hospital visit, and a plucked arm hair, strategically placed as trace evidence. I'll have to remember that one. So, I suppose this puts us back to the proverbial square one. Shall we compare leads and set out again, then?"

"Not yet," Jack said. "Wait for the fallout. See which way it blows. Shouldn't take long."

To Jack, "waiting for fallout" did not mean waiting as a group. He wanted to separate, then discuss leads by phone after Quinn found out what the Feds were doing about Moreland. Felix seemed inclined to agree, but Quinn argued that it made little sense when morning—and news—would be here soon enough. We should separate for the night, but reunite at breakfast so we could discuss our next steps together.

I understood Jack's concern. Spending as little time together as possible made sense. But after mulling it over for a few minutes, he agreed that breakfast—in our hotel room—should be safe enough. He'd contact them later with the address.

HSK

He stood in the stand of trees, binoculars trained on the front entrance to the psychiatric hospital. The agents had gone in that way, so he presumed they'd exit there, too, but every few seconds, he'd scan over to the other doors as well, just to be sure.

He'd taken the hair from Moreland months ago and stored it. Then he'd planted it on a scene, to support his later claim to be the son of Charles Manson. Whether it went further than that was supposed to depend on whether he'd need Moreland as a scapegoat. If he did, Moreland would die, in an apparent suicide, but not before confessing to the crimes. As for how a psychiatric patient had managed to commit them, that would be up to the Feds to puzzle out, formulating a theory to fit the evidence.

But now he'd had to use Moreland in a very different way, and couldn't help feeling a twinge of regret. He'd liked the Manson angle. It had served him well.

Back in 1969, when the Manson murders hit the news, he'd been just starting as a hitman, making the transition from stealing goods to stealing lives. Like most people, he'd followed the case with a mixture of revulsion and fascination. Yet in his case, it was revulsion at the killer's mistakes, and fascination at the uproar he'd caused.

The murders were a work of genius carried out by an idiot. How many times had he worked through Manson's crimes himself, imagining how much more panic they could have caused if they'd been done right . . . if the killer had left so little evidence that it looked as if he'd never be caught.

When he'd come up with this plan, he'd thought of the Manson killings. He'd considered reenacting them, but he didn't have the stomach for that kind of bloodbath. At his age, too, such theatrics seemed a tawdry way to get attention. So he'd done the murders his way, and added the Manson link to set people's minds and fears buzzing. It'd worked beautifully. But now the time for that game was past.

He'd tossed Moreland to the Feds early, so they'd know the whole Manson angle was a crock. Then they'd concentrate on their theory that the killer was a hitman. He wasn't worried about that—his cover was secure—but the increased pressure on the profession should make his colleagues think twice about coming after him. They'd turn their attention to protecting themselves, which was what they did best anyway.

Yet after he'd made his decision, he'd realized the tip-off could prove even more useful. It was all a matter of how the Feds played the hand he'd dealt them.

As he was considering this, the agents left the hospital. Disappointment thudded into the pit of his stomach. They were alone. He'd hoped they might have Benjamin Moreland with them. Not that he'd expected them to arrest Moreland, but he'd thought they might remove him for questioning, perhaps even take him into protective custody. That would have made things easier.

He shook off the disappointment. No matter. He could still use this. The Feds had been here, and staff could confirm that. Good enough.

In his letter, he'd promised a demand, but hadn't planned to make one. Just part of the game. Game ... A week ago it had been a mere plan. A simple plan for a simple, practical purpose. Now it had become so much more. A huge, intricate game, the patterns, possibilities and plays becoming evident only as it unfolded before him.

What if he made that demand? He wouldn't ask for much. Just a small token from the people of America. One that could never be paid, no matter how insignificant it might seem. But payment wasn't the point. It didn't matter. What mattered was the game, and this would take it to a whole new level.

TWENTY-SEVEN

"Very nice," I said, looking around our hotel room.

The living room of the suite was bigger than my bedroom back at the lodge. Better furnished, too. It even came with flowers—the kind that need water. The last time I had a hotel room with live flowers was . . . well, never. I was impressed all to hell.

"And a kitchen. Wow. Fridge, stove, microwave. Is this a hint about dinner? I should warn you right now, the only thing I cook is microwave popcorn. And I usually burn that."

I crossed the room and opened the door. Inside was a bed. One bed.

"For you," Jack said. "Couch folds out in here."

I opened the other door. "A Jacuzzi tub? Hot damn."

I walked to the counter, took the bottles of shampoo, conditioner, lotion and mouthwash from the basket they'd haphazardly been tossed into, and arranged them on the counter as Jack laid my bag on the bed for me to unpack.

"You like those?" he said, motioning at the tub. "You should get one. Use some of the money."

I laughed. "How big of a paycheck am I counting on?"

He shrugged. "Big enough."

I started refolding the towels, which had been put on the rack crooked and seam-side out. "I've considered a hot tub for the guests. Nothing fancy, but it would add to the 'romantic getaway' allure. The only drawback is hygiene. They don't strike me as the most sanitary things."

"Use chemicals, don't they? Keep 'em stocked. Change the water. Should be fine."

"We have plenty of fresh water, so that'd be easy enough."

"Then get one. For your room, too. A tub. Not the guest rooms. Yours."

I grinned. "I must be looking at a real windfall here."

"Just a job." He turned to leave. "Pizza okay?"

I said that it was, and he went to order while I washed up.

We spent a couple of hours discussing the case over the pizza, laying out scenarios and theories. There was lots of fodder for theorizing now, as if there hadn't been enough before. Why create a fake Manson connection? Had someone tipped off the Feds? Or had they figured it out, too? How was the killer going to react?

We debated the possibilities into the wee hours, and I loved every minute of it, like those nights with my dad. Not that Jack reminded me of my father—far from it. But it was nice to go back to that memory place again, and to have someone to go there with.

The next morning, I walked to my bedroom door and listened for Jack. Was he still asleep? I hoped so. I wasn't ready to face him yet.

I'd awoken in the aftermath of a dream. I'd been back in that closet in the hospital. Someone had been coming down the hall, and Jack had been whispering for me to stay still and quiet, and I'd been straining to hear footsteps, heart thumping, adrenaline racing. His hands had slid down my hips and under my skirt, lifting it and—

The dream hadn't ended there, but that was as far as I planned to remember it.

I knew where the dream came from—being stuffed into

that closet with Jack, in the midst of what had been a rather long dry spell. Still, knowing where it sprang from wasn't going to make facing him this morning any easier.

So I'd dressed as quietly as I could, and now I was hoping to sneak past him and head out for coffee before he awoke. Yet when I cracked open the door, Jack was gone.

There was a note on the table. I wiped the sleep from my eyes, then squinted down at the precise, black strokes. "Getting coffee. Back soon. Wait."

I *could* wait. Or I could take a cold shower. But there was something else I could do, too, something my body was screaming for almost as much as it'd been screaming for that dream. I stripped off my clothes and pulled on my jogging pants and T-shirt.

By "wait," I assumed Jack meant "Don't go home" or "Don't have breakfast without me." Sure, it could mean "Don't leave the hotel room," but that's the problem with one-word sentences—they're so open to interpretation.

I donned the wig, contacts, mascara and lipstick. Any more makeup than that and I'd be wearing it on my shirtfront by the end of the run. Then I amended his note, crossing off "Getting coffee" and replacing it with "Gone jogging."

Five minutes later, I was running along a downtown street, weaving past baby strollers and business suits. I doubted I'd make the full 10K. My legs might, but my lungs wouldn't. Ten kilometers of breathing in exhaust fumes and I'd be ready for the oxygen mask.

I liked to run every morning, but that hadn't been possible since this started. I didn't want to be seen jogging around Evelyn's neighborhood—not when no one else seemed to. That first morning at a motel I hadn't wanted to slow down the investigation by asking Jack if he minded me taking off for a while. So now I welcomed the excuse.

After a few blocks, I found myself stuck on a street corner, running on the spot, waiting for a very long light to change. A diesel delivery truck cut the corner too sharp and belched blue smoke into my face. I closed my eyes, and pictured falling golden leaves and an endless empty dirt road.

"You look happy," said a voice at my shoulder.

I tensed as I recognized Quinn's voice. He'd followed me? I forced a smile. "Hey, there. Small world."

The light changed. I started to walk across, but he waved me forward.

"Go ahead. Run. I can keep up." We broke into a jog. "When I got to your room, Jack said you were out jogging, so I thought I'd join you. Hope that's okay."

I slanted him a look. "What did Jack say?"

"I snuck out while he was in the bathroom."

"Smart man."

I navigated through the commuter crowd and crossed the road, Quinn at my heels. Once across, the bulk of the crowd turned left. I continued straight. Quinn jogged up alongside me.

"I thought this might be a good time to redo my introduction," he said. "I came off like a jerk yesterday and I'm sorry."

"You didn't like the idea of Jack bringing a stranger on board. I don't blame you. I think that's why he didn't want us to meet. Protecting your privacy—yours and the others."

We turned a corner.

"So you must be Evelyn's new protégée," he said.

"Why do you say that?"

"Well, because you're a—" He colored slightly. "Because I can be a sexist moron. Sorry. Again. I didn't mean to jump to conclusions. You're not Evelyn's, then?"

"No, I'm Jack's."

When he looked my way, brows raised, I sputtered a laugh. "I mean his protégée. Strictly business. Even 'protégée' is probably pushing it."

Another light. We waited in silence, then crossed.

"How far do you go normally?" he asked.

"Te—" I stopped myself before saying kilometers. "Five miles. Give or take."

"Every day, I'm guessing."

He flashed an appreciative glance down my figure. A nice glance—not a leer or an ogle. The appreciative part was good, too. After that dream, I was certainly in the mood for it. I even returned it, though more discreetly. He was wearing jogging pants and an old T-shirt with the sleeves ripped off, showing his muscles. Good-looking in a wholesome, athletic way, nothing to stop traffic, but enough to invite the gaze to linger . . . and enjoy.

He plucked at the sweat-sodden front of his T-shirt and pulled a face. "I definitely need to start doing more cardio myself. Soon, or I'll be skipping ski season this year."

"Cross-country or—" I stopped. "Sorry. I guess that'd be prying."

Quinn whooped a breathless laugh. "That's what happens when you hang out with Jack. You start thinking 'What do you take in your coffee?' might be too personal."

We turned the corner, then Quinn continued, "Sure, you have to be careful, but there's still stuff you can talk about. What are you going to do, say, 'Hmmm, I know Jack likes James Dean movies, nachos with chicken, and Bob Dylan,' and plug it into some national database to figure out who he really is? Even if I knew his name and social security number, what the hell would I do with it?"

"If you were caught, you might find a use for it."

"Cut a deal, you mean? Considering what he knows

about me, I'd be nuts to do that. Anyway, I don't think that telling you I like to ski is a major security violation. So, yes, I ski. Downhill, as you were about to ask. I keep meaning to try cross-country, but I never get around to it."

"Cross-country is a good winter substitute for jogging, though it can't beat downhill for the adrenaline rush. I always think of them as opposite ends of the spectrum. Downhill for getting the heart pumping, cross-country for relaxing."

We crossed at the lights, nearly getting knocked down by the draft of a car whizzing around the corner.

"Cross-country's more peaceful, I bet," Quinn said. "Without the crowds of hot-doggers racing around you."

"God, yes. Find a nice quiet trail through the woods, go out at night with the moonlight glistening off the snow— perfect."

"There's this club I go to, up in Vermont. They've got a trail along the river, and every year I tell myself I'm going to try it, but I can't get my buddies off the hills . . . or off the snow bunnies."

"Not many snow bunnies on the cross-country trails."

"Which is not necessarily a bad thing. Last year, we met this group of girls. They must have blown a grand each on their outfits, but they couldn't even lace up their boots right. We . . ."

". . . ride the helicopter to the top of the mountain," Quinn said as he held open the hotel room door for me. "Then they drop you off and you ski down."

"Heli-skiing," I said. Felix and Jack were watching CNN. "I hear it's amazing."

Felix glanced over. He looked different today—his hair

color the same, but his manner changed along with his clothes. A well-loved tweed blazer and slacks, hair slightly too long, glasses perched on the end of his nose, pale cheeks hollow—the college professor who doesn't spend much time away from his books.

"Jumping out of a helicopter and skiing down a mountain?" he said. "Sounds almost as much fun as swimming in a shark tank. But I suppose you two do that, too."

"Only if we have the right equipment," I said. "If you forget the blood-soaked bikini, there's just no challenge to it."

"Dee?" Jack cut in. "Breakfast."

"Oh, right. Should we order—"

"Pick up." He walked to the door. "Come on."

"I'll take the breakfast special," Quinn said. "Bacon, eggs, whatever. If I get toast, make it whole wheat."

"And what would you like in your coffee?" I asked.

He grinned. "I could tell you, but then I'd have to kill you."

"Cream and double sugar," Jack said. "Let's go."

TWENTY-EIGHT

We got as far as the elevator before Jack said, "You saw my note, right? It said 'wait.'"

"That was a note? I thought it was a haiku." I pressed the elevator button. "I left you a note in return, and stuck to the main street, so it was no less safe than wherever you went."

"That's not—"

"If you mean Quinn, it wasn't as bad as it looked. Yes, I know, one minute I'm worried about meeting the guy, and the next I'm chatting and laughing with him. But that's my way of handling situations like this. Morose and monosyllabic may work for some people, but not for me."

"Morose?"

"The best way for me to behave with someone I don't trust is to act like I trust them completely. They may let their guard down, but I don't. Ever."

As the doors opened, I could feel him watching me. We stepped on.

"Tomorrow?" he said. "You want to jog? I'll follow."

"You run?"

"Only if someone's chasing. I'll drive."

Over breakfast, Jack told us what he'd been doing earlier—checking his messages. And he'd had one, from Shadow. It seemed Sid, his twin brother, had indeed been taken into custody. Now Shadow had decided to make like his namesake and gone to ground, wanting nothing more to do with the investigation. He was in such a hurry that Jack didn't get a chance to ask whether they'd uncovered any leads or even what angle they'd been investigating.

Then came Quinn's news: the FBI was investigating Benjamin Moreland but not considering him a viable suspect. What did interest them was the killer's possible link to Moreland—how he'd gotten that hair.

After we discussed that, we moved on to our own investigation. Jack had me tell Quinn and Felix our progress to date.

"Not great," I said. "So far, they all feel like dead-ends."

"Shit," Quinn said. "At least you've *got* something to look into. With the Moreland lead gone, so's our investigation. How about we take some of yours?"

Jack shrugged. "Suppose so. Vigilantism. You want that?"

Quinn's lips tightened, but Jack only sipped his coffee.

"We'll take it," Felix said. "I'll also see what I can do to verify Baron's death. Damned shame, that. He was a good man once."

Jack nodded.

Since we were back to wearing our biker-duo outfits, Jack must have thought we needed to get in the right mind-set. After only an hour on the road, he stopped at the kind of place that gives the word "dive" a bad name. It wasn't even noon, and there was already someone lying on the floor. Probably passed out drunk, but in this place you could keel over dead and not be noticed until the flies started feasting.

There were a half-dozen men in the diner/bar, but only one even looked our way, and just to ogle me as we passed.

At a sharp look from Jack, the man returned to staring at the empty chair across the table, and lifted his coffee mug, taking so deep a swig I suspected it wasn't filled with java, which would explain why I couldn't smell fresh brewed coffee despite the mugs at every man's table. For that matter, I couldn't smell much of anything, just a faint whiff of mildew, as if the customers—even more disheveled and shabby than the tavern—were too well pickled to give off any odor.

Without so much as a glance around, Jack navigated to the darkened back hall.

"You've been here before, I take it," I whispered. "Please tell me it was on business."

"Yeah. Order a burger for a mark? Chef does your job for you."

The hall was nearly pitch-black. An exit sign at the end gave off the only light. After my eyes adjusted, I could see a chain on the rear door. The management must have been more worried about customers escaping without paying than escaping a fire. Although, from what I'd seen, I doubted they'd go anywhere even if the chairs under them were ablaze.

Jack led me to a phone booth, picked up the receiver and held it to my ear. Guess that meant I was doing the talking. I presumed he was holding it because he was wearing gloves and I wasn't, but I was glad of it for any reason. The receiver was so filthy I could barely bring my lips close enough to it to talk.

He dialed. Evelyn picked up on the third ring.

"Hey, Auntie E," I said, cranking my voice up a few octaves. "It's me!"

Not so much as a beat-pause. "Deedee, why hello, dear.

So good of you to call. And how's Jackie? Taking good care of you, I hope."

I looked around at the grunge-streaked walls. "You bet. He takes me to *all* the best places. So, auntie, remember how we were going to visit cousin Will? Before that thing came up? Well, Jackie and I thought we'd pay him a visit. But first, we wanted to see whether you wanted to join us, since it was your idea."

"Oh, that's very sweet of you, dear, but you kids don't want to travel all the way over here to pick me up. Go and see Will, and give him my love. Then you can stop here on the way back. I'd love to see you."

I glanced at Jack, who'd been listening in. "I'm not sure—"

"Really, I must insist." Her voice was still light, but her tone had taken on a steel core. "We have so much catching up to do."

Jack hesitated, then nodded. I told Evelyn we'd be there late this afternoon, then signed off.

"Jackie?" Jack said.

"She started it."

He shook his head and led me back into the bar.

At the jail, Jack didn't even bother with a cover story—just gave the guard his fake name and ID and said we wanted to speak to Nicky Volkv. Volkv agreed to see us. I guess after years in jail, he was just happy for a visitor.

From the moment we entered the jail, Jack became someone else, sliding into his aging-biker character as he hadn't bothered to until now. His head went higher, shoulders squared, stride taking on a hint of a swagger.

We sat on the visitors' side of the Plexiglas barrier for

five silent minutes before the door opened and the guard ushered in a tall man with graying dark hair and a milky-white left eye. Volkv squinted his good eye at Jack.

"I know you?" he asked.

"You should."

The briefest hesitation, then Volkv sat down. He folded his hands on the counter, gaze darting from Jack to me. It lingered on me, hungry.

"Leon Kozlov," Jack said.

Volkv reluctantly pulled his gaze from me. "You know Leon? How is the old son of a bitch?"

We'd expected Volkv to know about Kozlov's death. Even in jail, he shouldn't be that cut off, but from his open smile as we mentioned his friend, he was obviously serious.

"He's dead," Jack said.

Volkv blinked, then leaned forward, resting his mouth against his open hand. It took a moment before he looked up again.

"How'd it happen?"

"Hit."

I expected Volkv to laugh, or at least ask Jack to repeat himself. Someone paying to off an old thug who'd been out of the business for twenty years? Waste of ammo.

But Volkv just gave a long slow shake of his head. "Dumb fuck. I warned him. Last time he was here, he sat right there—same chair you're in, as a matter of fact, and I said, 'Leon, you dumb fuck, that ain't a retirement package, it's a death sentence.' You don't screw with those guys, you know what I mean?"

Jack nodded.

Volkv leaned forward. "Now you and I, maybe we ain't picked the kind of careers our mamas would want, but those guys? A whole other league. Not even part of the human race, if you ask me. Fucking psychos, every last one of them. You don't blackmail a psycho."

"Not unless you want to end up six feet under." As Jack switched to full sentences, I noticed the brogue had been replaced by a faint drawl, like a southerner who's worked hard to lose his accent.

Volkv jabbed a finger at the Plexiglas, earning himself a glare from the guard. He lowered his voice. "That's exactly what I told Leon. You don't fuck with a hitman." Grief flickered behind his eyes again. "Did he get a good funeral?"

"A big one. Standing room only."

"Really? So those Nikolaev bastards came around to show their respects, did they? I always told Leon he was smart not to tell them what happened. If they knew, they'd have bumped him off themselves, just to be safe. No loyalty, those fucks. I got this on the job"—he pointed at his blind eye—"they wouldn't even pay my doctor's bill. Fired my ass 'cause I couldn't see right no more."

By now I could almost hear my toe tapping with impatience. It was like seeing the carousel brass ring zipping by, as you try to reach a little farther, knowing that any moment, the music could stop and you'd lose your chance. Jack just sat there, hands never leaving the reins, as if, by being patient enough, the ring would come to him.

For the next ten minutes, he chatted with Volkv, letting the old con take the conversation where he liked, around and around, never veering any closer to the prize. I held my tongue only by clamping my mouth shut so hard my jaw ached.

"Russians ain't so bad," Jack said, relaxed in his chair, one arm hooked over the back. "I had to pick, I'd go with them over the Yakuza any day. Look at those bastards wrong, and it's permanent retirement time." He stretched his legs.

"Speaking of retirement, I don't suppose Leon's retirement plan is up for sale."

Volkv laughed. "So that's what you're after? You got balls, buddy. My advice would be the same I gave to old Leon: buy yourself a lottery ticket instead. Odds of cashing in are a hundred times better." He leaned forward. "You want the truth? Plan's not mine to sell. I never asked Leon for the details—my life might not be worth much, but it's all I got. All I know is that he saw something he shouldn't have. Some*one*."

Jack let Volkv ease back into small talk. Five minutes later, the guard announced our time was up. I made it as far as the parking lot before I let out a growl of frustration.

"Goddamn it! We were so close. A few more minutes…" I took a deep breath, retaking control. "Well, let's analyze what we've got. Kozlov crossed a hitman back in his mob days. As for how he crossed him—"

"He saw him," Jack said as he opened the car door.

I stopped, fingers grazing the handle, and looked over the roof at him, but he just climbed in and started the engine. As I slid into my seat, he continued, "Kozlov witnessed a hit. Probably the one that got him fired. Didn't just let his guy get whacked. *Saw* the hitman. Maybe even recognized him. Been sitting on it all these years."

"And he called in the marker?"

"Maybe. Or maybe Kozlov wasn't the only one retiring."

I frowned over at him as he pulled out of the parking lot.

"Gotta clean up before you retire. Clip the loose ends. Otherwise—" He shrugged. "No sense quitting. Always looking over your shoulder."

I took a moment to unravel this and fill in the missing parts. "You mean that if a hitman wants to retire to a normal life, he needs an exit strategy, to make damned sure there's nothing, and no one who can finger him?" I twisted to look at him. "Do you think that's what this guy is doing? Tying up all his loose ends by killing witnesses?"

"Could be."

TWENTY-NINE

When I rapped on Evelyn's door, she shouted a muffled welcome. We found her in the living room, tapping away on her keyboard, gaze fixed not on the monitor, but on the TV across the room. Before I could say hello, she gestured for silence and pointed at the television screen.

"—have confirmed the existence of a second letter, reportedly from the person responsible for the killings," a news anchor was saying. "In it, the alleged killer speaks disparagingly of the federal agents assigned to the investigation—"

"Disparagingly?" Evelyn snorted. "Like I speak 'disparagingly' about the damned property taxes in this neighborhood."

"—agents are defending their actions, stressing that at no time did they consider the psychiatric patient a viable suspect. However, as several staff members at the hospital have confirmed, the FBI has taken a serious and ongoing interest in Benjamin Moreland—"

Evelyn waved us to the computer. On the monitor was the letter from the killer.

Dear Mr. & Mrs. Citizen,

For two weeks now, I have been taking lives where I wish, and the federal agents assigned to catch me are no closer to their goal today than they were after the first death. In jest, I left a small trail of bread crumbs for them to follow—pages from a book, a letter claiming kinship with the subject of that book, a hair plucked from the arm of one who is indeed kin to that subject.

The joke is that the man to whom the hair belonged is one Benjamin Moreland, a schizophrenic who has been in a mental institution for the last six months. When I led the FBI to Mr. Moreland, I assumed they would see that it was a prank. Not only has he been in a secure facility since the crimes began, but he is diagnosed with a condition that would make it impossible for him to carry out murders as methodical and careful as these, as your experts will tell you. And yet, the FBI has turned their investigative efforts in his direction and are even now on the verge of arresting Mr. Moreland. This is how your premier law enforcement agency protects you.

So who can protect you? You can. I will ask for no more than you can afford—a laughably small price to pay for the safety of yourself and your loved ones.

"Scroll down," I said.

"That's it."

"But there's no demand. See if you can find a complete version—"

"That's all there is, Dee. I've searched every copy, and every summary. There is no demand."

Evelyn showed us a few sites where people were already debating the missing demand, and the significance of its absence. The prevailing theory was that the demand portion of the letter had been suppressed, that someone had managed to scare every news agency in the country into not printing it.

Bullshit, of course. The killer had intentionally held back his demand to leave people dangling. Let the panic mount, and the conspiracy theorists feed off it.

As for the ineptitude of the Feds, that was more misleading fear-mongering. He'd put the federal agents in the awkward position of defending themselves to Joe and Jane Citizen, who've read too many stories about inept, ineffectual or corrupt cops.

"Head games, Dee," Jack murmured. "Remember that. We're getting closer."

"Are we?" I said, unclenching my jaw, but keeping my gaze down, hiding the dark rage bubbling in my gut. "This throws a big wrench in our theory, doesn't it?"

Evelyn flicked off the monitor. "Tell me this theory."

I explained what we'd learned from Volkv.

When I finished, she nodded. "If that's *not* why Leon Kozlov was killed, it's a hell of a coincidence. Only one problem..."

"This"—I waved at the television screen—"screws it all to bits. If he's making demands, then he's not doing pre-retirement cleaning."

"Don't be too sure, Dee. That's isn't the problem I meant. How many witnesses have you left, Jack?"

"None I know of."

"I had one," Evelyn said. "My fourth job. When I told my partner what happened, he sent me back to clean it up, and I learned my lesson there. Make damned sure you don't have witnesses, or you might have to do something you'd rather not."

I nodded. "In other words, if the killer is as good as he seems, there's no way he should have left six witnesses... maybe more. So Kozlov is a coincidence?"

Evelyn shot off her chair and marched to her bookshelf. She grabbed a thin paperback. A second later it landed on my lap, the cover facing up.

"*A B C Murders*. Agatha Christie." I skimmed the blurb

on the back cover. "Oh, right, this is the one where the killer murders a bunch of people to hide a single—" I looked over at Evelyn. "You think he killed the others to cover killing Kozlov?"

"Former Russian mobster winds up dead, where's the first place the cops look?"

"Organized crime."

"A little extra effort, and Kozlov's murder is hidden. Plus, our hitman goes out with a headline-making bang. Not a bad way to retire."

"Killing five innocent people isn't what I'd call a 'little extra effort.'"

"You know what I mean. For someone who's spent his life killing people, a few more isn't going to matter. Most pros don't even see *people* anymore. Not the way you do, Dee." She looked at me, finger wagging. "And that's what could make you a hell of a hitwoman. Conviction. Purpose. Passion. Harness that and—" Her eyes gleamed. "You might even become better than me."

Her gaze locked mine, daring me to break away.

"Kozlov," Jack cut in. "We need more."

She looked at him. For a moment, no one spoke. Then she turned to her computer and got to work.

As Evelyn searched, we put together criteria for a list of potential hitmen.

"The Nikolaevs fired Kozlov in the early eighties, according to Little Joe," I said. "That means we're looking for a guy at least . . ."

"My age," Jack said. "Probably older."

"And judging by the language in that letter, I'd say he's well educated," I added.

"Age," Evelyn said, not looking up from her typing. "The style. It's overly formal. Not so much educated as an older person trying to sound educated."

"Educated in an era before e-mail, so he pays more attention to his word choices, composition, whatever." I looked at the printout. "He goes overboard. Wanting to sound smart, not be dismissed as some high school drop-out thug. Appearances are important. Could be self-esteem issues there, too. Proving himself, like with the murders."

"Wilkes retired yet?" Jack called over to Evelyn.

"Dropped out of the life years ago. And a plodder. His idea of creativity was toy handcuffs. We're looking for someone with vision."

"Add him anyway," Jack said to me. Then to Evelyn. "Mercury?"

"A possibility. He was definitely creative. Knew positions even I never imagined."

"Hank?"

"Mmm, he was pretty good, too. But he liked three-somes. Not my style. He's dead, though. Heard he got the death sentence from his doctor, went to Reno, blew his retirement fund on reserving a whole brothel for a week and died happy."

"How about saving us some time?" I said. "Just make a list of your former lovers."

"You'll need more paper."

"Riley's dead," Jack said. "Falcon's long retired. Not many left. Not at this age. Young man's game." He leaned back, as if searching his memory.

"What about Felix?" I said. "He's about the right age."

Evelyn shook her head, her eyes still on her computer screen. "He's been with Quinn and if he started taking off,

Quinn would be suspicious. Plus, Phoenix isn't the retiring type."

"Phoenix?"

"Felix. Phoenix is his work name. Any hitman with a moniker like that—a bird, animal, whatever—probably has a second nom de guerre for friends. Can you imagine chatting over beer with a guy and calling him 'Phoenix'?"

"So I can cross Felix/Phoenix off my list. And Quinn is obviously too young—"

"Ah, Quinn," she said. "What did you think of *him,* Dee?"

I glanced at Jack. "Okay, I guess. Seemed straight up."

"Oh, he is. As straight as they come." Her eyes glittered. "I bet you two will get along famously. You have so much in common, and not just a shared law-enforcement career. Quinn has another name, too, something with a little more . . . meaning, as much as he hates it. Perhaps you've heard of—"

"Scorpio," Jack said.

"Scorpio? That's Quinn's other—"

"No," Evelyn said. "Jack is telling us to move back to the list. Age-wise, Scorpio is a possibility, though you know him better than I do, Jack. Could he pull something like this?"

"Doesn't matter. Add him. This list—" He waved at the paper in my hands. "Probably finish with four, five names. This job? Not a high retirement rate. Check them all."

THIRTY

Two hours later, we were no closer to finding details of the hit Koslov had witnessed. Evelyn had put Maggie and Frances on it, to see whether their Nikolaev contacts knew anything.

"What about Little Joe?" Jack said as we ate dinner.

"The same Little Joe who laid a marker on my head? Oh, yeah, there's the guy you want to chat up about Nikolaev history."

"He'll talk."

"After excusing himself to go call the next name on his list? Or will he try a new tactic this time?"

"Nah. Not that creative. He'll stick to hitmen."

"That's comforting."

"We can handle it."

"We?"

"Yeah. Need your help. It'll be okay. Safe." When I didn't respond, he added, "No miniskirts."

"I'll think about it."

I saw the note the moment I walked into my room. It wasn't obvious, a small square of paper partly tucked under the bedside lamp. But when I stepped in, I automatically did a visual sweep. And so I saw the note—something that had not been there before.

I unfolded it. A newspaper article on white copy paper, printed from the Internet. I knew it came from Evelyn. Anything Jack wanted to convey to me, he'd say. Language might not be his forte, but I couldn't imagine him communicating any other way—certainly not through clandestine notes in my bedroom.

My gaze went first to the headline: "Accused Pedophile Freed."

I sat on the edge of the bed and read the rest of the article. It was taken from a Wisconsin paper and detailed the sort of crime that, while it makes headline news locally, rarely goes further, not because it is insignificant but because, quite simply, it happens too often to qualify as news.

A middle-aged man, leader of some youth organization, had been accused of molesting boys on camping trips in a list of crimes stretching back a decade, resulting—the prosecution had claimed—in two victim suicides. He was also believed to own a lucrative online child pornography business, and the police had found boxes of evidence in his home.

Unable to prove the business allegations, they'd settled for possession of child pornography, plus the molestation charges. Nothing stuck. His lawyer claimed the porn had been illegally seized, and a judge had agreed. That then excluded all photographic evidence of his molestation crimes from the trial. Left with only victim testimony—from boys who'd gone on to have their own run-ins with the police, psychiatric problems and substance abuse issues—a jury had decided this fine, upstanding citizen was being railroaded by ungrateful juvenile delinquents. Case closed.

Not an unusual story, though that didn't keep my hands from clenching on the paper as I read it. Then I read the small yellow paper attached to the bottom. A sticky note with numbers on it. A figure: $100,000.

I understood what I was holding. A job offer.

My first "target" had been a pedophile. Not that prostitute-killing thug the Tomassinis set me on, but the first criminal I'd ever hunted. I'd been seventeen, a few months from finishing high school, already making plans to attend police college.

The man had been accused of sexually and physically assaulting two boys in his apartment building, one six years old, one seven. He'd lived in Kitchener, a city a half-hour from our town, meaning the case had hit our papers, had been discussed—in detail—in our living room, over poker, those games I'd once catered and now joined, even getting a bottle of beer after my mother retired to bed, though my father drew the line at the rye and Scotch.

Over those poker games and from hanging out at the station, I'd heard more about the case than the average citizen. And I knew, as every cop in that part of the province knew, that the guy was guilty. But things had gone wrong. There'd been only two victims, one too terrified to talk and one who'd recanted his story at the last minute—some said his family had been bought off by the wealthy defendant.

I'd shared everyone's outrage and frustration, participated in the debates and agreed that this experience wouldn't scare the guy straight—if such a thing was possible for a pedophile. Yet my own feelings about it didn't go much deeper than that. Or so I'd thought.

A month later, I'd been at the rifle range with an older cousin, a constable on the Kitchener force. After Amy's murder, my father had introduced me to marksmanship. In it, I'd found a place where caution and planning were not only appreciated, but vital to success. Just follow the rules, work out every contingency and success is predictable in a way life never can be. Through my teens, marksmanship had been my favorite hobby—my outlet and my escape. But that day, I discovered something even better.

We were there, my cousin and I, at the range, when the accused pedophile walked in.

"That's him over there, Nadia," my cousin said, pointing out a pleasant-looking man in his late thirties. "Looks like he's getting some training. A little nervous maybe? Feeling like someone's gunning for him?" He snorted. "I wish. Bastard deserves a bullet—right through the nuts. That'd solve his 'problem.'"

I'd said nothing. I never did. I would participate in the debates and discussions on a purely philosophical level. But, taking my cue from my father, I never let it get personal, never let my frustration descend into wishes and threats. Not aloud, anyway. So I'd only nodded, and continued with my practice.

But in that moment, something happened. Maybe it was seeing that man. Maybe it was hearing my cousin's words. Maybe it was witnessing the man's fear—as he struggled to shoot a gun, trying to feel safe, when I was only twenty feet away, holding a gun myself and knowing—should I turn it on him—he'd never have a chance. Knowing that he'd be as helpless as the boys he'd abused.

Whatever the reason, at that moment I realized I had the power to do something. I wasn't thirteen anymore, helpless, hearing my cousin being raped. Only four years later, I had changed. I had power. I could fight and I could shoot, and I had the will and confidence to do both.

When the man left, I followed him. I'd driven my parents' car, so I told my cousin I was feeling unwell and he never thought anything of it. Even if he'd noticed the man leave before me, he didn't see a connection because I was just his teenage cousin, the one who drove seniors to church on Sunday and always had a friendly word for everyone.

I spent the rest of the day following the man. I took

notes. By the end, I knew where he lived, where he shopped and where he liked to park his car—in a quiet lane behind the school where he could watch the little boys playing tag.

He watched them. I watched him.

For three weeks, I followed him. Not every day—I had school—but every few days I'd head to the city and find him. Then, when I had his routine down, I considered what I could do. Considered what would be a proper punishment for his crimes, a sufficient deterrent.

I read up on pedophiles. Read about treatments. While the therapy sessions sounded very nice and proper, I'd heard enough stories about criminals and their misuse of the psychiatric system. Chemical castration seemed far more effective. Impossible for a teenage girl to pull off, though. So it would have to be true castration. I considered that for a long time, whether the punishment fit the crime, whether preventing future molestation would justify such an extreme measure.

As I studied, fear crept into my gut. The fear that I would be found out, that my dark thoughts would show on my face, in my manner. I imagined my father discovering my notes and my books, and that was almost enough to stop me.

But while I was plotting to castrate a pedophile, my world revolved as it should. My mother alternated between ignoring me and harassing me over imagined misdeeds. My brother just ignored me. My boyfriend still kissed me, still looked into my eyes and mangled misremembered love poems in a vain attempt to get into my pants. My friends still phoned, still sought my company, still told me their secrets. And my father still waited for me, at the station, every day after school. Waited for me to arrive, coffees in hand, and join him in his office, where we'd share our day before heading home.

If I'd changed, no one noticed.

So I continued to plot. Studied methods. Examined my target's schedule. Came up with a plan. How I would carry it out. Then I closed my books, burned my notes and placed an anonymous pay phone call to the Kitchener police, telling them about the man's voyeuristic habits.

Three months later, he was brought up on fresh charges stemming from surveillance. Justice was served.

And now, in my hands, I held another chance.

I read the article again. Looked at the man's picture.

I could do it. But where would it lead?

Did I want to go there?

Did I want Evelyn to be the one to take me there?

To Evelyn, I was a project. Something to be made better. Something to be used? Maybe. But a project nonetheless. And here, in my hand, was the lure.

I folded the paper and put it into my bag.

It was past two. I'd gone to bed an hour ago. I was coming out of the bathroom, heading toward my room when a shadow moved. I started, then saw Jack silhouetted in his open bedroom door.

"Oh," he said. "You were just—" He waved toward the bathroom. "Thought you were heading down."

I managed a small smile. "Trying not to, but losing the battle."

"Come on."

* * *

He waved me to the kitchen table and got out the cocoa and sugar containers. When it was made, he brought over my mug and sat across from me.

"You okay?" he asked.

"Sure."

He studied me. "That letter. Doesn't mean shit. We're getting close."

"Sure."

We sat there for a few minutes, the quiet broken only by the drumming of Jack's fingers. He cast a few glances at the window overlooking the driveway.

"Want me to grab your cigarettes?" I asked.

A tiny smile. "That obvious?"

"Stressful day." I lifted my mug. "This is my fix. I suppose Evelyn wouldn't be keen on you smoking in the house, but we can step outside if you'd like."

"Damned cold..."

"I don't mind if you don't. A little fresh air might help us sleep."

Jack lit a cigarette, took a drag and made a face. Then he took another one.

My soft laugh echoed through the backyard. "Tastes like shit, but it does the job, huh?"

"Yeah."

We were leaning on the railing, side by side, staring out into the night. There was a sharp wind coming from the north, but Jack had moved close, blocking it for me. I had my hands wrapped around my still-warm mug, sipping it as Jack smoked.

I longed to ask him about Evelyn. To tell him about her "offer." Not to set him against her, but to get his opinion, as the person who knew her best. When he said this was my decision to make, I knew he meant that. I also knew that accepting this job, accepting Evelyn's help, wouldn't mean giving up his. He'd never make me choose.

Would *she*? Maybe. As fond as she was of Jack, she wasn't one to share.

Two years ago, Jack hadn't wanted me becoming Evelyn's project. Why? What danger was there in accepting the tutelage of the woman who'd trained him, a person he still obviously trusted, still had a relationship with?

Good enough for him. Why not good enough for me two years ago? And what had changed now?

So many questions—and here, alone in the dark, I could have asked. I should have asked. But I couldn't find the right words. So we stood there looking out over the yard. I drank my hot chocolate, shared his cigarette and his company . . . and asked him nothing.

The next morning, Evelyn didn't mention the "offer." Nor did I. We had breakfast, then Jack and I got ready to go. Back to Little Joe. As Jack promised, I was miniskirt free. No high heels or push-up bras, either. My outfit was pretty much what I'd normally wear at this time of year—jeans, a turtleneck and a denim jacket. The disguise started at the neck, with Evelyn's long brunette wig and my new green contacts. I'd added a needle-thin scar under my eye, the kind of distinguishing feature that doesn't really stand out, but would be the first thing you'd mention in a witness ID.

Jack had dressed casually as well—in jeans and a thick pullover that, with some padding, bulked him out from well built to hefty. A sandy-brown wig and glasses, and he was the other half of a middle-class couple going to visit an old family friend in the nursing home.

As Jack drove, the radio station we were listening to faded. I flipped the dial and caught:

"—killer's demand was delivered to over fifty media outlets at 9 a.m. eastern standard time. The FBI has requested a publication ban until they verify that it is not a hoax, but fledgling network TNC has announced plans to air it in a special broadcast at ten this morning—"

I glanced at the car stereo clock: 9:43.

"Do you think any of the radio stations will carry it?" I said. "Or should I call Evelyn, get her to watch, maybe tape it?"

Jack was already steering onto the off-ramp.

"Where—?"

"Place with TVs. Lots of 'em."

Before us was a wall of television screens, all tuned to the nearest TNC affiliate. Between us and those screens was another wall—one of flesh and bone—as we stood in the midst of a mob seven or eight people deep, all crowded into the department store's home electronics department. Even the staff was there, in the first row, having weaseled through the crowd on the pretense of "monitoring the volume levels."

The store was already warm, and the added crush of bodies wasn't helping. Nor was the overpowering cologne on the young man to my left. I supposed the strong musky scent was intended to provoke some hormonal response, to make him irresistible to women, but it reminded me of the raccoon's nest I'd cleaned from the boathouse this summer.

"This is a special TNC broadcast—" a man's voice intoned.

As the crowd hushed, I lifted onto my tiptoes and leaned right to see past the head of a mountainous man in front of me. The announcer seemed to be explaining how the letter had been delivered, but I caught only a smattering of words through the whispers of the couple to my right. The text version of the newsman's words scrolled across the screen, and if I could just lean a little more to the right, I'd be able to— The man stepped squarely in front of me.

A hand reached around my waist and Jack tugged me over, squeezing me in front of him for a perfect view.

"Thanks," I whispered. "Can you still see the—?"

"Don't need to."

I knew he wasn't just saying that to be polite. He would have been content to continue on to see Little Joe, and get the update later. We were here for me.

After five minutes of recapping the delivery of this letter, and the contents of the one from the day before, the newscaster finally revealed the main prize—lifting a sheet of paper with such care and gravitas that you'd think it was the original Declaration of Independence.

"'Dear Mr. and Mrs. Citizen,'" he read. "'I will keep this brief. You already know that your law-enforcement agencies cannot protect you, so there is no need for me to spell out the danger faced by each of you, and your loved ones. My demand is simple. In return for a one-time cash payment, I will end the killings. I don't ask for a lot. It is perhaps the cheapest insurance policy you will ever buy. The cost: one dollar.

"'As an act of faith, all I ask is that the president of the United States appear on CNN before noon today and promise me that I will be paid one dollar for each adult citizen. If noon passes without that promise, I will make my own promise: one dead citizen by 12:01. And that is only the beginning.'"

There the letter ended. When the announcer stopped reading, the crowd didn't budge, either waiting for more or too stunned to move. Jack put his hand against the small of my back and prodded me out. We were in the parking lot before I spoke.

"One dollar for every adult? That's . . . hundreds of millions."

Jack nodded and reached for his keys.

"How would he transport that much money? You can't just pack it in a suitcase."

"Doesn't matter. Two hundred dollars. Two hundred million. Same thing. Can't be paid."

It took a moment to realize what he meant. "Because the U.S. government has a policy of refusing to bargain with terrorists. He must know that. Does he expect them to make an exception?"

"Maybe. Could just be a game."

"Asking for money he knows he'll never see? What kind of game is that?"

"Helter Skelter," Jack said, and pulled open the car door.

As we drove to see Little Joe, I remembered what Lucy had said at the lodge, about a hitman turned serial killer, and how tough that would make things on the investigators. We'd dismissed that possibility. These were cold, clean kills, with none of the earmarks of random serial killings.

But, in setting up his calculated plan to hide the murder of Leon Kozlov, the killer must have encountered something he'd never experienced as a contract killer—the thrill of fear, the power that came with chaos and the chance to play God.

Jack said it did happen. Usually it was the new hitmen who succumbed and, even then, they didn't fit the textbook definition of a serial killer, picking and hunting down victims, acting on some inner urge. They just didn't give a shit who they killed.

If you're willing to kill five innocent people to eliminate one potential problem, then what's to stop you from killing umpteen more to get what you want? "What you want" could be two hundred million or it could be the thrill of playing Death. Or it could be a last burst of glory before you slide into your golden years. Doesn't matter. You're just shifting pieces around a board, patiently moving toward your endgame while the rest of the world holds its breath and awaits your next move.

Lyndsay

"So he comes home last night with this wrapped box," Moira said as she plucked a brownie—her third—off the plate. "He hands it to me, and he's all puffed up, proud as can be—"

"Aren't they always?" Beth cut in. "As if they deserve a medal for being thoughtful."

"Not a medal," Lyndsay said. "A blow job."

The other women snickered their agreement. Moira settled back in her chair and waited for silence, obviously miffed at the interruption of her story. That was enough. The others fell in line like trained show dogs.

As they fawned over their queen, Lyndsay bit into her brownie. The first rush of chocolatey sweetness filled her mouth. As it settled, the aftertaste came through, the faintly bitter chemical taste of store-bought baked goods. *Revenge is like that,* she thought. Everyone called it sweet, and it was, at first nibble. Then the aftertaste kicked in.

"—picked up the box, and it's too heavy to be jewelry," Moira was saying. "So I think maybe Ted's trying to be cute again, putting something in the box to make it seem heavy. Then I open it up, and you know what I find?"

Lyndsay took another bite of her brownie. *Why the hell am I eating this thing?* she thought, even as she chewed it. *It tastes like crap, and I'll pay for the extra calories, but I keep on eating. Just like revenge.*

"It was a gun," Moira said.

Tina screwed up her nose. "Are you serious? What for?"

"To protect myself, in case this Helter Skelter killer comes calling."

The women let out a collective burst of laughter, and eased back in their chairs, all shaking their heads. Even Lyndsay, who rarely shared any opinions in common with her neighbors, had to agree. The thought of needing protection was preposterous.

They were safe here, and their husbands paid very well to keep them safe in their security-system–armed homes, in their ultraexclusive gated community, in this remote suburb, isolated from Seattle, and its big-city evils. Some of their husbands had guns, of course, but the women didn't need them. They lived here, socialized here, sent their children to school here, secure within the gilded cage of Oakland Hills, venturing out only to shop, and even then traveling in packs.

Ted was an idiot. But Lyndsay could've told Moira that. Once she *dreamed* of telling her that. Just after Lyndsay and her husband had moved in, when Moira had snubbed her—never ignoring her, of course, that would be rude—but making her feel welcome while sniping to the others behind her back. Then she would've loved to say, "Hey Moira, your husband is an idiot. . . . Believe me, I know. I've been fucking the loser." As revenge went, though, sleeping with Ted had proven as deceiving as the brownie—much less satisfying in reality than it had looked on the plate.

Lyndsay popped another chunk in her mouth and chewed so hard she heard her teeth grinding. As the other women nattered on about the Helter Skelter killer, Lyndsay gnawed through a second brownie.

By the time she finished, her gut was in full revolt, and she wanted to beg off staying to watch CNN, and find out whether this killer would meet his noon deadline. Who cared? She had bigger things to worry about—namely how to keep Ted from telling her husband, as he threatened to do if she broke it off.

But to leave midway through the killer-watch was out of the question. Lyndsay had fought for her place here, and she wasn't doing anything to jeopardize it now. She needed to think, so she offered to start a fresh batch of coffee for Moira while the others retired to the entertainment room.

Once they were gone, Lyndsay gathered the cups and plates and put them on the counter. Maybe if she gave Ted a taste of his own medicine, and threatened to tell Moira...

Lyndsay snorted. Like he'd care. Like *she'd* care. Moira would probably be glad—one more dull wifely function delegated.

Lyndsay picked up the bag of coffee beans and turned to the coffeemaker. Holy shit—was that a coffeemaker? It had more switches and digital readouts than a space shuttle. Was this where the beans went in? Did the machine grind them in there?

If she lost Austin— No, she couldn't, *wouldn't* lose him. Maybe if she diverted Ted, found him a new lover. That was an idea. She could—

Liquid splashed as she poured the beans in. She peered down to see them floating in the water reservoir and cursed.

As she studied the space-age coffeemaker, something hit her in the back, hard enough to slam her against the counter. In the stainless steel side of the coffeemaker, she saw the reflection of a man behind her. An older man.

The distorted image looked like Blake, Tina's husband, but when she saw her own reflection, blood flower blossoming on the chest of her white sweater, Lyndsay knew it wasn't Blake. *Jesus Christ,* she thought. *I do not have time for this.* Then her knees buckled, and she hit the floor.

* * *

He looked down at the body at his feet. A young blond woman, cover-model gorgeous with centerfold tits. Amazing what money could buy. He wondered whether two hundred million would buy him one of those, and almost laughed. Two hundred million would buy him one for every day of the week...and extras for Saturday night. Too bad he'd never see the money.

He could hear the women chattering in the other room. So close and yet, at the first click of an Italian leather pump, he could be through the pantry, and out the back door. Unbelievable how easy it had been, even in a place that sold security as a way of life. Disappointingly easy.

He took two things from his pocket—a page from *Helter Skelter* and a dollar bill. He bent to put the page in her pocket, then stopped. Did he really need this calling card anymore? No. The Feds would know it was him—the act itself was proof enough. So he kept the page, but dropped the dollar bill, letting it flutter down onto the dead woman.

THIRTY-ONE

When we reached Little Joe's retirement home, Jack parked in the side lot; the one reserved for overflow guests. The regular lot was almost empty, so I didn't know why he chose that one.

To get to the place, we had to take a path through a patch of woods. Jack was at the trail's edge before he realized I wasn't behind him. He waved—as if I might not have understood that I was supposed to follow. When I didn't move, he walked back to the car. I rolled down my window.

"I like my life, Jack. Sure, it's a little screwy, but I'd really like to keep it for a while longer. Going in there, after the last time, doesn't seem the best way to prolong my term on this earth."

He opened the car door. I didn't move.

"You trust me?" he asked.

"Sure, but—"

"Then get out. I'm going to fix this."

"That fix doesn't involve prematurely ending the life of a Mafia don's brother, does it?"

A look. That's all he gave me. Just a look.

I threw up my hands. "Well, I had to ask. The last time I had a run-in with Little Joe, it ended with body disposal, and I like to be prepared."

He headed for the home.

There were three people at the front desk—a nurse, a receptionist and a young man who looked like an orderly.

They were so engrossed in their conversation they didn't notice us come in.

"—think he'll do it?" the receptionist was saying.

"Of course he will. He has to. Otherwise, no one will take him seriously." The orderly glanced at the wall clock. "Right now, someone, somewhere is enjoying the last few minutes of their life."

"Someone, somewhere is always enjoying the last few minutes of their life," the nurse snapped. "Hundreds of people will die in the next ten minutes, and if we start panicking over that one, we're giving him exactly what he wants."

The Helter Skelter killer. What else would they be talking about as the clock hands hit noon, reminding me that no matter how close we got, it would be too late for at least one person.

My throat tightened, breath catching, as if the oxygen content in the room had plummeted. Jack's hand tightened on my elbow.

"We're here to see Joe Nikolaev," he said with a standard midwestern accent.

The receptionist and the orderly both glared at him for disrupting their death watch. As the nurse turned off the radio, the orderly looked from Jack to me, then scurried off, probably to find another radio. Jack's gaze followed him.

"I'm sorry," the nurse said. "I'm afraid Mr. Nikolaev is no longer with us."

"No longer—?" I began. "Oh—oh, geez. We hadn't heard. When did it happen?"

The receptionist sputtered a laugh, covering her mouth as she did.

The nurse glared at her, then turned a wry smile on us.

"I'm sorry. We need to be careful what we say in this business, don't we? I meant he's not here anymore—at the home. His family took him out yesterday." She lowered her voice. "He didn't seem too happy about it."

"Caused a real uproar," the receptionist muttered.

"Transition can be difficult at that age," the nurse said. "I'm sure Joseph will adjust."

That hitman Joe sent after me had said Boris Nikolaev had had enough of his brother's screw-ups, the same thing Evelyn had heard. If Boris had found out about Joe's slip of the tongue—and the failed hit—well, then the only thing Little Joe would be adjusting to was life at the bottom of a six-foot hole.

"Thank you," I said. "We'll try to stop by his brother's—"

"Toilet," Jack said.

I glanced at him, brows raised.

He continued. "Before we leave, you needed the toilet. Don't forget, because we have a long drive." He turned to the nurse. "Is there one she can...?"

"Right down this hall. Third door on the right."

Jack put his hand against my back. "I should use it, too."

When we were out of earshot, I whispered, "I'm assuming you want to search his room. Do you know which it is?"

He tugged a tissue from his pocket and used it to open the bathroom door, then peeked inside. "Go in. Open the window. Then cough."

"Cough?"

He propelled me through the doorway. "Glove up. And don't lock."

The door closed. I looked at the lace-curtained window. Better follow instructions, and get the explanation later—if he cared to give it.

I snapped on latex gloves and cracked open the window. On the other side was a screen. I suspected bathroom air quality wasn't the reason he wanted this open, so I lifted the sash as far as it would go, unlatched the screen and pulled it inside. Then I coughed. After a moment's pause, the door eased open and Jack slid in. I grasped the window edge, preparing to climb out, but he waved me back.

He moved to the window, then crouched to look out under the privacy glass. A sweep of the yard, then he climbed through. I waited for the all-clear and followed.

A fifteen-foot dash to a shed, and we ducked behind it.

"The orderly," he said.

And that's all he said, as if it should explain everything. After a few moments of thought, I understood, but sometimes I wished he'd give my brain a break and let his tongue do some of the work instead.

I remembered the look the young man had given us before hurrying off. If Boris Nikolaev knew Little Joe had let something slip about that old hit on the senator, and he knew we'd terminated Joe's hired gun, he'd know there was a good chance we'd come back. Easiest way to make sure he found out about it would be to bribe the orderly for a tip-off. Yet, by the time Boris got someone here, we'd be long gone . . . which meant he probably had someone nearby or even on the property, waiting for a call.

Less than two minutes after we got behind the shed, the rattle of the bathroom door sounded through the open window. A figure appeared at the bathroom window. He ducked and peered out. I squinted to get a better look, but all I could see was his mouth, the rest of his face hidden under the bill of his ball cap.

The man scanned the lawn, then disappeared.

I glanced at Jack. He motioned for me to wait. The front

screen door slapped shut. A stocky figure in a Cleveland Indians jacket hurried off the porch and cut across the lawn, then headed into the trees, toward the lot where we'd parked.

Jack grabbed my elbow and pulled me along at a jog. We looped behind the home and straight for the wooded path the thug had taken. Now, it would seem to me that the time to make a run for the car was *before* Nikolaev's thug got to it, but maybe that was just too simple for Jack.

We skirted the wooded side field. Before we reached the path, Jack stopped. He surveyed the semidark forest, then prodded me into a thick patch.

We had to move carefully. The chill of the last few days had fulfilled its promise with an early morning frost and here, out of the sun, the undergrowth was still covered with a thin sheen of it, crackling with every ill-placed footstep. The thug didn't bother with stealth, and we could hear him as easily as if he had maracas strapped to his legs.

"Wait." Jack turned to go, then glanced back. "Duck down. Stay hidden."

"And then what?"

"Don't let him see you."

He must have seen me already, but I knew Jack's order had nothing to do with being overprotective. As the female half of the duo, I made the better target. And if I didn't play "good victim"? I'd humiliate this thug, as Evelyn and I had done to Bert at the motel, and that would lead to the same result—we'd have to put the boots to him and intimidate him into giving up whatever information Jack hoped to gain.

While that thought didn't bother me, Jack was my boss, the senior partner. I didn't want to disrespect him by challenging him, not on this.

As for staying put, though, that was another thing. Jack might not be accustomed to working with a partner, might not understand a partner's duties, but I did.

I crept forward, watching my step. The undergrowth was thick here, and I nearly stepped on a shallow puddle coated with ice.

Jack had stopped halfway to the parking lot, waiting in the bushes. A few minutes later, the thug returned, walking at a brisk clip back to the home. As he passed, Jack swung out, silent as a wraith, came up behind him and barrel pointed at the base of the man's skull.

"Turn left and walk," Jack said.

The man gave a tight laugh. "Into the woods? So you won't have as far to drag my body? I ain't making it easier for you."

"I wanted you dead? Be there already. Got a message for Boris."

"And you want me to play delivery boy?"

"You don't want to? Fine. I'll use the next guy."

The thug let Jack steer him into the woods—on the opposite side of the trail. I crept as close as I dared, waited until they had their backs to me, then darted across the open path.

Jack stopped in a clearing. I found a spot ten feet away, with a good sight line. He made the thug kneel, hands on the back of his head, then trained his gun on the guy's skull base. I aimed mine at the thug's right shoulder—a disabling shot.

"You said you got a message for Boris," the guy said.

"Houston."

"Wha—?" The thug tried to look over his shoulder at Jack, but a gun poke stopped him.

"That's the message. Houston."

"What the hell does that mean?"

"Boris knows. Tell him this is my business—"

"Who the hell are you?"

"Houston. He'll know. And my business? No concern of his. His business? No concern of mine. Got it?"

"Got what? That's not a message. It's code or some—"

"Repeat what I said."

The thug sighed but, with prompts, repeated it.

"Good," Jack said. "Boris comes after me again? I'll know you fucked up the message."

Jack let the thug go, then slipped into the woods to make sure he left.

The moment the guy's car pulled out, Jack looked directly at where I was hiding. I stepped out, expecting to be lambasted. But he only waved me toward the car.

"So is that the last we'll hear of Boris Nikolaev?" I asked as I climbed into the car.

"Better be," Jack muttered. "Damned inconvenient."

I shook my head and reached for the radio dial.

"Won't change anything, Nadia."

I looked at him, fingers on the knob.

"Find out now. Find out at Evelyn's. Won't change what happened." His gaze slanted my way. "You *know* what happened."

I nodded and turned on the radio.

THIRTY-TWO

As promised, the Helter Skelter killer had taken another victim at noon. As for whether he struck on the dot of noon, I'll leave it for the more dramatically inclined reporters to speculate. What I do know is that the victim was found less than ten minutes past noon, when her friends called into the kitchen to see why she was taking so long with the coffee. At the time of the murder, they'd been tuned to CNN waiting for news of what was unfolding a few steps away. The irony of that would be lost on no one. Of everyone waiting for news of the next victim, one person *became* that news.

The audacity of the killing was lost on no one, either. Not only had he struck in an occupied home, but one with a state-of-the-art security system, in one of the most supposedly secure gated communities. The message was clear— if I can get to her, I can get to anyone.

That promoted exactly the kind of paranoia that gated communities preyed on. I'd pulled a hit in a "high security" private club, in the middle of a golf tournament, and let me tell you, I've done harder—much harder.

But of course the media was already playing it up, making it sound like he was some kind of phantom who'd slipped past not only the armed guards at the gate, but a fully armed home security system.

Fully armed, my ass. How many people rearm their system when they're indoors entertaining, with friends coming and going? My guess was that the homeowner had reactivated it when she'd learned of the murder. If the system had been off, the Feds would figure it out, but I doubted *that* tidbit would make it to the six o'clock news.

Jack needed to call Quinn before we got back to Evelyn's, so he stopped at a Cracker Barrel near the state border. I went in to grab coffees to go, then got sidetracked by the display of old-fashioned candy. When I returned to the car and found Jack wasn't back, I put the coffees and candy inside and went to look for him.

Jack was twenty feet away from the phone booth, standing by the edge of the parking lot. When I walked up behind him, he looked back at me, his eyes unreadable behind his dark shades.

"What happened?"

He looked my way, but said nothing.

"Quinn told you something, and now you're trying to figure out whether—or how—you should tell me." My mind leapfrogged to the obvious. "Another killing. Already? He just finished—"

"Not yet."

I stopped. "Not yet what? The killing, you mean? He hasn't done it yet, but he's announced it already? Come on, Jack, don't make me drag it out of you two words at a time, or I swear—"

He motioned for me to sit with him on the edge of the restaurant porch, and started talking.

The FBI knew where the killer was going to strike next. While it would have been nice to claim that they'd deduced this through painstaking hours of statistical and behavioral analysis, the truth was far more disturbing. They knew because he'd told them.

According to Quinn, the FBI agent leading the investi-

gation, Martin Dubois, had received his own letter from
the killer. In it, the killer had promised to take a victim tonight, at a recently reopened historic opera house in Chicago. He didn't dare them to stop him, but the challenge
was obvious.

"So what you were debating was whether to tell me in
advance or not, wasn't it? Quite possibly our best chance
to catch this guy, and you don't think we should bother
showing up."

A kernel of rage rolled around my gut. I could feel Jack's
gaze on me, studying me, appraising my reaction. I closed
my eyes to slits, then took a deep breath. Took another.
Opened my eyes and looked at him.

"Could be a setup," he said, words coming slow, deliberate, almost as if guiding me back on track.

I considered that. Saw the truth in his words. "Playing
with the Feds. Leading them on a goose chase."

"Playing, yeah. Goose chase . . . ?" He pulled off his sunglasses. "Helluva challenge."

"Killing someone in a busy public place—after you've
given the FBI a heads-up? That's not just a challenge. What
better way to prove that no one is safe than to tell the Feds
where you'll strike next, and still pull it off."

"Yeah."

"So you think he's really going to do it?"

A long pause now, really thinking it through. Then a
nod. "Yeah. Think he's gonna try."

My nails dug into my palms as I kept my voice steady,
dispassionate. "Are we going to be there to stop him?"

"Gonna try."

* * *

Jack called Quinn back. Quinn and Felix had already planned to be there—not that Jack had been about to tell me that before we made up our own minds. As he slid into the car, I stared out the window. After a few minutes of his driving and my window gazing, he said, "You okay?"

"Just thinking of something and feeling stupid."

"'Bout what?"

"Quinn." When he didn't answer, I glanced his way. "When you told me he was a cop, I figured you meant 'cop,' like me—like I was. Street cop. Maybe detective, but definitely local or state. But now he tells us about this tip-off. A beat cop gets the drop on an unpublicized tip-off to the FBI? Right." I shook my head. "Quinn's a Fed, isn't he?"

"FBI?" He shrugged and started to say something that I knew from his expression would be, if not a complete disavowal, at least suitably neutral.

"FBI, CIA, DEA, NSA, or whatever other acronyms they have. You know what I mean. Federal level."

"That's a problem?"

I twisted in my seat. "Yes, it's a problem. You tell me he's a cop, and I figure he's from some little force in Podunk, Maine. *That* I'm comfortable with. But a federal agent?" I shook my head. "Yes, I know, federal, state, local, he's still a cop, so you didn't lie, but you knew what conclusion I'd draw, and you let me draw it."

"He's clean."

"Says who? Says you? A federal agent has federal jurisdiction. Federal contacts. Access to federal databases. I'm not comfortable—"

"Nadia? His story's solid. He's not a plant. Not a threat, either. He flips? I flip harder."

I remembered what Quinn had said earlier, that Jack had more on him than vice versa.

"Not a threat," Jack repeated. "He was? Wouldn't have let you meet him."

I leaned back in my seat. "I know. It's just...federal makes me nervous. It's a cop thing. On the streets, you don't deal with them that much. Every now and then, we'd have the horsemen ride in, scoop up a case—"

"Horsemen?"

"RCMP." When his look didn't change, I said, "Mounties. Mounted police."

"They still ride horses?"

"Only in parades...and tourist photo ops."

"The red uniforms?"

"It's suits these days. Disney owns the uniform copyright anyway. I once asked a Mountie whether his dress uniform tag said 'Property of Walt Disney.' He wouldn't tell me, but he did offer to let me take his off and check for myself."

Jack shook his head. He pulled into the slow lane, and set his cruise control two miles over the speed limit. Then he looked at me. "About Quinn. Makes you nervous? Best thing you can do? Keep your distance."

"You mean stick to business. No socializing, no chatting, no jogging together..."

"Right."

I shook my head. "You said he was clean, and I trust you." I glanced at him. "You did say that, didn't you?"

A hesitation, then a soft exhale. "Yeah."

We'd agreed to meet Felix and Quinn at a baseball diamond in Chicago. When we arrived, Quinn and Felix were right inside the gates. I saw Quinn first, a tray of hot dogs and sodas in his hands, wearing worn jeans and a T-shirt that pulled tight over his broad shoulders. His gaze lighted on me, and he grinned. My stomach did a little flip. I blamed it on the smell of the food.

"Got you a hot dog," Quinn said, thrusting it out like a bouquet of roses.

Beside me, Jack made a noise, half grunt, half sigh.

"Don't glower, Jack," Quinn said. "Got you one, too."

I took mine with thanks. Jack just looked at the tray.

Felix walked up behind Quinn and raised a half-eaten hot dog. "I can assure you, Jack, they're quite fine. He isn't trying to poison us...yet."

"One could argue that all hot dogs are poisonous," I said, as we fell into step and headed for the bleachers. "If you eat enough, they have to be at least as lethal as arsenic."

"Shhh," Quinn said. Then he held out the tray again. "Jack, have another."

"Someone's in a good mood," Jack said.

"Someone's in a fucking fantastic mood. We are finally going to nail this bastard."

Quinn grinned at me, and I felt an answering rush of excitement. I was finally on my target's trail, so close I could narrow my eyes and visualize him in my scope.

When I smiled back, Quinn's grin grew and he swung out of the way to let me head into the bleacher row. He tried to follow, but Jack cut in front of him. Quinn waited for Jack to pass, then darted into the aisle below, passed us and vaulted over the bench to sit on my other side, still grinning, looking like a kid who's outwitted the teacher. I couldn't help laughing.

"You think he'll show?" I said, as we settled into the bleacher seats.

"I sure hope so, because if he does, he's toast." His eyes

gleamed. "This bastard has taken his last victim. We're bringing him down and I cannot fucking wait to see it."

"Got that impression," Jack said.

Quinn only rolled his eyes, enthusiasm undimmed, so stoked he was practically bouncing in his seat. As I watched him, I felt a pang of envy. Quinn felt no need to emulate Jack and treat this with quiet professionalism. I could only sit there, basking in his fire, struggling to remember what it felt like to be that open, that unguarded.

Felix pitched his trash into the distant can with perfect aim. "I know you're hoping to be the one to snap on the cuffs, Quinn, but remember, there's a good chance it won't be us."

"That's fine. Sure, I'd love to take him down myself, but if it's the Feds or the locals, good enough."

"He'll be caught," I said. "And that's all that matters."

As he nodded, our eyes met.

"Great idea," Jack said. "But a plan would help."

"Already got one." Quinn pulled two pieces of cardboard from his pocket, then fanned them, and leaned closer to me. "If you don't have any plans for this evening, I thought maybe we could take in an opera. I hear it's going to be a good show. Chock-full of danger, adventure, mystery . . . and, if you want, maybe we could even see the opera afterward."

I smiled and plucked the tickets from his hand. "So what are these? Forgeries?"

"Uh-uh. With tonight's security, it's the real deal or none at all. The theater's only about two-thirds full, so I nabbed these easily enough." He glanced around me. "We can get more for you guys if you want."

"Really?" Felix said. "You see, Jack, we aren't invisible over here after all."

"Hey, I included you two. You can come in if you want, but I figured two in and two out would be better. It makes sense for Dee to be one of the two going in and, well, if she's going to have a date, I'm the natural choice."

Felix arched a brow. "You are?"

"You know, the age thing," Quinn said.

"Jack and I will pretend we didn't hear that."

"You're forgetting something," Jack said. "Partners. Dee—"

"—is your partner," Quinn said. "But—"

"She's worked with me. Not *does* work. *Has* worked."

I folded my napkin and tucked it into my empty hot-dog box. "Jack's right. I know his style and with something this big, I need a familiar partner. I do agree two of us should go in, so if Jack would rather not, then I guess you and Felix—"

"Nah," Jack said. "Two guys? People still notice."

"A man and a woman would be less conspicuous, par-ticularly if we pick up fake wedding rings. As for the age difference, at these events, it's pretty much a given. Older guys, second wives—" I caught Jack's look. "Not that you're *older*. Well, older than me, but—" I checked my watch. "We'd better move if we're going to do this. I'll need a dress."

"Nice save," Felix said. "And, yes, you will need a gown. This opera house evidently has a black-tie dress code for these opening weeks. Jack will require a tuxedo."

Quinn snorted a laugh, but Felix cut him off before he could say anything. "There's a shopping plaza nearby with suitable shops for formal wear. I'm sure Jack can select his own, but if Dee requires any assistance—or merely a sec-ond opinion—I can help. I have some experience shop-ping there for formal gowns."

Quinn looked at Felix, brows raised.

"I find women's wear an excellent disguise," Felix said. "Particularly evening dresses."

Quinn kept staring.

"I have had lady friends in Chicago, Quinn, and have escorted them to the symphony and such, occasions for which women often appreciate new evening wear."

"Oh."

Felix shook his head. "While poor Quinn works that out, may I suggest we move straight to shopping? That should give him time to recover, then retrieve the blueprints and security details."

We finished our hot dogs, and left.

THIRTY-THREE

Jack checked us into a motel on the outskirts of Chicago. Felix and Quinn would presumably find one elsewhere. I could tell Jack wasn't comfortable with the prolonged time together, but there was little we could do under the circumstances except keep our guard up and remember that there was no reason for anyone to be tracking *us*. Had this been a job, that would be a concern, but here, attention was focused on our target, and no one was looking for us.

The opera curtain was ninety minutes away, and the doors would open in forty-five. I was ready to go, dress on and hair fixed in the best updo I could manage with bobby pins and a hand mirror. Jack had showered and shaved, but still had to throw on his tux, so I left him to do that and went outside to find Quinn.

It was dark already, and the motel poorly lit, but I located him on the other side of the lot, leaning against the fence, watching the highway traffic whiz past. He'd changed into black jeans and a black hooded sweatshirt—dark enough for recon work outside the theater, but common enough street wear not to attract attention. He'd also switched to dark hair, and from his profile I could see that he'd added a beard and mustache. Guess he wanted a little more of a disguise in case he bumped into someone from the FBI task force. Further proof that I was right about him being a Fed. FBI or DEA was my guess. A field agent—he didn't strike me as a desk jockey—but he obviously still had enough clout to get all the info we needed without raising eyebrows. And the clout to get the time off.

As my heels clicked across the asphalt, Quinn turned. He stared. Then he stared some more.

I laughed. "Don't tell me I look *that* different."

"No, just...wow."

I blushed.

"You look good as a redhead," he said. "That must be closer to your natural—I mean, it suits you."

"Thanks."

The wig was redder than my normal hair—and longer. The dress was mint-ice-cream green. The tag had called it sea-foam or something like that, but it reminded me of mint ice cream. Felix and I had debated the merits of black over colors and, while black would doubtless be the shade of choice and I'd have blended into the crowd more by wearing it, it would also increase the chances that Jack would lose me.

So we'd picked this—a simple, formal dress in pale green, nothing revealing or flashy...although by the way Quinn was staring, you'd have thought it was fire-engine red with a neckline plunging to meet the hem. It'd been a while since a guy had looked at me like that. Jack had grunted something when I'd put it on, which could have been "nice," but could just as easily have been gas.

"Is Jack really wearing a tux?"

"He will be soon."

Quinn laughed. "This I gotta see."

I grinned. "Should be interesting. Thank God Felix is there to help, because I suspect Jack doesn't have a clue how to do the tie."

I don't think he heard any of that. As soon as I grinned, his gaze locked with mine.

"You have a great smile," he said, then blinked. "I mean,

you look great when you smile. Not that you look bad when—"

Before he could muddle his way out, a figure appeared from the shadows. Quinn looked over at Jack and, if he'd been about to make some jab, he stopped. It was my turn to stare. Jack didn't look nearly as uncomfortable in a tux as I'd expected. It even suited him, giving the harsh angles of his face an air that was less rough and tumble and more sharp and sophisticated, but still slightly dangerous. He had foregone a wig in favor of putting more gray in his black. Bright blue contacts added a splash of color. He looked fine...better than fine. Of course, I wasn't telling him that—not when my outfit had only warranted a grunt.

Jack turned to me. "You forgot these."

He handed me a pair of gloves—not latex, but green silk. One advantage to formal dress—it gave you an excuse for gloving up and hiding fingerprints. For himself, he would use a form of liquid latex. It worked pretty well, but was far from perfect, so whenever possible, I'd be opening doors tonight.

As I pulled on my gloves, Felix joined us. I had to do a double take to recognize him. That afternoon, he'd looked as I remembered him from Indiana—tall, thin and ginger-haired, fussy, professorial. The man in front of me looked like he was ready to join the senior's mall walk—gray-haired, pasty-faced, slightly stooped and pot bellied, dressed in a navy jogging suit and new sneakers. An old man trying to prolong his life with some much needed exercise.

"We all set then?" Quinn said. "Any last-minute obstacles need tackling?"

"Besides the lack of a suitable method of communication?" Felix said.

"Yeah, I know it'll be a bugger without it, but even Jack

agrees. The Feds may be monitoring frequencies, and there isn't a radio or phone I'd take the chance with."

"I know of one," Felix said. "Unfortunately, no courier could deliver it from Moscow in time. However, we may wish to consider splurging if we fail to roust this man tonight."

Quinn's face darkened. "It ends tonight. Between us and the Feds, he doesn't stand a chance. A few hours from now we'll be celebrating, not ordering extra equipment." A sudden smile and he turned my way. "Speaking of celebrating, I know a place, has the best suds and deep dish in town."

"Think I'd be overdressed?"

"Definitely, but you won't hear me complaining." He glanced over my head. "How about it, guys? Up for a little postassignment partying?"

Felix arched a brow. "Oh, were we included in that invitation?"

"Of course. Not like Jack would let me take Dee without him." His gaze shot back to mine. "Is it a date then? Say... midnight?"

"Only if I can buy the first round."

"Haven't caught him yet," Jack said. "Don't get cocky."

I looked at him, my smile fading. "It isn't cockiness, Jack. It's confidence... and a generous helping of hope."

He nodded and, for a minute, we all stood in silence. Then Jack jangled his keys.

"Time to go."

A half hour later we were rounding the corner, the opera house in sight, a crowd at the doors, moving slowly. Jack eyed the crowd, then motioned me aside and took out a cigarette. Earlier he'd grumbled about the habit, calling it the worst a hitman could have. I wasn't sure I agreed. It certainly came in handy—a convenient excuse for standing around outside without drawing attention to yourself. Unlike that hitman at the jail, Jack could pull it off. No one watching would mistake him for an amateur smoker.

He lit the cigarette, took a drag, then said, "We okay?"

"Sure. Aren't we?" I stepped to the side, out of the path of an oncoming foursome. "Is something bothering you? Something we missed?"

"Nah."

His gaze slanted away, as if this wasn't what he'd meant and he was trying to reword it. After another drag, he looked at me.

"*You* okay?"

"Me? Sure. Not having second thoughts about getting involved, if that's what you mean."

A small shake of his head, coupled with a look that said he'd never make that mistake. A third drag, then he passed the cigarette to me. He let me inhale, exhale, and waved it off when I offered it back.

"Might not get him," he said, voice low, though no one was around. "Gonna try. Sure as hell gonna try. But... might not."

"Like Quinn and I said, we don't care who does the take-down, us or the Feds. Yes, I'd rather be the one..." I paused. "You mean— This is about that talk outside the motel— Quinn and I going on about getting this guy, making our victory celebration plans." I felt my gaze harden. Blinked it away. "You're worried that I'll get cocky. Overexcited. Over-eager. That I'll screw up."

"'Course not. You're a pro—"

"Quinn and I were just blowing off steam, okay? Some of us need to do that. And, yes, I suppose *showing* it is un-professional—"

"I never said—"

"I know we might not get this guy tonight. I know maybe no one will. And I know that if we stand a hope in hell of success, it's going to take calm, controlled, focused effort. There's no room for grandstanding, for cowboy bullshit—"

"That's not—"

"I'm ready, okay? If you think I'm not, then just say so, and I'll walk away now."

He looked out over the road and, for one long minute, I was certain he was going to call me on that, tell me to walk away. Could I do it? My heart hammered at the thought, fingers trembling around the cigarette.

"Line's going down," he said, waving at the crowd. "Better get inside."

As we climbed the steps to the new opera house, we were caught in a stream of high-school students—a band or music class—led by a woman talking excitedly about the production to come. I knew why the police hadn't issued a warning and yet... well, I couldn't shake the urge to grab that teacher and tell her to get the kids out of here, get as far away as they could.

The truth was, as cruel as it seemed by *not* letting people know of the threat, the police were doing their best to end that threat... for everyone else. This was their first chance—an excellent chance—of catching the Helter Skelter killer.

If they'd refused to play along and canceled the show, any criminal psychologist could predict the killer's next move. Ruin his game, and he'd do something worse, as payback. Here, they could monitor every variable and ensure the guests' safety.

Once inside the doors, we found ourselves funneled into a line through a portable metal detector and a wand-wielding guard.

"My bag?" sniffed a matron at the front. "No, you may *not* paw through my bag, young man."

The queue ground to a halt.

"Oh, come on," I muttered. "They're not worried about the flask you stuffed in there."

Jack craned his neck to see around the mob. After a moment, a guard took the woman and her party aside to let others pass though.

"Unbelievable," huffed a diamond-dripping woman about my age. "It's opera, not a rap concert."

"There's a whole industry getting rich off this terrorism nonsense," said the gray-haired man at her side. "Did I tell you what happened on my flight to Tokyo last week? They body-searched first-class passengers. First-class! As if any of us..."

He continued to bitch about the injustices visited on the upper classes, but I turned my attention to mentally reexamining Quinn's blueprints of the opera house. One front entrance, one staff entrance, one delivery door and three fire exits. Easy to guard and, according to Quinn, guarded they were, with no one allowed in or out any way but the front door tonight.

According to Quinn's source, even staff had needed to pass through those main doors earlier, with the metal detectors and bag search. That would likely be the ruse the killer would use—pretending to work here. With a new business, employees would still be accustomed to seeing unfamiliar faces and wouldn't question one more. If that was his plan, he'd have found himself out of luck. There had been a manager at the door, ticking off names, and if a new or replacement worker showed up, the Feds had turned him away.

We made it through security without incident. We weren't armed. Too risky. The Feds would probably have wand-waving agents inside, too. Not having a gun made me uneasy, but I knew the killer wouldn't have risked bringing one in, either. He wouldn't need to. A real pro doesn't need a traditional weapon to do his job.

Once inside, we veered left. Quinn said the Feds were setting up base in a storage room behind the bar, so that's where I wanted to go first. Get an insider's feel for security precautions, and we'd see where the holes were.

It took some wrangling, but we found a spot where we could, with the help of listening devices provided by Felix, hear what was going on in the FBI's control room. We arrived just as they received a call from the front door, about a woman refusing to let them search or scan her evening bag. It could have been the same woman we'd seen, but I suspected they'd been dealing with similar complaints all night.

"I don't care if she's the wife of the goddamned president," a man boomed. "No one gets in without a search and if you can't handle that, then find someone who can." He signed off. "Fucking unbelievable. Old bats thinking we're going to swipe twenty bucks from their handbags, delivery men too lazy to carry boxes to the front door, but if something goes wrong, they'll be the first to raise a stink, calling the papers to complain that we weren't doing our jobs."

"Nothing's going to go wrong, Marty. A woman couldn't get groped in here without us knowing about it."

"Yeah, but if she does, I'll have ten deadweight rookies in here asking me what they should do about it, while that fucker has free run of the building."

The door creaked open.

"What the hell are you two doing back—?" the first man boomed.

"There's been a seat mix-up," a woman said. "An elderly couple is in ours—"

"Then tell them to move!"

The women continued in the same calm voice. "The usher feels it would be less intrusive if we took the seats beside them—"

"I told you where to sit! We picked out the sight lines to cover every—"

"We've checked the sight lines and they'd be the same."

"I don't care. You sit where I assigned you, and if there's someone there, then you move them. Why the hell you couldn't figure that out without bothering me—"

"Because you asked to be apprised—personally apprised—of all complications."

"This isn't a complication, Chin. It's ass-wiping, and you can damned well do your own."

The door clicked shut. I looked over to see a young couple in formal wear heading back to the foyer.

"Idiot," the woman muttered.

"He's under a lot of pressure," her partner said. "He saw what happened to McMillan, and he knows if this goes bad, he's next."

"Stress, my ass. Dubois is in his element. He wants to be in control so he can take full credit if he pulls this off. But if he doesn't, you can bet your ass it'll be everyone else's fault."

Jack touched my arm and motioned that we should

move on. I had to agree. All we'd accomplished here was overhearing Martin Dubois, the agent now leading the investigation after the last one had been "reassigned." The guy might be a jerk, but he seemed to be doing the job.

As we walked through the lobby, I hoped that the undercover agents wouldn't be as obvious to the killer as they were to me. The janitor emptying a quarter-filled trash can. The extra barman, who did nothing but wipe the counter and polish glasses. The couple lingering in a T-intersection, talking but never looking at each other. Still, if the killer did "make" them, maybe that wasn't such a bad thing. He might realize he didn't have a chance.

Next, Jack and I scoped out all the potential blind spots—places *we'd* pick for a hit. We started with the bathrooms. The moment I walked in, I knew it was covered, by an agent playing washroom attendant, pumping lotion onto a matron's hands and apologizing when the squirt dribbled onto her shoe instead. Oh, the joys of undercover work.

Despite the on-duty agent, I gave the bathroom a once-over, seeing it with a hitman's eye. No closets, no windows, the dividers too low to crawl under, the stalls too small to hide in. By the time I finished using the toilet, I was satisfied enough to strike this "blind spot" off my list.

I scrubbed my hands, my mind fully aware of my surroundings yet skipping forward, planning my next move.

He was here. My target. In this very building.

I was on the trail, his scent in the wind. The real thing. Out there. Waiting for me.

And while maybe that should have had me as puppy-dog excited as Jack seemed to think I was, I felt calm. Perfect control, the kind I'd never felt off the shooting range. Everything in focus. Sharp focus—smelling the soap on my hands, hearing the squeak of shoes on the linoleum, seeing the flash of red as the woman beside me painted on fresh lipstick.

I looked at myself in the mirror. No signs of stress—no beading sweat, no parted lips, breathing hard. Just a woman enjoying her evening out and looking forward to the pleasure yet to come.

I turned to the agent at the door, passed her a smile and a tip, and walked out.

Grace

In the movies, things were always so much more dramatic. Put this scene in some Hollywood blockbuster, and there would be a deviously elaborate solution to the challenge he faced, maybe explosives hidden inside a seat, rigged to detonate when the soprano hit her first C. In real life, sometimes even the most difficult situations had solutions that were almost laughably simple.

How would he kill someone in an opera house, with only one way in or out, patrolled by dozens of top FBI agents, all devoted to stopping him? By hiding behind a door. His only tool? A pair of panty hose. Not worn on his head, like some cinematic killer. In his world, disguising yourself from your target was ludicrous—if he lived long enough to talk, then you damned well deserved to get caught.

One glance at the opera house blueprints and he'd known where he'd hide—behind the door in the one room the Feds couldn't be inside: the handicapped washroom.

He'd been preparing for tonight since he'd first leaked the Moreland arrest. He'd bought the tickets before making the call—two, knowing they'd later search for single-ticket purchases. He'd walked right in the front door, among a group of retirees, even talking to them, as if he was just another old man out for a night of culture. Then straight to the bathroom. He'd limped in with his cane—for the benefit of anyone who saw his destination. Once inside, he'd had to tamper with the lock, to be sure he could relock it as he left. Then he'd positioned himself, turned out the light, leaned over . . . and unlocked the door to await the next visitor.

Laughably simple.

Grace steered her wheelchair around a group of middle-aged matrons who looked as if they'd rather be anywhere but here. A social-duty event. Grace remembered those, dragging David along, kicking and screaming, telling him he couldn't ignore an invitation from the CEO, even if it was the company's twentieth outing to *The Nutcracker*.

She hit a wrinkle in the carpet and the wheelchair veered, heading straight for a young woman in a green dress. The woman's companion tried to pull her out of the way, but she grabbed the wheelchair handles, stopping and steadying it.

"Thank you," Grace said. "Still haven't gotten the hang of this darned thing, I'm afraid."

"And I'm not much help," said a voice behind her.

She twisted to see Cliff hobbling over on his cane, two champagne flutes precariously clutched in his free hand. The young woman took the glasses from him. She handed one to Grace, then waited until Cliff was settled before passing back his.

Cliff thanked her, then chuckled. "We make a fine pair, don't we?"

"Do you need any help getting to your seats?" the woman asked. "I don't see a ramp."

Her companion's gaze slid to the side, as if anxious to move on.

"Thank you, dear, but we'll be fine," Grace said. "This place is supposed to be accessible, so they must have a ramp or elevator hidden somewhere."

"Enjoy the show, then," the woman said, and let her companion lead her away.

Cliff found a quiet corner and they sipped their champagne and watched the "preshow show," the parade of patrons, from the well dressed, to the badly dressed, to the barely dressed. Cliff's murmured commentary kept her in giggles, as always. For fifty years, no one had ever made her laugh like Cliff could. Her husband, David, had been a wonderful man, and she'd loved him dearly—still missed him every day—but when she needed a good chuckle, she'd always looked to Cliff, David's childhood friend and business partner.

There'd never been anything between them while their spouses had been alive. Never considered it. But as the grief had faded, they'd realized that there might be more between them than the shared love of a good laugh. Their children and grandchildren had encouraged the relationship, happy to see the "old folks" bonding in companionship and mutual support. As for romance, well, there was bound to be some hand-holding, maybe the odd kiss on the cheek, but that was it. After all, both would see eighty in a year or two.

Had the kids known the truth…Grace smiled. With Cliff, she'd discovered a passion she'd thought lost to age. Even with his bum knee and her recent hip break, they managed just fine.

"What are you thinking, Gracie?" Cliff's voice was a growling purr as he leaned over her. "That glint in your eyes tells me I might want to skip the show."

She was opening her mouth to reply, when an usher passed, telling people it was fifteen minutes to curtain.

"Time for me to find a bathroom," Cliff said. "That

wine at dinner went right through me and this"—he lifted his empty champagne flute—"didn't help. How about you?"

Grace paused. She hated using public bathrooms with this wheelchair. Darned awkward. But there was no way she'd make it until she got home after the show, and the hallway congestion would be impossible at intermission. Better to get it over with now.

"So who goes first?" Cliff said as Grace wheeled into the bathroom hall. "Flip for it? Or..." He grinned down at her. "Maybe we should go together. I'm sure you could use a hand."

"If we do, will we get to our seats in ten minutes?"

"Probably not."

"Then save that thought for another time."

"Don't think I won't."

A sly smile up at him. "Good." Before he could answer, she waved at the bathrooms. "Seems we don't need to flip for first dibs after all. There are two of them. You know you're in a place that caters to us old fogies when..."

He smiled. "Too true. You take the first, then, my lady, and I'll meet you in a few minutes." He snuck a look her way and waggled his brows. "Sure you don't want some help?"

"Oh, I want it... but I don't want to be rolling into the auditorium after all the lights go out, or I'll break my neck."

He pushed open the door for her and she navigated inside.

He heard the knob turn and tensed, hose strung between his hands. The door opened, hiding him behind it. He pressed himself against the wall, waited until the door was swinging shut, then lunged.

He checked outside the door, then stepped out, letting it close—locked—behind him. As he strolled past the other handicapped washroom, the door opened and a woman in a wheelchair maneuvered her way out.

As Grace waited outside the bathroom, the usher came by, announcing five minutes to performance time. She glanced at the door. Yes, some things weren't as speedy at seventy-eight as they'd been at eighteen, and she hated to rush him, but she really didn't want to be navigating the aisles in the dark. She rapped on the door. When Cliff didn't answer, she rattled the handle.

"Cliff?" she said, as loud as she dared. "It's me."

Sill nothing. His hearing was fine, but she knocked louder, just in case. Her gut went cold. Why wasn't he answering? She tried to calm herself. Her mind offered up a dozen logical explanations, but her gut shut them down. Something had happened. A fall, a stroke, a heart attack—just like David.

"Can I help?" A middle-aged man paused in his sprint from the washroom to the front hall.

"My—someone's—I need a—an usher. Someone who can open the door. Quickly!"

He glided into the front foyer. People were still streaming in, and a few were heading out for that last-minute cigarette. He thought of joining them, but knew he couldn't.

Ushers were right there, watching each exit with disapproval, warning people the opera would begin soon. He might get all the way to the car before the Feds found the body—or he might not get down the steps. Safer to do what everyone else was doing and head into the auditorium.

As he walked, his gaze passed over the crowd and snagged on a face with a split-second of "Hey, don't I know...?" But when he zeroed in, that spark of recognition faded. The man was in his late forties, an investment banker type, with that lean, slightly hungry look. On his arm was a younger woman, maybe thirty. Typical, especially here, amid a sea of trophy wives, but this didn't look like your average "secretary turned spouse." He let his gaze linger and didn't worry about being obvious—he wasn't the only one looking. She wasn't a knockout. Just... pretty. A pretty redhead with a smile that turned heads, and sparked more than a smile or two in return.

She was chatting away animatedly, and her companion—he checked the man's finger and amended that—her *husband* was listening to every word, turning now and then to nod at her, the hard edges of his face softening each time he glanced over. The doting husband. The investment banker and the... kindergarten teacher, or maybe a pediatric nurse—she had the cheerful vibrancy of someone who worked with children. Probably had a few of them at home, tucked away with the sitter for the night.

A pang of remorse ran through him. If only *she* could have been his victim. Now, that would have been a coup. The world would be appalled by the death of the old man, but someone like this, they'd be outraged. They'd *demand* action. Parade her crying children on television, her grief-stricken husband, her shell-shocked co-workers and neigh-

bors, all telling the world what a kind, caring woman she'd
been, and the nation would demand that the killing be
stopped. As the regret over lost opportunity washed over
him, he passed the couple, so close he could have reached
out and—

The woman said something and her husband gave a low
chuckle. Hearing the sound, he froze in midstep, then
turned, slowly. That low laugh had triggered a connection
in his brain, and he realized he'd been too quick to dismiss
the gut-level recognition. He *did* know this man. Had
known him well, once upon a time. He told himself he was
wrong—he had to be—but his gut refused to believe it.

Still, the coincidence had to be just that—a coincidence.
But as he replayed the last minute in his head, he saw the
"banker's" gaze, in constant motion as he'd walked, watch-
ful, scanning, searching.

He glanced over his shoulder and found the couple in
the throng. The woman's grip tightened on the man's arm.
Their eyes met. Her head tilted to the left, toward a side
corridor, and they veered that way, still talking, as if they'd
been heading in that direction all along. He remembered
that Internet chatter about hitmen teaming up to find
him, and his gut tightened with an unexpected jolt of pain.
So it was true. And this was who it was.

"But not for long, Jack," he murmured. "Not for long."

By the time the usher arrived, a crowd had gathered at the
bathroom door. Two men argued over the best way to open
it—credit card or a hard shoulder shove.

Just open it! Grace wanted to scream, but the words
jammed in her throat and all she could think about was
Cliff's laugh and David, slumped on the garage floor, dead

from a heart attack, just minutes after he'd kissed her good-bye. A split second, that's all it took, and your world was shattered.

"Oh, God, please, please, please," she whispered under her breath.

The usher arrived—two ushers, and two security guards, and two men in suits, guns flashing under their coats as they loped down the hall. Security? Armed men? What about paramedics? Where was the paramedic? Was there a doctor here? There had to be a doctor in this crowd, all these people, standing around doing nothing while Cliff was—

A hand closed on her arm. She looked to see a red-haired young woman crouching beside her. The same woman she'd almost crashed into earlier. Her husband was off to the side, scanning the crowd. Looking for his wife? No, his gaze touched hers, but moved past.

"Cliff," Grace whispered. "He's—he was in the bathroom. I knocked. He's not—"

She couldn't finish. As the young woman tugged off her glove and took her hand, genuine anxiety flooded her eyes. The woman opened her mouth to say something, but just then, the bathroom door swung open. Through the crowd, Grace caught a glimpse of a fallen figure and a shock of white hair. She gasped, but the sound came out as a whimper.

She slammed her wheelchair forward, into the legs of the person standing in front of her. The young woman leapt to her feet and started clearing a path. Then someone grabbed her shoulder. She reached to push the hand off.

"Gracie?"

She stopped and, for a moment, couldn't move. Then slowly, she looked up. Cliff was leaning over her, face tight with concern.

"What happened?" he asked. Then he saw the figure in the bathroom. "Did someone—?"

She grabbed his hand and pulled him down to her in an embrace.

"I thought—" she began. "Where were you?"

"The bathroom was locked, so I used the main one. Helluva lineup, too."

She hugged him again, then looked for the young woman, to thank her, but she was gone.

THIRTY-FOUR

As Jack led me to the foyer, I breathed deeply, struggling to ground myself, but the air seemed so thin I could barely find oxygen. If there was a floor beneath my feet, I couldn't feel it. The blood roaring in my ears drowned out all sound around me.

I felt . . . nothing. Numb. Distantly aware of my feet stumbling on the carpet, Jack's fingers tight around my arm, my hip scraping against the wall, bumping along in a cushion of shock.

I'd failed. In the same building as the killer, less than a hundred feet away, and I hadn't stopped him.

"Might not have been him," Jack murmured, lips close to my ear, hand still around my arm, supporting me. "Old guy. Maybe a slip-and-fall. Heart attack."

I shook my head.

"Don't know that. We'll check. But we don't know."

"Dollar bill," I managed to get out. "On the floor."

Jack's lips parted in a curse. My chest tightened and the world pitched sideways. His fingers clenched around my arm, but I barely felt the pressure, as if he was holding me through a down-filled parka.

I saw his lips move, but heard only the pound of blood in my ears. I saw myself running, running through a forest, heart pounding so hard I thought it would burst, pain lashing through me. Running for help. Helpless myself. Couldn't stop him. Couldn't—

I ricocheted back so fast I gasped. The fog cleared, and something else took its place—something so hard and so dark that I dipped into darkness again, blinded. But not by shock, but by rage.

This wasn't over. He'd succeeded, but he hadn't won, hadn't escaped. I wasn't thirteen and I wasn't helpless.

I spun to face Jack. As I did, a voice in my head screamed for me to be more careful. Don't let him see how angry I was. Don't give him any reason to suspect I wasn't in perfect control, the consummate professional.

"Can I— Can I get a drink?" I whispered, gaze down. "Some water?"

He steered me to the bar. They'd closed, but the bartender took one look at me and handed Jack a glass of ice water. We stepped off to the side and I gulped it, feeling the shock of the cold hit, reviving me.

"S—sorry," I said. "Just— Warm. It got warm."

I gulped the rest of the water, filling my mouth with ice, closing my eyes and biting down on it. Yet it did no good. My blood ran so hot sweat broke out along my hairline, stinging as it dripped into my eye.

I had to find him. Make him pay. He thought this was a game? I'd show him a game. I'd track him down and I'd catch him, and then I'd wrap my hands around his neck and squeeze the life from him. And I wouldn't turn away. I'd watch him die, and I'd savor every moment.

Jack cleared his throat and my gut went cold as I realized he was standing right there, watching as I'd let the mask crumble. I rubbed my hands over my face, mumbling about the heat. He didn't say a word and when I looked up, met his gaze, his expression didn't change.

As I swallowed, Jack's gaze moved away to track a middle-aged man hurrying for the doors. The man hailed friends standing outside, waving them in from their cigarette break, and Jack relaxed, nodding slightly. I realized that's what he'd been doing, not watching me, but looking for the killer. Too preoccupied to notice me. Better things on his mind. More important things.

The buzzer sounded.

"We have to go," I said, searching for a trash can. "Get out of here before the show starts. He's done his job. Now he'll run—"

"No, he won't."

"But—"

"Too risky. He'll be in there."

"Wha—?"

Jack waved at the line of patrons filing into the opera. I looked around, realizing that nothing had changed, no one was panicking, screaming about a murdered man in the washroom.

"They aren't telling anyone what happened, are they? Everyone who was there thinks it was an accident. And if there's no mass exodus—" I swallowed, then swung my gaze to the auditorium doors. "He'll have to go inside. Watch the show like everyone else."

Jack nodded, took my glass with one hand, my elbow with the other, and led me over to join the line.

I don't know how I made it to my seat. My heart started racing the moment I stepped through those doors—walked into the same auditorium where my target now sat. The thought of sitting down and doing nothing about it was... indescribable.

Jack moved closer, his knee pressing against mine, hand going to my thigh as he leaned over to say something. I could feel the heat of him, smell the cigarettes on his breath. His lips moved, but I couldn't hear what he was saying, the noise around us too loud, the blood pounding in my ears not helping. I watched his lips move, stared at them, mesmerized by the sensual curve.

I sat there, watching him, smelling him, feeling his hand on my leg, until that was all I *could* sense. Something built inside me, an ache, sharp, urgent. A primal voice whispered that this would do, that *he'd* do—a suitable substitute, a way to slake my frustration, reach out and touch him—

I realized what I was thinking. Felt it like a slap that jolted me out of my thoughts, face reddening, cheeks heating. I looked away. Jack's fingers only pressed into my thigh, getting my attention.

I didn't look, but heard him now, telling me to watch for the killer, study the audience before the lights went down. It took a moment for my thoughts to unsnarl and to realize what his words meant. I glanced around, searching for men in the right age group . . . which described 90 percent of the male patrons. I tried narrowing it down to those sitting alone, but there was no way of knowing because hardly anyone "sat alone"—with no one on either side of him. The killer would be smarter than that anyway. If he'd somehow ended up with an empty seat on either side, he'd just move over, joining another party. As Quinn had said, this wasn't a sold-out show. There was at least one empty seat in every row.

A hopeless task. But a task nonetheless. Busywork. Keeping my mind occupied, that surging frustration at bay. Exactly what I needed. To Jack, it was just being efficient. Making the best use of our time.

At intermission, I wanted to find out what the Feds were doing, if they even knew this was a hit yet, but Jack was having none of it, and I had to admit he was right. We couldn't be caught hanging out too close to the FBI agent plants, hoping to overhear their conversations.

"Come on," Jack said, tapping the cigarettes in his pocket and jerking his chin toward the mass of patrons streaming outside. "Gotta talk to Felix."

We walked along the sidewalk, getting as much distance from the other smokers as possible without looking suspicious.

"How will they find—?" I began.

"Already did. Don't look. Just keep walking. I'll stop. Next to an alley exit. Turn toward the street."

"With my back to them in the alley. Got it."

When I was turning, I caught a blur of a face. Quinn, judging by the height. His dark clothing blended with the shadows.

Jack positioned us so we were standing side by side, partly turned toward one another, our backs to the alley as we watched the traffic.

Jack smoked while I told Quinn and Felix what had happened. To anyone driving by or watching from the opera house, I'd seem to be speaking to Jack. When I finished, Quinn let out an oath.

"So he did manage it," Felix murmured. "We thought as much when we noticed the agents stream into the street after the show began."

"So they're out here?" I said, scanning the road. "They think he left."

Jack passed me the cigarette. As I took it, I caught a glimpse of Quinn. He'd moved to the edge of the alley, still in shadow, but behind Jack now. He frowned as he watched me raise the cigarette to my lips.

"Yes, it's a nasty habit," I murmured. "And one I'm sup-posed to have quit but, sadly, I'm not above temptation."

I smiled as I spoke, but his expression didn't change. He watched me take a drag, then pass it back to Jack.

"Can't spring for a fresh smoke for Dee, Jack?" he said.

Jack grunted, and my cheeks heated as I realized what Quinn had been gawking at. Not the cigarette, but the sharing. I'd never really thought much about it, and I knew Jack was only being considerate. He knew that as an ex-smoker, I'd refuse a full one, but could reason that a few puffs didn't count, like a dieter taking bites from someone else's dessert. To an outsider, though, the shared cigarette might seem rather...intimate.

"So where are they?" I asked, looking around.

"Most went back inside," Quinn said. "But a few are still patrolling the perimeter, stopping people who look like they might be leaving."

As I turned left, my heart skipped a beat. "Someone like that?"

Jack followed my gaze to see silver-haired man cutting briskly through the smoking crowd. He checked his watch, as if hurrying off to do something before the intermission ended.

"Son of a bitch," Quinn said. "What do you want to bet...?"

"I don't," Jack said. "Watch, Dee. Don't react."

"I know."

He held out the cigarette again, and this time, I'll admit, thinking of Quinn's reaction, I hesitated before taking it. But I did take it, if only for the nicotine hit.

The man crossed the road, walked past us on the other side and ducked into an alley.

"Felix?" Jack said under his breath.

"I know, Jack, but we can't. If Quinn and I cross that road, we're going to be seen. We can try looping around—"

"Do that." Jack retrieved the cigarette and stubbed it out on the wall, then dropped it into his pocket and took my arm. "Let's go."

We walked about fifty feet farther down the road, bringing us past the alley. Jack was curbside, so he looked down it.

"Still there," he said. "Walking."

We crossed, jogging between cars, then backtracked.

Jack's arm tightened around my waist, getting my attention. "Your turn."

I looked down the alley. It was dark, but I could see the silver-haired man had passed through into a well-lit parking lot on the other side. I swallowed the urge to tear after him and told Jack. He only nodded, still moving.

"Find another way," he murmured. "Lane up here."

"And, judging by that parking sign, it leads right where we want. Can—" I stopped and rephrased. "Should we turn down it?"

Jack hesitated, then nodded. As I passed the lane, I started veering that way, my gaze fixed on the entrance, a tunnel that would lead me to—

"What the fuck is this?" a man's voice echoed. "I was taking a piss, okay? You try getting to the bathroom in there."

There, partway down, two cops had a guy spread-eagled against the wall. He was beefy, with a crew cut, no older than me, wearing a rented ill-fitting tux.

"You guys had better explain to my date why I'm not in there, 'cause if she thinks I cut out on her, after I blew five hundred bucks..."

One of the officers saw me watching and gave a "move along" wave.

"Fuck," Jack muttered as we continued past. "You see another route?"

"No, and I'll bet you Mr. Silver Hair didn't get stopped by the cops. Too old to fit their damned profile."

Jack stopped and exhaled, pretending to watch traffic for a break to cross.

"Maybe if we walked back and took the same alley he did. It's not the safest move, but we need to go after—" I stopped as I turned in the direction of the alley. "Or maybe not."

There was the silver-haired man, jogging across the road, a cashmere cardigan in his hand. His wife, waiting on the other side, took it and pecked his cheek. Then they headed into the opera.

"Fuck."

I took a deep breath, working past the sharp disappointment. "I second that. So should we—?"

The intermission buzzer sounded.

"Head back in," Jack said. "Try afterward."

Our postshow plan was to get outside ahead of the crowd and watch for any middle-aged men exiting alone. Sounded great. Failed miserably. We even split up, and each of the four of us followed a lone man over forty-five . . . only to discover he was just bringing the car around for his wife or girlfriend.

Chances were that the killer wouldn't walk back alone to his car. He'd follow someone as far as he could. So when our first idea failed, we tried hanging out in the main lot, looking for men veering off from a group. Again, abject failure.

Finally, as the last of the opera-goers dispersed and we started looking obvious standing around, we admitted defeat and headed back to the motel.

THIRTY-FIVE

Earlier this evening I'd envisioned two possible scenarios. One, the killer would see he had no chance at success, and cut his losses. Two, he'd try, fail and be caught. Even when I'd considered the possibility that he'd kill someone, I'd been certain he'd be caught before he could escape. To succeed, and so easily, without a single apparent slip ... I'm an optimist, but there's a point at which realism and optimism collide, and we'd reached it. Tonight only proved that we were in over our heads and it was starting to seem that nothing short of handing over two hundred million would stop the killings.

I didn't remember the trip to the motel or the walk to the room. The next thing I knew I was sitting on the edge of the bed, staring at myself in the mirror. I'd run my hands through my hair so many times I must have looked like Medusa—all snaky curls and jutting bobby pins. I'd caught my dress in the car door and dragged the hem over ten miles of wet road. I looked like bedraggled alley cat. And I didn't care.

Fixing my wig and my dress wasn't going to change what had happened tonight and would happen tomorrow and every day after that because all our running around solving the puzzle was for nothing if we couldn't stop this bastard. I'd been right there, less than a hundred feet away when he'd killed that man, and there hadn't been a damn thing I could do about it.

Failure. Complete, abject failure.

A rustle across the room. Then a cigarette package

appeared, hovering over my lap. I shook my head and it vanished.

"You want a drink?" Jack asked.

I wanted to say no, but I knew he was trying to be considerate, so I nodded. I thought he'd meant he'd grab something from the minibar—assuming there was one. When the door clicked and I turned to see him leaving, my mouth opened to say "Please don't go." But before I could get the first word out, he'd left. And the room got very, very quiet.

Just me. Alone with my thoughts when I so desperately didn't want to be.

Someone rapped at the door. I didn't even check the peephole, just yanked it open, thinking Jack had forgotten something. Heart tripping with relief that he'd returned.

Quinn stood there, deep lines etched between his brows.

"I thought you'd left," I said.

"I have a bit of a drive and I'm . . . not ready to make it. I circled back, and I saw Jack leaving as I was pulling in. I thought maybe you could—we could—use some company."

"Yes." The word flew out before I could think about it. When I did, I considered my options, and the risks of each. "Let's head out, but I'll need to leave a note for Jack and stay close."

He stepped in, but left the door cracked open.

"Is Felix in the car?" I asked as I found paper.

He shook his head. "I dropped him off at a motel. We don't . . . I stay somewhere else."

"Makes sense. Safer, I suppose."

"Nah, that's not it. Well, I suspect Felix is happier splitting up, but I—with my job—I can't just take off for parts unknown even when I'm on vacation. I need a base. Anyone checks up on me, I need an alibi, even if it's just a hotel clerk saying he saw me that morning."

"Sorry. I didn't mean to pry."

A small smile. "You didn't. I explained of my own free will. Not exactly top secret." He leaned back against the wall. "I don't usually have this problem. My jobs, I keep them closer to home, work around my schedule. This?" He shook his head as I finished the note. "Major finagling. When Jack called, I'd finished a big case, hadn't really started anything new, and had vacation time banked so I was able to take off on short notice."

He went quiet then, gaze moving away, fingers tapping the dresser.

"I'm going to guess it's not an open-ended vacation," I said. "How much time do you have left?"

"Not enough." He exhaled softly. "That's one reason I was really counting on..."

"Finishing this tonight."

He nodded. "A few more days and I'm out of here. And once I'm gone, I don't know how much help I can be, even with information."

Without Quinn's FBI sources—and Quinn himself—our investigation would be in trouble. I put the note where Jack would see it, then followed Quinn out.

Beside the parking lot was a pool. The sign said Closed for the Season, but judging by the moss-lined cracks in the concrete walls, it had been closed for a lot of seasons. Of the surrounding security lights, three were dead and two were flickering with their last breaths, but the last still held on. I walked under that one. Close enough for Jack to find me easily, and the angle let us keep an eye on the parking lot and anyone approaching.

I lowered myself to the cement, legs dangling over the pool's edge. Quinn sat beside me.

For a minute, we just gazed at the pool and the layer of trash that blanketed the bottom. Pizza boxes, pop bottles, beer cans, a running shoe...whatever people or the wind had dumped inside.

Quinn pointed at the sneaker. "Whenever I see that, I always wonder how the shoe got there. A pair, I can see. Maybe you take them off to swim or go barefoot and forget where you left them. But how do you lose one shoe? Wouldn't you notice?"

Using my toes, I worked the strap off the back of my opposite heel, and let my left shoe fall into the darkness below. Quinn gave a soft laugh, and tugged his off. It hit the bottom with a squishy thump.

"One high heel and two unmatched sneakers," he said. "Now that's a mystery."

I managed a smile and glanced over at him. His gaze met mine, and I saw something in it that sent a slow burn through me. I was suddenly aware of how close he was sitting, almost brushing me, close enough to feel the heat from his body, and I remembered sitting in that opera house, Jack beside me, my body telling me the perfect substitute for a thwarted hunt. A way to chase the shadows from tonight and still the thoughts pinging through my brain. Something I could cling to, a warm body and a dip into the mindlessly physical.

I could use this. In every way, I could use this.

The attraction was there, and I didn't need to worry about either of us expecting anything. One night. No strings. I looked at him, and felt the hunger burn through me. Then I looked away.

Too risky. I told myself Jack would worry if I disappeared for a few hours with Quinn, but that wasn't the risk I was thinking of. I couldn't trust Quinn. Didn't want to trust him. Even for a night.

When I looked away, I expected Quinn to find an excuse to go inside. Instead, his hand slid into mine. I glanced over at him, but he was staring into the depths of the pool.

"They should have closed the handicapped washroom," he murmured, not looking up.

"They couldn't. Not both of them—not without causing an uproar. In some places you could, and no one would complain, might not even notice. But that place was 50 percent retirees." I gazed out into the night. "They should have posted a guard. Maybe closed one and watched the other. There were guards at the end of the hall and in the main bathrooms, but it would have been easy for him to slip into a handicapped one, unlock the door after a minute and have no one notice he didn't leave."

I glanced over at him. "Do you think he did that on purpose? Targeting someone who was handicapped? Or was it just the easiest way?"

"Maybe one of the easiest, but I'm sure he thought about it. Probably has a whole goddamned list drawn up— little tick boxes to make sure he doesn't overlook any target group."

There was an anger and bitterness in his voice that made me squeeze his hand.

"You get it, don't you?" he said softly. "They don't. Jack and Felix—" He shook his head. "Jack, cutting out on you the second he can get away. And Felix, calm as can be. To them, this is just business. Got a hitman causing trouble, that's bad for business, so you take him out. Doesn't matter how many people get killed in the meantime."

"I think they care," I said. "In their way. Maybe Jack doesn't show it but—"

"You know what kind of work Jack does, don't you? What kind of hitman he is?"

"Sure, I've—"

"You pay him, he whacks someone. No questions asked."

"Isn't that what most hitmen do? I mean, that's the job description, right? Hired killer."

"And is that what you do? Take money to kill anyone, anytime, any way? Like hell. Now, I have no idea how you operate, but that's not it, and it doesn't take a genius to see that. Someone handed you fifty grand to off some random guy in a handicapped washroom, you'd tell him to go fuck himself. Hell, if someone offered me fifty grand to do it, I'd be tempted to put the gun in *his*—" He stopped. "You know what I mean."

I gave a half-shrug, knowing he was heading into territory where I didn't dare follow.

He leaned down to catch my eye. "You do know what I do, don't you?" A small laugh. "No, I guess that's a stupid question. The only way you'd know is if Jack told you and he sure isn't about to tell you, because he doesn't *approve*."

"Approve of what?"

"You know I'm a cop. Not exactly a state secret. And you probably wonder how I justify playing both sides. Maybe I'm just a corrupt son-of-a-bitch who gets off on doing exactly what I'm supposed to be fighting. The truth is, being a cop is what got me into this business, seeing the crap that—"

He stopped. A figure had rounded the front corner of the pool, emerging from between two minivans. It was

Jack, his white dress shirt bright against the darkness, his jacket open, tie off, bottle dangling from one hand.

"Dee?" He stopped in the gateway and lifted the bottle.

"She'll be right there," Quinn said. "Just give us a—"

"What're you back for?" Jack said as he approached. "Forgot something?" He looked down at our hands, face unreadable. As I pulled my hand back, his gaze lifted to Quinn's. "Forgot to say good-bye? Think Dee's a bit old for a good-night kiss."

Quinn pushed to his feet. "Maybe, but I figured one thing she *could* use, after tonight, was someone to talk to. Someone who might even talk back."

"Playing Boy Scout again?"

Quinn's mouth tightened. "Don't call me that."

"Then don't act the part." Jack turned to me, bottle raised. "Coming?"

Quinn met my gaze. "You don't have to."

"I should," I murmured as I stood. "I'll see you later."

He hesitated, then nodded. When Jack turned back to the motel, I reached for Quinn's hand and gave it a quick squeeze before hurrying after Jack.

Back in the motel room, I waited for the door to close, then turned to Jack, hands raised in defense.

"Before you say anything, let me point out that I was on the grounds, in a public place, under a spotlight, where you could see me and I could see anyone approaching. Plus I left you a note. If that's not safe, I don't know what is."

"Staying in your room? Alone?"

"He was upset about tonight and he wanted someone to talk to. Is that a crime?"

He answered by pouring shots of whiskey into plastic glasses.

"What about Felix?" he said as he handed me one.

"What *about* Felix?"

"Quinn wanted to talk? Could talk to Felix." He paused. "Couldn't hold his hand, though. Felix might complain. But maybe not. You never know."

"He wasn't—" I shook my head. "It wasn't like that."

"Looked like that."

"He was *upset,* Jack. When people are upset, sometimes they just need someone around, some human contact."

"So that's what he wanted. Contact."

I felt myself blush and covered it by gulping my whiskey. Big mistake. The second it scorched my throat, I coughed, sputtering whiskey everywhere.

Jack shook his head and handed me a tissue. "Not much of a drinker, huh?"

"It went down wrong."

"Huh."

"Not like this dress wasn't a write-off to begin with. If it's okay with you, I'm getting out of this thing and taking a shower—"

I got halfway to the bathroom before his fingers closed lightly around my wrist.

"Maybe Quinn was upset. Maybe he was lonely. But give him the chance? He'd do the same tomorrow night. And the next night. He's interested. He's going to make sure you know it. Staring at you. Complimenting you. Holding your hand. It's inappropriate." He paused. "Quinn can be careless. Not with work. He's good at that. But other stuff? Personal stuff? Shows too much. Lets his guard down. Careless."

Don't you ever want to be careless, Jack? I wanted to ask.

He continued, "You're here on a job, Nadia. Both of you. He should respect that. Hitting on a colleague—"

"—is inappropriate. I get it. Don't worry. I'm not giving him my phone number until all this is over."

From the look on Jack's face, you'd think I'd suggested taking up a third career as a street whore.

"I'm kidding," I said. "Please. You think I'm here to widen my dating pool? A hitman boyfriend—exactly what my life needs."

He grunted "good"—or something like that—then downed his drink and gestured at the bathroom. "Shower's yours."

I laid my drink down and walked into the bathroom.

After we both showered and retired, I lay there, eyes open in the dark, afraid to close them, knowing those dark dreams waited.

I could hear Jack across the room, his breathing slowing, hitting the rhythm of sleep. Or so I thought until a half hour passed and, without a hitch in that steady breathing, his polyester comforter whispered, pushed back. A crackle of joints. A soft sigh. The muffled thump of his feet hitting the carpet. I feigned sleep and listened to his footfalls as they rounded his bed, then paused at the end of mine.

I peeked just enough to see his faint silhouette in the near-dark room. It hovered there, at the foot of the bed, then moved on to the bathroom. The creak of the door shutting. The click of the light—turned on only after the door was closed, always considerate. I lay on my side, watching that glowing rectangle under the bathroom door. The toilet flushed. His feet passed through the rectangle.

The gurgle of water finding its way up the pipes. Then the light went out, door opened.

He started past my bed, hesitated and came back, walking up to the side. As I lay there, eyes shut, I could hear him breathing, only feet away. Watching me. I knew this should concern me—a man standing by my bedside when I'm supposed to be asleep—but I didn't feel concern. Couldn't. Just lay there and listened to him breathing.

A catch in the rhythm, then the muffled sound of footsteps as he moved closer. I cracked open my eyes to see him bending over, still keeping a respectable distance, but getting a closer look.

"I'm not asleep," I said.

The sound of my voice didn't seem to startle him. He just grunted, "Yeah. Thought so. Wasn't sure."

I opened my eyes to see the outline of his face, one strip—from eye to chin—illuminated by the moonlight streaming through the crack between the curtains.

"Can't sleep, either?" I said.

"Nah. Too . . . busy."

He went quiet again, just standing there, so still that even that strip of moonlight over his face didn't budge. After a moment, he said, "You wanna go out?"

"You need a cigarette?"

He shook his head. "Just . . . out. Somewhere."

I rose on my elbows and yawned. "Probably not a bad plan. As for where, at this hour, that could be a problem."

"Got an idea."

He left it at that. When I nodded, he grabbed his bag and headed for the washroom, telling me to call when I was dressed.

* * *

We drove in silence, the lights of the city soon fading behind us. I recognized the route as the one we'd taken into Chicago, but knew we couldn't be leaving, not with our bags still at the motel.

Jack turned down a road where, earlier that day, we'd stopped for gas. He drove slowly down the dark back route, as if looking for something, but there was nothing to see. We were in a wooded area, with the occasional sign warning us this was conservation land.

After a couple of miles, he made a three-point turn and headed back, then turned off on some kind of service road, little more than two ruts leading into the forest. The entrance was so faint, I'd missed it the first time, but Jack turned in with the confidence that said he'd already seen it.

The car rocked down the ruts, brush scraping the sides and undercarriage. He drove past the forest edge, then stopped and killed the engine.

Jack got out of the car. I followed. I didn't ask why we were here. I was enjoying the anticipation of not knowing. I was in the mood to turn off my brain, stop trying to figure it out and just let myself be surprised.

Awaiting instructions, I stood alongside the car, listening to crickets and the distant, unmistakable yowl of coyotes. The hairs on my neck rose at the sound, eerie and mournful. I closed my eyes and drank it in with the rich smell of wet earth and dying foliage.

An ache grew in the pit of my stomach, casting me back twenty-five years to my first "away" summer camp, lying on my cot, smelling marshmallows on my fingers, thinking of hot chocolate and home. I stood there, taking in the smells and the sounds of the forest—the smells and sounds of my lodge, of home—and with that longing, the weight of the evening lifted, fluttered away on the breeze.

A sharp click of the opening trunk.

I walked back to find Jack uncovering a rifle case.

"Target practice?" I said.

"Yeah."

I looked out, into the forest, black a mere five steps beyond the moonlit clearing. "Kind of dark, don't you think?"

"That's the point." He hefted the case out. "Do much night shooting?"

"Not enough."

A grunt, as if this should answer my question, which I suppose it did.

He handed me the flashlight. "Got your gun?"

I peeled back my jacket to show him.

"Good."

He took out the twenty-six-ounce bottle of whiskey from the motel and passed it to me.

"I'll carry, but I'm not partaking," I said. "Guns and alcohol don't mix."

"That's the point."

He shut the trunk. As that light disappeared, I turned on the flashlight and cast it over the dark woods. He waved me toward them, then set out on a narrow path. A few steps, and we were in the forest. We passed a campfire pit near the edge, ringed with beer cans.

The forest closed around us, the sounds of the crickets vanishing under the crunch of dead leaves underfoot. A few more steps, and Jack continued the discussion as if he'd never left off.

"Drink on a job? Big no-no. But sometimes? Don't have a choice. Can't always have a cola, nurse a beer. Job might mean you gotta drink."

I stepped back to let him lead as the path narrowed, but he waved me on again.

I said, "So you need to know how it will affect your reflexes and your judgment. How to counter the liability. Like shooting at night."

The path forked. Jack's fingers pressed against the back of my jacket, prodding me to the left. Ahead I could see a moonlit clearing.

"Might never need it," he said. "But gotta know how. Perfect chance comes? Nighttime? Or had a beer? A coffee? Know how to compensate? Won't lose the opportunity."

He stopped in the clearing, put the rifle case on a stump and opened it. Inside was a takedown rifle and nightscope. He handed me the scope.

"Holy shit," I said, turning it over in my hands. "I've got scopes at home, but this is high-tech. James Bond territory. Yours?"

"Nah. Gadgets and me? Don't mix. That's Felix's area. And his scope."

He held out the rifle for me to attach the scope, but I was still examining it, a slow smile creeping onto my face.

"Thought you'd like that," he said. "This is done? We'll talk to Felix. Get you some stuff."

I could feel my grin stretching, thoughts of the opera house fading, almost gone now—belonging somewhere back there, in the city. Here was the forest, with its reassuring sense of home, of calm and order. And here was something for me to learn, to focus on, to enjoy. A diversion. Which was, of course, the point.

I finished setting up the rifle and played with it for a while under Jack's tutelage. Once I had the hang of it, he tried a few rounds, then we put it away. Onto the handguns. That was the real practice. I'd used nightscopes—if nothing so fancy—but I had little experience shooting a handgun in the dark. Night-vision goggles would help but, as Jack had said, this was more about preparing for found opportunities, those times when you see the chance to hit a mark, but something is less than perfect, like the lighting or your blood alcohol level.

"Need a target," Jack said. "Something we can see..."

"Hold on."

I ran back to the campfire pit and gathered all the silver-label cans, took them to the clearing and let them clatter into a pile by the stump.

"Now, to do this in proper hillbilly style, we're supposed to drink the beer, then shoot the cans, but we'll have to settle for empties and whiskey."

"Works for me." He squinted into the darkness. "Set 'em up over—"

"Uh-uh. This is supposed to be a challenge, remember?" I drew back my arm, ready to pitch the can. "Whenever you're ready..."

"Fuck no."

I turned a grin on him. "You think *this* is too challenging? Wait for the whiskey shots."

He laughed, a low rumble that was an actual laugh, maybe the first I'd ever heard from him. Then he took out his gun. "Five bucks."

"Oh, getting serious now, are we?"

His eyes sparkled in the moonlight. "Nah. You want serious? Wait for the whiskey shots."

I laughed and threw the can, closing my eyes as I did, hearing the crack of the gun, then the sharp ping of the can. When I looked, he was walking to the beer can pile, moving with his usual slow, deliberate gait, never in a hurry. He bent...then whirled fast, whipping the can without warning.

"Cheat!" I yelled as I fired.

The bullet zinged through the can. Jack shook his head. "Fuck."

"If you want an advantage over me, you're going to need to do better than that."

I passed him the bottle. He uncapped it and took a slug, then paused, letting the alcohol settle into his stomach before handing it back.

"Ten bucks," he said.

"You got it."

He got the can, too.

Our shooting, predictably, grew less impressive the more whiskey we consumed. Jack gave me pointers on overcoming the imbalances, but it was less a serious practice than "Let's get a feel for this"...with a generous heaping of horseplay.

I pulled into the lead quickly, but lost ground the more I drank, with Jack seeming to hit his "low point" early, then staying there. Earlier Jack had said I didn't seem to be much of a drinker. I suspected the same went for him. It took less than half a bottle to get us both pretty wasted—well beyond the point where we'd ever attempt a hit.

As for Jack, I must admit I was curious to see him drunk. He was one of those guys you can't imagine stumbling and slurring. And he didn't, his feet and tongue steady even as I could see the alcohol taking its toll.

I'll admit, too, that I was curious about how the alcohol might affect his tongue in other ways, but the only thing it did was make his brogue more pronounced. He didn't start waxing eloquent...or even use more pronouns. Nor did he delve into tales of his sordid youth, as much as I would have loved to hear them.

What did happen was not what I expected. As he drank, that edge I'd seen earlier, when he put on the tux, that hard, dangerous "something" that I glimpsed every now and then, slid to the fore. Not an angry drunk. If anything, he was quicker with a laugh or a joke. Just that edge peeking out, that look in his eyes, in that set of his jaw that said he wasn't someone you wanted to cross.

Maybe, seeing that, I should have been worried. At least wary. If anything, it was almost comforting. I saw it, and I recognized it, and it didn't bother me. With a man like Jack, a career killer of his caliber, you know there has to be something hard, something dangerous under that calm, impassive exterior. Seeing it and seeing no anger there, feeling no sense of danger directed at me was oddly reassuring.

The last thing I remembered that night was Jack's voice, his thick brogue making even his clipped sentences almost musical as he told the story of a job gone by. I'd been up a hundred dollars in the betting, but almost falling over drunk, and he'd suggested I sit, close my eyes, rest for a minute. While I did, he told his story and I hung there, fighting sleep, clinging to his words, wanting to hear the end and then ... thankfully dreamless sleep.

The next morning I awoke on the forest floor, Jack's coat draped over me. He was propped against a tree—more dozing than sleeping—and roused when he saw me up. We gathered our things, including the beer cans, then headed off in search of breakfast and news.

The morning papers mentioned the killing. Just mentioned it. Few details had been released, and certainly nothing about the killer's "challenge." I suspected the Feds were scrambling to come up with a way to break the news themselves, with their own slant.

As for us, we'd go back to doing what we'd been doing all along, pursuing our leads in hopes that we'd roust the killer from the rear, through his identity and contacts in the underworld. Far from a foolproof plan, but it was a damned sight better than sitting on our hands waiting for more people to die.

HSK

He watched the typed messages scroll up the screen and, with each, his hands gripped the chair arms tighter. He'd logged in for a quick check before he dropped off his next letter at the courier's. In it, he forewarned the Feds of his next night-time strike—an overnight train to California. He'd even provided the train number. That should be fun, and hopefully more challenging than the opera house. On the way he'd make his daytime hit. He hadn't worked out the location or the specifics yet, but he knew what he wanted: a young working-class male. And it was probably time for another visible minority.

But now he was reading something that had sent all thoughts of his plan from his head. The big news on the boards? Little Joe Nikolaev was dead. He wanted to believe the timing was coincidental, but a smart man assumes connections exist until he can prove otherwise.

Rumor had it that Little Joe opened his mouth once too often. One of tonight's posters claimed to know a middle-man who'd been approached by Little Joe about a job just a few days earlier. Sounded like wannabe bullshit...until he read the next lines.

REDRUM: LJ wanted him to whack two broads. First thing I thought was: whores. LJ buys himself some company, blabs too much pillow talk, wants them offed. No big deal. Only one of them was old enough to be my grandma. The other was younger but, still, doesn't sound like whores to me.

He stared at those lines, watched them jiggle up the screen, pushed by the flurry of responses that came after them.

Evelyn.

His fingers dug into the chair arms. Now the pieces clattered into place. Rumors of hitmen on his trail. Jack showing up at the opera house, with a young female partner on his arm—Jack, who never took partners. A young woman and an old lady show up at Little Joe's, asking questions that put a price on their heads.

Evelyn, the goddess of destruction, always looking for disciples to sacrifice on the altar of her ego. Evelyn and her schemes, endless schemes, sucking you in, then tossing you aside when something new and shiny caught her eye.

A snap of her wrist and she'd yanked her favorite hound back to her side, foisted her new acolyte on him, then set the pair on his trail.

He could be wrong. There were plenty of assumptions in that argument. But a careful man took action before action was required. If Jack was on his trail, and if Evelyn knew about the Nikolaev connection, then he had a tap to shut off . . . before it leaked.

He looked at the letter. Could he still do it? Not that particular train, but he'd find another. He wasn't about to let Evelyn spoil his plans.

THIRTY-SIX

"Gallagher," Evelyn said before her door even closed behind us. "Maurice Gallagher called the hit on Sasha Fomin, the one Kozlov witnessed."

And with that, she swung us back on the trail without a word about what had happened in Chicago. The opera house murder had yielded no clues, so she'd plowed past it. An inconsequential distraction from the hunt.

"Gallagher in Vegas?" Jack asked.

Evelyn snorted. "Where else? That spider hasn't left the Fortuna in thirty years. As long as he's alive, that's where you'll find him. Hell, even when he isn't alive, that's where you'll find him." She looked at me. "He's built himself a mausoleum inside the casino. You meet some strange ones in this business. More than our share of psychiatric case studies."

"Go figure," Jack murmured. "Guess we're off to Vegas, then."

"Should be a quick trip. You've built up enough credit with Gallagher, all the work you've done for him."

"Been awhile."

Her head shot up. "He hasn't been calling you?"

"He calls. I don't answer."

"What? You get a client like Maurice Gallagher on the line, you thank God for a steady income, Jacko. You don't go telling him you're too busy."

"Don't tell him that."

"Good."

"I tell him I'm not interested."

"You what? For fuck's sake, Jack!" She turned to me. "About those psychiatric case studies? Case in point."

"Is this going to cause a problem, Jack?" I asked. "If he's pissed off at you—"

"Not pissed off. Just not happy. We'll work around it."

Evelyn opened her mouth, but Jack cut her off by grabbing my suitcase.

"Better repack," he said.

"Do I need the push-up bra?"

"It's Vegas."

"Damn."

I'd really hoped to avoid my makeover for a few hours, but Jack insisted that we arrive and leave in character. Made sense, but *he* didn't need jeans so tight they gave him a wedgie with every step.

Jack wore a golf shirt, chinos and loafers. Quite preppy... until you slicked back the dark hair, undid all three buttons on the shirt and added a half-pound of gold—chain, watch, rings, earring, even a tooth. Toss on mirrored sunglasses, and you took the persona from banker to loan shark. A five-minute trip to the bathroom and you'd be back to banker.

My outfit wasn't nearly so versatile. I got a blowzy blond wig, painted-on jeans and cowboy boots. No five-minute change was making that more respectable... or more comfortable.

When we got to the airport, there was a guy soliciting donations outside the terminal doors, tucked behind a pillar, out of sight of security. When I saw the red pot beside him, stuffed with dollar bills, I thought *Huh, a bit early for the Salvation Army Christmas drive, isn't it?* Then I saw the sign beside the pot: Your Dollar Accepted Here.

I slowed, and steered Jack closer to read the smaller print. *Protect yourself today,* it said. *Pay* your *dollar, and sign the list.*

"Fuck," Jack muttered. "What's he gonna do? FedEx the cash?"

"And the list, don't forget, because I'm sure the killer is checking ID first."

"Con artists. Fucking bottom-feeders."

I looked around. "I should notify security."

"No time. People are stupid enough to pay..."

He didn't finish, just shrugging as if to say that you couldn't rescue people from stupidity, and he wasn't about to waste his time trying. So I waited until he was in line to check in, then zipped off to the bathroom, with a side trip past the security office. Sure, you can't save people from stupidity, but at least you can stop others from getting rich off it.

"You want the window seat?" I asked as we boarded the plane.

An odd look crossed his face. He mumbled a gruff "You take it," grabbed my overnight bag and hoisted it into the compartment. By the time he lowered himself into the seat beside me, I was almost done straightening and rearranging the in-flight magazines. I pulled an overlooked empty peanut bag from under the seat in front of me, then glanced around for a place to put it.

The light came on for us to fasten our seat belts. As I reached for mine, I noticed Jack's hands as he fastened his, fingers trembling slightly. I looked at him, but his gaze was down, intent on securing the belt.

We listened through the obligatory safety spiel, then the plane began takeoff. As I shifted, getting comfortable, I happened to glance Jack's way. He'd gone dead white... almost as white as his knuckles, gripping the chair arms like they might fall off if he let go.

"You're afraid of flying," I murmured, lowering my voice. "Why didn't you say—?"

"No choice. Too far to drive."

"Can I get you any—?"

"Talk to me."

That was one thing I could manage, so I did.

Once in Vegas, we had to make a few stops. First to a safe drop where Jack kept disguises and equipment, including guns. Then to a hardware store, where I could find the material I needed to carry out our plan.

The Fortuna was the kind of casino frequented by three types of gamblers: old pros who hate the glitzy big operations, problem gamblers kicked out of the big operations, and lost tourists. It was off the Strip. Dated from when the mob ruled Vegas, it looked as if it hadn't been renovated since, and wore its age like a badge of pride. If you wanted flashing lights and fruity drinks and gorgeous girls you went elsewhere. The Fortuna was for gambling.

As we moved through the room, I was struck by the difference between the Vegas I'd seen in advertisements and movies, and the reality. Maybe somewhere on the Strip there were casinos filled with handsome couples, grinning and cheering and having the time of their life, but here gambling seemed more a life sentence than a vacation. Those sitting at the antiquated slot machines looked like extras from a zombie flick, eyes glazed, faces ashen as they fed the coins and pulled the handles. The tables weren't much better, everyone crowded around, expressions solemn, gazes fixed on the worn green cloth. At some tables, only the tinkle of the dice and the murmur of the dealers' voices broke the quiet. Then we came along...

"But you promised," I squealed as Jack dragged me to the blackjack table. "I wanna see Celine."

Jack leaned down to my ear and hissed loud enough for everyone around to hear. "Shut the fuck up, or the only thing you'll be seeing is the inside of the hotel room."

I sniffled. Jack laid down a hundred-dollar bet and tried to snake his arm around my waist, but I sidestepped away.

"Come on, baby," Jack said, his hand sliding to my rear. "Gimme some luck."

"You said this trip was for me."

"You give me a couple hours and we'll see Celine, Newton... Hell, you can play with the fucking white tigers if you want, okay, babe?"

He started playing... and losing, a hundred bucks at a time, then two hundred. He won the odd hand, but most of his money went back to the dealer. Wasn't long before a server sidled up with a tray of free drinks... the least they could offer for such a generous donation.

"Uh-uh," I said, patting my still-flat stomach. "No booze for this baby. I got six more months and I'm sticking to it."

Jack gave a proud papa grin and patted my stomach. "That's my girl." He shot the grin around the table. "Our first... and I'm here to win a room full of baby furniture."

A murmured round of congratulations on the first point,

tainted with skepticism on the second. The server returned with a soda for me and a Scotch for Jack. He made a show of taking a big gulp, but very little of the liquid left the glass before he surreptitiously slid it aside. My soda was supposed to be Coke. Judging by the taste, though, they'd substituted a no-name brand, then further cut costs topping it up with tap water.

After a few more rounds, Jack's luck changed. Drastically. I knew he was cheating—that was the plan—but I have no idea what he did, only that he started winning big and winning often—too big and too often to be healthy. All eyes were already on us, with our role-playing, and he hadn't won more than his sixth round before a beefy hand closed on his shoulder.

"A word with you . . . sir," the guard rumbled.

"Sure," Jack said. "If it's congratulations."

Another guard flanked him, and both took hold of his upper arms to escort him away.

"Oh no," I moaned as I scampered after them. "You didn't. Tell me you didn't."

"Shut the fuck up," Jack hissed over his shoulder.

"You promised!" I whacked him with my purse. " 'Not this time, babe,' you said. 'I'll play straight, babe.' You don't know *how* to play straight, you no-good . . ."

And so we left the casino floor and headed for the security wing, Jack under armed guard and me running along behind them, alternately sobbing and railing. As we passed through the doors, a desk guard leapt up, probably to tell me to wait outside. Then he apparently decided this was one domestic dispute he didn't want to get in the middle of, sat down and busied himself with his logbook.

It wasn't until we hit the "holding" room that the guards stopped me, one stepping into my path as the other took

Jack inside and closed the door. I didn't try to follow, just snuffled and wiped my arm across my streaming nose.

"You can wait over there, ma'am," the guard said. "He might be awhile."

"I can't believe he did this. He promised! This whole trip was for me, he said. 'Cause I've been so sick with the baby. For me, my ass. How could he—?" I clutched my stomach. "Oh, I don't feel so good."

"There's a bathroom—"

"Uh-uh, if I start puking, I'll never stop. I just need to sit down."

He quickly pointed me to a small room. I spent only a couple of minutes in there, sniffling and moaning, then bolted for the door, hand over my mouth. The hall guard didn't say a word, just got out of my way and waved in the direction of the washroom.

Once in the washroom, I did some retching, and tossed cupfuls of water into the toilet for effect, but I doubted the young guard came close enough to the door to appreciate my efforts. Still moaning and snuffling, I stood on the counter and wriggled the ceiling tile loose. Next I pulled the climbing gloves from my bra, and slid them on. Then I took out my key chain, unhooked my penlight, put it between my teeth and heaved myself up into the ceiling.

"Are you sure it's removable ceiling tiles?" I'd said to Jack. "If they've plastered since you were last there, we're in trouble."

"Gallagher doesn't redecorate. If it works, it stays."

This plan was my idea. Jack had his own—which went something along the lines of "cheat, get caught, get taken into the secured area and demand to see Gallagher." And my role? Just play along in the casino, then enjoy my evening gambling while he risked broken fingers with

Gallagher's security team. When I'd suggested this enhancement, I'd expected him to balk, but he'd only thought for a moment, then said, "Yeah, that's better." The balking came later, as we'd prepared our strategy, and he'd realized how much danger I was putting myself in.

"It's no worse than your plan," I'd said. "With yours, you're relying on the guards to deliver your message . . . and Gallagher to accept it, rather than take advantage of the chance to beat the crap out of you for refusing his jobs. With mine, I do the delivery, and Gallagher has no choice but to accept it. Worst thing that can happen? I can't get to Gallagher, and we'll be back to your idea."

"Or Gallagher gets you. Holds you hostage."

"He has to catch me first."

When Jack didn't smile, I'd said, "You seriously think he can take me that easily? I'm careful, Jack. One wrong look from the guy, and I'm back up in that ceiling. See if he can follow me there."

"Wouldn't fit."

As I squeezed into the gap between the beams and the floor above, I saw Jack's point. Tight quarters up here. Not bad, though. I'd been in worse.

Still, Jack hadn't seemed satisfied, kept poking and prodding, making sure I was prepared.

"I can do this," I'd said finally, exasperated. "If you didn't think I could, why let us get this far with the plan?"

Silence. After a moment, he'd said only, "Be careful."

"I always am."

Something had passed though his gaze, but he'd dropped it before I could get a good look.

I checked my compass. North-northwest was that way. Down on all fours again, flashlight between my teeth, and

I was on the move. Dust swirled up with every step. Despite the contacts, my eyes watered, and more than once I had to stop and chomp down on the flashlight to swallow a sneeze.

"Take this," Jack had said, thrusting the map at me. "Keep it handy."

"I won't need it," I'd said.

"Humor me."

I had, but I didn't take the map out now. I didn't need to. In high school, I'd spent a summer working as a guide in Algonquin Park, and the first thing I'd learned was not how to repel black bears and blackflies, but how to memorize maps. Nothing destroys tourists' confidence—and a guide's chance at a tip—so much as having her stop in the middle of an endless expanse of forest to pore over a map.

From below came muted whispers of conversation against the backdrop of the constant whirs and dings of distant slot machines. As I crossed one room, the sound changed to a steady clinking, a river of chips going through a mechanical counter—the sound of broken marriages, busted kneecaps and shattered lives. Never saw the appeal of gambling. Not with money, anyway. The risk of parachuting or white-water rafting is one thing—you know the odds are in your favor. But casino gambling? Just take a look at the owners, and how they live, and tell me where you think all that money is going.

I supposed it was all about the threat of risk and the possibility of reward. But the risk of financial ruin was, for someone who'd been there, not enough to get my heart pumping. Not like this—the thrill of true danger, crawling into the unknown.

Regular spelunking is risky enough. But there, in a cave, you have partners who can go for help and, most times, the biggest danger you face is broken bones. Here, if I fell, I'd be exposed as a thief or, worse, an assassin. Men like Gallagher didn't handle either by simply breaking bones.

And with spelunking, it's all about the journey, the thrill of knowing every move you make could land you in a crevasse, that you can try your damnedest to control every variable, but you still leave something to chance. The goal is the simple satisfaction of survival. Here, there was more. Not just increased stakes, but an actual prize. A name that could rip the mask from the Helter Skelter killer.

Crawling through this ceiling was the ultimate extreme sport. Or, perhaps, only the precursor to it.

As I moved, the clatter of coins gave way to slurping, interspersed with moans set to a sound track of "yeah, baby, that's right, baby, uh-huh." I listened for the familiar wocka-wocka music of a seventies porn movie. Yes, I knew what porn movies sounded like. When you've worked in a testosterone-dominated occupation, you have two choices: lecture the guys on the political incorrectness of watching porn with a female co-worker or laugh it off with cracks like, "Hey, how come *my* pizza delivery boys are never hung like that?"

As I shimmied forward, being careful not to disturb the video watchers below, a shaft of light glimmered up through a fist-sized hole in the ceiling tile. Below it, I could see a balding head. The rafters on either side had pipes running over them. No detours possible. Damn. I eased back onto my haunches, took the flashlight from my mouth, turned it off and tucked it into my pocket. Then forward again, relying on the hole for light. I inched to the edge and peered down.

Below was a middle-aged man, his hands wrapped around a bleach blond head bobbing in his lap. He continued his porn star dialogue and she continued slurping, making way more noise than was necessary for the act—at least, as far as I remembered it. I was tempted to look around for the video camera. The man groaned and exhorted the woman to "Take it in. Take it all in," which, from my vantage point, didn't look very difficult. I crawled over the hole. Not like either of them was going to look up anytime soon.

As the live porn sound track faded, I put the penlight back in my mouth and pushed on. Only a few more rooms to cross now. In spite of the racket from the distant casino and the filth of seriously overlooked housecleaning chores, more than once a sudden grin almost sent my flashlight tumbling to the ceiling tiles below.

"Spelunking," I'd said when Jack had expressed some doubts about the wisdom of rafter-crawling. When his look demanded an interpretation, I'd said, "You know. Exploring caverns, caves, natural tunnel systems, that sort of thing."

His look didn't change.

"It's a sport," I'd said.

He'd shaken his head, as if unable to believe anyone would voluntarily do such a thing.

"What about getting down?" he'd said. "Long jump. You fall? He'll hear."

I'd rolled my eyes. "I'm not planning to fall . . . or jump. I'm going to abseil."

The look again. When I'd opened my mouth to explain, he'd lifted his hand and shaken his head. "You can do it? Good enough. Just be careful."

I paused for another compass check, realized I'd veered off at the last turn and backed up a few steps. Then there it was: the final marker—a tangle of wires that snaked the feed of every security camera into Gallagher's room. He'd be alone. Both Evelyn and Jack had sworn there was little question of that. Seemed Gallagher was antisocial as well as agoraphobic. He spent his nights locked in his control room, watching his money roll in.

Despite their assurances, I wasn't taking anything on faith. I stretched out across two rafters, grabbed a third with one hand, then lowered my head down as close to the ceiling tiles as I could get without slipping. A moment's pause, to double-check my balance, then I reached down with my free hand, hooked my fingertips around a tile edge and eased it to the side. It moved less than a half-inch, just enough to open a crack to the room below. And there sat Maurice Gallagher.

"He's a big guy," Jack had said.

He wasn't kidding. Evelyn had called Gallagher a spider, and I couldn't imagine a better metaphor. Gallagher was obese, at least four hundred pounds, with sticklike arms and legs, and a too-small, round head. He wore his dyed red hair slicked to each side, the part a blazing white stripe of pasty flesh that made his two patches of hair look like giant arachnid eyes. A spider, perched in his lair, watching his prey buzz about in the casino, entangling themselves in his web.

I wriggled back onto my main rafter, being careful not to make any noise, then crawled to the east side, where I'd find the bathroom. Next I took off my belt. It was a blue rope wrapped three times around my jeans, plus a length of chain and a ring clasp. A very practical fashion statement. I wrapped the chain around the rafter, attached the abseil ring, then looped the nylon cord through, and knotted it.

Again I braced myself on three parallel rafters and leaned down, tugging the tile up and out of the way. The whole time, I kept my eyes closed, concentrating on sound—how much I was making, and how much was coming from the adjacent room. One squeak of Gallagher's chair and I was out of there.

Once the tile was moved aside, I took hold of the cord and lowered myself through the hole. I aimed for the toilet seat, which, thankfully, Gallaher's mother had taught him to keep down. My sneakers made contact, but I kept rappelling down until my full weight was on the seat and I had my balance. Then I slid to the floor, leaving the rope dangling in case I needed to make an emergency exit.

THIRTY-SEVEN

The bathroom door was closed. I eased it open and used my makeup compact to scout the room, keeping it tilted down so a stray reflection off the mirror wouldn't give me away. Jack had said the call button for security was on Gallagher's right. I located it, then turned my attention to Gallagher. He had his back to me as he scanned the bank of screens, his head swiveling from left to right, then back again.

His gaze moved at such a constant rate that if it wasn't for the measured breathing, I'd have suspected Gallagher had indeed croaked, and I was looking at an automated version of him. I could even time his visual scan. Eleven seconds from one side to the other.

I waited until he began the right to left scan, counted off five seconds and slid forward, moving between him and his call button. Then I waited. It wasn't until he scanned all the way back from left to right that he saw me

"Hi," I said.

He didn't jump. Didn't dive for the call button. Didn't even blink. Just looked at me, gaze moving from my head to my feet, as slow and impassive as if I was a row of security screens. Then he eased back in his chair.

"If you've come to rob me, young lady, you've made a very serious mistake." His voice was high pitched, almost squeaky. "There is no money here and you will not get anything from me but a one-way ticket to jail."

"Jail?" I said.

"I was being polite."

"Ah. Well, if I was here to rob you, I'm very unprepared."

I lifted my hands, stood and turned around. "No money bags, no cans of mace, not even a gun."

"So I noticed," he murmured. "Yet you must have a weapon hidden somewhere on that pretty body. I'd bet on it."

"How much?"

He tilted his head, gaze traveling over me, studying me with a scientist's eye. "Unarmed. That is most . . . peculiar." His gaze lifted to mine, head slanting the other way. "I do hope, my dear, that you didn't intend to use your body as your weapon because, I assure you, I am quite immune."

"Well that's good, because when it comes to the Mata Hari routine . . ." I shook my head. "Hopeless. Guns are really more my thing, but that just didn't seem right. You want to talk to someone, you don't pull a gun on them. Very disrespectful."

"Quite so." He leaned back in his chair. "So you wish to talk? And what would a young lady like you want to talk to me about? Employment, perhaps? An interesting way to go about it. Much more . . . personally revealing than dropping off a résumé."

"Actually, it's an employee I want to talk to you about, not employment. A former employee, that is." I gestured at the row of screens. "Camera number six. Recognize him?"

He looked for a few seconds, then shook his head.

"Try this. Pick up the phone, dial 555-2978."

"And say what?"

"Nothing. Just try it. Please."

He did. The phone in Jack's pocket vibrated, and he looked straight into the camera, and mouthed something.

"Jack," Gallagher said, twisting the name into a curse.

"He said you might not be happy to see him. That's why

I'm here doing the talking instead of him. Well, that, and I'm much better at talking."

"So I noticed. I take it then that you are a..." He let the sentence fall away, as if he couldn't come up with a "polite" term for what I did.

"Right," I said. "I'm working something with Jack, and we need something from you."

He laughed, the sound a nails-on-chalkboard screech. I waited through it, then continued.

"And yes, Jack knows he's in no position to ask for a favor, which is why he sent me with an offer. An exchange of information. Seems you hired someone a while back to make a hit, and he double-crossed you."

Gallagher's eyes narrowed. "No one double-crosses me."

Gallagher locked gazes with me, but I just sat there, and waited him out.

"Double-crossed me how?" he said finally, mouth barely opening to let the words out.

"He told the mark about the hit, collected a tidy sum for the info, waited until the guy skedaddled to Europe, then came back, told you it was done and collected again."

"And Jack expects me to pay for the name of this traitor?" A tight laugh. "My dear, all I'd need to do is run a more thorough verification of the hits I've called."

"Sure, but Jack thought this might be faster. A *lot* faster, considering you're a high-volume customer." When Gallagher hesitated, I went on. "How about this? I tell you what we need and you decide if it's worth it?"

Another hesitation, then he waved for me to continue.

"Twenty years ago you bought a hit on a man under the protection of the Nikolaev family. The man's name was Sasha Fomin. We'd like to know who you hired for the hit."

Gallagher waited. When I didn't go on, his lips pursed.

"And that's it? Jack wants to know who I hired on a twenty-year-old contract?"

"If you remember…"

"Of course, I remember, my dear girl. I don't forget anything. Including an insult. You make sure you tell Jack that."

"Jack insulted you by refusing to take your jobs? Well, he's lining up a whole battalion of enemies then. Between you and me, sir, I think the guy has a serious attention deficit problem. Does a job here, a job there, gets antsy and moves on. He doesn't mean any disrespect… he just can't seem to keep at one thing for very long. I think it's his age. Been in the business too long. I'm already counting the hours until he tosses me aside."

Gallagher said nothing but I could see he was digesting this. I had no idea how loyal Jack was to his regular employers, but Gallagher wouldn't know, either—Jack didn't go around bragging about his clientele. If Gallagher thought he wasn't the only one Jack had abandoned, that should lessen the insult. After a minute, Gallagher relaxed into his chair.

"And that is all Jack wishes to know? The name of the man I hired?"

"That's right."

"I can hardly imagine what use he'd have for such information. The man is no longer even in the business. Retired a year or two ago." He met my gaze. "And he had the civility to inform me of his retirement, and apologize for any inconvenience it might cause."

A mini-tornado whipped up in my gut. Retired a year or two ago? That fit our profile. But if Gallagher respected this man, felt some allegiance to a loyal former employee—

"Wilkes."

I remembered that name. It was the first one Jack had thought . . . and the one Evelyn had dismissed.

"Wilkes?" I repeated, to be sure.

Gallagher waved his hand. "After John Wilkes Booth, I suppose. These men are hardly creative geniuses. Still, it's better than 'Jack.' Anything is better than Jack. Anyway, Jack knows him. They were . . . comrades of a sort, back when Jack was more . . . approachable."

No question then. This was the same Wilkes—Evelyn's former lover.

I related what Jack had told me about Gallagher's traitor. Gallagher accepted the information without any reaction, then called the security room and told them to release Jack. Once Jack was out, Gallagher called him and passed the phone to me, so I'd know he was safe before I left.

"Mind if I use the front door this time?" I said.

"Be my guest. A last word before you go . . ."

"Hmmm?"

He met my gaze. "You appear to be a bright young lady and I have no doubt you are quite capable at your chosen occupation. Choosing Jack as a mentor speaks well to your intelligence. However, a continued . . . alliance with him would not. There are three kinds of people in this business, my dear. Those who play the game, those who cannot and those who will not. Only a fool aligns herself with the last. You'd do well to remember that."

"I will. Thank you."

"Should you ever be in need of employment, you know where to find me."

* * *

Success. I hadn't realized how much I'd needed that after the opera house. I walked out of that casino with such a spring in my step I attracted the notice of a prostitute standing outside, waiting for winners. She gave me a once-over, as if thinking maybe my gender wasn't a complete deal breaker. I flashed her a wide smile, and she sighed before resuming her vigil.

I stepped into the side alley where I'd agreed to meet Jack. He was there, smoking one of his hated American cigarettes, his free hand drumming against the wall. When he saw me, he exhaled a long stream of smoke, then ground out the cigarette and dropped the butt into his pocket.

"You okay?" he said, squinting through the darkness.

"You're the one I should be asking that. Lose any fingers?"

"None I needed." His gaze slipped to my hand. "Where's your gun?"

"I didn't need it."

"Nadia . . ."

"What?"

"You do *have* the gun, right?"

"Sure."

"I mean now. On your body. Not back in the hotel room."

"Would you have taken a gun?"

"Couldn't. Guards found a gun on me—"

"You know what I mean. If it had been *you* going to see Gallagher, would you have taken a gun?"

He lifted his hand to his lips, as if forgetting he wasn't still holding his cigarette. A scowl, then a sharp shake of his head.

"You get anything?" he asked.

"Gallagher went for the deal. He remembered the Fomin hit and he said it was done by a regular of his, someone who just recently retired. A hitman who goes by the name Wilkes."

For a second, Jack said nothing, then he breathed a long, low, "Fuck."

"That's the guy you thought of first when I started rhyming off a profile of the killer. The guy that Evelyn said couldn't be responsible."

"Yeah."

"Do *you* think it could be him?"

Jack paused, gaze emptying as he thought it over. It took about a minute, then he gave a slow nod. "Yeah. Age is right. Haven't heard much from him lately. Could have retired. He's good. What'd Evelyn say? Technically adept. So... Gallagher still pissed?"

"At you? Yes. But I told him it was an attention deficit problem, and that helped."

"Attention...?" A twitch of his lips. "I don't want to know, do I?"

"Probably not, but it eased you a step out of his bad books." We started for the sidewalk at the front of the casino. "Though he did warn me about you. Said you're a bad influence."

"Am I?"

"Apparently, you're not a player."

"There's a game?"

"Yes, and you're not playing it."

"Never was good at games. Too many rules."

"You seemed darned good at one game, at least. A little card-sharking in your past, I'm guessing?"

"Better a casino than a bank."

"What's that I hear? An *ethical* choice?"

"A *safety* choice."

"Bullshit. You get caught robbing a bank and no one's

going to put a bullet in your brain. Is that the sort of thing Gallagher hired—?" I shook my head. "None of my business. Sorry."

"Yeah, it *is* your business. Especially if Gallagher's gonna offer you employment." He glanced my way. "He did offer, didn't he?"

"Yes, but the answer would be no, regardless of what kind of work it was. It's like I've been telling Evelyn—with the Tomassinis I know what I'm getting and I'm getting enough of it. No need to go elsewhere."

We hit the sidewalk beside the casino and Jack nudged me toward the parking lot, keeping quiet until we'd turned into the empty lane.

"With Gallagher? Never know what you're getting," he said. "Doesn't matter. Not to him. He gives you a name—"

"Sir!"

A young man in a casino uniform was hurrying toward us.

"Sir," he said, lowering his voice as he drew nearer. "I have a message from Mr. Gallagher."

Jack nodded.

"He says he has more information on the man you were asking about. There's someone he wants you to talk to. He's arranged for a meeting tonight."

"Where?"

"At a condo on H.G. Wells Boulevard." He pulled a piece of paper from his pocket. "Here's the address."

Jack took the paper, unfolded it, read it and frowned. "Where the hell is this?"

"In one of those new master-planned subdivisions. Adventura, they call it. In the north."

"Near Centennial Hills?"

"Closer to Aliante."

Jack studied the paper for a moment, frowning as if he was having trouble reading it. The lighting, while not great, was decent enough so I knew eyesight wasn't the problem. I peered down the alley. Too long and empty for someone to be lurking down there. As I moved to the mouth, Jack stalled, asking the kid for better directions. I peeked, then moved out, standing watch and hoping no one mistook me for a hooker. A quick survey of the street showed people coming and going, but no one hanging about suspiciously. I glanced back at Jack and nodded.

After a few seconds, his voice floated along the alley, so soft I had to strain to hear him. "You said Mr. Gallagher gave you this message?"

"Not Mr. Gallagher personally, sir. I've never seen Mr. Gallagher. No one does."

"So it was an employee?"

"I don't know. I was on the door, and some guy came by with the message, and gave me a hundred bucks to deliver it."

"Huh." The crinkle of paper. "That hundred bucks? Look something like this?"

"Yes, sir."

"You take that then. Matching pair. Now describe the guy."

"Uh . . . I didn't really get a good look at the guy. He *was* a guy. I know that. Or . . . well, I'm pretty sure . . ."

That's all the kid could recall—that it had looked like a man. Size? Not noticeably big or small. Age? Maybe forty . . . or younger . . . could have been older, too. Distinguishing features? He thought the guy might have been wearing glasses. Short of hypnosis, that's all we were going to get out of him. Listening in, I could tell he was worried about losing that hundred, and scrambling to come up with enough to keep it.

"I'm sorry, sir. I just wasn't— I wasn't paying attention."

"Busy looking at Benjamin Franklin's face instead?"

A sheepish laugh. "Yeah. You, uh, want your money back, I guess . . ."

"Keep it. Guy comes around? Asks how it went? You delivered the message. Seemed like I was going. Never asked any questions."

"Yes, sir."

THIRTY-EIGHT

"You handled that well," I said as we got into the car.

"Do what works. Drop a few bills? Play it cool? Sometimes good enough."

"Safer and easier than throwing people to the ground and pointing guns at their head."

A shrug as he started the engine. "Depends on the circumstances. At Little Joe's? Didn't see me offering the guy cash. Depends on the person, too. Sometimes, though..." He shrugged. "Might feel better to toss them around but...

"It won't always get me the results I want, and I'll have a lot harder time going back if I want more. With that kid, making nice and tossing him some cash was definitely the way to go. That's someone I *wouldn't* have wanted to rough up...even if it might teach him a lesson about taking money from strangers."

I looked out the window. "I take it we're going to that meeting?"

"Not much choice. You want to stay out—"

"No. If you go, I go. You're right. We need to know what this is about and the only way to do that is to play along." I glanced his way. "I'm assuming you don't think we're really going to meet a contact who can give us more information on Wilkes."

Jack snorted. "Meeting a stranger? In a condo? Might as well ask me to meet him in the desert. And bring my own shovel."

* * *

On the way to the condo subdivision, Jack explained what he thought we'd find there. He was sure the welcoming party would come bearing guns, baseball bats or tire irons. What he *wasn't* certain of was who'd issued the invitation. He laid sixty-forty odds on it being Gallagher. The other possibility was Boris Nikolaev.

Apparently Jack wasn't as confident as he'd seemed about how his message to the Nikolaevs would be received. Issue a simple, respectful message of professional courtesy, assuring them that he wasn't interested in their business, so they shouldn't be interested in his, and they *should* back off. But he'd heard Boris could be a hothead, quick to see insult where none was intended.

As for how the Nikolaevs could have dispatched someone here so fast—well, telephones work pretty quickly. If Gallagher knew the Nikolaevs were looking for Jack, it would take one phone call from his end, and one phone call bounced back to a Nikolaev associate in Vegas, and they could have someone at the casino before I'd even made it outside.

"Is it just me, or is this getting really annoying?" I said.

"Fucking annoying."

"I think we should just call up all the nice mobsters in the country and tell them, 'Look, we're trying to catch a rampaging killer here. Do you think you could stop putting contracts on our heads? Just for a day or two? Please?'"

"It'll stop. Tonight."

I glanced over at him, but he was looking straight ahead, face hard. I nodded and leaned back in my seat.

After a moment he said. "Earlier. About Gallagher. Kind of jobs he wants. You should know."

"I don't plan to ever call on him for employment."

"Still, you should know. Gallagher wants someone dead?

You don't ask why. Sometimes it's card sharks. Sometimes it's unpaid debt. Sometimes..." He shrugged. "Sometimes, you don't wanna know. For a while, that was okay. Didn't give a shit. Figured someone's gonna take the contract. Might as well be me."

He turned left, heading toward the highway. "Eventually? Decided it didn't need to be me. Didn't need the money. Didn't need the grief. Things change. Ten, fifteen years ago? Didn't matter. Now...?" He shrugged. "My jobs these days? Some you wouldn't touch. I'm not like you and Quinn. Don't come from the same place. Don't see things the same way."

So how *did* he see things? I longed to ask, but when I opened my mouth, I couldn't think of any way to word it that wouldn't sound like prying.

Jack slanted an expectant look my way. "You gonna ask? Or you don't want to know?"

"Uh, sure, I'd love to know. I just didn't want to— Well, it didn't seem right to just come right out and ask, but I'm certainly interested if you want to tell me."

A slight downturn of his lips. A frown? Didn't he just *offer*—?

"Better not," he said after a moment. "Not my place. Ask him. He wants you to know. Tried to tell you. Shouldn't have interrupted."

Huh? What was he talking—?

I replayed his first comments, about him not being like Quinn or me. *That's* what he thought I'd want to know, more about Quinn, how he was like me. I'd assumed he just meant because we'd both been cops.

When I said I was interested, he thought I meant in Quinn's story, the one he'd interrupted at the motel. Was there a way to clear up the confusion? To say "Oh, I thought you were talking about yourself"? Ask him about himself. But if that wasn't what he'd been offering...

Before I could figure out a way to continue, Jack passed me the map and put me in charge of finding our destination.

We found the new condo complex—so new it wasn't even finished. A security van was parked at the far end, the lone occupant's head down, reading or dozing. Jack pulled in, headlights off, and slid the car into the equipment lot between a crane and a bulldozer.

Across the road a billboard exhorted home buyers to "Experience the adventure. Live life in the heart of the game." As I cracked open my window, I was hard-pressed to feel the adventure...or the life. The stale stink of dust filled the air. Empty window frames stared out like dead eyes. Sheets of plastic covered the board studded walls, the eerie *slap-slap* of the plastic the only sound.

I closed my window.

"Not quite the scenario we expected," I said. "Too open. Too...empty."

He nodded, gaze scanning the complex.

"Do you have a plan?"

"Working on it."

"May I make a suggestion?"

"Always."

I proposed we handle this as a two-man police raid, using a variation on standard procedures for infiltrating unoccupied buildings. Unlike an occupied area, here there was a good likelihood that our welcoming party wasn't at 510 H.G. Wells Boulevard at all, but in an adjoining townhouse, or even across the road, watching for us through a sniper's sight.

The condos were row houses, with two basic styles—carport to the left and carport to the right. That meant we could investigate the one beside it, and expect to find the same floor plan reversed at 510.

Jack removed his gold; I put away the blond wig and jewelry—things that could catch the light. Then I scooped up dirt from the unfinished roadway, added bottled water, and we daubed it on our faces. I would have loved a Kevlar vest, but apparently the wire in my push-up bra was all the body armor I was getting. So I donned my gloves, took a deep breath and opened the door.

"Forgetting something?" he said.

I looked at him.

"Gun." He reached under his jacket. "Here. Take my backup."

"That's okay—"

"*Take* it."

As he thrust the gun at me, I opened my jacket and showed him the Glock. "See? I didn't leave it back at the hotel."

"Yeah. Just in the car."

He got out. I followed.

Desolate. Some words evoke images; others, emotions. Desolate is a shivers-up-the-spine word, full of loneliness and emptiness. And, as we approached unit 510, the word sprang to mind and lodged there.

Empty houses stood stark against the darkness, looking not half finished, but half ruined. Tarps over the windows and roofs billowed like spirits chained to the houses, flapping and slapping in the wind as they struggled to fly free. Behind us lay the desert, sand blowing in to reclaim the subdivision.

I shivered. Jack glanced over at me.

"Cold?" he whispered.

"A little," I lied.

"It's the wind. Better inside."

The modern condos loomed around me, scarier than any moldering Victorian mansion. I knew they weren't haunted—stuff like that doesn't bother me. You have to believe in the supernatural to be frightened by it. What spooked me was the desolation, as if it were a force that could reach up and swallow me.

We started at the last house in the row, secreting ourselves in its rear shadows, and creeping toward unit 510. We stopped at the unit to the left, and slipped behind the tarp to the largest window. Like most of the others, the glass hadn't been installed yet and the frame stood open.

Jack laced his fingers to help me through.

THIRTY-NINE

Inside, I paused to let my vision adjust and give me time to focus, pushing past the frustration. My heart was thumping.

We had work to do, a solid lead to follow—a *name* even—but we were stuck here chasing down another would-be attacker. Somewhere out there, Wilkes was stalking his next mark and I would fail, again, to stop him. Fail to save another victim, not through my inexperience or ineptitude, but because some two-bit thug was holding me back. Well, this thug wouldn't walk away.

When my eyes adjusted, I looked around to locate all the entrances—all the ways someone could sneak in here and see me—but the whole main level was a big entry point. The interior walls were naked stud-work. There was one front door, one back door, a basement door, a half-dozen open windows and a stairwell leading to the second level.

I moved to the wall adjoining this unit to the next—the route I hoped to take into unit 510. It was drywalled. Figures. The compound hadn't been added yet, so I moved my gloved fingers over the boards, testing their resilience and peering through the cracks. The drywall was securely fastened. Jack could probably rip off a piece, but not without creating enough racket to alert anyone waiting for us next door.

Something whispered behind me—the soft sound of a carefully placed foot. I wheeled, gun going up. Jack lifted his free hand. He'd come in the window, obviously deciding I needed closer backup. I nodded and motioned for him to follow, so he could stand at my back while I examined the wall farther down. We slipped through the wall studs into what looked like the kitchen. There, alongside the counter, the drywallers had left a bare two-by-three-foot section, presumably waiting for something to be roughed in.

While Jack covered my rear, I crouched to examine the hole. The gap was partly drywalled on the other side, but there was a spot big enough to squeeze through—big enough for *me*. I straightened and gestured at the hole. As Jack ducked for a better look, something thumped overhead.

I froze, eyes narrowing as I looked up. For a moment, all was quiet. Then it came again, the faint thump of a foot on uncovered floorboards . . . right over our heads.

Jack's gaze shot left. I gestured at the stairwell, the only obvious route to the second floor. I mentally raced through my image of the exterior, then leaned over to Jack, and whispered an idea.

"Where?" he mouthed.

I took a moment to figure it out, then pointed. His gaze flicked up, and I could see him processing the second-floor plan, working out the logistics. Then he nodded and waved me off.

Once I was through the hole between units, Jack hunkered down beside it, giving me cover while protecting his own back. For a minute, I didn't go anywhere, just stood there, looking and listening. Just because we knew someone was upstairs in unit 508, didn't mean there wasn't anyone in 510.

Like its neighbor, this unit was all open stud-work, meaning the only thing between me and a potential attacker was the darkness—but that worked both ways. Once I was reasonably confident that I was alone, I moved forward, gun ready, steps soundless as I moved toward the stairs.

Construction had progressed further on level two, making travel easier in some ways, tougher in others. Without Jack's cover, I had to take it slow and careful. With my back to the wall, I crept down the hall, peeked through the master bedroom door, then darted over to the balcony. Here the patio door had been installed, but didn't yet have a lock—or handle. I eased it open, crept onto the balcony and moved to the far right end.

A few feet away was the balcony for 508, where we'd heard the steps. Crossing the gap would have been easier—and safer—with proper tools, but I made it. Once across, a look through the glass door assured me the bedroom was empty. Within seconds, I was inside and across the room, pressed against the wall beside the hall doorway.

The footsteps had come from the northeast corner of the unit, right across from the master bedroom. I strained for a sound from that direction. None came. I tapped a fingernail against the drywall. A second tap answered. All units in position. I counted to three, then silently swung through the doorway.

The hall was empty. A split second later, Jack wheeled around the other end, gun drawn. He nodded. I lifted my hand and counted down: three-two-one. We each moved to cover the next doorway. Mine was the bathroom. No one was in it. I glanced at Jack. He shook his head.

With the next countdown, he swung into the entrance to the room where we'd heard footsteps, with me covering him from anyone coming down the hall. A soft grunt told me the bedroom was empty.

I squeezed past him, leaving him covering the door, and

moved into the room. A quick check out the window. I shook my head. All clear.

While Jack kept me covered, I crouched and took out a penlight. Shielding it with my free hand to limit the reach of the light, I examined the floorboards. The thick layer of drywall dust showed the ghost of many feet, and two sets of recent prints, made after the last of the dust had settled. One set was mine. The other crisscrossed the room a few times, then ended at the window.

As I bent to examine the window, Jack tapped my shoulder and shook his head. I arched my brows. He gestured at one of the footprints. Misshapen, as a few of them were, with an extra bump-out near the heel, as if the walker had slipped in the dust.

"Retraced his steps," Jack whispered.

He motioned for me to get the window open.

"Make noise," he said. "Be obvious."

I nodded. Jack slid soundlessly back to the door, and I started working on the window. I was careful not to be *too* obvious about it, but didn't take pains to open it quietly. Jack motioned for me to keep up the ruse and disappeared around the corner.

I got the window open, then stage-whispered, "Here, let me go first."

I grunted, playing Jack hoisting me into the window.

"Shit," I whispered. "It's a helluva drop. Give me your hand and lower me down."

Another grunt. Then the crack of a gunshot. I wheeled away from the window, realizing as I moved that the shot came from the hall, not outside. A second shot—returned fire. As I sprinted across the room, two more shots came in quick succession from the second, farther gun.

As I neared the door, gun drawn, I could see Jack inside

the bathroom doorway, diagonally across the hall. He had his gun up, listening. Seeing me, he jerked his chin, telling me our assailant was down the hall. I motioned, asking Jack if the gunman was far enough away for me to cross my open doorway safely. He nodded, and I flipped to that side. Then we waited.

I heard it first, the slap of a foot brought down too quickly. I gestured to Jack, telling him the gunman was on the move. Then I motioned a plan. He hesitated, then nodded.

I counted to five, leaned into the hall, making myself a target, then jerked back. The gunman fired. Jack fired. A hiss of pain. Return fire, receding, covering the sounds of retreat. Only when I heard the distant sound of feet racing down the stairs did I peek to check on Jack. He was already in pursuit. I hurried after him.

Wilkes

Wilkes huddled under the tarp, back against a lumber pile, gun drawn to blast the first shape that came near him. Gone to ground. Holed up like a rabbit.

God, wouldn't Evelyn love to see him now?

No. She wouldn't. Wouldn't care one way or the other. She'd just sniff, as if to say "What do you expect?"

His hands trembled, but he told himself it was rage, not fear. The fury of a wounded lion cornered by a sniveling jackal. He'd set the trap at the window, assuming they'd draw the obvious conclusion and climb out. Jack would let the girl go first to help her down. Such a gentleman. Then Wilkes would have swung around the corner, opened fire and rid himself of an annoying little scavenger.

That's all Jack was—a scavenger. A jackal. Fed scraps by Evelyn, petted and pampered until he thought he was good enough to compete with the lions. One swing of Wilkes's paw and he could have brought Jack down twenty-five years ago. Should have.

Wilkes shifted, inhaling sharply as pain knifed through him. Two shots. How the hell had Jack managed to hit him twice? He knew the answer in a heartbeat. Because he'd screwed up.

These past two weeks he'd prided himself on the care he took, on the control he exercised. Easy enough when it was a stranger at the other end of his gun barrel. But when given the chance to take down Jack, that cold layer of detachment had evaporated, and he'd been running on hate and adrenaline. He'd moved quickly, carelessly. Unforgivable.

He wouldn't make the same mistake again. At least he'd had the sense to back down after he was wounded. Neither shot was serious, and that was all that counted . . . even if it meant he was forced to crouch here, bleeding like a stuck pig, when he should be hunting Jack.

A fresh burst of rage, and he inhaled again, sharper, clearing his head, then peeked out. Where were they? Maybe he'd been wrong. Maybe they weren't searching for him. He must have hit Jack at least once. Must have. Maybe he was lying in a pool of blood right now, the girl bent over him, desperately trying to staunch the flow.

The thought cheered Wilkes enough to push to his feet. He staggered forward and tugged back the tarp for a better look.

"Blood here." Jack's distant whisper carried through the silence. "Got a trail."

Didn't *sound* like he was bleeding to death.

Wilkes clenched his jaw hard enough to feel a jolt. As he took another step, the pain from his side and shoulder flared. He gritted his teeth and pushed past it. No time for weakness. He had to get out there and—

The pain was so intense he stumbled, hands smacking the tarp as he broke his fall.

"—hear that?" the woman's voice whispered.

Wilkes pushed up straight, both hands on his gun to steady it, waiting for one of them to appear. But all went silent, even the sound of the flapping tarps from earlier gone as the wind had died. He surveyed the construction yard. It was dotted with piles of lumber, covered drywall, bricks . . . a dozen places to hide.

Did he expect them to waltz over here, letting him get a clean shot? Did he really think Jack was that stupid? He wanted to. God, how he wanted to. But he knew better.

He checked his watch: 11:48. No more time to waste. As much as he'd love to stick around and see this through, he had a train to catch.

He hadn't made it to his car. He'd got about a quarter of the way when he'd picked up the sounds of pursuit. Knowing he was in no condition to outrun them, he'd taken the first port of refuge: the security guard's van. He'd known it was open—he'd left it that way after he'd killed the guard.

The perfect hiding place. He'd positioned the guard so, from a distance, he appeared to be dozing. Jack wouldn't dare come close enough to see otherwise. He'd spot a sleeping guard and avoid the van, assuming his quarry would do the same. So now, hunkered down in the back, tying makeshift bandages on his wounds, Wilkes only needed to wait Jack out.

He checked his watch. Could he still make the train? He had over an hour's drive just to reach the station. He fought the first prick of panic. He'd still have time. Jack wouldn't search for long, not with the girl in tow.

They'd left. They'd finally left. Wilkes checked his watch for the hundredth time in the past hour, his rage so white-hot that sweat streamed down his face.

No, it wasn't too late. He could drive to the next station. He could—

Impossible. He'd calculated it, recalculated it with every possible variable in his favor and knew he'd never make it on time.

Take another train. Kill another victim.

And, while he was at it, he'd send the Feds a congratulations card, for scaring him off his promise, making things too hot for him to pull the promised hit. That's what they'd assume.

He'd failed.

No, not failed. Changed his plan. He was toying with them. He never even got on the train. Couldn't have, because he'd been in Vegas, killing a security guard.

He smiled, took out his wallet and removed a dollar bill, rubbing it between his gloved fingers to make sure he only had one. Then he reached into the front seat, laid it on the guard's lap and—

And looked down at the bloodied shirt he'd stripped off.

His gut went cold.

He fought the panic back. He'd been careful. Even the shirt was folded, unbloodied side down. But if he made this an HSK kill, the Feds would rip this van apart. A single blood drop. A single hair. Even an eyelash. They'd comb the building site, too, and he knew from Jack's words that he'd dripped blood somewhere.

He swallowed. Fresh rage enveloped him.

In a flash, he was back in that house, in that hall, seeing Jack down the hall illuminated by the moonlight. His face hard. Emotionless and cold, as if he knew he'd make his shot. Jack hadn't feared starting a gun battle in an empty house because he knew he'd instinctively cover all the contingencies, that even if he wasn't hunting a mark, he'd have covered his traces.

So damned perfect. Jack wouldn't have panicked and crawled into this van, bleeding.

Wilkes shook off the thought. He'd leave this as an unmarked killing, and he'd be safe. That meant the Helter Skelter killer couldn't strike in or near Vegas tonight—couldn't take the chance of the murders being linked.

It didn't matter. He'd make up for it. Something bigger. Better. Splashier. Let the Feds think he'd been pulling their strings with the train hit, making them dance. He'd do it right next time.

Then he'd take care of Jack.

FORTY

We searched for longer than we should have. If I needed further proof that Jack was as frustrated by this "interruption" as I was, this was it. After a thorough sweep, we should have left, in case the dozing guard awoke. Even more dangerous was our pursuer himself, possibly holed up somewhere, gun poised, ready to blast if anything crept past his hiding spot. That *I* realized this first—when the black fury over losing our prey lifted long enough for me to take stock of my situation—proved how furious Jack was.

When I did realize it, I felt a lick of fear, worried that if I suggested we should quit, he'd turn that anger on me. Yet I didn't get more than a whispered "Jack, I think—" out before he was nodding and nudging me to a quiet spot, where he said the very words I'd been ready to speak, as if he'd already realized we should leave and had just been holding out a few minutes longer before surrendering.

And it *did* feel like surrender. Jack said our target had probably left, and I agreed, but we both knew neither of us believed it. Even if we suspected it, we wanted to be sure, to cover every square inch, hunt until dawn drove us off.

It was a silent drive to the hotel.

Instead of letting me sink into my black thoughts, the quiet refocused my attention. Jack was just as angry, just as frustrated as I was, and what I felt was the overwhelming need, not to join him, but to pull him out of it. Help him as he'd helped me last night, after the opera.

Yet last night, he'd initially seemed uncertain how to help, leaving my room to buy a bottle. Only later did he hit on the perfect diversion— And so now I sat there, wishing I knew him better, knew how to help.

When we finally reached the hotel and got inside, I said the only thing I could think of.

"You got him. Shot him, I mean. For all we know, he's holed up, dead."

Jack shook his head, tossing his keys on the dresser, rattling as they collapsed in a heap.

"Fucked up," he said.

"You? I never even got off a shot."

He shrugged off his jacket and tossed it on the chair then, with a glance my way, picked it up and laid it neatly across the back. I watched him, measuring the set of his jaw, the force of his footfalls as he crossed the room. He sighed, rubbing the back of his neck, vertebrae crackling. Then he kicked off his shoes, thumping one-two on the carpet.

"Fucked up," he said again, as if he'd never paused the conversation. "Back at Little Joe's place. That punk. Message wasn't enough."

"We don't know that. This was more likely Gallagher's man—"

"Doesn't matter." He lowered himself onto the bed, springs squeaking. "Ten years ago? Woulda put a bullet in him. Never thought twice. Punks like that? Can't let them think they bested you."

Another neck rub. "But like I said tonight? Ten years ago? Don't much like who I was then. Things I did. These days? Try to find other ways. Sometimes? Go too far."

"Even if you had killed that guy the other day, that's not to say the Nikolaevs wouldn't have sent this one ... if that's who did send him."

Jack opened his mouth, as if to argue, then said, "Gotta get some sleep."

"Can you? I mean, I'm not sure *I* can so if there's anything I can do..."

He paused and I could tell he was ready to lie and say "Nah, I'm good," but then he glanced my way, hesitated a few more seconds and said, "Talk to me."

I managed a wry smile. "Now that I can do, as you well know—though, after I get going, you probably wish I came with a shut-up button."

He met my gaze. "Never."

I felt my cheeks heat. Didn't know why, but felt the blush anyway as I stumbled on. "If it's war stories you're looking for, I'm afraid I can't match yours. Mine are all pretty much 'find Mafia thug, kill Mafia thug.' Good for putting you to sleep, though..."

"None of that shit. Just tell me..." He shrugged. "Talk about the lodge. Your plans. Where you want to be in five years."

"Still open for business."

A quarter-smile. "Yeah. I know. You will be. Must have plans, though."

"Tons of them."

"Tell me."

And so I did. Babbled on about the lodge, my plans for it, and he listened, even prolonging the conversation with questions and suggestions. Absolutely meaningless drivel that we managed to invest with all the gravity and consideration we gave to our investigation plans.

After ten minutes, we were stretched atop our respective beds, heads on the pillows. Jack had his shirt off, jeans still on, half ready for bed but not prepared to make the full commitment. Another twenty, and his questions came slower, as he relaxed, lack of sleep from the night before catching up with him. Ten more and he was gone, snoring softly, as if exhausted.

I slipped from bed, tiptoeing, knowing how easily he woke. I took a blanket from the closet and laid it over him, as he'd done with his jacket the night before. Then I changed into my nightshirt, turned off the lights and crawled into bed.

"Nadia..."

Running. Lungs on fire. Heart pounding. It hurt. Hurt so bad. Pain ripping through me. Couldn't think about that. Couldn't think about *me*. All that mattered was Amy. Gotta get home. Gotta tell my dad...

Hands grabbed me, strong hands. I fought, kicking, biting.

"Nadia..."

Arms going around me, holding me still. Restraining me. No! Wouldn't let him touch me again. Wouldn't let him—

"Nadia!"

I slammed awake, head flying back, gulping air. For a moment, I seemed to hang there, between sleep and waking, not sure where I belonged. Then I felt the arms around me, bare skin hot against mine. I blinked. A face appeared, black eyes, tousled black hair, black beard shadow framing a frown...Jack.

I jumped, arms flailing, one catching him in the jaw hard enough that the smack resounded through the tiny room.

"Oh, geez," I said, scrambling up. "I'm sor—"

"Deserved it," he said, rubbing his jaw. "Shouldn't have startled you."

He sat on the edge of my bed, still dressed only in his jeans.

"You were having a nightmare," he said.

Wisps of the dream fluttered back to me. "I was. I'm sorry. I didn't mean— Did I wake you?"

"Yeah. That's what I'm worried about. Losing a few hours of sleep." He met my gaze. "Seemed like a bad one. You were . . . screaming."

I rubbed my eyes. "Sorry."

"Stop that. Fuck." He shook his head and went silent, as if considering something, then, slowly, turned to meet my gaze. "You were calling for your cousin."

"My—?" The word jammed in my throat. "You know."

"Yeah. Evelyn."

Of course. I'd already suspected she'd found the case. It wasn't difficult—almost any article on the Franco incident mentioned my past.

I rubbed my throat. His gaze went there, and stayed there. I yanked my hand away.

"That's where you got it," he said. "Isn't it?"

His fingertips brushed the faint scar on my throat.

"N—no," I said, backing up and instinctively ducking my head, covering the mark. "That's just— Kids' stuff. You know. Goofing around, doing what our parents always tell us not to do. I learned my lesson. Anyway, I'm sorry I woke you and—"

"Papers don't say anything about you."

"Papers?"

"Your cousin's murder. The articles. Said you escaped unharmed."

"Amy—" I swallowed. "She was prettier, more mature. So he picked her first and . . ."

"Left you alone?"

I met his gaze. "Yes."

In the silence that followed, I sat there, mouth slightly open as I struggled for slow, easy breaths. He stared out across the room, and rubbed his lower lip. Twice his gaze swung my way and I froze, certain he was going to ask another question.

The third time, his gaze came to rest on my throat and I struggled to keep my chin up, letting him look.

"What'd you do?"

"Wha—?" The word came out as a squeak. I coughed. "What?"

"The scar. Looks like a knife wound."

I managed a laugh, a little too high-pitched, but he didn't seem to notice, his expression unchanged.

"If anyone asks, that's exactly what it is," I said, forcing a smile that felt like baring my teeth. "It'll give me some street cred. Truth is, I sliced it open climbing a barbed-wire fence."

"Huh."

"Stupid kid tricks, huh?"

I pried my grip from the bottom sheet, twisted to sit up more and found myself caught in the covers. I looked down to see them tangled around my bare legs, my oversized T-shirt bunched up around my stomach, underwear on full display.

I yanked my shirt down. "I think I need more roommate-friendly sleepwear."

He didn't answer. Just sat there, studying me, then after a moment, his gaze dipped away and he shrugged, gesturing at his bare chest. "I'm not any better."

"Well, between the two of us, we're fully dressed."

"Yeah."

He stayed there, gaze fixed on something across the

room. I tried not to stare... but, well, he was sitting right there, in front of me, so he was all I *could* see, his head tilted slightly, face in shadow, strong jaw set, dark beard stubble somehow emphasizing the planes of his face, making it rougher, sexier. Yes, sexier, as much as I hated to admit it, even to myself. He looked damned good half naked, with the muscled chest and arms of someone who stays in shape because he has to, not necessarily because he wants to. Nothing showy, just lean and hard and sexy as hell.

And here I'd been lying in bed beside him, my shirt riding up around my stomach, more than half naked, and he hadn't so much as snuck a second look... if he'd even noticed at all. That stung.

As I pulled back and tugged the covers over my legs, he looked over sharply, as if startled.

"You tired?" he said.

"No, and it wouldn't matter if I was. Once I start having the nightmares, they don't end until I stop sleeping."

He nodded. I adjusted the sheet some more, but he still didn't get up. His hand moved to the space between us, bracing himself, and his bicep flexed. The skin there was rough, unnatural, and when I looked closer, I could make out the ghost of a surgically erased tattoo, a symbol of some kind, invisible from more than a few inches away.

My gaze slid off his arm to another patch of disfigured skin over his breast. A star-shaped pattern of quarter-inch circular burns. I'd seen marks like that before, and knew immediately what they were. Cigarette burns—the lit end held against the skin, applying enough pressure to scorch but not to put out the flame. A crude torture tactic. These marks were old, the burns faded to skin color.

Jack followed my gaze before I could look away.

"War wounds." His mouth opened again, as if considering saying more. It shut, then reopened, but he only said, "Old."

"So I see."

Again, that hesitation, lips parted, debating the urge to say more. Again, he stopped himself. Again, he restarted.

"Hungry?"

"What?"

"You hungry? We could get breakfast. Catch an earlier flight."

Figures. Here I am, waiting for a great personal revelation, and he's just trying to figure out whether it's too early to suggest breakfast.

"Well, I'm up," I said. "But you're the one whose sleep was disturbed, so if you'd rather catch another couple of hours—"

"Didn't disturb me."

"Okay, then. We might as well get going. As for breakfast—" I checked the bedside clock. Four-ten. "Our chances of finding a place serving food at this time are pretty slim."

"It's Vegas."

"Right. Breakfast it is then."

I shifted up in bed, but he still made no move to stand until I tapped his leg. As he turned, I saw a pair of fresh scratches clawed across his back.

I touched them with my fingertips. "Did I do that?"

"Hardly mortal."

"Geez, I'm—"

"Don't say it."

We put on our disguises, but didn't play them up to full effect. It was four-thirty in the morning, and neither of us was in the mood to take on the guise of a character who made our skin crawl.

By four-forty-five, we were seated in the corner of a diner, as far as we could get from the other patrons, most of whom were nursing coffees in silence, recovering from a long night of drink or disappointment.

As I rearranged the containers on the table, Jack thumbed through the menu. Under the harsh florescent lights, he no longer looked sexy. Just tired. Very tired, the creases over his nose turned into furrows, shadows under his eyes, skin pale against the beard shadow, the black threaded with gray.

"At least now we know who we're looking for," I said quietly.

A slow nod.

"But it doesn't really help, does it?" I laid down my menu, and traced my finger over the cartoon pig on the front. "All we have is a name, and it's not even a name; it's an alias."

"Evelyn knows his name."

"His real name?"

"Yeah. Evelyn knows everyone's name." A pause. "Well, most everyone."

"But not yours."

"Not for lack of trying."

The obvious segue here was to talk about Evelyn and her relationship with Wilkes. Back when we'd been compiling the list, Wilkes had been the first name to Jack's lips. But Evelyn had dismissed him in a heartbeat.

His wasn't the only name she'd dismissed, and we hadn't discounted any of them. Given Evelyn's reaction to Baron, her fast and strong opinions on our suspects hadn't seemed out of character. And yet . . .

I thought back to when we'd gone after Little Joe's first hitman—Bert—and how she'd tried to stop me. Had it been more than a test? Had she worried that the hitman might be someone she knew? Someone she hadn't wanted me going after?

Could Evelyn be *involved*? Could that be why she'd been so adamant about joining the search, to keep an eye on our progress? I didn't know her well enough to form an opinion. Someone at this table did, and I knew I had to ask, but wasn't sure how I could. Whatever his quarrel with Evelyn over me, there was a deep history between them, an almost parental relationship. What if Jack couldn't bring himself to consider the possibility—

"For two hundred million?" he said. "Or a decent cut? Yeah. She'd do it."

I blinked. "Wha—?"

"Evelyn. The big question. Could she be part of this."

"Was I talking out loud?"

A tiny smile and shake of his head. "We were talking about Evelyn. Her and Wilkes. You went quiet. Looked worried." He shrugged. "Doesn't take ESP."

"And you think the answer is yes? That she could be involved?"

He sipped his coffee. "Gut reaction? No. But that's not good enough. Question's there. Needs an answer. From the head. Not the gut. Could she?" He stared out the window at the passing cars. "Not impossible."

"You think, if someone offered her a cut of two hundred million—"

I stopped and realized what I was saying. How many people would help a killer if it meant a share of that kind of money?

I continued, "But she has to be smart enough to know the government would never pay that much—"

"She is. But is this it? The final play? Maybe there's more. Some...way of getting it. Even a partial payment..." He paused, still watching traffic. "Bigger question? Would she work with Wilkes? Can't see it."

"So you think we should—?"

"Dismiss it? Can't. Like I said. It's a question. Needs an answer. How?" He tapped the menu. "Eat first."

The server approached, refilled our coffees and started to leave again. We had to call her back to place an order. She seemed a bit put out, as if this shift demanded little more of her than carrying around a pot of fresh coffee and that was how she liked it.

After she left, I said, "Back to Evelyn knowing Wilkes's real name. How much good will that do us?"

"Depends."

"On how much he still uses it for anything."

"Yeah."

I sipped my coffee. "Maybe you don't know Wilkes as well as Evelyn does, but you must have some opinion on this exit strategy of his. Was his original plan to just cover Kozlov's death? Kill off the only witness? Maybe because Kozlov *had* tried to activate his blackmail retirement plan. Or is this where Wilkes was headed all along? *His* retirement plan. Try to earn himself a huge pension and get rid of Kozlov as a bonus?"

"Doesn't need a pension. Put in all these years? At this level? Unless you got bad habits, you got money. I do. Evelyn does. Fucking all you have. But you have it."

"And Wilkes didn't have any 'bad habits' when you knew him? Drinking, gambling, drugs?"

"You get bad habits? You don't last. Get desperate. Get caught. Small shit? Drink too much Friday nights? Play the ponies Saturday afternoons? Yeah, sure. Doesn't dent his paycheck."

"So he's developed a jones for the killing, is that what you figure?"

Jack sipped his coffee, then nodded. "Yeah. Fits him. Fits the situation, too. Retiring, all that."

"One last bang before you go?"

He leaned back in his seat, fingers tapping against the side of his mug. "More like figuring out you got no place to go. All this work. For what? To retire? To what? Go fly-fishing? Buy a condo in Florida? Take a cruise? Guys like Wilkes. Like me. Like Evelyn. This is it. You get this far because this is all you got. Some guys have more. Kids. Girlfriends. Wives. Bunch of wives, more like. But they're pulling jobs for five grand. Kill-the-cheating-bitch shit. Real money comes with real risk. You don't do that with kids, wives, whatever."

I opened my mouth to respond, but he kept going, leaning forward now. "That's why I tell you, you got it right. Something else besides this. The lodge. Your life there. Ever comes a time? You have to choose?"

"I know what I'd pick, Jack. There wouldn't be much sense in keeping this job and losing the lodge when the main reason I have this job is for the lodge."

"Keep it that way."

Our orders arrived. I sliced into my egg and cut a clean stroke through the solid yolk…a yolk that was supposed to be over-easy. I carved a line around the yellow and took a bite of white.

"Seems like you've given this some thought," I said after a moment, my gaze still on my plate. "Retiring, I mean."

When he didn't answer, I glanced up, hoping the question hadn't offended him, but he was in the midst of chewing. He finished, then said, "Did. Past tense. Couple years ago. Thought I was ready. Realized I wasn't."

He sliced into his ham steak. "It's like any job. Whole time you're looking at the exit door. When will I have enough? Money, I had. Still young enough to enjoy it."

"That's important."

"Yeah. But enjoy it how? Piss off to some tropical island? Lay on the beach all day? Work on my tan?"

I grinned. "Hey, you could always pull a Brando. Retreat from the world, buy an island and set up your own little tropical kingdom. Build up a harem, laze around getting laid and getting fat."

He gave me a look that said he'd as soon stick lit match-sticks under his fingernails.

"Seriously, though, there must have been something you wanted to do, something you always planned to do when you retired."

"Travel."

"Now that'd be cool."

"You like traveling?"

"I'm really more of a homebody, but it would be nice to see the world once. Visit all the places you've read about."

He laid down his fork. "Seeing Paris in the spring. Strolling the Great Wall. Standing under the pyramids in the moonlight. Sounds great. Reality? Standing by a mountain of broken rock. Shoes full of sand. Sweating my ass off. Worrying about my pocket getting picked. Surrounded by strangers..." He shrugged. "Waste of fucking time. Might as well buy a book. Look at pictures."

"I wouldn't care. Sand, heat, pickpockets... it'd all be atmosphere. I'd just like to say I saw the pyramids."

His gaze met mine, studying me, his fingers tapping the

side of his mug, probably trying to decide whether he should ask if I wanted a coffee refill.

"Maybe..." he began. "Sometime? You wanna go? I'd go with you. See the pyramids—"

A crash across the diner cut him off.

FORTY-ONE

I twisted to see a red-faced man in a cowboy hat, a toppled canister of sugar at his feet, standing beside two uniformed officers on coffee break.

"Now, just calm down, sir," the one officer said, keeping his voice low.

"I'll calm down when I get some fucking answers! And the answer I want is why the fuck I can't pay this!"

He thrust out a piece of green paper. From here, I could barely see it, but I knew what it was. A one-dollar bill.

"Shit," I breathed, closing my eyes.

"It's one fucking dollar," the man continued. "I can find this much by digging through my sofa cushions. Do you think there's a person in this room who wouldn't pay this insurance policy?"

"I wouldn't," said the first officer's partner as she swiveled her chair to face the man. "And do you know why? Because, if I did, what would stop a thousand other freaks from doing the same thing? If you pay once, you have to keep paying."

I could feel myself nodding, but a glance around showed I was the only one.

"What you have to do, sir," the second officer continued, "is put that dollar back in your pocket, go home to your family, look after them, and trust that we will look after you, and the FBI will catch this guy."

"Catch him?" a woman yelled from across the diner. "The FBI has their heads so far up their asses they're investigating drooling lunatics. They can't even stop him when he hands them a schedule and directions."

"Yeah," a man's voice boomed. "Tell that poor old fart in Chicago how safe he is. Can't even take a crap without getting killed. And what about that Indian yesterday? Did the killer tell the Feds where he was going to be then, too?"

"I wouldn't know," the first officer said. "The FBI is conducting an independent investigation and we—"

"And you're sitting on your asses eating doughnuts!"

A rumble went through the smattering of diners. As my hands clenched my mug, Jack's knee brushed my leg. He jerked his chin toward the door, a twenty already on the table. When I hesitated, he caught my eye and shook his head, and with great reluctance, I stood. Around me, people continued to shout questions and abuse at the two officers. A few were already on their feet. Jack's fingers wrapped around my upper arm. He leaned into my ear.

"You can't help. Not now."

I resisted for a moment, then yanked my gaze away and let him lead me from the diner.

So we knew there had been another killing since Chicago, and that the public knew about the opera house, too. All yesterday I'd avoided papers and radios and TVs, struggling to concentrate on the task at hand. Even now I did my best to resist. I walked past the newsstand at the airport terminal, tuned out other passengers' conversations, even looked away from a big-screen TV tuned to CNN when the ticker flashed "Helter Skelter killer." Like Jack said—and said often—knowing didn't help, didn't get me any closer to catching him.

On the plane we decided what we'd do about Evelyn. We were halfway to her house when Jack pulled into a strip mall.

"Want a coffee?" he said.

I shook my head.

"Need to use the bathroom," he said, opening his door. "Smoke shop down there. Could grab a paper."

I sat there a minute after he got out, wondering whether I should hold out, *could* hold out, then pushed open the door, went in and bought a paper—well, three of them, two nationals and a local. As I was paying, I noticed the rows of cigarettes behind the counter, at least half of them in packages I didn't recognize.

"You have a lot of foregin brands," I said, waving at the display.

"You name it, I got it," said the old man behind the counter. "Whatcha looking for."

"I'm not sure. Something...Irish? Maybe English. Probably an older brand, been around awhile. I know what the logo looks like..."

"Then we'll find it."

When I climbed into the car, Jack was already back. I put down the bag with the papers and took out a smaller one, then did up my seat belt.

"Candy?" Jack asked with a small smile.

"Uh-uh." I pulled off the bag with a flourish.

His brows arched. "How'd you figure out—"

"Keen detective work. You seemed a little stressed after that flight, so I figured it might not be unwelcome. We're not really 'on the job' right now so..."

"Appreciate it. Better not smoke in here, though. Bring the papers."

* * *

We found a picnic table behind the strip mall. Jack shook out a cigarette and had it lit before we were seated, and went through another before we finished our reading.

The killer's last known victim had been killed at noon the day before. William (Billy) Curtis, a twenty-eight-year-old Nebraska construction worker, pushed off the high-rise he'd been working on. At first, police thought it had been an accident...until the coroner found the lone dollar bill in his pocket. While the papers spent little time dwelling on the victim, they *were* speculating over one thing: had the Feds been tipped off about the killing?

I slapped down the paper. "Just because he forewarned the Feds of the opera house plan doesn't mean he's going to keep doing that. He can't. It'd be stupid."

Jack took out his third cigarette and lit it.

"My guess is that the opera house was tougher than he expected, and that's the last time he's going to pull something like that."

Jack nodded, head tilted, holding the lit cigarette a hairsbreadth from his lips.

"And the problem with that theory is...?" I said.

He took his time tapping off the ash on the picnic table before responding. "Wasn't a warning for Nebraska. Couldn't have been. An occupied building? Sure. Just a construction crew. Nah. They'd have caught him."

"Which proves my point. There was no warning."

Jack stared out across the trash-strewn strip of grass, smoked half the cigarette, then stood.

"Gotta call Quinn."

* * *

When Jack returned, he sat down across the table, hand going out for the spot where he'd left his cigarettes, then shaking it off and stuffing the pack into his pocket.

"There was a tip-off, wasn't there?" I said.

"Train. Last night. Promised to kill a passenger."

"But he didn't?"

"Everyone accounted for."

"So either the tip-off was a fake—"

"Quinn says no."

"Then he failed. I can see that. It'd be very hard to pull a hit on an enclosed vehicle. He must have realized he'd overshot and backed off."

"Maybe. Maybe he missed the fucking train. Wilkes never could keep time." He stared off into the distance for a moment, then gave a sharp shake of his head. "Doesn't matter. He fucked up. That's good."

"So are the Feds going to release the note? Make it sound like they managed to abort the attack? That'd be a nice win for them, and right now they could use it."

"Quinn doesn't know. Doesn't think they've decided. They've got another problem. Bigger concern. Another tip-off."

"Another? Goddamn it. That's going to put them in a corner. Did he intend to make the train hit and something went wrong, in which case they should put all their efforts into dealing with this new one? Or are the tips red herrings now, keeping them busy chasing phantoms instead of pursuing the investigation?" I looked at Jack. "Maybe missing the train hit was part of the plan. Get the Feds second-guessing him, splitting up their manpower."

"Could be. That's what they're doing. Main team is ignoring this one. They'll go back to investigating. Put a secondary team and local forces on security detail."

"Where's the hit supposed to go down?"

"Homecoming parade. Late this afternoon. West Virginia."

I was still shooing the dogs from the gate when Evelyn appeared on the back porch.

"Girls," she growled.

They fell over each other getting out of my way. I unlatched the gate, walked in, then closed it behind me.

"Where's Jack?" Evelyn asked.

"He took another flight. He said he had to check something someplace else and he'd meet up with me later."

She waved me into the house. "You two have a falling out?"

"I don't think so." I set down my bag and tugged off my shoes. "Why? Did he call?"

"No, but I can't see him splitting up. There's no reason to take separate flights—you two aren't on a job. If he wanted to check something, why not take you with him?"

"So it seems odd to you, too, huh?" I moved into the living room and sat down. "I thought he'd at least try to persuade me to go with him but . . . well, he's been acting weird."

Her eyebrows shot up. "Weird? Jack? I can use a lot of words to describe that man's behavior sometimes, but weird isn't one of them."

"I know. Normally he's so focused. But he seemed distant last night, almost . . . rattled. Ever since he talked to Maurice Gallagher."

Evelyn went rigid, then settled back into her chair, taking awhile to get comfortable, trying to hide her initial reaction. When she spoke, her voice was calm. "I warned him, didn't I? About crossing the old spider. I suppose Gallagher threatened him…" She let the words fade, frowning, as if thinking. Putting two and two together?

"Were you there?" she asked.

"When Jack talked to Gallagher? No, he didn't take me in."

"Not to the meeting maybe, but into the casino? Could Gallagher have seen you with Jack?"

I wasn't sure where she was leading, but not in the direction I wanted. "I don't think so. Whatever upset Jack, it had to do with the name Gallagher gave him."

"The hitman Gallagher hired and Kozlov saw?"

I nodded. "Jack wouldn't tell me who it was, but…I don't know. Maybe it was a friend of his."

"Jack doesn't have friends. He might know him, but wouldn't care enough to get 'rattled.'"

"Well, something sure upset him." I stood. "I should unpack my things."

I headed upstairs. After laying down my bag, I retrieved my gun from its hiding spot, where I'd left it before we'd gone to Vegas. Then I slipped from the room, closed the door loud enough for Evelyn to hear and crept to the top of the stairs to listen.

If Evelyn was involved, the reason for Jack's "odd behavior" in relation to the name would be obvious. According to him, she'd take advantage of my temporary absence to do one of three things. The first two, he said, were most likely: make a phone call or send an e-mail. The third…

Soft taps sounded across the wooden hall floor, then stopped. A double clump, as she removed her pumps and laid them down.

The click of the hall closet door. The rasping whoosh of a box being pulled off the shelf. A moment of silence. Then an unmistakable sound.

"Hall closet." I could hear Jack's voice as we'd discussed this on the flight. "Top shelf. Box with some scarves. Keeps a gun there."

One of several guns secreted around the house, he'd explained, listing all the locations.

"You're upstairs? Hall's most likely. Hear her get it? Leave."

A shadow crossed the bottom landing.

"Evelyn?" I called.

The shadow retreated.

"Yes?" she replied.

"I'm going to take a shower. Wash away some of this jet lag."

"All right."

I walked backward into the bathroom, locked the door, thumped around a bit and turned on the shower. Then I retreated to my hiding place, making sure no shadow or mirror reflection gave me away.

This wasn't what Jack wanted, but I didn't think he was the best person to make that decision. Even when he'd been convinced Evelyn hadn't been involved, he'd tried to figure out way to confront her himself, take me out of the equation. When it became obvious there was no way to do that, he'd instructed me to go into the bathroom, run the shower ... and escape out the window, which overlooked the porch roof. Whatever happened, I was not to confront Evelyn myself.

Worried for me? Or her?

Did I pose a danger to her? That depended on whether she'd done anything to deserve it. But even if she was involved in this, I'd stay my hand, for Jack's sake—let him handle this, as was his prerogative.

When he'd asked me to sneak out the window, I hadn't

agreed—just let my silence suggest I did. I'd had no intention of backing down from a confrontation. Even if Evelyn was guilty, I could control my instincts and step aside for Jack when the time came.

After a moment, the lock on the door clicked open. A pause. Then the sound of the handle turning. I adjusted my grip on the gun.

A faint squeak as the door opened. A blur of motion, Evelyn swinging around the doorway, gun trained not on the shower but behind the door.

I stepped from the alcove by the toilet. She spun, gun going up, lips twisting in a hard smile that didn't reach her eyes.

"Clever girl," she said. "Not quite clever enough, though."

"I managed a draw. I'd say that's pretty good."

I could have dropped her while she was turning, but I didn't say that.

"Where's Jack?" she asked.

Her gaze was on my hands, watching for movement. Mine stayed on her eyes. I'd see her decision there before her trigger finger responded.

"You think I'd tell you?" I said. "So you can shoot me, then—"

"If you don't tell me where Jack is in five seconds, I *will* shoot you, and then you'll be in so much pain you'll tell me anything I want... but it won't be anything comparable to the pain you'll be in if I find out you've done anything to him. Now, where is Jack?"

A shadow filled the doorway behind her.

"Right here," Jack said. "Don't turn. Just look in the mirror."

She did. When she saw Jack behind her, with a gun

pointed at the back of her skull, something indecipherable flashed through her eyes. Then she blinked, and said, "Et tu, Brutus?" A glance my way. "Well, if Jack's alive and pointing a gun at my head, this obviously isn't what I thought it was."

"And what was that?" I asked.

"First?" Jack said. "Evelyn? Gun on the floor."

She flashed a smile at him through the mirror. "Making you nervous, Jacko?"

She raised her gun, pointing it at me, but her eyes stayed on him. A look passed between them, unreadable from my angle. Then Evelyn lowered her weapon, crouched and laid it on the floor.

—

FORTY-TWO

Downstairs, Jack sat with his gun on his lap, a polite reminder.

"You said this wasn't what you thought," I began. "And that would be . . . ?"

"I hadn't made up my mind," Evelyn said.

I waited for an explanation, but she only eased back in her chair and slanted a look at Jack, who grunted, as if her meaning was perfectly clear.

"So what the hell *is* this about?" Evelyn said. "I can't even imagine what I could have done to deserve both of you pulling guns on me."

"Gallagher talked," Jack said. "Gave Dee a name."

"Dee? But she said . . . Okay, so this must be connected to that name. What could—?" She paused. "Gallagher didn't finger me, did he? Now, that would explain this reaction, but it's obviously impossible. I was with Dee for one murder and couldn't have done the others then gotten back here in time to meet you two."

"Wilkes."

"The killer is Wilkes— Bullshit. Gallagher is pulling your—" She studied our faces. "And if I continue like that, I'll only convince you I'm involved. You honestly think I'd cover for that loser, Jack? Partner with him on a job this big?"

"Had to know."

"The only person I'd trust on something like this would be you. Wilkes ranks at the bottom of my former partners and protégés. I still say he could not be responsible. He doesn't have the ingenuity—"

"Forget ingenuity. Technical skill?"

"Well, yes, but—"

"Could have quietly killed Kozlov. Not easy. Not impossible, either. Didn't need this . . . exit strategy. Wanted more. Had something to prove."

"Well, yes, theoretically that would fit Wilkes—"

"Gets a taste for power. Control. Gets drunk on it. Full of himself. Challenging the Feds. Making impossible demands. Playing head games. Thinking he's winning. Now he's somebody. Finally somebody."

Evelyn sighed, then shook her head. "Son of a bitch. So now we need to find him. That's not going to be easy."

"Jack says you know his name," I said. "His real name. Is that going to help?"

"I trained him well," Evelyn said. "If he's using a name, it's probably not his own. If it is his own, any information you'd find with it would lead to a dead end. Even at the absolutely best scenario—he's forgotten everything I've taught him and has a house registered under his real name—we aren't going to show up there and find him. I'll do the search and give you what I find, but right now, he's out there—" She waved at the window. "Setting up his next attack. We need to figure out what that is."

"We might already know," I said, and told her about the missed train tip and the next one, in West Virginia.

"He fucked up with the train," Evelyn said. "Personally, I like your idea, Dee, fulfill a promise, break a promise, get the Feds running around like chickens with their heads cut off. Brilliant—and exactly what I'd do. You, Jack or I could pull that stunt without giving a shit who thought we'd 'failed' the train hit. But Wilkes? Not a chance." She lifted three fingers. "One: he's single-minded. Two: he lacks creativity. Three: he's got a balloon ego."

"Balloon ego?" I said.

Jack grunted. "One prick, it deflates."

"Something did go wrong with that train hit," Evelyn said. "As for *what*, it's moot. What matters is that he'll be mad as hell right about now. He's going to be at that parade, and he's going to make a hit, and if the Feds are standing this one down, then I'd sure as hell recommend we be there."

"To do what?" Jack said. "Needle in a haystack."

"True," I said. "But do you know the best way to find a needle in a haystack? With a magnet."

Evelyn chuckled. Jack went still for a minute, then his gaze shot to mine, eyes hardening.

"Better not be suggesting—"

"That we draw out the needle ourselves? That's exactly what I'm suggesting."

"You are *not* setting yourself up to become the next victim," Jack said.

I considered commenting on the length and completeness of that sentence, but the look in his eyes said this wasn't the time.

"Jack's right," Evelyn said. "Wilkes has established a plan and he's already 'done' any type you could play. We need to bait the trap with something he doesn't have yet, something he won't be able to resist."

She looked at Jack.

"Because he knows Jack?" I shook my head. "Sure, he might go for it, off a fellow hitman, but—"

"It's been over twenty years. A bit of work and he'd never recognize Jack. What he *will* recognize is a prize missing from his collection. A tough guy."

Jack snorted.

"You know what I mean. A biker, a hood, muscle, all

roles you've done many times before. There are a million guys out there right now, bragging in bars about how they'd take down the Helter Skelter killer if he ever came near them. Give him one of those, in a setting that'll make an easy kill, and he'll pounce on it, to prove that nobody is safe . . . and reinflate his ego after the train fiasco."

FORTY-THREE

———

It was a five-hour trip and we didn't have time to stop for lunch, so we grabbed sandwiches on the way. We were almost to West Virginia when we had to pull into a gas station to fill up, and for Jack to use the washroom. I eyed the attached convenience store, considered getting some candy for the stakeout. But I had a more important use for the time alone with Evelyn.

I waited until Jack headed into the store to prepay for gas, then shifted into the middle of the seat, so I could lean forward and talk to her on the front passenger side.

"So, I suppose after what happened today you'll be rescinding that 'offer' you made?"

"Because you held me at gunpoint?" She smiled. "I consider it a logical and important step in a developing relationship with any good student. I'm sure I'll give you cause to do it again and, if I don't, then you're not the sort of hitwoman I'd care to mentor."

"Ah."

As I eased back into my seat, she peered under the headrest at me. "Is that disappointment I hear? Don't tell me you're hoping I'll retract the offer, save you from having to make the decision. I expected better of you, Dee." Her gaze studied mine, then she smiled. "Or, I suppose, this was just a good excuse for bringing up the matter, since I haven't done so myself."

"Just checking. Seeing whether it still stood."

"It does and, as you haven't said no, I presumed you're still considering it, which is good enough for me. If that offer doesn't suit your tastes, I can get others. Someone with your talent is wasted on Mafia punks."

When I said nothing, she tilted her head, gaze boring into mine. "I'm giving you a chance to really quench that thirst, Nadia. Take out people who even *I'll* agree have lost the right to walk on this planet."

I didn't miss the switch from Dee to Nadia. A calculated reminder of how much she knew about me. If I called her on it, though, she'd only claim a slip of the tongue, so I said, as evenly as possible, "I'm not a vigilante."

"So you've said."

I turned my gaze to the window, watching Jack start pumping the gas, then looked back at Evelyn. "What would you get from it?"

"A cut, of course. Money is always good." She eased back in her seat, gaze returning to the windshield. "When I got into this life, I only wanted three things. Money, power and respect. A girl like you, comes from a nice middle-class background, born after the so-called sexual revolution, gets a good education, takes on a man's job. I'm sure it wasn't as easy as we might hope, but it was possible. These days, girls don't know what it is to want those things and know you've got a snowball's chance in hell of getting them. I fought like you couldn't imagine and got everything I wanted. But it wasn't enough."

A long pause as she watched Jack fill the tank.

She continued. "They say that man gains immortality through his children. I don't have any. Never wanted them. What I *do* have are students. I take raw clay and I fashion something remarkable."

"That's what you want to do with me. Make me better."

A laugh so sharp it startled me. "Oh, you don't like that idea, do you? You can play the cool professional, act like you don't give a shit what anyone thinks, but you've got your share of ego, of ambition. You're just good at hiding it. Reminds me of someone else." Her gaze slid to Jack, now walking to the bathroom. "What I can make you, Nadia, isn't *better*. It's famous. Legendary. Reach the point where you can do exactly the kind of work you want and nothing else."

I stared out the window, watching Jack as he returned.

"He's still with me, isn't he?" Evelyn said, as if reading my thoughts. "I haven't damaged him. Haven't made him anything he didn't want to be. Jack doesn't hang around because he feels *obligated*. He wouldn't do that and you know it. So if I'm good enough for him..."

Jack dipped his head, peering into the car, gaze shooting to Evelyn, as if he could see us watching him and talking.

"I'll let you think about it, Dee," she murmured. "Take all the time you need."

For over an hour, I'd been standing in front of a fifth-story window, watching the parade route fill. To pass the time, I mentally ran through ballistics tables, recalculating the distance, velocity, trajectory, wind drift, making sure I had everything right.

I'd have rather been in one of the taller office buildings down the street, but if there were SWAT team snipers here, that's where they'd be. And even if there weren't, the Feds would be checking out the best perches in case Wilkes was trying for a sniper shot himself. So I had to make do with one that was third rate.

Having to take the shot standing didn't make the situation any better. The higher up you get, the less stable you are. Ideally, I'd be on my stomach. Given that the window was four feet off the ground, lying down wasn't an option. So, as any good sniping manual would tell you, I should have used the materials at hand to create a level and sturdy four-foot-high platform. Works great, if you're on a SWAT team . . . not so great when you're a professional killer who can't leave any trace and may have to abandon your perch at a moment's notice.

So I'd shoot standing, as I usually did. Not only was it the least steady position, it was the hardest to hold for an extended period. Since I used it the most often, though, I'd trained for it, doing most of my practice upright—the off-hand position. To alleviate some of the unsteadiness, I used a sling. A dark-colored loop of nylon, the sling attached to a swivel at the end of the gun stock, near the barrel. I put my left arm through the opposite end of the loop and pulled the keeper along the strap until the loop was snug against my biceps.

At this distance, it was possible—if unlikely—that someone on the parade route could look up and see a silhouette in the window. To reduce the risk, I wore a brimmed hat, beaten into a shapeless lump, so my head wasn't a rounded dome. Mosquito netting over the front of the hat darkened my face and helped it blend in with my black clothing. I'd also draped a larger swatch of netting over the window, to further darken and blur my silhouette. For the window itself, I'd cut out a pane. Breaking glass makes noise. Lifting the sash looks suspicious. If you see a closed window, you assume all the panes of glass are there.

I could see Evelyn's hat weaving through the crowd. It was pink and old-ladyish. For Evelyn, I'm sure that was a fashion torture on par with my push-up bra, and judging by the look she'd given me when I found it for her, I was in for some serious payback. But it made her easy to track, and that's all that mattered.

I needed to be able to find her in a split-second survey of the parade scene because my attention had to remain focused on the main lure, Jack. He couldn't wear anything as obvious as a pink hat. Fortunately, tracking him wasn't the issue because he'd staked out a table at the edge of a licensed patio, where he nursed a pint of beer and read a motorcycle magazine. If he attracted the attention of anyone who looked as if he could be Wilkes, Jack would fold up his magazine, vacate the patio and head for the alley beside it, which was right across from my perch and lined up for a perfect shot. Alternately, if Evelyn spotted Wilkes, she'd get Jack's attention and he'd make his way to Wilkes, while staying within my line of fire.

Wilkes could be planning a sniper shot himself, but according to Evelyn, he was crap at distance shooting. Besides, if he wanted to reassert his credibility with the Feds, firing from a safe distance would be a cop-out. Just in case, though, I'd been careful to pick a spot with no surrounding high buildings.

As I was thinking this, something thudded over my head. My first reaction was an instant gut-clench, accompanied by a vision of Wilkes standing at the window over mine, his scope trained on Jack. My second reaction was a stifled laugh. There *was* no floor above mine—just a roof, one with a sloped front and a high lip, unsuitable for shooting.

From overhead came the distinct sound of gravel crunching underfoot. I gave myself a mental shake. Nerves are a sniper's worst enemy. The slightest tremor, and you might as well put the rifle back in its case.

I checked my pulse. Steady. Good. Now concentrate on—

A chirp from the rooftop exit hatch.

Maybe it was only my mind playing tricks, but until I reassured myself of that, my shot was in jeopardy. I took one last look at Jack, then checked my watch. Six minutes to parade time. I laid down my rifle, slipped out of the sling, then spread my tarp over my gear—the fastest way to hide it.

As I pulled out my handgun, I ran though the description Evelyn had given for Wilkes—late fifties, six foot one, big-boned. The rest didn't matter—a disguise could change hair and eye color, make him older and heavier, but shorter or significantly younger were impossible.

It was only then, as I visualized him, that the full impact of what was happening hit. This man, now sneaking into the building, could be Wilkes. The Helter Skelter killer. My target.

I was transported back to the opera house, to that hour when I'd been so sure we'd get him, and I felt again that excitement, that rising sense of oddly calm anticipation. Senses heightening, muscles tensing, pulse hitting a steady rhythm, sliding into that perfect zone.

In that hour at the window, I'd known who I hoped to find in my scope. Yet I never *felt* it. Too distant a target, too cerebral a goal. What I loved about distance shooting—that total control—also robbed me of this, that delicious moment of knowing that in a few minutes, I'd see my target's face, hear his gasp of shock, smell his fear.

As a loose ladder rung creaked, I pictured him, frozen in midstep, the creak seeming to ring out like a gunshot. He'd listen for any responding sound from below, then start down again, slower now, testing each rung first. Finally, he'd reach the bottom. A few steps and he'd be at my door, turning the handle . . .

The soft click of the latch. Good. Now look out into the hall. Make sure it's clear, then step out . . . oh, better close the door behind you.

Click.

Silence.

He was in the hall, looking, listening. No sign of the Feds—if they had a team camped out on this floor, he'd hear it; there was no need for them to be quiet when they were just pulling stakeout or sniper duty from a fifth-story window. Hearing nothing, Wilkes would start forward again, looking for the best window, which was right here, in my room.

I flexed my grip on my gun and smiled.

At least three minutes of silence passed. Still listening for an occupying force? Wilkes hadn't struck me as the nervous type. Maybe the pressure was getting to him. Another two minutes, then a floorboard creaked. Still *sneaking* down the hall, expecting trouble?

Another creak. He'd be at my door in a few seconds . . .

Silence.

From my vantage point, I couldn't miss seeing anyone passing the doorway. So where was he? Being cautious was one thing, but he was moving so slowly—

I stopped, imagining not Wilkes, but an officer from the security detail canvassing the building. But if Wilkes wasn't in this hall, that meant Jack was in danger, down there trying to lure in a killer, confident that I was watching his back.

My gaze tripped between the window and the door. Just a few seconds. Let them pass the door and move on. Dear God, I hoped they moved on.

I watched the doorway, tensed for the first shadow. I lowered my gun barrel to leg height. No, too risky for an impulse shot. I might hit his femoral artery. A shoulder shot? That had been my first choice with Wilkes, but would I risk it on a cop? Could I even shoot one?

Silence from beyond the door. Awaiting backup? If so, I had time to move away from the door and...And what? Jump out the window? Hide. I could get behind—

A shadow moved across the door opening. I could make out a filthy sneaker and an arm clad in a battered leather jacket. Hardly standard wear for law enforcement. An undercover officer?

I stayed against the wall and waited for him to step inside. Then I'd knock him down and get the hell out—

The shadow crossed the open doorway. Through the crack behind it, I saw a young man, maybe twenty, dressed in ill-fitting clothes that screamed charity wear. He cast a nervous glance through my doorway, then scuttled down the hall.

It *could* be an undercover officer, but if so, he should have stepped into this room to conduct a thorough search. Through the crack, I watched the young man continuing down the hall, peering into some rooms, ignoring others, haphazardly searching. Not a cop but a junkie spooked by the police presence outside and looking for a safe, quiet hole to shoot up.

All this for a goddamned junkie who probably wouldn't have even noticed me standing at the window with a rifle?

I swallowed a burst of rage, reminded myself I had a bigger concern. When the figure reached the end of the hall, I sprinted for the window, looked down...and saw an empty table.

I whirled and grabbed my rifle. Then I spun back to the

window, my gaze going to the alley. It was empty. From here, I could see right to the end. I swung back, visually retracing the path from the alley to Jack's chair, but saw no sign of him. A server was at his table now, holding his half-empty beer glass as she wiped his table.

Heart thudding, I scanned the crowd for Evelyn's pink hat, and found it a few storefronts away. I slowed my survey of the crowd, searching for Jack's light brown wig, bearded face and leather jacket. But people were moving off the road and crowding onto the sidewalk as the distant sound of music announced the beginning of the parade.

Out of the corner of my eye, I saw Evelyn glance up. I waved my arms. She lifted her hand to shield her eyes. I grabbed my gun-cleaning cloth—the lightest-colored item I had. I waved it, then gestured toward Jack's table. When she saw that empty chair, she stiffened, and I knew she understood. She jabbed her thumb down, then pointed at me and jabbed down again. *Come down.*

I hesitated. I could see better from up here—then I understood: if she'd looked up here for me, Jack was likely doing the same. He'd check for my shape at the window before he got near Wilkes. If I wasn't ready, better that he shouldn't see me at all and know something was wrong.

With one eye and my gun aimed at the door, and both ears on full alert, I pulled the tarp off my gear and stuffed it into my rucksack. Then I unloaded the rifle and slung it across my shoulder—dismantling it was too loud and too time-consuming.

I hurried to the door and peered out. All clear. A pause, a deep breath, another check, then I sprinted down the hall. Keeping an eye out for the junkie and anyone else, I retraced my steps down to the first floor and out the back exit.

* * *

I never should have left that window. I *never* should have left that window.

Even as I beat myself over the head with the chant, I knew if I hadn't left my post, I could have been seen. There had been no way to know it was only a junkie until it had been too late. What I *should* have done was arranged an emergency alert plan, told them that if I had to leave my window I'd stick a piece of paper on the pane, so when Jack looked up he'd know he was unprotected.

From the door, I headed into the back alley. As I ran, I stripped out of my gear and haphazardly wiped the camouflage makeup from my face, then stashed my rucksack and rifle behind a trash bin and kept going.

As I stood at the junction of the sidewalk and alley, a float rolled past. The men's swim team, clad in Speedos and goose bumps, enduring the cold as they basked in the hoots and catcalls of the students and alumni lining the street. My face had to still be streaked with paint, but I attracted no more than a casual glance. If there were near-naked young men on a float, then a face-painted alumna on the sidelines didn't look out of place.

I strained to see over the crowd and, for once in my life, wished for high heels or platform shoes, anything that would help me spot that pink hat bobbing along in the mob. When Jack had vetoed the use of cell phones, I should have insisted we have something for emergency communication.

"I hate backup plans," Evelyn had said. "If you have one, it makes it acceptable to screw up the original."

Maybe that was true, but under these circumstances, a fallback plan wasn't an escape hatch, it was a safety net.

The parade was in full swing, and I doubted it would last much longer. Was I too late? Not unless a man could drop dead on the sidewalk and no one noticed. Maybe the Feds were right and there would be no hit at the parade. Or maybe Wilkes hadn't seen Jack. Or maybe he had, and decided to strike elsewhere. At least Jack was armed and knew what was happening. I just had to keep—

There! Across the street. A bearded profile over a leather jacket moving behind a cluster of drunken alumni. Now how was I going to get across the road? In the middle of the parade? Run like hell . . . that was the only way, as much as I hated doing anything that might call attention to myself. I elbowed my way to the front of the crowd, with murmurs about "someone holding my place" and plenty of apologies.

Maybe the streaks of face paint made it easier, but I managed to get through the blockade. Perched on the curb, I rolled on the balls of my feet, counting the seconds until the float was just far enough past—

I darted out between the photography club float and the woodwind band. I dashed for the curb. As I neared it, I caught the stare of a man about twenty feet away. An older man, late fifties, just over six feet tall, big-boned. In that second I knew I'd accomplished what Jack had failed to do: attract the attention of a killer.

My heart slammed against my rib cage. Wilkes. Right there.

I had to make him chase me.

As the thought formed, my heart rate swung into rapid acceleration. Lure him away. Make sure he was the one. Let him think he was in control, the great hunter stalking his innocent prey. And then . . .

I grinned.

I jumped onto the curb and started making my way to

the rear of the crowd. Would he follow? As Evelyn had pointed out, Wilkes had done my demographic. But if it was an easy kill? If I made it an easy kill? A seeming guarantee of success?

I had to make this easy. Too easy to resist.

As much as I longed to scan the crowd for his face, to see his reaction, I didn't dare. I walked fast, eyes straight ahead, chin high, striding toward some imaginary rendezvous point.

When I neared the point where he'd been standing, the urge to look into the crowd was so strong I had to force myself to glance the other way. As I did, I caught my reflection in the window of a storefront. Behind me was the crowd. After a moment's searching, I saw that face again. Watching me. Curious. Considering...

I suppressed a shiver of excitement, shoved my hand into my pocket and slid it around my gun. Then I wheeled left and headed into the alley.

FORTY-FOUR

When we'd first arrived that afternoon, Jack and Evelyn had done a full reconnaissance sweep, checking every street, alley and nook. With my extra setup work, I'd only had time to map out two escape routes from my building perch. That should have been enough. I just needed to know how to evacuate my perch in an emergency. They were supposed to be the ones luring Wilkes into an alley.

Those routes I'd investigated were across the road, and my chances of getting Wilkes there were slim to none. So I had to do something I hated—blindly walk into the first suitable-looking alley I crossed.

When I stepped into that alley, I looked toward the first intersection and thought of nothing but getting there...as fast as possible. For that thirty-second trip, Wilkes could come around the corner and shoot me from behind, and there wasn't a damn thing I could do about it.

I could argue that a gun hit made no sense. It was too risky this close to the sidewalk. Shooting someone in the back was a coward's ploy, and unlikely to impress the Feds. Plus, considering he'd invited the police, he wouldn't take the chance of walking around carrying a gun.

Dirt crunched as my pursuer rounded the corner behind me. I kept my pace fast but steady. Speed up and he'd know I heard him. Just a few more steps...

I hit the first corner and took a split second to look each way, searching for the nearest doorway or second corner, getting Wilkes far enough from the crowded street. The alley intersected with another about fifteen feet to my right, so I turned that way. I crossed the first half of the distance in a few long strides. From the occasional whisper of his shoes on the dirt, I knew my pursuer was still behind me. Yet he seemed to be moving slowly—slower than I expected. Being cautious? Or wasn't it Wilkes?

I was convinced it was him, but I could leave no chance I would, in my eagerness, shoot an innocent man.

The man I'd seen could have been a random pervert or mugger, more than willing to follow a woman into an alley. It might not be the man I'd spotted, but Jack or Evelyn or a cop seeing me turn into the alley and following. Or it could be some drunken student who'd slipped from the parade for a piss break. And if it was the latter, then I sincerely apologized for what I was about to do, and hoped his full bladder could withstand it.

When I reached that next junction, I'd round the corner, then get up against the wall and wait, gun drawn. Wilkes would turn—

I hit the corner...and found no corner to turn. What I'd thought was the junction of another alley was a doorway—with a recess so shallow I couldn't even duck in and hide. As I slowed, my gaze swung forward again, looking for a second option. Ahead, less than a dozen feet away, a real alley intersection, one I could see from this angle wasn't another dead end. But Wilkes was too close. He'd never let me get that far. My only option was to break into a run and escape.

Run and he'd know he'd been made. And, like any good hitman, he would back off.

Run and I'd lose him.

I stared at that intersection and knew I should do it. Escape and try again later. But everything in me rebelled at the very thought.

Run like a coward? Like a helpless thirteen-year-old girl?

Run and let him kill someone else, sacrifice another life for mine? *Never* again.

I saw my chances, knew they were far from perfect, maybe even far from good, and I made the only choice I could.

I slowed down.

Gravel crunched behind me. Right behind me. I spun and saw Wilkes closer than I'd expected. Saw the wire raised above my head. My gaze met his and, for a split second, I saw his surprise and dismay.

He twisted behind me again, and the wire swung down. For one second, as the metal flashed, something inside me went wild with fear, seeing not a wire, but a knife. Then my hand tightened around the Glock and the feel of it jolted me back. I started to raise the gun, but my brain screamed "too late," and I let it drop inside my pocket. Both my hands shot up, palms up, just in time to block my throat as the wire came down.

The wire sliced into my palms and I let out a soft gasp. Instinctively I pushed it away, but it only bit in harder. For a second, we just stood locked in indecision, our hands occupied, unable to let go. My first urge was to kick backward. But I stopped myself before my foot left the ground. Kick and I'd lose my balance. Lose my balance, and I risked letting go of this wire, and the second I did that, it was through my windpipe and into my carotid artery.

I unclenched my right, releasing a stream of blood down the inside of my wrist. With the slick blood, my hand slid free. Then the wire jerked up. If I wasn't going to lose my balance, he'd do it for me. I swung my hand forward, then drove my elbow into his gut.

My elbow made contact just as he kneed me again and my legs gave way. I let them give way. Let myself crumple forward onto the wire just as he stumbled back from my blow, grunting, as if I'd hit him harder than I thought. He released the wire and I pitched face-first to the ground.

"Hey!"

The shout rang down the alley, followed by the pound of running footsteps. Young male voices. Multiple running footsteps. I ignored them and flipped over, my hand going to my pocket for my gun. As I rolled, I saw Wilkes poised over me. But he'd frozen in place, head up, hearing the approaching voices and footsteps. Our eyes met. His filled with rage and frustration and, again, I drank it in.

He wheeled. I pulled out the gun. Swung it toward his fleeing back. Smiled as I watched him trying to run, but faltering, as if still feeling that blow to the gut. Such an easy target. I allowed myself one delicious shudder. Then, finger on the trigger—

A pair of legs jumped into the way, running out from a side alley.

"Whoa!"

My rescuer backpedaled, but stayed in my line of fire . . . and Wilkes disappeared around the next corner. I flew to my feet, but hands grabbed me.

"He's gone. It's okay. He's gone."

I turned, snarling, ready to shove this kid out of my way and tear off after Wilkes. But then I saw the boy's face, eyes wide with terror—innocent—and it was like a bucket of ice water. I'd missed my opportunity. Now I was on the ground, a gun in my hands, blood streaming down my arms, surrounded by a bunch of college kids who thought they'd just saved me from a killer.

I had to play it out, get away safely, then go after Wilkes. Find him again and catch him before he killed someone else in my place.

I looked at my gun and widened my eyes, as if surprised

to see it there. Then I backed against the wall, hands going around my knees, feigning shock while making sure all my blood went on my pants, not on the ground where a crime scene team could find it.

One of the kids dropped down beside me, his hand going to my shoulder.

"You're safe now," he said. "We called the cops. They'll be here in a minute."

My head shot up, and I didn't need to fake my reaction. My brain scrambled for an excuse and latched onto the first one it came across.

"No," I said, pushing to my feet. "No—no cops. I'm—My dealer. I was here meeting my dealer. I'm carrying. I can't—"

"It's okay," the boy said. "They won't care about that."

"Oh, God, I can't—I have to go. If my husband finds out—"

They tried to calm me, but then someone called from the end of the alley, asking whether we needed an ambulance, and in the ensuing confusion, I shoved the garrote wire in my pocket, gave a last scan for evidence, pushed to my feet and bolted.

I followed the same path Wilkes had taken, praying he'd hit a dead end or run into a crowd and would circle back for another escape route. I'd just rounded the first corner when I heard feet on gravel. Behind me? In front of me? I couldn't tell and was about to look when a pebble pinged off the top of my head.

I glanced up to see Jack on the roof two stories above. He motioned to the nearest fire escape. I shook my head and kept going, on the trail, after Wilkes, so absorbed in my task that I saw Jack swing down the fire escape, moving fast, but didn't comprehend the meaning of it until I was passing the bottom, and he grabbed my arm.

Fingers so tight they'd leave bruises, he hauled me up the ladder. Too confused to struggle, I followed as best I could, my feet fumbling for purchase on the rungs, barely touching one before being dragged up to the next. At the top, he yanked me over the edge.

I tripped and sprawled onto the gravel.

"Wilkes," I managed gasping for breath. "I—"

"I saw."

"I need to get—"

"He's gone."

"But I can find him," I said, still gasping, my pounding heart not letting me relax enough to catch my breath. "Before he takes someone else, before he escapes."

I started to rise.

Jack planted his foot on my stomach, then leaned over. "He's gone. I followed. Lost him. Think I'd be here otherwise?"

"You don't understand, I need—"

"Too fucking bad, Nadia. This isn't about what you need."

The fury in his eyes made the hair on the back of my neck rise and I almost backed down. But then I imagined Wilkes below, running, escaping. Jack was wrong. He didn't understand, and I wasn't going to sit here and take this, even from him.

I pretended to relax, as if giving in, then shoved Jack's foot off. I started scrambling up, then saw something metallic flash in front of my face and looked up to see a gun pointing down.

Had there been anything in my bladder, I think I would have lost it, not because I was staring down the barrel of a gun, but because of who I saw on the other end. Jack. Pointing a gun in my face. For one horrible moment, I thought

I'd been tricked, that Jack was involved, that he was work-ing with Wilkes—

"It's too late, Nadia. Listen."

"I've listened to you enough—"

"No," he growled. "Not me. *Listen*."

The distant sound of voices carried up to the roof, but I couldn't make out any words. Then the distinct sound of a cop shouting orders.

"You staying?" he said.

I nodded.

He lowered the gun.

I swallowed. Got my thoughts under control. "I'm sorry. About leaving my post. Believe me, Jack, I didn't try going after him myself and leave you out there unprotected."

"I know. Evelyn told me."

"I heard someone on my floor and I had to leave the window, then when I got back, you were gone and Evelyn wanted me to come down—"

"Doesn't matter. Had to change plans. That's fine. But this—" He jerked his chin toward the alley. "Leading him in? No backup—?"

"There wasn't time for that. I got his attention, Jack. I didn't mean to—I certainly wasn't trying to. I was looking for you and he saw me, and I—"

"Where's your gear?"

I told him.

"Stay here." He headed for the ladder, then paused and looked back at me. "I mean it. You leave? You go after him? Pull this shit again?"

He didn't finish, gaze dipping from mine, rage re-treating.

"I'll stay," I said. "I promise."

He nodded, then disappeared down the ladder.

* * *

Jack returned with a change of clothing—a full campus-gear outfit of sweatshirt, khakis, ball cap and knapsack. As I dressed, he stuffed my clothes and wig into the knapsack. We wouldn't keep them, but we had to dispose of them outside the city. I battered my cap in the gravel a bit, so it didn't look so new. Then I cleaned the rest of the grease-paint off my face and wiped my hands as best I could.

Through it all, Jack said not a word. I could feel his temper smoldering, waiting only for a spark from me to ignite. So I was keeping my mouth shut. It was only when I was cleaning my hands that he acknowledged I was there, walking over and yanking my hand, none too gently, for a closer look.

"Keep them clean," he said. "Needs a first-aid kit. Might be awhile."

"That's okay." I paused, then decided to risk it. I'd done something wrong—very wrong—and I needed to know what it was. "I don't think I left any trace. Well, there might be a few drops of blood if they look hard enough…"

"Doesn't matter. They're after him. Not you."

"Is it the witnesses? They didn't get a good look at me. I kept my face down and—"

"You were in disguise."

"No one would have made me for a pro, if that's what you're worrying about. Not Wilkes and not those college kids. Wilkes just got a victim who fought back. He never saw the gun. The kids did, but not in any way that would seem like anything other than a victim defending—"

"I saw. Looked fine."

"Then what—?"

"Evelyn got your gear. We'll head straight to the car. Merge with the crowd. Stay beside me. You see a cop—"

"Act normal," I said. "Don't avoid him, keep my gaze up, maybe look curious, wondering what's going on, but act like everyone else seeing cops swarming around."

He hefted my knapsack and started across the roof, leaving me to catch up.

FORTY-FIVE

When the Feds learned that Wilkes had tried to take a victim—and left a missing witness—they'd probably erect roadblocks. But if they had, we didn't see them. We did see cops, fanning out to search the crowds leaving the parade route, but our back-street path kept us—and probably Wilkes—out of their way.

When we reached the car, Evelyn was already there, with my gear in the trunk. As we approached, she got out of the driver's side. She looked from me to Jack, and waved me to the passenger seat, then reached for the back door. I shook my head and crawled in the back.

Jack got into the driver's side, leaned over Evelyn and opened the glove box. He pulled out the napkins and hand wipes we'd stashed in there after lunch.

"Clean your hands," he said, tossing them over the seat at me.

"I've already—"

"Clean them again."

As he started the car, Evelyn twisted and caught sight of my cut hands.

"Christ, what happened to you?"

I glanced at Jack.

"He didn't tell me anything," she said. "Just came over to where I was supposed to meet you two, threw me the keys, told me where your gear was and stalked off."

"I met Wilkes."

She blinked, then glared at Jack. "Well, *that's* not worth telling me about." She looked at me. "So what happened . . . and start at the beginning."

I told her.

"So now he's missed two scheduled hits," she said. "Plus he has an eyewitness...a victim who fought back. Probably saw you and decided to skip the demographics and take the easy mark." She chortled. "Oh, he'll be mad now. Spitting mad."

"And off-balance. We need to keep him there. If we act now, we can use it to our advantage and end this."

Jack's hands clenched around the steering wheel. "We'll end it. The old-fashioned way. Legwork. Stop this shit and—"

"That's not *fast*, Jack."

Our eyes met in the rearview mirror. His were ice cold. "And this is? Running after him? Facing him down in alleys? Almost getting killed?"

"I had him. If you saw it go down, you know I had him."

"Where I stood? Looked fifty-fifty."

"Seventy-five/twenty-five. At least."

"So that's okay? Twenty-five percent chance of getting killed? Fuck, yeah. Why not? Goes bad? Who gives a shit? You don't."

"What the hell is that supposed to mean?"

Jack went silent, his gaze turning back to the road.

"Oh, don't you dare," I said, taking off my seat belt and moving to the edge of the seat. "If you have something to say, have the guts to say it."

He said nothing. I clenched the edge of the seat. Goddamn him. Challenge most guys with that, and they'd rise to the bait. Not Jack. Never Jack.

"Pull over," Evelyn said. "You and Dee need to have a chat."

He kept driving.

"Jack..."

When he didn't answer, Evelyn thumped back against the headrest.

"Okay, fine, do it your way. Dee? The next time you get a chance like that, you go ahead and take it. You want this guy taken down more than we do, so any risk you take is your decision, and we support that—"

Jack turned the wheel so sharply I smacked into the door panel. The car slowed at the side of the road. Without a word, Jack got out and headed for a dirt track leading into a cornfield.

Evelyn looked over the seat at me.

"Go on. You won't get another chance."

Brown cornstalks whispered in the breeze, empty and dying, waiting to be mowed down for next year's crop. Through them I could see the back of Jack's jacket.

"I'm here," I said.

He didn't move. I walked through the rows to come out in front of him.

"I'm here," I said. "So talk."

He only stared at the setting sun.

"Okay, you *don't* want to talk. You just want Evelyn to shut up, and you know what, Jack? That's fine with me. We can stand here and pretend we're having it out, then go back and tell Evelyn everything's fine. But the next time you decide to take some cryptic jab at me? Think about whether or not you plan to follow through. And if the answer's no?" I met his gaze. "Then shut the fuck up."

He didn't so much as blink. Just held my gaze for a moment, then looked away. So I guess that meant we were waiting it out, and that was fine with me. Anything to avoid a fight.

I gave it five minutes, then said, "Good enough. Let's go back to the car."

I made it two steps.

"Back there," he said. "In that alley. When things went bad. What'd you do?"

"Do?"

"When it went off course. Could have run. Didn't."

I turned to look at him. "Run? And let him shoot me in the back?"

"Gun wasn't out. You'd know that. Too risky. Cops everywhere. Even if it was? Could have made it."

"Made it where? I was in the middle of an empty alley."

He stepped closer. "Second alley. Ten feet away. You saw it."

"It looked a lot farther than ten feet from where I was standing and maybe that's my fault, but I sure as hell didn't see an escape route and just ignore it, if that's what you meant."

"Yeah. That's what I meant."

He met my gaze and, in his look, I knew he'd seen through my lie—knew I'd seen a chance to escape and rejected it.

I broke away, and continued, "As for getting caught, I misjudged—and yes, I admit that I screwed up. I thought I could turn and get the jump on him, but he was right there."

Jack nodded, gaze down, as if studying a mole hole at the bottom of a cornstalk. Without looking up, he spoke again, his voice quiet. "Let's say... sake of argument. You saw the alley. Knew you'd make it. Would you?"

I considered lying, but from that look in his eyes, he already knew the answer.

I squared my shoulders. "Not while I saw a reasonable chance to catch him."

"What's reasonable? Greater than zero?"

I opened my mouth, then snapped it shut, and forced out a calm tone. "Reasonable is whatever I decide it is because, as Evelyn said, it's my risk to take. Maybe you don't like that, but I'd never endanger you or anyone else, so I don't see the point of arguing about it."

His eyes darkened. "No, you don't, do you? You die? Who gives a shit? No one to care."

"No one—?" *Don't let him bait you. Just ease back.* "I guess that's right. It's not like I have a husband and kids at home to worry about."

"Got no one. Few friends. Everyone else pissed off after Franco. Never came back."

My nails dug into my palms. "Thank you so much for reminding me of that, Jack."

"Didn't mean it like that. Was just—"

"Pointing out that no one would notice I'd died today?"

"No. Just meant—What happened to you. Lost everything. Family. Friends. Career. Future. Whatever you thought your life was going to be? Gone. Won't come back."

"Well, when you put it that way, maybe I shouldn't have stopped Wilkes. Just let him put me out of—"

"You want this bad. Knew that. But I fucked up. Didn't realize *how* bad. How far you'll go."

"How far—?" I could barely get the words out, my heart hammering. "I want *what* so bad? To kill myself? I am not—"

"Suicidal? Nah. But it happens? It's a risk? You'll take it. Won't let it get in the way."

"Get in the way of—?" I swallowed the rest, swept aside the cornstalks and headed for the car.

"Dee..."

I didn't answer.

"Nadia..."

I picked up my pace.

I climbed into the backseat. Evelyn turned to look at me, then sighed.

"He wouldn't talk, would he?"

"Oh, he talked."

Another keen-eyed study. Another sigh. "And it was one of those times when he does, and you're left wishing he'd kept his mouth shut." She shifted to face me. "Jack isn't very good at expressing himself."

"I think he expressed himself very well."

I looked out the windshield. There was no sign of Jack. I glanced at my watch.

"He's just walking it off," she said. "He hates confrontations. I remember this time, years ago, a middleman was bad-mouthing Jack behind his back and..." She noticed my wandering gaze. "And you're really not in the mood for 'insight into Jack' stories, are you? In that case, I'd suggest we discuss something that it takes very little insight to know he's not going to want to discuss. Our next move."

"It'll need to involve me. Up close and personal with Wilkes again. I'm the eyewitness who got away."

She nodded. "And this whole thing started because he wanted to shut up his last—and only—witness. Meaning if he can get a shot at you, preferably before you go to the Feds, there will be no luring involved—he'll jump hurdles to get to you."

"Question is: how to make sure he finds me?"

"I have an idea for that, but Jack will absolutely hate it."

"At this point, not a concern."

She looked at me, and her mouth opened, as if she wanted to say something, then she gave a sharp shake of her head.

"He's a big boy," she murmured. "Okay then, here's what I'm thinking...."

By the time Jack returned to the car, fifteen minutes later, we'd hammered out the skeleton of a plan. When it was time to tell him, I let Evelyn do the honors. As he listened, his face darkened. He let Evelyn get into it, then interrupted.

"Involving the Feds is stupid." He looked at me. "That your idea?"

I smiled. "But of course. If it's stupid, it must be my idea."

"I didn't say—"

"We can't just make Wilkes disappear. You saw the scene in that Vegas diner. People need to see a body, to know this is really over. They need resolution. *We* need resolution or every pro is still on the Feds' hit list."

"And no, it wasn't Dee's idea," Evelyn said. "It was mine. If this agent in charge is as ambitious as Quinn says, he'll make the trade. He gets the glory of the arrest, and in return, plays down Wilkes's past, doesn't portray him as a psycho hitman. Things go back to normal. Sure, the cops still want us gone, but they won't be seeing us all as potential serial killers. That's what we've been trying to do all along, isn't it? Get back to business as usual?"

"Pulling Feds in—"

"One Fed. Maybe two if he needs someone to hold his hand. As for exactly how he'll manage it without involving his team and his superiors, that's his problem."

"This okay with you?" Jack said, twisting to look at me, eyes unreadable. "Taking Wilkes down by yourself?"

"Sure, Jack. Why not? A chance to catch a killer and redeem my sorry life, and if I fail, well, it's not like anyone will give a damn if I turn up in a Dumpster somewhere."

Evelyn looked at him. "What the hell did you say to her?" When neither of us answered, she leaned back into her seat. "Oh, boy. This will be fun."

Next we had errands to run. Jack phoned Quinn to summon him and Felix to West Virginia. Then we drove out of town to dispose of my things and pick up supplies. By the time we got to our hotel, it was evening, and my mood had lifted. We had a plan, and I was an integral part of that plan, so there was no time for sulking.

As for Jack, well, he was quiet, maybe still simmering, or maybe just gone back to his normal self. Either way, I wasn't dwelling on it.

I walked through the door joining the two hotel suites Evelyn had checked us into.

"Better digs than *he* puts you up in, I'll bet," Evelyn said, shooting a look at Jack.

"We had a nice place in Ohio," I said. "Real flowers, Jacuzzi tub . . ."

Evelyn sniffed. "And a heart-shaped vibrating bed? Classy, Jacko."

"Do you want this room?" I asked, moving into the bedroom doorway. "Or I guess if the other has two beds, you and I should take that—"

"This one's yours. You took on Wilkes today, you deserve something special, and this hotel is my way of saying 'good job.'" She glanced at Jack. "You can take the sofa."

I shook my head. "We all need a good rest tonight. There are four beds—"

Evelyn cut me off with a sigh. "Fine, share my room with me. You don't snore, do you?"

I thought about the nightmares, but Jack said, "She's fine." He paused. "Or she will be. Gotta get those hands fixed."

I picked up the drugstore bag he'd laid on the table. "I'll do that now."

"Can't bandage your own hands." He took the bag from me. "Sit down."

"I'll be unpacking," Evelyn said, and left.

Jack was still cleaning my wounds when Felix rapped at the door. Jack opened it. Quinn walked in and stopped dead, staring at my hands.

"Shit, are you okay?" he said.

I nodded.

"How did you—?"

"Garrote wire."

Felix stepped up beside me and frowned down at my wounds. "A garrote wire can be tricky to use. The instinct is to wrap it around your own hands, but if it's sharp enough, then you see the damage you can inflict."

"This isn't— I wasn't using it on someone; he was using it on me."

"And you managed to get your hands under it? Excellent reflexes. However, it does beg the question..."

"Who the hell tried to garrote you?" Quinn said as he crouched and took my hand.

Jack waved him aside and took his place, then unrolled the bandage.

"Wilkes," he said when I was slow to answer.

"Wilkes attacked you?" Felix said as he sat in a chair. "So he knows we're in pursuit? That could lead to some difficulty—"

"Doesn't know," Jack said. "Picked Dee as a victim. She—" A hard look my way. "Lured him in."

Before anyone could comment, Evelyn walked from the other room. As Felix and Quinn greeted her, Jack inspected the cleaned wounds.

"So you decided to join the hunt," Quinn said, flashed a smile at Evelyn. "Getting a little too exciting to ignore? I bet— Ah, wait. The anonymous 'concerned party' who's paying our wages. Guess I should say thank you."

Evelyn said nothing, but from the look that crossed her face, she had no idea what Quinn was talking about. I'd never suspected Evelyn was the person funding the job— she wouldn't hire a group of hitmen for a nonprofit expedition. But if it wasn't her . . .

"Stop squirming," Jack said. "Gotta get this fastened."

Quinn sat on the sofa. "So Dee lured Wilkes into a showdown?" He grinned my way. "Way to go."

Jack shot him a look, but Quinn continued, "You went mano a mano with the infamous Helter Skelter killer. The first victim who fought back. Did he say anything? Too busy getting his heart out of his throat, I bet."

Jack scooped up the bloodied cloths, wrapped them in the empty bag for later disposal and took them back to his room. I crouched to clean up the first-aid supplies. Quinn slid down beside me to help. As he leaned over for the scissors he whispered, "I'm jealous." I laughed. We both reached for the spare tape roll. I got to it first, but he pretended not to notice and grabbed for it, ending up with my wrist instead. A quick grin and quicker squeeze, and he released me.

"You'll have to tell me all about it later," he said.

I smiled. "We'll see."

As I straightened, I caught Evelyn watching us.

"When Jack called us in, he said you have a plan," Felix said. "Care to share?"

Felix liked the plan. Quinn wasn't so sure. I understood his reticence. What he and I knew, and the others didn't, was that we were expecting a federal agent to do something no agent should ever consider. However often one might see movie cops playing lone cowboys, it didn't work that way in real life. You're trained to be a team player, and there are plenty of checks and balances to make sure you stay that way—like Quinn having to provide a hotel name and phone number while on vacation.

But, as Quinn conceded, if there was a guy who might go for this, it was Martin Dubois. He amended the plan somewhat, building in protections that might sway Dubois, make him feel safer. Even then he warned that we were taking a chance—that Dubois wouldn't agree, would double-cross us, would back out at the last moment. But we knew that. All we could do was guard against it.

Quinn left to set his part into motion. While he was gone, Evelyn, Jack and Felix compared notes on Wilkes, as they remembered him. Not a conversation I could join, so after twenty minutes I wandered off to the other side of the room to check out the room service menu. Last thing I'd eaten was a sub on the drive to the parade.

"Hungry?" asked a voice at my shoulder. Quinn. "I'll bet

you are. Confront the man the whole country is searching for, and no one even buys you dinner."

"Did everything go okay?" I asked.

"It's started. Now we have to wait for a response. Don't worry. If what I hear about Dubois is right, he'll at least hear us out."

"Good."

Quinn glanced over at Evelyn, Jack and Felix.

"They're talking about Wilkes," I said. "I can't help them there."

"Me neither." He took the menu from me. "We can order from this if you'd like, but I saw a place down the road. What do you say I buy you dinner?"

"Sure," I said.

I grabbed my wallet, shoes and jacket. As I got ready, I glanced Jack's way, waiting for him to notice I was leaving, but he was engrossed in the conversation.

Quinn called out a "going to grab a bite," and I thought I heard Evelyn respond, but he only closed the door and ushered me down the hall. If Evelyn or Jack had wanted to stop us, they could have made it to the door before the elevator arrived. No one did, so I took that as permission to leave.

FORTY-SIX

"You know you're going to have to kill him," Quinn said as he speared a chicken ball.

We were in Felix's hotel room—a small one a few doors from ours. Jack might not have minded me going out to eat with Quinn, but I imagined he'd have something to say about our choice of dining area.

Our plans for the restaurant had gone south when we realized it closed at eleven, and we'd arrived at eleven-thirty. That left McDonald's or a take-out Chinese place. I'd picked takeout, meaning we needed a place to eat. When Quinn suggested Felix's room, with a hands-lifted "just to eat—no ulterior motives," I'd agreed.

If Jack was right, the greatest danger I faced being alone with Quinn was that he'd rethink that "no ulterior motives" bit. That I could stop . . . if I wanted to. So far, he'd kept his word, lying on the opposite side of the bed, with boxes of food laid out between us, as we talked.

"You have to kill him," Quinn said again when I didn't answer. "If not you, then me or Jack, but someone has to. It has nothing to do with 'the bastard deserves to die.' Give me a choice, and I'd rather see him rot in jail than get a quick ticket out. Problem is, there's no guarantee he'll go to jail. You and I know that better than any of them."

His eyes met mine and I knew he was searching for some look or reaction that would confirm a suspicion.

I wound up a forkful of noodles. "The justice system isn't perfect. Everyone knows that."

As I slurped noodles off my fork, Quinn caught my gaze

and I let him have it, holding it for at least ten seconds. Finally, he let out a sigh, breath hissing through his teeth.

"Fine, so you've *heard* things can go wrong. Cops fuck up, lab fucks up, prosecutors fuck up, juries, judges... everyone's human, and as hard as people try, sometimes they make mistakes. Wilkes'll get himself a defense lawyer who'd put Manson himself back on the streets if it meant a new car for his mistress."

I shrugged. "Everyone's entitled to a fair trial and someone has to make sure they get it."

"If the case even gets to trial. The way we're stringing this thing together, even a pro bono suit could find grounds for dismissal."

"Sure, but—"

"I'm not knocking the plan. I can't think of an airtight way to do it, either. But it's a problem, and the question is: what are you going to do about it?"

I put down my fork. "The question is: can I see a way around it? Do I have a problem with killing Wilkes? Of course not. But what's more important to me is making sure everyone knows he's been caught. If he just drops off the face of the earth, this won't ever go away. The Feds will keep pouring money and man-hours into solving it. The newspapers will keep reminding people that it's unsolved— in other words, that the Feds 'fucked up.' Every time a potential suspect turns up, you risk the public taking matters into their own hands. Sure, it'll die down eventually, but you can bet that on every anniversary for the next decade, the media will bring it back up, reignite the fear. Then there's the whole issue of copycats—nutcases thinking they can win instant infamy by pulling one hit and claiming the rest as their own."

"I'm not saying we off him and dump the body. But

what if we could toss Dubois a dead suspect instead of a live one?" When I didn't respond, he added, "I know, it wouldn't be as easy as it sounds, but take some time later and give it some thought. Run it by Evelyn and Jack. See what they think."

"I will. And if we can't come up with a way to kill him before we hand him over, we could arrange it afterward." I looked over at Quinn. "I'm sure someone would be able to make sure Wilkes never sees the inside of a courtroom... someone who knows how to do such a thing."

Quinn went still. "So Jack told you what I do?"

"Jack didn't tell me a thing. He said it wasn't his place. I had a hunch."

"That obvious, huh?"

I took a forkful of rice before answering. "I've... heard of things like that. As a cop, you must see things go wrong. Maybe someone offers you money to make it go right." I shrugged. "It might not seem like such a bad idea."

He shifted on the bed before continuing. "If that did happen, you'd think it would need to be something really big that set him off, wouldn't you? One of those awful cases you might see once in a lifetime, the kind most cops go their whole careers and never see."

I thought of Wayne Franco and his victim, Dawn Collins, and concentrated on getting out the last grain of rice.

He continued. "But it wasn't anything like that. It was the kind of situation you see so often you almost start forgetting what a tragedy it is, and you sure as hell stop expecting anything like justice to come of it. Woman leaves her husband, guy threatens her, she takes out a restraining order, calls the local cops a few times... sure, they try to help, but there are other priorities. And it seems like half the time when cops *do* respond, the couple is making up in the bedroom when they get there."

"But this wasn't one of those times, was it? He killed her."

Quinn nodded. "It wasn't my case—that's not . . . it isn't the kind of work I do. But I knew the woman's father—a friend of my dad's—and my dad asked me to be there, to explain stuff to the parents. The bastard walked. He leaves the courtroom, grinning and high-fiving his buddies, while her parents are crying, her oldest kid just staring into space, and I'm thinking how goddamn unfair it all is, but that's really all I think because I've seen stuff like that so many times before. Afterward, we're in the parking lot, and her father asks me to do him a favor."

"Set things right."

Quinn nodded.

"And you did."

"Nope. Told him two wrongs don't make a right, and I understood how badly he was hurting, but this wasn't a road he wanted to go down. Two days later, the bastard's dead, the old man's in jail, his wife tries to kill herself, and the kids . . . well, you can bet those kids are fucked for life. And it could have been avoided if I'd taken that job instead of spouting some 'turn the other cheek' crap that I knew was bullshit."

"So that's what you do then," I said. "Vigilante for hire."

Quinn looked at me. His eyes were blue that night. Whenever I saw him, they were blue. I doubted that was his normal color, but he always wore the same contacts when he knew we'd be meeting—the same contacts, the same hair color, the same overall disguise—as if he wanted to show me something consistent.

With Jack, I could look him full in the face and still not have the faintest clue what was going on behind his eyes.

The doors were closed. With Quinn, there were no doors, probably never had been, and I could imagine that it had only taken one look around for the victim's father to know the best person to approach with his offer.

Now, as Quinn watched me, his feelings were written over every feature—the creases around his mouth, the line between his brows, the anxiety in his eyes as he mentally replayed those words "vigilante for hire," and tried to interpret my tone.

I moved the take-out boxes aside, folding each and laying it on the table.

"So, you, uh..." He rubbed his chin. "You think..."

"What do you want me to say, Quinn? That I'm impressed? That it puts you a cut above guys like Jack? Like me?"

He grabbed the last box. "No. Absolutely not. I don't kid myself that it's some noble cause. I get paid for it... well, not always, but, yeah, you're right. Vigilante for hire. Maybe it's a fucked-up way of looking at the world if I think that makes me any better than the guys I off. I just... That's what I do, and I wanted you to know..." He let the sentence trail off.

"Because...?"

He scooped up the forks and shrugged. "Maybe I just wanted you to know because I wanted you to know."

I watched him as he dropped the forks into the garbage, his hand hovering there a moment even after the forks had thumped into the bottom, as if reluctant to turn toward me, dragging the distraction out as he tried to think of what to say next. His jaw tightened and relaxed, as if practicing a line.

My gaze slid down to his arm, muscles so tense I could see the tendons against the fabric of his shirt, and I had to fight the urge to slide over there, put my hand on the dip between his shoulder blades, rub away the tension. I resisted, but not because I was afraid where that would lead, because I was pretty sure where it would lead and, at that moment, I was almost as sure I'd let it. I held back because I couldn't tell him it was all right, when I wasn't sure that it was. But there was one thing I could say, and honestly, so I did.

"Thanks," I said. "For telling me."

A half-smile and a nod, then he moved back onto the bed. As he did, his hand brushed my foot, stopped, and squeezed in a slow rub.

"You might not want to do that," I said. "I spent half the day in boots."

A burst of laughter, not—I'm sure—because it was terribly funny, but just because it gave him something to laugh about. He took a better hold on my foot and kept rubbing.

When I arched my brows, he laughed again.

"Don't worry. This isn't step one to seduction. I meant what I said earlier. I won't push."

"No, you said you didn't have any ulterior motives."

"And I don't. There's nothing at all secret about my motives. I think I've made them perfectly clear."

"Ulterior motive doesn't mean 'hidden agenda.' It means planning to do *more* than you let on. In other words, bringing me here for more than dinner."

"Damn."

I smiled and shook my head. When he let his hand wander up my calf, I gave another head shake, then another smile.

"Not that I'm averse to the idea in general . . ." I said.

"But this isn't the time or the place. I know that, despite what Jack thinks."

"He said something to you?"

"With Jack, it's not what he says. It's all about the body language, which has been screaming 'don't even think about it.'" He moved back. "This is probably a dumb thing to ask, because even by bringing it up...But I have to, because I know how it probably looks, me chasing you when I have a beef with Jack, and I wouldn't blame you for thinking this is all part of that, another bit of the...you know, rivalry."

"Well, if it is, then you're wasting your time because there's nothing going on between Jack and me. Like I said, to him, I'm a partner, maybe a student, but that's it."

"Yeah, I knew you two weren't...well, I didn't *know*, but I figured if there was, he'd be doing more than shooting me nasty looks. And I can't imagine—You don't seem the type who'd be here if there was someone else."

"I thought I was just here for dinner."

"And talking." He slid over to me. "Talking's good."

"And dinner was good."

"Wasn't bad. Not exactly the victory meal I had in mind..."

"Better than McDonald's."

"That's good."

He leaned over and kissed me. The first touch was soft and light, his lips barely brushing mine, ready to move back fast at any sign of rejection. I hesitated and, for a moment, we seemed to hover there, lips touching, looking at each other. Then I closed my eyes. His arms went around my waist, mouth pressing against mine, lips parting.

He leaned into me, not squeezing, not pulling me closer, just...kissing. A very nice, sweet kiss. No pressure, no urgency. Like embers in a campfire, you can see the glow, feel the heat, but there's no danger there, not unless you want it.

When that first spark ignited, Quinn's tongue darting into my mouth, testing, hands sliding to my rear, a low, almost inaudible groan rumbling up from his chest, I knew if I wanted to stop it, this was the time. But I didn't want to. I wanted to close my eyes and drop . . . and I couldn't.

I didn't break the kiss, but I must not have reciprocated the way he'd expected, because he pulled back his head, eyes glazed and hooded.

"No go, huh?" he said.

"I'm sorry," I said, disentangling myself.

"Not your fault." He sat up, concentrating on tucking in his shirt. "If you don't feel it, nothing you can do about that."

I gave a ragged laugh. "Oh, I feel it."

His gaze shot to mine, lips curving slightly. "Yeah?"

I kissed him lightly. "Trust me, that's not in question. But our timing really sucks."

He laughed, put his hands around my waist and pulled me onto his lap. "The others wouldn't appreciate it if we showed up tomorrow too tired to pull this thing off." He nipped my earlobe. "And something tells me, if we start this, the night's not going to be over anytime soon."

I shivered and tried hard—really hard—not to think too much about that. He ran his teeth up my ear, and I ducked away.

"Enough." I laughed. "I'm trying to be responsible here."

"One of us needs to be."

He slid his hands under the hem of my sweatshirt, tickling my sides, his grin threatening to take his hands farther north. I scrambled backward. He grabbed my hips, toppling me down on my back, then moved over me, on all fours above me, crouched there, grinning.

"Not going to make this easy for me, are you?"

"That depends. Am I *close* to getting a yes?"

"That depends. Can I be upstairs in about thirty minutes? Before Jack comes looking for me?" I arched my head back and pointed at the suitcase on the floor. "And before Felix wants his room back?"

"Shit. Forgot about that." He tickled his fingers across my belly, where my sweatshirt was riding up. "Hmmm. Part of me is screaming to take what I can get. But there's that other part that's saying if I do, that might be *all* I get. Thirty minutes isn't really enough to make a lasting impression...." He met my gaze. "And I want to make a lasting impression."

Something inside me flip-flopped and I'm sure I blushed.

His lips lowered to my ear. "We could just make out for a while. Hands-over-clothes rule?"

I sputtered a laugh. "I haven't heard that since high school."

"I have maturity issues, in case you haven't you noticed. Is that a yes?"

"Hands over clothes it is."

"Does it still count if I take *mine* off?"

I put my hands on the back of his neck and pulled him down.

Quinn did manage to get his shirt off, but I didn't complain. Otherwise, he stuck to his rules—just kissing, a relaxed, sensual intimacy that, in some ways, I needed more than sex.

After about ten minutes, Felix unlocked the door, but

the chain stopped him from opening it. He must have figured out what was going on and called that he'd be in the lounge, and for Quinn to come get him when he was "unoccupied."

We lay there for another minute, Quinn's hand resting on the curve between my waist and hip.

"When this is over . . ." he began. "I know I can't exactly ask you out to dinner and a movie, but I *would* like to keep in touch. It doesn't matter how. Cell phone, e-mail, whatever you're comfortable with. I just want . . . I'd like to stay in touch, whether anything comes of it or not. It'd just be nice. To talk sometimes."

I smiled. "It would be. Nice, I mean."

"Good." A light kiss, then he pulled back.

"I should go," I said. "Jack's probably pacing by now, figuring I've done something stupid again and wound up in a ditch somewhere."

"More like figuring I've *put* you in a ditch somewhere. Go on then. Get a good night's sleep."

FORTY-SEVEN

By the time I got upstairs, it was past one. I opened the door. The sitting room was dark. As I slid inside, I realized this was Jack's room, now that I'd moved in with Evelyn. I started to back out, but before the door closed, I remembered something else, namely that I didn't have a key card for the other room.

I tiptoed to the door joining the other sitting area. As I drew near, I heard voices. Typical hotel—you can shell out for big suites and nice views, but don't expect soundproofing. It was Evelyn talking, though I could only hear snatches of the conversation.

"... to do about it? ... sit back and feel sorry ..."

A low rumble. Male, probably Jack, but too low to hear clearly. I considered knocking, but didn't want to interrupt. Maybe I could watch TV, turn it up loud enough so they'd know I was here, in case they were waiting for me. And the blare of a TV would be less intrusive than a polite knock?

Evelyn again. "Fine, *brood*, not sulk ..."

Jack answered, still unintelligible. As I reached out to knock, Evelyn's voice grew louder, her words coming clearer. I rapped anyway, but she continued. "... need to *take* what's yours."

Another rumble.

Evelyn sighed. "... not yours, then. So change that. *Do* something."

I took the handle and turned it, slowly, checking whether the door was open. It was. One final knock.

Evelyn continued. "If you think *he's* going to let this blow over, and just walk away afterward, you've got a hell of a shock coming—"

As she spoke, I eased open the door, then gave one last, loud knock, and she stopped in midsentence. I poked my head through the opening.

"Sorry," I said. "I tried knocking, but I guess you couldn't hear me. I just wanted to let you know I'm back. I'll wait over here..."

Evelyn pulled the door open and I nearly fell in. Jack stood across the room, arms crossed.

"Everything...okay?" I asked.

Jack uncrossed his arms, but Evelyn beat him to an answer.

"No, everything is not okay," she said, looking at him. "But, apparently, it won't be fixed anytime soon. Not that it matters. Fuck up this chance and I'm sure one will come around again...in another twenty, thirty years."

"The plan, you mean?" I said as I closed the door behind me. "Has something gone wrong? Quinn hasn't heard from Dubois, so—"

"The plan is fine...or as fine as we can make it at this point."

"Maybe not," I said. "Quinn and I discussed something, a possible change."

I told them our thoughts on the "final" solution.

"Yeah," Jack said. "Been thinking that. It's a problem. Not just Wilkes getting off. He's arrested? He'll talk."

"About you and Evelyn. Damn it, I didn't think—"

"Doesn't matter. We can handle that. Cops know we exist. You? Still an unknown. I want to keep it that way."

"Fine, but I still say you guys are in more danger. He won't hesitate to use whatever he knows as leverage and, if that fails, he'll just give it away to make your lives difficult.

That settles it, then. We can't hand him over to Dubois while he's in any condition to talk."

"Easy enough," Evelyn said. "We amend the plan so we hand over a corpse instead of a suspect. No big deal. You kill Wilkes, and Dubois will claim he did it in self-defense."

And there it was. Easy as could be. "You kill him, Nadia." I didn't even have to suggest it.

I said, "With the ambition angle, we have some leeway. Dubois might see the danger of bringing in a dead man, but he'll see the advantages, too. 'Top federal agent takes on notorious serial killer in a fight to the death...and wins' makes a lot better copy than 'Top federal agent apprehends suspect.'"

"No need to decide anything until morning, so let's take the night to think about it. In the meantime..." She glanced Jack's way.

Jack hesitated, then looked at me. "You tired? Got a smoke or two left." He took the pack from his pocket. "Should get them gone."

My gut twisted. I knew what he really wanted—to finish our argument from earlier, the one I'd walked away from.

"When the hell did you start smoking again?" Evelyn asked Jack.

"Never stopped," he said.

"I haven't seen you light up in years."

"Don't do it in front of you."

"But you'll do it in front of Dee? You really *do* know how to treat a lady. Take her outside in the middle of the chilly night, so you can blow smoke in her face? At least find someplace warm. There's a lounge downstairs. Order a drink, relax, have your smoke if you need it...."

I shook my head. "I don't drink before a job. And I'm beat. I'm just going to go to bed, okay?"

I didn't wait around to find out whether it was okay, just grabbed my bag and headed for the bathroom. When I came out, Jack was gone.

Evelyn started for the bathroom, but I stopped her.

"You know what Quinn does, don't you?" I said. "His angle."

A small smile. "The Boy Scout?"

"Is that his other pro name?"

She moved back into the room and sat on her bed. "Yes, but I wouldn't suggest you use it unless you want to piss him off. Seems vigilante types have this odd aversion to having it thrown in their face."

I ignored that and pressed on. "But if this is his angle, vigilantism as you call it, and he's obviously far more into it than I am, why not take him?"

She grinned. "If I were thirty years younger, Dee, I'd take him in a second. But that's just libido talking. As a student? He'd be . . . adequate. Nothing more."

"But he *is* a vigilante. And a true believer, not just some guy taking advantage of an underserviced wedge of the market."

"Still trying to wriggle out of this without making a decision, Nadia?"

"Of course not," I snapped, a little harder than I meant, annoyed by her switch from Dee to Nadia. I covered it by continuing. "You said you want me because you're interested in this 'angle' of mine. But Quinn has it, so I think I'm entitled to ask a question or two."

"And make sure I'm not misleading you? Tricking you into something?"

"I'm being careful."

"Good girl. So why you and not him? Fair question. For Quinn, it's all up here—" She tapped her head. "Cerebral.

He sees injustice and, as a cop, as a moral man, he's outraged. But there's no fire here—" She patted her stomach.

"But Quinn's good. Even Jack admits it."

"Technical skills, attention to detail, creativity, brains, all that can make you a damned fine hitman, and Quinn has it all. But to be better than fine, to be *legendary,* you need that drive. Me, I had some, but not on your scale. I've only ever seen that kind of fire once, a different sort—the worst case of 'fuck the world' rage you've ever seen. Without training? Suicide. You take too many chances, trying to dowse those flames. You burn yourself up." She met my gaze. "Seen any symptoms of that lately, Nadia?"

I said nothing. She pushed to her feet, muttering about her knees, then wished me good night and headed to the bathroom.

I didn't sleep. Couldn't. That never fails. If you have a big day coming, and you know you need your rest, then you won't be able to find it, and the longer you lie there, the more anxious you get, which only keeps you awake.

What really kept me awake that night, though, was my conversation with Jack. I believe in honesty. Always have. But brutal honesty is, well, brutal. It rips the scabs off wounds you've tried so hard to heal.

He hadn't said anything I didn't already know. No matter how hard I'd worked to get my life back on track after Wayne Franco, that track was closed to me forever now. I'd never be a cop again. Marriage, kids, a house in the suburbs—none of it had ever ranked very high on my list of life goals, but there's a difference between not wanting something and not being able to have it.

Sure, I could find a guy willing to overlook my past—I'd

had plenty who'd offered—but I wasn't as willing to let anyone try, not after Eric. And I was never bringing a child into this world to grow up under the shadow I'd cast. If I really wanted those things, I could move to another country and start over, under a new name, but that was something I'd never more than fleetingly considered.

There were people who would give a damn if I didn't come back from this trip. Emma and Owen and a handful of friends, like Mitch and Lucy. A pitiably small group, none of the ties as close as those I'd once had. I no longer let people get close, not after everyone who should have stuck by me didn't. My mother, my brother, my lover, my friends, my extended family—some tried to hang on after "the Incident," but none tried very hard and when I'd finally packed up and left, I'd heard a collective sigh of relief.

If I died on this mission, I couldn't help wondering whether my funeral would be like Kozlov's, where news cameras outnumbered the mourners. That's a shitty thing to realize...and a shittier thing to make someone realize.

Damn Jack.

After two hours of tossing and listening to the hitches in Evelyn's breathing as my restlessness disturbed her sleep, I grabbed a pillow and blanket, crept from the room and set up on the sofa.

About thirty minutes later, I drifted off. But when sleep came, it didn't come soundly, and the moment I lost consciousness I slid right into my nightmare.

I was out of that endless forest and running through a field. I could see the Millers' house ahead. I'd stop there, call my dad—

Something flashed over my head. I looked up, and saw

the wire. My hands shot up to block it, but it flew down, passing right through my outstretched palms and into my throat.

I couldn't breathe. I kicked and flailed, but the wire only cut deeper. Then it changed. Not Wilkes's wire, but a knife point, digging into my throat.

Aldrich laughed.

No! He couldn't have followed. He'd finished with me and was busy with Amy now. I had to get help. To save her—

"Save her?" His voice whispered in my ear. "You aren't saving her, Nadia. You're running away. Abandoning her."

"No!"

As the word ripped from my throat, the world dipped into black. Something whispered across my cheek. A touch, a hand, brushing back my sweaty hair. Cool skin against mine. The faint smell of soap.

"Nadia . . . ?"

I opened my eyes. Jack sat on the edge of the sofa, his hands smoothing my hair.

I groaned. "I'm making a habit of this, aren't I? How many partners have you had to comfort after nightmares?"

"Don't work with partners."

"And this is why, isn't it?"

A small smile. He traced his fingertips down my cheek, then stopped, his gaze flicking to his hand as if surprised to see it there. He pulled back and shifted to adjust my blanket.

"Sorry," I said. "Two nights in a row . . . that's not normal for me."

For a moment, he crouched beside the sofa, gaze averted, as if thinking. Then his eyes swung back to me. To my throat. To the ghost of a scar. I pulled the blanket higher. His face turned from mine. Then he pushed to his feet.

"Gotta get you to sleep."

He walked toward the minibar.

"Uh-uh," I said. "Booze isn't—"

He took out a bottle of brown liquid and held it up. "Saw this earlier."

"Yoo-hoo?" I said, squinting at the label. "What's in it? Looks like chocolate milk, but..."

"Thought it was." He looked at it and frowned. "Not sure. Huh. Ingredients..." His lips moved as he read the list. Then his frown deepened. "Still not sure."

He put the bottle down. "Let me go downstairs. Find you some real stuff. Heat it up."

"Ah, hot chocolate. Now I get it." I sat up. "Here, we'll use that. I'll just stand back from the microwave, in case it's explosive."

He waved me down. "Stay."

He poured the stuff into a coffee mug, and microwaved it for me. As he brought it over, I gestured at the cigarette pack on the table, where he'd tossed them down earlier.

"You didn't finish them, I see. Go ahead if you want."

"Nonsmoking room."

"I think you've broken worse laws."

"Yeah. But I'd feel bad about this one."

He handed me my mug and sat beside me on the sofa.

"So, you talked to Quinn tonight," he said. "He tell you? About himself?"

"That he's a vigilante hitman? I'd already figured that."

He studied my expression. Then he grunted, fingers tapping against the cigarette pack. A hungry look down at it, then he stood, crossed the room and tossed it on the counter.

"What did you think would happen, Jack? That I'd hear what Quinn does and say 'hey, sign me up'?"

"Nah. Just..." He shrugged. Didn't finish the sentence.

"I didn't need to hear it from Quinn to know it *was* an option, that there's a market for that kind of thing."

"Yeah, I know."

He sat down. I sipped my hot Yoo-hoo, and tried not to make a face.

"Tastes like shit?" he said.

I managed a small smile. "Yes, but it gets the job done." I took another sip. "About tomorrow. I'd really like— I know you're not the person to talk to about it, because you have problems with the whole plan, but, well, Evelyn, Quinn... I can talk to them but I just don't feel..."

I looked at Jack. "Whatever happened today, however much we disagree about that, I trust you and I'd really like your input. I plan to pull this off, Jack. Without getting myself killed."

"I know." He leaned back into the cushions. "Talk to me."

So I did.

FORTY-EIGHT

I woke up in the bedroom I was sharing with Evelyn. Last thing I remembered, Jack and I had finished discussing the plan and moved on to talking about ... I had no idea what we'd moved on to, because I think that the moment I had the plan straight in my head, I fell asleep. Jack must have carried me into the bedroom.

I rolled over and checked the other bed. It was empty. The clock read 8:12. I shot up with a curse. Of all the days to sleep in ...

I could hear Evelyn in the main room, saying something about Dubois and the contact call. Was there a problem? I scrambled up and threw open the door.

"Have we heard back—?"

I stopped. Evelyn sat on the sofa, in conversation with a man. Only that man wasn't Jack. It was Quinn. And I was standing in the doorway, half-naked, no wig, no contacts, no makeup. Quinn's gaze didn't go to my face first, though. It went to my chest. Or, more accurately, to my torso, emblazoned with the Ontario Police College logo. His eyes lifted to mine. He blinked, realizing I wasn't wearing a disguise, then looked away. I backpedaled and slammed the door as Evelyn let out an oath.

Evelyn opened the door without knocking.

"Shit, that was a stupid move," she muttered.

I glared over my shirt collar as I pulled it on. "Yes, I've been making a lot of stupid moves lately, but thanks for clarifying that."

"By 'stupid move,' Dee, I meant mine. I should've warned you Quinn was here."

I tugged on my jeans. "Well, I should have woken up enough to think about checking before throwing open the door."

"I don't think he got a good look at you. He did the right thing—turned away."

"It's not my face I'm worried about. It's this." I lifted the police college shirt for her to read before I refolded it into my bag. "That he *did* see."

"Shit."

A soft knock at the door.

"Dee?" Quinn.

I asked him to wait while I looked around for my wig and contacts. When I had them on, I called a welcome. He slid inside. Evelyn hesitated, then left. Quinn stood there as I pulled on my socks.

"I'm sorry," he said.

"Hey, you didn't do anything wrong. You just glanced up when the door opened. And thanks—you know, for looking away when you realized I . . ."

I let the sentence fade, and picked up my toothpaste. Before I could slip into the bathroom, he grabbed my hand.

"Dee? Whatever I saw? There could be a few explanations, and I have no intention of trying to figure out which one is right."

"Thanks."

"How about a trade-off?" He smiled. "One question. Ask me anything."

When I shook my head, his smile faltered.

"Sure. Okay. I mean, maybe there's nothing you want—"

"Your eyes," I said, managing a small smile. "What color are your eyes?"

His grin returned full wattage. "Sure. I can do that—better than that." He dropped his head forward, reached up and took out his contacts. "There."

He looked at me. His eyes were light green, the color of new grass.

Quinn moved closer, his head tilting, lips moving down toward mine—

The door banged open and we both jumped back.

"Evelyn told me," Jack said, by way of introduction. He started crossing the room, then met Quinn's eyes. A grunt, and his gaze dropped to Quinn's hand, still cupping his contacts.

"Christ's sake," Jack muttered. "Show-and-tell? This isn't kindergarten."

"He was just—" I began.

"Leaving," Jack said. "I need to talk to Dee."

"It wasn't Quinn's—"

"Fault. Yeah. I heard." He jerked his thumb at the door. "Go call your sources. Dubois doesn't respond by noon? We call it off."

Quinn put in his contacts, then squeezed my hand and left.

"There was no need to talk to him that way," I said. "He didn't do anything wrong."

"Besides taking out his contacts?"

"He felt bad, and he wanted to reciprocate—"

"Yeah. He wants to reciprocate. Middle of a fucking job. Starts playing 'I'll show you mine.'"

"Actually, I think I showed him mine first."

"Not on purpose." Jack moved closer, the edge leaving his voice. "You okay? Evelyn said he saw you. Saw your shirt."

"Which I should have never brought with me. A dumb

move, but it . . . helps me sleep, and sometimes that's more important than being careful."

"I've seen the shirt. Had a problem with it? Would have said so. Back to the question. You okay?"

"I'm shaken, but I guess it's a good lesson for me to be careful all the time, and not relax my guard when I'm with just you and Evelyn."

"Yeah. Gotta be careful with Evelyn."

A small smile. "But not you?"

"Not unless I open my mouth. Then I'm dangerous." He paused. "About yesterday—"

The door swung open.

"Jack? Dee?" Evelyn called. "Dubois bit. He's in."

"Now the fun begins," I murmured.

We'd arranged for our point person to meet Dubois at eleven thirty. Just because he'd agreed to speak to us didn't mean he'd agree to our plan, but we couldn't wait to find out. We had too much prep work.

"I ordered the radios yesterday," Felix said as we ate a late breakfast in our hotel room. "I called this morning and rerouted delivery to a plaza outside town. Quinn? Would you be able to pick those up later?"

"Will do."

"Need a safe house," Jack said. "Motel would work. Prefer a house."

"Easily done," Felix said. "We'll locate several for rent, with immediate possession, scout locations, and select one."

"Hole up in a place for rent?" I said. "Sounds good, but there's a risk factor, isn't there? If someone decides to show the place—"

"We'll rent it," Felix said. "Cash for a month."

"Is that—?"

"Safe?" He smiled, and switched to an upper-class British accent. "Hello, I'm Dr. Patterson, and I have a rather…odd request to make. I'm visiting your university and, well, I must admit, I loathe public housing. I believe you have a lovely little place for rent on Main Street? If it wouldn't be too much of an inconvenience, I'd like to let it for the week. I'll pay you for the entire month, of course, in advance."

"Works for me," I said.

"And it has worked for me more times than I can count."

"Let's get moving on that," Jack said. "Dubois comes through? I want keys within the hour. Need time for a thorough examination. No surprises."

Dubois

Martin Dubois stirred his coffee, tasted it, then added another sweetener. As he lifted the cup to his lips, he looked over the rim at the clock. Eleven twenty-nine. He'd wait until eleven thirty-five, no longer. Maybe eleven forty, but only if he didn't finish his coffee before that. He drank slower.

The message had come in last night. An e-mail, sent to his personal account.

> Missing a witness? We have her but I think you'd rather have the man who tried to kill her. If so, we can deliver. This is a private transaction. You'll get your man and all the credit, and we'll ask for very little in return.
>
> If you wish to discuss this further, please respond to the e-mail address at the bottom with a time and place.

Attached to the e-mail was a photo of a bloodied garrote wire. No one knew that's what the killer had tried to use. The kids thought he'd been strangling her with a rope, which hadn't explained her bloodied hands. The wire looked like the same gauge used on the Lee woman. That made sense.

He'd tried to trace the e-mail, of course—using what

resources he could without arousing suspicion—but the trail ended at a dead account. So he'd done the only thing he could: responded with a time and place. Here and now.

They'd expected him to come alone. He hadn't, of course. He was ambitious—not crazy. But he'd told the young agent accompanying him only that he was meeting a witness in a public place and wanted backup, then positioned him across the room, where he could watch for trouble, but couldn't overhear the conversation.

Had it been any other case, there would have been a team of agents with him, ready to take into custody whoever showed up. But this was the case of a lifetime, one that every agent dreamed of—a dream that was fast turning into a nightmare.

They hadn't blamed him for the Chicago killing. That had been his free swing. Then he'd had his entire team on a train to California . . . and the killer took a victim in Nebraska. Strike one. So he'd pulled them back into the investigation, and sent a skeleton crew to organize security at the West Virginia parade. And the killer had not only shown up in West Virginia, but left an eyewitness who just up and walked away. Strike two. He had twenty-four hours to produce that witness. If not . . . strike three.

Now he had a shot at getting her. That would redeem him, for a while. But if he could go all the way? Bring down the Helter Skelter killer? That would hit the ball out of the park, home run, bases loaded . . . safe forever. He could ride the wave for a few more years in the bureau, retire with full pension, maybe even tour the lecture circuit.

The bell over the café door tinkled. He glanced up. In walked an older woman. White-haired, elegantly groomed, the country club type. He was about to look away when she caught his gaze . . . and headed straight for him.

Goddamn it. She'd recognized him. And now she was coming over to tell him what a horrible job he was doing, and someone had to catch this criminal and, in her day, by God, they would have nabbed him after the first murder, if not before—

The woman dropped something onto the table. The garrote wire. He looked up at her, his mouth open, but nothing coming out. She took the seat opposite his and shrugged out of her coat.

He looked down at the wire.

"It's clean," he said, because he couldn't think of anything else to say.

"Yes, the boys wanted to leave the blood on it for you, but if you get blood in a silk pocket, it just never comes out." She met his gaze. "You didn't really think we'd leave our girl's DNA all over it, did you?"

"Your girl?"

"Your witness?"

She was looking at him like he was an idiot. A twenty-year veteran, and he was gaping at a source like a rookie. He slapped down his mug hard enough to slosh coffee over the edge.

"Where's my contact? If this is someone's idea of a joke—"

"It's someone's idea of covering your ass, Dubois. You're a public figure, in a public place . . . talking to a nice old lady. Probably calming her fears about this big bad killer. Even your boy in the corner is still busy watching the door for whomever you're supposed to be meeting."

He shifted in his seat. He had to take the upper hand—or at least find it.

"So who do you represent? I need to know who I'm—"

"A group of publicly minded individuals who've been

chasing this madman for you. Protecting their . . . business interests."

"What kind of business—?"

"What kind of business do you think your boy is in?"

"Who knows? Bunch of experts swear he's—" Dubois stopped. "A professional kil—"

"Smart experts. And if he was a member of said profession, there would likely be other members of said profession more than a little annoyed with the heat he's bringing down." She looked at him. "Who better to stop a killer?"

"So who the hell are you?"

She smiled. "Their fairy godmother . . . and I just might be yours, too. Let me order a coffee and run a little business proposition past you."

"So that's it," she said as she finished.

"And I somehow do all this without involving my team or my supervisors? This is the FBI, lady. I can't wipe my ass without filling out a triplicate requisition for new toilet paper."

She shrugged. "If it can't be done, then we'll find another way. Lure him in ourselves, take him down and notify the papers, telling them where to find the body—"

"Let me think about it."

"I'm sure you'll come up with something. No one said it would be easy, but the reward . . ." Another shrug. "Worth the cost, I'd say. If you need to involve someone else, one other person from your team, we understand that. Share the risk and share the glory—your decision."

"You still haven't told me the price. No, wait, let me guess. Prisoners. You want me to release some of your buddies we picked up while looking for this guy. Don't bother asking, because I don't have the kind of authority—"

"Keep them. If they've fucked up enough to get caught, that's not our concern."

He leaned back in his chair and studied her. "If it's not prisoners, it must be amnesty. Your guys want a few 'get out of jail free' cards. Some old cases closed—"

"My boys don't need free passes. Any cases you have on them have been shelved for lack of evidence and lack of interest. Let me save us both some time. We want one thing: this guy's name removed from our ranks. Once he's yours, he was never one of ours."

He thought about that for a moment. "You mean you don't want word of his former occupation getting out."

"A simple request that will make things much tidier for us."

He waited. She sipped her coffee.

"That's it?"

An arched brow. "Well, I could ask for two hundred million, but I suspect the answer would be no. So that's it. A fair and honest bargain, made in good faith. Do we have a deal?"

He hesitated, then nodded.

FORTY-NINE

The press conference was scheduled for 4 p.m., and by two, the announcement was on every local radio and TV station, and probably half the stations across the country. If Wilkes wanted to know whether the Feds had found me yet, he'd be tuning in. If he hoped to make sure I wasn't around for a police lineup or court case, he'd have stayed in town to take care of that...and would be at that press conference.

Evelyn, Felix and Quinn took off on their various tasks, making sure everything would run as smoothly as possible. Jack, Felix and I concentrated on the house. It was a row house in an area rife with student housing. As we'd seen with the Vegas condos, a row house limited access to the front and back, meaning Jack and Quinn could cover it. Student housing meant that it would either be near-vacant for homecoming, or there'd be parties nearby to cover any noise.

We searched the house from top to bottom and made a list of every possible entry point. Then we narrowed the list down to the most likely ones. The upstairs windows would be too difficult to get into, especially for a man approaching sixty. The basement one was too small. The best candidate was the patio door. The backyard was enclosed by a privacy fence, so once he was over that fence, he was out of sight.

We closed the vertical blinds so he could work on the patio door without being seen from inside. That also meant he couldn't take a shot from outside—a bonus. We closed every blind in the house to solve that potential problem.

Plus I'd be wearing body armor. That sounds a lot safer than it really is...a pro like Wilkes would know body armor was a possibility with a secured witness, and he'd aim for my head. But if he didn't have a chance to aim, the armor would help.

We closed off every room that we didn't need, and Jack applied something to the hinges so they'd squeak if the doors opened. With the shades drawn and doors all closed, the house was nearly dark, even at midday, and we moved furniture around, putting side tables in the halls, chairs just beyond doors, wrinkling area rugs, nothing that looked too out of place, but giving Wilkes things to bump into or trip over as he made his way through the house.

It would drive me crazy, having rumpled rugs and cock-eyed furniture, but if he stumbled or bumped something, it would be another way to let me know he was inside. We could have done more, rigged up an alert system of some sort, but if he found it, he'd know this was a trap.

Once the house was set, and I'd memorized the layout well enough to navigate in the dark, we ran through the plan, every variation of the plan, and every conceivable obstacle to the plan. Only when Jack was certain he'd left nothing unconsidered did he declare we were ready to bring in the others...and lunch.

Over lunch, we went through the plan with Evelyn, Felix and Quinn, and we all tried to poke holes in it. There were a few, but nothing that gave me any real cause for alarm. Finally, it was three thirty. Jack wanted everyone in position before the press conference.

Felix left me my radio, and showed me how to operate it. Quinn tried to stall, and I knew he wanted a private good-bye, but Evelyn took him aside to help her check on something.

They waited in the front room while Jack gave me last-minute instructions. Once they were out of earshot, he turned my way.

"You okay?"

I managed a weak smile. "As okay as I'm going to be."

"It'll be fine. Got everything covered." His gaze shot to me. "Did, didn't we? Everything covered?"

"It's fine, Jack."

"Things don't go as planned? Get out. Don't try a second time. Get him outside. Got Evelyn and Felix. Both good distance shooters. He runs? Got me and Quinn. Fast enough on our feet. Faster than him, at least."

I nodded.

"You want me here? Maybe we could—"

"No. The plan makes the most sense as it is."

We stood there, the silence thick and heavy.

"I know you don't want me to do this, Jack."

A moment's hesitation. "No. No, I don't."

"What happened yesterday, it wasn't— I was just—"

I stopped, realizing it would do no good to argue. He knew what had happened in that alley. If the lengths I'd gone to had surprised him, my motivation had not.

Yesterday he'd said he knew I wanted "it" bad, but didn't realize how bad, how far I'd go. Now I understood what that had meant. All those times I feared I'd let the mask slide and my rage show, then seen his reaction—no reaction at all—I'd told myself I'd dodged the bullet, kept my secret. But if he hadn't reacted, it was because he hadn't been surprised, had already seen what drove me. Saw it, accepted it, let it be . . . until I almost got myself killed.

I remembered what Evelyn had said the night before, about another student. "Worst case of 'fuck the world' rage you've ever seen."

I looked at Jack. "I won't screw up again. All things considered, we both know I'm not the best person for this, but I won't let you down."

"Not worried about that."

"Whatever you may think, I'm not suicidal."

He rubbed his hand over his mouth. Then his eyes met mine. "I know what that's like, Nadia. Lose everything. Everyone. It makes a difference. Not like you'd jump in front of a bullet. But things go bad? First thing people think? Who they'd leave behind. Parents, wives, kids . . . Don't want to let them down. But if there's no one there . . ."

"It's easier to take that risk," I said softly. "I won't do it again, Jack."

He nodded, gaze down, but had he looked up, I knew what I'd see. Doubt.

"I screwed up yesterday, on a whole lot of levels," I said. "But I have it under control this time. I swear."

He nodded. Hesitated. Opened his mouth to say something else, then Evelyn popped through the doorway. She saw us and stopped. A murmured apology, and she started to withdraw, but Quinn poked his head in, too.

"Jack? It's almost ten to."

Jack nodded. "Gotta run."

"You can take another minute—" Evelyn began.

"Gotta be in position before Dubois gets here." He looked at me. "Everything will be ready. It goes bad—"

"I bolt. You cover me. I got it." I touched his arm. "I really do."

He nodded, then everyone left. And I was alone.

Four o'clock, and the press conference, came very quickly. The furnished house had a television, so I tuned in. The conference took place in town, and was open to both media and locals. Wilkes would be there, if not in the audience, then close enough to overhear everything, anxious for firsthand news on his witness.

Dubois played his part perfectly. It started as a "no news to report" update, then he received an emergency call about the witness. After relaying the news to the press corps and the assembled audience of locals, he whispered something to the agent beside him, probably telling him to take over, excused himself and left.

I turned off the TV. Now my waiting began. Evelyn had instructed Dubois to get into his car and start driving. Felix would already be hidden in the backseat with the directions. Giving them to Dubois early would have been asking for trouble.

The route was as uncomplicated as we could make it, so Wilkes could follow. Dubois was instructed to "drive normally," that is, not to speed and risk losing him, but not to go too slowly and look suspicious. He was presumably en route to meet a critical witness. He wouldn't dawdle. Meanwhile, Evelyn would be tailing him, providing countersurveillance, should any agents or members of the press decide to follow Dubois. If they did, that could delay his arrival even more . . . if not permanently abort the plan.

Should everything work out, my cue would come when the front door handle turned, signaling that Dubois was there. Then he'd hurry back to the car, as if he'd forgotten something, and I'd be on, waiting for my big moment.

There was no sense trying to figure out how long it would take Dubois to get here. Overestimate and I'd be caught off guard. Underestimate and I'd start worrying that something had gone wrong.

I adjusted the police scanner in the living room. It wasn't

tuned to the frequency the Feds were using. Even if we could find that, we didn't need to. The scanner was just a prop, set slightly off station so Wilkes could hear police-type chatter, but static choked out the words.

At four forty-seven the front door handle rattled. I stood poised in the living room doorway and blocked out the police scanner buzz as I waited for the next signals, as Felix had explained them to Dubois. First, he'd jangle the handle. Second, he'd open the door, just a few inches, then slam it shut again. Finally, he'd turn and walk past the front window, where I'd see him and know, if all three events occurred, that it wasn't someone delivering pizza flyers.

The doorknob turned. It opened. And . . .

The clomp of footsteps, a firm one-two. Then the door clicked shut.

He'd come inside.

I tensed, fingers tightening around my gun. Had Wilkes figured out the right house before Dubois arrived? Jack had included that in his list of possibilities—the drawn blinds could give it away as soon as Dubois's car slowed a few doors down. But to walk in the front door? That was ballsy.

The squeak of shoes. Following the siren's call of the police scanner. Too late to back up to my post down the hall. No problem. You want contingency plans? Jack had dozens of them.

I ducked into the living room and crouched behind the entertainment stand we'd moved into position facing the doorway. I could aim my gun right through the opening above the TV, which was turned off so it wouldn't attract

Wilkes's attention. He'd slip up to the doorway, and look at the recliner beside the scanner—

Footsteps sounded in the hall. Not moving very quietly, was he? He stepped into the doorway. My finger touched the trigger...

"Jesus Christ!" I hissed as I stepped from behind the stand.

A flicker of surprise as Dubois's gaze slid over me, as if I wasn't what he'd envisioned, then his face went taut.

"Change of plans," he snapped. "This is my roust. You're standing down."

"The hell I—"

I swallowed the rest. Any moment now, that patio door could open and Wilkes could walk through. I glanced at the recliner and considered suggesting Dubois take a seat, provide me with a real guard to draw Wilkes's first fire. The thought cheered me enough to push back the surge of frustration.

"Stand down," Dubois said.

I resisted the urge to flip him off. No time for confrontation. No time to get him out of the house. The best solution? Compromise. And fast.

"We think he'll come in the kitchen," I said, speaking softly and quickly. "The radio should draw him in here. You can lie in wait—"

"Don't tell me where I'll lie in wait."

"Fine. You pick then."

I turned and headed for my bathroom hiding spot, trying not to snarl as I stalked off. Of all the stupid stunts. We'd arranged it this way to protect Dubois. All the glory and none of the risk. And this was how he repaid us? There are capable, bright agents all across the nation...and we had to wind up with an idiot.

This was a possibility Jack hadn't accounted for. We'd discussed the chance that Dubois would back out before the press conference, or on the way here, or before he got out of the car. Or that'd he'd get overeager and rush in too soon afterward, before we could leave. Or that our departure would be met with squad cars. The thought that he'd walk through that door and demand to take down Wilkes himself had never crossed our minds. Why? Because it was stupid!

As I brushed past Dubois, he made a move to stop me. I turned a glare on him.

"You want to take him down?" I whispered. "Then get ready. Before he comes through that door and finds us bickering in the hallway."

Dubois returned my glare, but let me pass. When I got to the bathroom, I looked back and saw him ducking into the living room. In other words, he was counting on Wilkes coming through that patio door into the kitchen. And if he didn't? Well, that was Dubois's problem. I wouldn't stand back and watch him get shot, but nor was I going to risk losing Wilkes to ensure Dubois's safety.

I slipped into the bathroom and looked around. Still a good hiding spot, with only one door and a window too small for Wilkes to climb through. I got into position, then turned on my radio, keeping the volume down, unit at my ear.

"We know," Jack said before I could speak. His voice was hard, words clipped. "Can't worry about it. You in position?"

"Affirmative," I whispered. "Quinn?"

"Here."

"Wire?"

A soft exhale, and I knew he'd been worrying about the same thing: whether Dubois was wired, either with a single partner backing him up or as a full operation, with a battalion of agents waiting to swoop in. There was no way to know for sure, and given how Dubois had treated me so far, he wasn't about to submit to a search.

"Fifty-fifty," he said after a moment.

"Shit."

"Forget it," Jack said. "Have to. Visitors show up? We'll know it. Warn you. Get you out. Meanwhile? Watch what you say. Stay on task."

An hour later, I was still waiting. Finally, I heard footsteps in the hall. Heavy footsteps. I sighed, but took up position anyway, in the corner by the door, gun drawn, watching through a mirror over the sink. Sure enough, within seconds, Dubois appeared.

I considered shooting him. Nothing fatal. Maybe a bullet through the right shoulder. Whoops, you can't fire a gun with a wounded shoulder? Guess we'd better get you out of here. Next time you're in a house with an armed stranger waiting for a serial killer? Don't come creeping down the hallway.

"Get back in position," I said through my teeth.

"It's been an hour. He's not showing up."

"No? Well, maybe that's because you're in here, and he needs to plan a little. If you'd left, he would have made damned sure he got in here before you returned."

"So this is my fault?"

I didn't dare answer that.

"Stand guard," I said. "I'll call my partners, and see whether anything's changed from their end."

FIFTY

"You gotta get him out of there," Jack said.

"You think I haven't tried? If you can do better, then I'll hand the radio over, because I want him gone even more than you do, but he won't go without a fight...and a fight will give Wilkes the perfect opportunity to strike."

"Or run," Jack muttered. "He hears arguing? He'll suspect a trap. Fuck."

"So I should...?"

"Stick to the plan. Holding pattern."

I lowered the radio and turned to Dubois. "Agent Dubois? Nothing's changed on their end. There's no sign of him outside, so they want us to stay the course."

Dubois's eyes narrowed. When he reached for the radio, I pretended not to notice, turning my attention back to it, tightening my grip. He paused, then stalked to the dining room.

"Back on track," I said to Jack. "For now...though I'm not sure how much longer he'll take orders from me."

"Dee? Quinn here."

"Hey."

"I was just going to say you're doing fine. Dubois won't like you running the show, but don't forget, he's on his own. Outgunned and outnumbered, and if we don't pull this off—out of a job. He's taken a big risk and broken a shitload of rules. He can't go back without Wilkes's head on a stick. As long as he knows that's what you want, too, and you don't get in his face too much, he'll toe the line."

"Good. Thanks."

I signed off and resumed my position.

* * *

Another hour passed. The light on my radio flickered. I turned it on and said hello.

"Me," came the response.

The reception in the bathroom wasn't clear enough to recognize the voice, but the terse greeting gave it away.

"He's waiting for night," Jack said.

"I was starting to suspect that."

"If Dubois left? He'd have taken a shot. Now? Too late. Damage done."

"Because he'll assume Dubois has already interviewed me, so there's no need to rush into a house that might be full of federal agents. Speaking of the Feds, they must be looking for Dubois and his car is right—"

"Evelyn hot-wired it. Moved it."

"I'm guessing you don't want me to stay in this bathroom all night. I could, if you think I should—"

"No. He'll wait for night. Expect you to be sleeping. Guards resting."

"Do you want me to go upstairs and stake out new positions?"

"Yeah. Me and Quinn? Going scouting. Wilkes has to be around." He paused. "You should eat."

He was right. Eating was the last thing I wanted to do, but I had to keep my blood sugar up. I'd brought a rucksack of food—trail mix, protein bars and water—and I told him I'd make myself a meal.

"Threw some candy in there, too."

I laughed. "Thanks, Jack."

"Go on, then. Talk to Dubois. Bring him up to speed." A pause. "But hide the food. Fuck him."

* * *

And so the night began. We expected Wilkes to wait until past midnight, when whoever was going to sleep would have drifted off. That meant Dubois and I had time to get ready, which we did ... separately.

Maybe the guy had just been in charge too long, or maybe he couldn't stomach the thought of partnering with a criminal, but he made it clear this wasn't a team effort. So we split territory—I got the upstairs and he got the down.

My plan was simple. If Wilkes wanted a sleeping victim, I'd give him one. The old pillows-under-the-comforter trick, which was a hell of a lot tougher without pillows and a comforter. The house came with furniture, but not bedding. I had to jury-rig something using a couple of towels and a sheet I found in a box in the basement, plus cushions from the living room. It wouldn't fool anyone who got close, but in the dark, it would get Wilkes in the doorway. I'd be in the closet waiting.

I don't know what Dubois's plan was, and I knew he wouldn't tell me if I asked. So when everything was ready, and it was only eight o'clock, I sat on the bed, munched my snacks, drank my bottled water and kept in radio contact with Evelyn and Felix.

Quinn and Jack were still on the prowl, presumably without result. Since they'd given their radios to Evelyn and Felix, though, one of them could have been ambushed by Wilkes and be lying in a backyard somewhere. I tried hard not to think about that, and to remind myself they were both experienced hunters, but I felt a lot better when my radio flashed at eight forty-eight, and Jack came on, telling me he and Quinn had returned.

They had scoured every bit of land within sight of the

house, and found no trace of Wilkes. Quinn thought he'd given up. Felix thought he hadn't been able to follow Dubois. Jack thought he'd hadn't fallen for the trap in the first place. Evelyn told us all to pipe down and be patient. So we waited.

While Quinn and Jack took a breather, Evelyn and Felix went on patrol, in the hope that if the guys had missed a nook or a cranny, fresh pairs of eyes would find it. An hour later, they got back with nothing to add. Even Evelyn now suspected our trap had failed. We'd hold on until morning, then come up with something new.

"You need sleep," Jack said as I yawned into the radio for the umpteenth time.

I laughed.

"I'm serious."

"One, I'm waiting for a professional killer who wants me dead. Falling asleep tops the list of stupid things I could do. Two, it's not even ten."

"You're tired. Three nights, almost no sleep. Wilkes waited this long? He's waiting until late."

"Jack's right," Quinn cut in on the other radio. "He'll be waiting for as many people in that house as possible to fall asleep, and be deeply asleep. My guess is you won't see him before two. And if you're tired now, you'll be beat by then. Can you catnap?"

"Sure, but—"

"Then we'll give you a half hour. Leave your radio on, and we'll wake you up at ten thirty."

I hesitated.

"You're okay, Dee. Everything's covered. Jack has your

front, and I have your back." A pause, then he sang. "*For a fee, I'm happy to be your backdoor man.*"

I sputtered a laugh.

"That didn't sound right, did it?"

"I think that's a whole different kind of pro."

Jack came on. "Suppose you want a story."

"Oh, I've got one," Quinn cut in. "You'll like it. A little tale about Martin Dubois. This isn't the first fix he's gotten himself into, but the last time he was lucky, managed to wriggle out…"

Dubois

Dubois looked across the room at the girl. Unbelievable. It wasn't even ten thirty and she was asleep, as if she was home in bed after a long day's work. And this was the same girl who'd lured a killer into an alley? Planned to take him on all by herself? Spent two hours poised in the downstairs bathroom like a pointer holding position on a duck? But, hey, night comes and the killer hasn't shown up yet? Yawn, I'm getting sleepy...and this bed looks so comfy. He was surprised she hadn't ordered pizza and a video.

Professionals, his ass. They reminded him of his stepson, who had ADD or whatever they called it these days. Put the kid on a task and he'd go full blazes on it for an hour and then...oh, look, a pretty butterfly. Didn't matter what so-called specialists said, what the kid needed was discipline. That's what differentiated real cops from these "detective wannabes."

He looked at the girl's hands on the pillow, beside her gun and radio. She was still wearing her gloves. Damn. He'd hoped to get a print. Maybe if he could slip off the wig and snag a hair...but just his luck, it wouldn't contain a DNA tag. And what the hell would he do with it? Ma Barker from the coffee shop had made it clear that "her boys" weren't going to give him the chance to turn the tables on them. If he tried, she had their conversation on tape.

At the time, he hadn't cared. Hadn't cared about anything. Rushed in headfirst. But that wasn't his fault—they hadn't given him enough time to think, only to react. Now, it looked as if he'd be heading home with no Helter Skelter killer to explain why he'd lied on camera and fucked off midinvestigation...

He ground his teeth. Something had to be done. His gaze traveled to the radio—her connection to the guys running this show. As long as she was in charge of that connection, she was in charge of things within these walls. He should have taken it from her, by force if necessary, hours ago. Yet, as the situation had unraveled, even as he'd raged against the loss of control, some panicked part deep inside him had been happy to cede that control, to continue hoping they could pull this off.

If everything went tits up, he could claim he'd been duped and kidnapped. That wouldn't work if he'd had the radio all along. But now, as failure seemed imminent, he was seeing a new way out. Yes, he'd been duped and taken hostage, but he would redeem himself by handing over, not the Helter Skelter killer, but a handful of hitmen.

Time to take back what rightfully belonged to him: control.

He took a few careful steps. No floorboards creaked, and she seemed to be sleeping soundly. Another step...

Her eyes flew open.

In that split-second, Dubois measured the distance between them, assessed his chances of lunging across it and disarming her before she fully awoke—

Her hand was already on the gun as she rose, her eyes clear and alert.

"Agent Dubois...?"

"Any news?" he said, gesturing at the radio.

"No."

"Let me know if there is."

"Of course."

He backed out of the room, shutting the door, but not pulling it tight enough to engage the latch.

Wilkes

Wilkes watched Dubois leave the room. The girl listened until his footsteps receded down the stairs, then crept from the bed and grabbed a hardcover book from the almost-empty bookcase. She propped the book against the door and went back to bed. If Dubois returned and found the door shut tight, he'd know she was suspicious and back off to try something else. If she left the door cracked open, he'd assume she'd bought his story and try again ... only to knock over the book and alert her.

Wilkes allowed it was clever enough, but the agent was an idiot—easy to fool.

He pulled back from the probe eyepiece and swiveled his neck, working out the kinks. Then he stood, as much as he could stand in the low-roofed attic, and stretched his legs. Getting too old for this ... but it wouldn't be much longer now.

As he moved, pain shot through his side. The wounds from Jack's bullets. One had been little more than a graze, the other going straight through muscle. Neither critical. He'd get them checked out soon enough, but in the mean-time, they were slowing him down, something he didn't need. If not for those wounds, he wouldn't even be here— he'd have taken the girl down in that alley yesterday. Jack's fault. But he'd pay for it soon enough.

He looked across the room at the small attic dormer window and resisted the urge to slide over and look out. He knew he wouldn't see Jack. But he was out there, watch-ing the house, making sure their girl stayed safe.

For the hundredth time in the last few hours, he wished

it was Jack down there instead of the girl. Not only could he have paid him back for that fiasco in Vegas, but killing Jack would stick it to Evelyn in the only place that cold bitch would ever feel it. But, if he couldn't kill Jack, then perhaps, as revenge went, this wasn't such a poor substitute.

He'd seen the way Jack had looked at the girl in the opera house. At the time he'd chalked it up to good acting, but now he preferred to believe otherwise. Jack didn't take partners. Wouldn't even work with *him* when Evelyn had suggested it. But now that had changed, and he wasn't just working alongside someone, but taking her everywhere, keeping her close, trusting her to watch his back. And that someone was an attractive younger woman. That was significant. It had to be. And if it was, then killing this girl just might hurt Jack more than any bullet.

Kill the girl. Hurt Jack. Maybe even sting Evelyn a little, robbing her of a new prize pupil at an age when she wasn't likely to see many more.

He wanted to be there when they realized they'd lost her. Not just lost her, *sacrificed* her. He'd tried to tell himself that he would never have fallen for their scheme, that even if he hadn't recognized the girl, he wouldn't have slid into the trap. But in all honesty, he wasn't so sure. It was a clever ruse. Evelyn had always been so damned clever, so quick to rub it in. Now she'd see she wasn't the only one.

When he'd arrived, after following Dubois from the press conference, he'd lamented his lack of supplies. He hadn't been prepared for this, and had to make do with the few things he'd had hidden in his rental car, all designed to kill one person. He had no idea how many people were in there. Was it just the girl and the one FBI agent? Or had Evelyn cut a deal with the Feds, meaning there'd be a house full of them? Or were Evelyn and Jack themselves in there, waiting for him? He wasn't stupid enough to sneak down and find out, not when he had the perfect perch.

A bomb would have been ideal. Blow the whole house up. Then it wouldn't matter how many Feds were guarding the girl. But all he had was a tiny thing that wouldn't do any good unless he put it right under her bed, and the explosion would have the Feds locking down the place in seconds. Then, while he'd been waiting, he'd slipped into the empty house next door, up to the attic and with a bit of work on some rotted boards, slipped through to the adjoining one. And there he'd found the answer to his prayers: the access door that led into the walk-in closet of the master suite . . . a master suite with a gas fireplace.

He checked his watch. Twelve minutes to go. Time to find himself a good, safe spot to watch the fireworks.

FIFTY-ONE

For five minutes after Dubois left, I lay in bed waiting for his return. Then I sat up. I knew I needed to give it longer than that—he'd be waiting for me to fall back to sleep before returning—but something was niggling at the back of my brain, pestering me to get up.

I checked the clock. Still seven minutes before Jack or Quinn would wake me. Maybe that was it—like waking just before the alarm goes off, wanting to grab a few more minutes but unable to squelch that inner clock saying it was time to get up.

I reached for my radio to call them and say I was up. As I swung my legs over the bedside, the smell hit me. Faint . . . but familiar. A memory flash. I'd been eight. Brad and my mother had gone out, and I'd wanted to cook dinner for my dad. That was the only time I'd ever heard my father yell at my mother, when he'd come home, and found me alone . . . passed out on the floor because I'd forgotten to turn off the gas after making his meal.

I leapt to my feet so fast I tripped and nearly dropped my gun. I recovered, and raced out the door. So this was Wilkes's plan—knock everyone unconscious and make easy work of the killings.

As I hit the hall, I heard the hiss of gas, not from downstairs, but from a bedroom. The gas fireplace in the master suite. I started to run, then checked myself. It could be a trap.

I lifted my gun then looked down at it and froze. Fire into a room full of gas?

I stuffed the gun into my holster, so I'd have both hands

free . . . and so I wouldn't instinctively fire if I saw Wilkes. As I holstered the gun, I thought of the radio. I'd left it in the room, running on instinct and thinking only of my gun. I considered going back, but that steady hiss of gas changed my mind. Shut that off first, then worry about the radio.

I stopped before reaching the doorway, and let my eyes adjust to the near dark as I listened. The hiss of gas from within covered any sounds, but that would work both ways. I reached into my pocket and made sure I had my penlight handy. Then I peered around the doorway.

The room was empty. In a sweep, I took in every place a man Wilkes's size could hide. Dresser—too low. Bed— see-through iron headboard. The closet. It would have to be the closet. As I slunk along the wall, I paused to take out my penlight. Then I moved alongside the door.

Empty hangers clinked as I swung the door open. A walk-in closet. Empty except for a forlorn handful of hangers and a couple of plastic storage containers. The storage containers were stacked in the middle of the large closet. I looked up to see an attic access hatch above that stack. Was that how he'd come in? Shit!

I backpedaled out of the closet. My gaze flew to the hissing fireplace. Get that turned off first, then—

I took one step and froze. There, at the base of the fireplace, was a little box. On the box, a timer, a simple windup timer. And it was about to go off.

Dubois! I had to get to him—

No time!

"Dubois!" I screamed. "Get out!"

I grabbed the nearest thing, a brass planter with a fake tree. I seized the thin trunk with both hands, and swung the planter at the window. It flew through the glass, the planter sailing free into the backyard.

One brusque sweep with the tree to clear the glass from the sill. Then I threw it aside.

"Dubois!" I screamed, voice cracking.

I backed up and took a run at the window. Grabbed the sill—vaulted through—a whoosh behind me—searing pain—a smack like an airbag going off—the force of explosion propelling me out the window—ground flying up to meet me—darkness.

I came to with a jolt, my limbs flailing as if I was still falling. I tried pushing myself up. A sudden "Oh, my God!" wave of pain, and I fell face-first to the grass again.

I had to get up. If Wilkes saw me fly out that window—

Quinn— Quinn and Felix. They were out here somewhere, watching the backyard. Had they seen—?

Another boom, and the night lit up. I craned to look over my shoulder. The house was in flames, the windows and doors yawning holes. Quinn and Felix would see that and assume I was still inside, that I'd been caught asleep.

Did Dubois make it? I couldn't worry about that. Had to get up. Find—

Wilkes.

I reached for my gun. The holster was empty.

I started looking around wildly as I pushed up onto my elbows. A sharp throbbing coursed through my wrist. My right wrist. My gun hand.

Doesn't matter. Just find the damned thing and worry later about whether you can fire—

Something moved across the lawn. A tall broadshouldered figure. Quinn!

My lips were parting to call a greeting, then something in the house flared and the flash of light illuminated a face under pale hair. Wilkes. Looking right at me. Heading for me. A slender barreled gun dangled at his side. Even half-stunned, my brain coughed up an ID before I could ask it for one. A Ruger Mark II with a suppressor.

Fury coursed through me, so strong I had no hope of beating it back. Couldn't even form a clear thought. Could only glower up at Wilkes like a cornered beast. Then I saw the gun glide down, moving into position, and my brain snapped back on.

Don't fight the anger. Use it.

A gun like that is made for contact hits. Small caliber, inaccurate with the suppressor, still noisy if fired from a distance. He'd want to walk right up to me and put the gun to my head. I had a chance...

I moved into a crouch, my gaze on Wilkes. He smiled, close enough for me to see the flash of his teeth. Then he aimed. I rolled just as he fired and the bullet tore a furrow in the grass inches from my shoulder. A second shot as I rolled the other way.

I scrambled to my feet as I came out of the roll. Pain shot through my ankle. Just sprained, I told myself, even as the ripping pain screamed otherwise. Didn't matter. Pain was nothing. An obstacle. Not a barrier.

I dove for the nearest shadow cover—the row of hedges alongside the fence. A bullet struck the middle of my back. The armor protected me, but the impact was like someone giving me a hard shove. I stumbled. My ankle gave way. I pitched forward.

No! Fall and you're dead. Get into those bushes. Now!

I pulled myself out of the stumble as a bullet grazed my upper arm. Three lurching steps, and I dove into the bushes.

A shot smacked into the fence boards. Wilkes let out a muttered oath.

Not used to firing that thing at a moving target, are you? I thought. Not used to firing more than one shot, either. And time was ticking. A house had just exploded. Cops, fire trucks, ambulances, they'd all be here . . . if Jack and the others didn't beat them. Wilkes was running out of time, shooting too quickly, wasting his ammo, firing at a moving target in the dark, the only light the flickering flames from the burning house, casting shadows every which way, hiding me better than total darkness would.

I could turn the tables, use his impatience and the flickering light and the shadows to my advantage, then—

Then what? I didn't have a gun. To take him down without a weapon, I needed to get close enough to physically attack him. While the thought of putting my hands around his neck sent a delicious shiver through me, I knew I stood little chance of getting close enough to do it.

Little chance . . .

A deep part of me seized on that, said "It's still a chance, good enough, take it!" But I'd promised Jack. Sworn I wouldn't do this again.

Still darting from bush to bush, dodging Wilkes's shots, I drew deep breaths, slowing my heart, reminding myself of my promise.

If I took this chance, and I lost, then maybe that didn't mean as much to me as it should, maybe I'd say the risk was worth it, maybe I could even convince myself that Jack wouldn't realize I'd broken my promise. But one thing I did know. If I went down, Wilkes would get away. He'd have no reason to hang around, and any chance that someone else would catch him—Jack, Quinn, Felix, Evelyn, the cops—would evaporate. He'd be free again, all because I couldn't fight that need to stop running and strike back.

Best thing I could do was stall him. Wait for help to arrive. But the yard wasn't that big, I was wounded, and he still had time to get off plenty more rounds. Eventually a shot would be serious enough to take me down just long enough for him to walk over and put a bullet through my head.

Goddamn it, if only I had my gun! Why couldn't I see it out there? Why couldn't I trip over it racing across the yard? If I had that, I could take the upper hand, put a bullet into this bastard so fast—

But I didn't have a gun and all the wishing and raging in the world wouldn't change that. Those same flickering flames that were making it hard for Wilkes to see me were making it impossible for me to see a black gun on the ground. Even if I could find it, would it work after the fall? Then there was my wrist. I could brace my hand or shoot with my left, but both would throw off my reflexes and accuracy. Too many ifs. I couldn't waste time—and focus—searching for the gun.

One thing I knew for certain: from now on, I was wearing a backup weapon.

I dove and weaved through the perimeter shrubs, missing some shots, getting gazed or hit in the chest armor by others. With every few steps, I stumbled. Any minute now, my ankle would give out for good.

How many shots had he taken? My brain blurted an answer. Seven— Another *pffttt* just above my head. Eight. He had ten rounds. Eleven if he'd chambered a round and topped up. Plus he'd be able to reload quickly, and probably even carried a backup weapon. Making him run out of ammo sounds good in the movies, but it wasn't going to work here.

So now what? Jack's voice echoed in my head, and I knew what he'd say. *Run.*

I was injured, with no working weapon, and no backup. As much as I hated to run—oh, God, how I hated to run!—if I didn't, he'd kill me, then escape. My best chance was to make a break for it. Not escape him, lure him. Play fleeing prey and he'd follow. Why? Because if it were me doing the chasing, I'd follow. To run was to surrender. He had to fight, kill, win.

To keep this chase going, I needed to get out of this yard. Problem was, the only way out was over the fence. Jack had chosen this setup for my safety. No one had ever considered the possibility that I could get trapped here.

Wilkes fired, the shot zinging so close to my head I swore I felt it pass.

Over the fence it was.

I didn't have time to worry whether my ankle could handle it—I had to make it work. One quick look and I found the biggest bush—one I'd just squeezed past. I steeled myself, turned sharp and raced back, ignoring the pain. The second I was behind that bush and hidden in its shadow, I grabbed the top of the fence, swinging myself up, grimacing as my wrist screamed in protest. For that split second, as I crested the fence, I was exposed. All I could do was keep my head down.

He fired. The shot hit my shoulder, stopped by the body armor, but the impact was almost enough to make me lose my grip. As I flipped over the fence, something snagged my foot. I kicked. Fresh pain as my injured foot made contact. An *oomph.* Wilkes released his hold, and I toppled, face-first, over the fence.

I hit the ground and clambered up. I could hear Wilkes scrabbling over the fence. A split-second survey of the yard. Also fenced. No way out until I reached the end of the row...vaulting over a half-dozen more fences. Couldn't do it. There was no "if" or "maybe." Couldn't. I had to take cover.

Unlike the other yard, here there was no long hedge to hide behind. There had been at one time, until student tenants moved in. Abuse, neglect, whatever the cause, there was nothing more than a few clusters of bushes left, none big enough to do more than cower behind. The house was dark, meaning unless I was somehow lucky enough to find the patio door unlocked, I wasn't getting out that way.

A siren wailed.

I should surrender this fight now. Step aside. Let the cops come in and roust Wilkes, take him down. I should scream loud enough that I'd raise the alarm.

But what if my screams brought someone back here? An innocent bystander rushing in to help? I could not risk anyone else's life. This had to end here. Now.

I hobbled for the largest clump of bushes, right up against the house. Whatever I did, I couldn't still be out here when Wilkes hauled his ass over that fence. I dove behind the bush.

Through the leaves, I saw him swing to the ground. He turned, took in the yard in one sweep and headed right for my cover.

Could he see me here?

You idiot, there's only one place in this yard big enough to hide you. Where else would you be?

A rock. I needed a—

As I felt around the ground, my fingernails clinked against something cold and smooth. A bottle. An empty glass bottle. I could have laughed. Thank God for student tenants.

Gaze still riveted to Wilkes, I gripped the neck of the bottle with my uninjured left hand and swung the base against the concrete foundation. As it smashed, Wilkes jumped, startled.

I wheeled from behind the bush and charged. Made it three strides before my ankle gave way, but as I sprawled forward, I smacked full-weight into Wilkes.

His gun fired. I felt pain. Didn't know where. Didn't care. We both went down. I saw his face below mine. Saw his neck, a pale strip in the moonlight, took aim, gripped the bottle neck, and slashed down with everything I could.

Blood spurted. He fell back. I twisted and grabbed his gun. He wrenched it, finger squeezing on the trigger, but I pulled it away easily as his grip slackened. I put the barrel to his temple. He looked at me. I pulled the trigger.

FIFTY-TWO

With Wilkes's exit strategy permanently aborted, it was time to worry about ours.

Dubois was dead. Jack had found his body when he and Quinn had gone into the house, searching for me. I felt bad about Dubois. Yes, I'd tried to warn him. Yes, he'd accepted the risk when he came into the house. But I still regretted the outcome.

We didn't hide Wilkes's body. Evelyn sent a letter to the Feds, just in case they mistook Wilkes for some poor senior citizen who got caught in the cross fire. I'm sure they would have figured it out eventually, but the nudge—and his real name—would help. As they unraveled Wilkes's story, they'd probably find out about his former occupation, so all the work we'd done to avoid that was for naught. But Wilkes was dead, and we weren't. Good enough.

Felix and Evelyn stayed behind to clean up any loose ends and watch for unexpected fallout. Quinn and I wanted to help, but Jack refused. We were the most vulnerable—the youngest, and least experienced, plus we both had "normal" lives and "normal" jobs, and he wanted us to go back to those right away.

Before I left, Evelyn took me aside. She wanted a method of contact. I wasn't comfortable giving it, but it was a case where refusing was more dangerous. She offered her training services, but seemed content to leave it at that, not pushing the point…yet.

Jack drove Quinn and me into Pennsylvania the next morning. Our first stop was the hospital. A half-day later, I walked—okay, hobbled—out with a reset ankle and wrist. I'd broken both.

I also had a nice collection of bruises plus a couple of bullet grazes. Jack had taken care of the grazes right away. He cleaned and bandaged them, and we came up with a cover story, in case someone at the hospital noticed the bandages and asked. They didn't.

Once out of the hospital, I hid my wrist cast under my coat sleeve as best I could. The bandaged foot was bad enough; I didn't need to call extra attention to myself.

When we got to the airport, Jack went to buy our tickets. Quinn helped me to a seat in a quiet corner, and bought me a coffee and muffin. He started to pass me the coffee cup, then stopped and opened the lid first. When he began peeling the wrapper off the muffin, I laughed and took it from him.

"Hey, don't—" he began.

"It's my wrist, not my hand."

"Still, I don't think—"

"I'm okay."

He hovered on the edge of his seat, as if expecting me to fumble and dump coffee into my lap at any moment.

"I'm *okay*."

"I know, I just feel—"

"Really bad. I've heard it. Heard it from you, heard it from Felix, heard it from Jack, even heard something like it from Evelyn. It was my choice to go in there. Unforeseeable circumstances, and no one's to blame . . . except Wilkes and Dubois, but neither is in much of a position to take his share."

"Well, I still feel—"

"Really bad."

A small laugh. "Okay, I'll stop saying it." He reached out

to take my coffee before I could set it down, but backed off at a mock-glare. Then he shifted in his seat.

"So, what I said the other day...Is it still...? About keeping in touch, I mean. Jack's sure not going to give me a way to contact you, so this is probably my last chance to..."

He let the sentence trail off.

I grinned. "Ask me for my phone number?"

"That'd be nice, but I know I'm not getting it. How about e-mail?"

We discussed it for a minute and each decided to set up a new account. I suggested we use other names, to keep things separate. After I gave him one for me, he thought about it for a few seconds, then sighed. "I'm no good at this stuff. Umm, maybe...geez, I don't know..."

"Backdoor Man?"

A laugh. "*Your* backdoor man. I'll use it. You won't mistake me for anyone else with that."

Quinn looked left and I followed his gaze to see Jack approaching. He leaned toward me.

"So, you know, keep in touch, okay?" A grin, and he sang, *"Pick up the phone. I'm always home. Call me anytime."*

I grinned back. *"Just ring 362-4368?"*

"I lead a life of crime."

Jack, who'd heard the end of the exchange, looked from one to the other, blank-faced as we laughed.

"AC/DC?" I said.

Still blank.

" 'Dirty Deeds Done Dirt Cheap'?" Quinn said. "Our anthem. Or if it isn't, it should be."

"Yours maybe," he said. "I'm never cheap."

Waving the tickets, Jack motioned Quinn aside. We said a quick good-bye, and Quinn promised to be in touch.

Jack caught that, and he looked at me, but said nothing, just gestured for Quinn to walk with him.

They headed for the domestic flights area, Jack talking and Quinn nodding. Then Jack passed him his ticket. Quinn shot me a final grin, hoisted his carry-on and merged into the flow of passengers.

Jack walked back to me.

"Got an hour," he said. "Cutting it close for security."

I nodded and he helped me to my feet. As I arranged my crutches, he looked back to make sure Quinn had disappeared, then led me to the international flights gate.

"Jack?"

"Hmmm?"

"Before I go. There's something..." I paused, looked around, then led him to a quieter corner. "Evelyn offered me a job going after some pedophile." I paused. "Vigilante work."

I studied his expression, but he gave nothing away, only nodded, as if this was no surprise.

"You knew?"

"Knew she would." A pause, then he looked at me. "You didn't take it. Didn't say no, either."

"I... couldn't. Either way. Not yet. She said it didn't matter, that if this one falls through she'll find me another."

He nodded, again not surprised. After a moment, he said, "You want my opinion."

"If I could."

A longer pause now, staring out at the passengers hurrying by. Then, slowly, he turned his gaze back to mine. "Could argue for. Could argue against. Don't think I should do either." He lowered my bag to the floor. "Whatever you decide? I'm here. Won't tell you which way to go. Won't let you walk off a cliff, either."

I considered that, deciphering it, then said, "Meaning it's an honest offer, as far as you know. She isn't setting me up for anything."

"Honest enough. I'll make sure of that. You wanna say yes? Let me check the job first. She won't trick you. But..." He shrugged, letting the sentence trail off.

"She's not above fudging the truth a bit to lure me in."

"Yeah."

He checked his watch. I took the hint and started walking. He steered our path away from the other passengers.

"Bring the cash next trip?" he said, voice still low.

"Cash?"

"Your cut. Assume you want cash. Easier if I bring it. For crossing the border. Unless you need it now."

"I don't want your money, Jack."

I waited for him to protest, to say someone else had financed the job, but he didn't seem to notice my wording.

"You earned it," he said.

"I don't—"

"You *earned* it. More than anyone. You need it, too. More than anyone."

"I don't, Jack. You know why I did this and it has nothing to do with a payment."

"Yeah, but—"

"I don't want your money."

He hesitated. A flicker of consternation as he realized what I'd said, and that I'd said it before, and he hadn't denied it. He opened his mouth as if to argue, but realized it was too late, and settled for rubbing his hand across his mouth.

Another pause, then, "I don't need it, either. You earned it. I want you—"

"You want me to have it? Then I'll tell you how you can give it to me: take me on an all-expenses paid trip to Egypt."

He looked at me.

"You did suggest that, didn't you? In Vegas? You were asking whether I'd come with you to see the pyramids someday, but we were cut off before I could answer. Well, it's yes. If you were serious, that is. If not, well, I guess you can buy me a trip for one."

"No, that'd be good." Another mouth rub. "Yeah." He looked up. "But your stuff. For the lodge. Gazebos, hot tubs—"

"It can wait."

"Shouldn't. I'll bring the money. You get your stuff. Egypt?" He shrugged. "That'll be the bonus. You earned it. Won't be right away, though. Got some jobs."

"No rush. If we could do it during a slow period at the lodge, that'd be great."

"Yeah. I'll do that. Let you know. Work something out." He paused. "That'd be good." Another pause, then he looked at the security gate. "You gotta go."

He helped me get my bag onto my shoulder. Took a moment for me to adjust the extra weight with the crutches, but then I was ready.

Still I hesitated.

I wanted to ask him why he'd done it. Why he'd paid for the job. But if I did, I knew what he'd do. Shrug and repeat some variation on what he'd said back at the lodge: that what was bad for the business was bad for everyone *in* the business.

I didn't doubt that had figured into his motivation. Was there more?

I thought of Jack, paying Cooper when there'd been no offer of money in our "deal." Paying that kid at the casino for information he hadn't been able to give. Why bother? Because, to him, it had been the right thing to do.

As a hitman, he'd been in a position to stop Wilkes, and hire others to help. So he had. Why? Maybe just because it was the right thing to do.

"Gonna miss your flight," he said.

I wanted to say "forget the flight." I wanted to get out of this line, this airport, take him someplace and talk to him. *Really* talk to him. But as I looked into his eyes, so unreadable he might as well have been wearing shades, I knew it wouldn't be as simple as Evelyn said. "Ask him and he'll tell you" only applied to the superficial. For anything with any meaning—not just this but any of the questions I really wanted answers to—I wasn't getting them. Maybe not ever. Certainly not now.

Another moment's hesitation, then I said, "See you around?"

He nodded. "Of course."

And that, I supposed, was the best I could hope for. So I adjusted my bag, nodded a final good-bye and headed through the gate.

If you enjoyed

EXIT STRATEGY

and have not yet read Kelley Armstrong's
tense supernatural novels
then please read on for

BITTEN . . .

HUMAN

I stood at the door before ringing the bell. It was Mother's Day and I was standing at a door holding a present, which would have been quite normal if it was a present for my mother. But my mother was long dead and I didn't keep in touch with any of my foster mothers, let alone bring them gifts. The present was for Philip's mother. Again, this would have been very normal if Philip had been there with me. He wasn't. He'd called from his office an hour ago to say he couldn't get away. Did I want to go alone? Or would I rather wait for him? I'd opted to go and now stood there wondering if that was the right decision. Did a woman visit her boyfriend's mother on Mother's Day without said boyfriend? Maybe I was trying too hard. It wouldn't be the first time.

Human rules confounded me. It wasn't as if I'd been raised in a cave. Before I became a werewolf, I'd already learned the basic mechanics: how to hail a taxi, operate an elevator, apply for a bank account, all the minutiae of human life. The problem came with human interactions. My childhood had been pretty screwed up. Then, when I'd been on the cusp of becoming an adult, I'd been bitten and spent the next nine years of my life with other werewolves. Even during those years, I hadn't been locked away from the human world. I'd gone back to university, traveled with the others, even taken on jobs. But they'd always been there, for support and protection and companionship. I hadn't needed to make it on my own. I hadn't needed to make friends or take lovers or go to lunch with coworkers.

So, I hadn't. Last year, when I broke with the others and came back to Toronto alone, I thought fitting in would be the least of my concerns. How tough could it be? I'd just take the basics I'd learned from childhood, mix in the adult conversational skills I'd learned with the others, toss in a dash of caution and voilà, I'd be making friends and chatting up new acquaintances in no time. Hah!

Was it too late to leave? I didn't want to leave. Taking a deep breath, I rang the doorbell. Moments later, a flurry of footsteps erupted inside. Then a round-faced woman with graying brown hair answered.

'Elena!' Diane said, throwing the door open. 'Mom, Elena's here. Is Philip parking the car? I can't believe how packed the street is. Everyone out visiting.'

'Actually, Philip's not – uh – with me. He had to work, but he'll be along soon.'

'Working? On a Sunday? Have a talk with him, girl.' Diane braced the door open. 'Come in, come in. Everyone's here.'

Philip's mother, Anne, appeared from behind his sister. She was tiny, not even reaching my chin, with a sleek iron gray pageboy.

'Still ringing the doorbell, dear?' she said, reaching up to hug me. 'Only salesmen ring the bell. Family walks right in.'

'Philip will be late,' Diane said. 'He's working.'

Anne made a noise in her throat and ushered me inside. Philip's father, Larry, was in the kitchen pilfering pastries from a tray.

'Those are for dessert, Dad,' Anne said, shooing him away.

Larry greeted me with a one-armed hug, the other hand still clutching a brownie. 'So where's—'

'Late,' Diane said. 'Working. Come into the living room, Elena. Mom invited the neighbors, Sally and Juan, for lunch.' Her voice lowered to a whisper. 'Their kids are all out West.' She pushed open the French doors. 'Before you got here, Mom was showing them your last few articles in *Focus Toronto*.'

'Uh-oh. Is that good or bad?'

'Don't worry. They're staunch Liberals. They loved your stuff. Oh, here we are. Sally, Juan, this is Elena Michaels, Philip's girlfriend.'

Philip's girlfriend. That always sounded odd, not because I objected to being called a 'girlfriend' instead of 'partner' or anything as ridiculously politically correct. It struck me because it'd been years since I'd been anyone's girlfriend. I didn't do relationships. For me, if it lasted the weekend, it was getting too serious. My one and only lengthy relationship had been a disaster. More than a disaster. Catastrophic.

Philip was different.

I'd met Philip a few weeks after I'd moved back to Toronto. He'd been living in an apartment a few blocks away. Since our buildings shared a property manager, tenants in his complex had access to the health club in mine. He'd come to the pool one day after midnight and, finding me alone swimming laps, he'd asked if I minded if he did some, as if I had the right to kick him out. Over the next month, we'd often found ourselves alone in the health club late at night. Each time, he'd checked to make sure I was comfortable being alone there with him. Finally, I'd said that the reason I was working out in the health club was to ensure I didn't need to worry about being attacked by strange men and I'd be defeating the whole purpose if I was nervous about having him there. That had made him laugh and he'd lingered after his workout and bought me a juice from the vending machine. Once the postworkout juice break became a habit, he worked his way up the meal chain with invitations to coffee, then lunch, then dinner. By the time we got around to breakfast, it was nearly six months from the day we'd met in the pool. That might have been part of the reason I let myself fall for him, flattered that anyone would put that amount of time and effort into getting to know me. Philip wooed me with all the patience of someone trying to coax a half-wild animal into the house and, like many a stray, I found myself domesticated before I thought to resist.

All had gone well until he'd suggested we move in together. I should have said no. But I hadn't. Part of me couldn't resist the challenge of seeing whether I could pull it off. Another part of me had been afraid of losing him if I refused. The first month had been a disaster. Then, just when I'd been sure the bubble was ready to burst, the pressure eased. I forced myself to postpone my Changes longer, allowing me to run when Philip was away on overnight business trips or working late. Of course, I can't take all the credit for saving the relationship. Hell, I'd be pushing it if I took half. Even after we moved in together, Philip was as patient as he'd been when we were dating. When I did something that would raise most human eyebrows, Philip brushed it off with a joke. When I was overwhelmed by the stress of fitting in, he took me to dinner or a show, getting my mind off my problems, letting me know he was there if I wanted to talk, and understanding if I didn't. At first I thought it was too good to be true. Every day I'd come home from work, pause outside the apartment door, and brace myself to open it and find him gone. But he didn't leave. A few weeks ago he'd begun talking about finding us a bigger place when my lease was up, even hinting that a condo might be a wise investment. A condo. Wow. That was almost semi-permanent, wasn't it? A week later and I was still in shock – but it was a good sort of shock.

It was mid-afternoon. The neighbors were gone. Diane's husband, Ken, had left early to take their youngest to work. Philip's other sister, Judith, lived in the U.K. and had to settle for a Mother's Day phone call, phoning after lunch and speaking to everyone, including me. Like all of Philip's family, she treated me as if I were a sister-in-law instead of her brother's girlfriend-of-the-hour. They were all so friendly, so ready to accept me that I had a hard time believing they weren't just being polite. It was possible they really did like me but, having had rotten luck with families, I was reluctant to believe it. I wanted it too much.

As we were washing dishes, the telephone rang. Anne answered it in the living room. A few minutes later, she came and got me. It was Philip.

'I am so sorry, hon,' he said when I answered. 'Is Mom mad?'

'I don't think so.'

'Good. I promised to take her to dinner another time to make up for it.'

'So are you coming over?'

He sighed. 'I'm not going to make it. Diane'll give you a ride home.'

'Oh, that's not necessary. I can take a cab or the—'

'Too late,' he said. 'I already told Mom to ask Diane. They won't let you out of that house without an escort now.' He paused. 'I really didn't mean to abandon you. Are you surviving?'

'Very well. Everyone's great, as always.'

'Good. I'll be home by seven. Don't make anything. I'll pick up. Caribbean?'

'You hate Caribbean.'

'I'm doing penance. See you at seven, then. Love you.'

He hung up before I could argue.

*　*　*